David F Burrows was born and raised in Suffolk. He lives there to this day with his wife Jenny. They have two grown up daughters and three grandchildren.

Having had a few short comedies published over the years David still looked on his writing as a relaxing fun hobby. Now that he is semi-retired, he has had a lot more time to devote to his writing, resulting in the unique Fish Bone Alley Series of short stories. This is the third book in the Fish Bone Alley collection. The first was published in January 2019.

To find out more about David and his work please visit his website at: www.dfburrows.co.uk

Fish Bone Alley 3
Bullington Castle

David F Burrows

Platen Publishing

978-1-9164050-4-2
Illustrations by Steve Royce Griffin
www.steveroycegriffin.co.uk

David F Burrows
www.dfburrows.co.uk

Published by Platen Publishing an imprint of David F Burrows, 2020

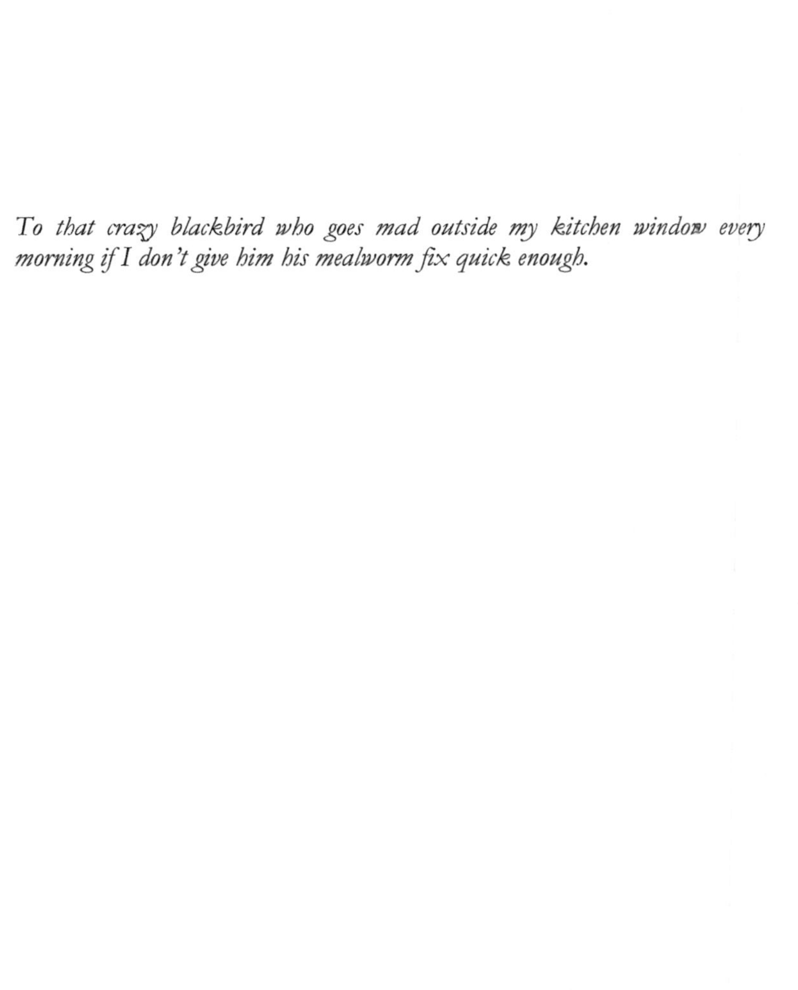

To that crazy blackbird who goes mad outside my kitchen window every morning if I don't give him his mealworm fix quick enough.

Contents

The Case

We are in Clumps office. The cheap stuff is out, so whatever's going on it isn't that serious and subsequently shouldn't be that dangerous. But then you never can tell.

"Not for me, sir," says Head as Clump is about to fill the glasses.

Clump shoots Head a puzzled look, "Are you ill?"

"No, sir. I'm just cutting down on the booze."

"Why?"

"Well, sir it can't be good for you continually drinking copious amounts of strong liqueur before lunch, during lunch, after lunch, before dinner, during…"

"As you wish," cuts in Clump. "And you, Inspector do you also wish to abstain?"

I am tempted, but Head's right, we do drink far too much. "Um… To be honest, sir although I don't intend joining the Temperance Society, I think it would be a good idea to cut down and to cut it out completely before lunch."

To our amazement Clump puts the bottle and glasses back into the draw and slowly but pointedly shuts it. "Right, let's get down to it. Cornwall, Sergeant what do you know about Cornwall? And take note, I only want sensible answers."

"It's famous for dumplings and pasties, sir," smiles Head.

"And pilchards," adds I.

"What about swedes and turnips?" says Head. "They grow tons of the stuff and are known as swede, turnip and dumpling heads."

"You are mixing up your counties, Sergeant," grates Clump. "I believe Norfolk and Suffolk are famous for swedes, turnips and dumplings. What else?"

"Smuggling," says I. "The area is notorious for smuggling in booze and tobacco from France."

"Good answer, Inspector. Well done. Although I am of the opinion that the problem isn't anywhere near as prolific as it once was.

"Ship wrecking," says Head. "I read a book once about how the Cornish used to lure ships onto the rocks during storms, brain all the crew and run off with the cargo."

"Excellent," beams Clump. "As you are both obviously well informed about the Cornish way of life, I am sending you down there for a few days."

"What for a holiday?" says Head.

Ignoring him Clump says, "Have either of you heard of a place called Bullington Castle?"

We shake our heads.

"Bullington Castle is owned by The Earl of Bullington, who is a personal friend of mine. While his wife, Countess Constance, just happens to be Mrs Clumps younger sister. They have a problem gentleman that the local constabulary has been trying to solve for the past month or more without even a smidgen of success. What is that problem you ask?"

"What is that problem?" asks Head.

"Shut up, Sergeant," snaps Clump. "The problem is attempted murder, gentlemen. Lord Percival Bullington, the eldest son and heir apparent to the Bullington Estate has had three attempts on his life. Attempt one consisted of someone taking a too close for comfit pot shot at him while he was in a cornfield. Attempt two consisted of someone jumping out of a hedge and firing an arrow at him while he was out riding…"

"Red Indians?" queries Head.

Clumps bushy eyebrows meet, "They don't think it was Red Indians, Sergeant, but Robin 'bloody' Hood may have had something to do with it. Sometimes, Sergeant you really do stretch your luck. Now, either you start taking this seriously or I shall have you suspended on no pay. Do you understand me?"

"I was merely…"

"Well don't. Attempt three occurred two days after attempt two. Lord Percival was making his way outside the castle when a huge chunk of masonry was pushed from the parapet, just missing his head and landing at his feet where it embedded itself several inches into the ground. Since then Lord Percival has remained in the castle for his own safety, while the local constabulary investigated the incidences."

"Obviously to no avail," puts in I.

"Exactly. Therefore, you two will be going down there to take over the investigation. Any questions?"

"What about my Chloe?" demands Head.

"What about your Chloe?"

"Can she come with me?"

"It may be summer, Sergeant and the weather glorious at present, but this is work. You are not going on a bloody jolly, you are going to investigate a series of serious attempts on someone's life, so why on earth do you think I would sanction your wife joining you to cause you all manner of distractions?"

"Because she is about seven months pregnant, sir and I don't want to be too far away from her in case something happens."

"I can understand that, Sergeant. But what good is a husband when it comes to pregnancy and giving birth? I will tell you, no bloody good whatsoever. The only man a pregnant woman wants to see is a qualified gynaecologist. In short, someone who can truly help her should anything go wrong."

"But I could help her by being there should she give birth early."

"Are you mad? Trust me, Sergeant when I tell you it is imperative that you are not there when she gives birth, unless you wish to see a side of your wife you never dreamed of seeing in your worst nightmares. As the pain and discomfort of giving birth increases with every 'push' so she will start glaring at you through accusing eyes that say this is all your fault. She then follows on verbally with such as: 'You're never going to do 'that' to me again, so don't even think about it as I am never going to go through this again. It's all right for you, you, bastard, you had the easy bit. I want a divorce so I can become a nun. God, what my poor mother suffered. And so on."

"But surely you advocate a husband at least trying to comfort his wife at such a time, sir?" says I. "Didn't you try and comfort Mrs Clump when she gave birth to your children?"

"No. I avoided it like the plague and went to the pub on each occasion." Suddenly he appears rather thoughtful as he scratches at his beard, while fixing Head with questioning eyes before counting the fingers on his hands. "Correct me if I am wrong, Sergeant. Did I or did I not attend your wedding five months ago just after Christmas?"

"You did, sir."

"And you are saying that your wife is about seven months gone?"

Head goes red, "Um… Correct, sir."

"I see. That being the case, your attempt to emotionally blackmail me into allowing your wife to accompany you on the trip to Cornwall, is denied, as you should have kept it buttoned up until you were married. You will just have to make sure your wife is left in capable hands while you are away should anything happen."

"Fear not, Sergeant," says I. "Chloe can move in with Betty while we are away."

"She'll still have her work to do."

"Gentlemen," grates Clump. "Let us exit the domestic doldrums and get back to the matter in hand." He slaps a folder on the desk. "Here are your instructions and reports on the case thus far, along with train times and where you will be billeted, etc-etc."

"Where are we staying?" asks a miserable looking Head.

"At a rather grand rustic inn called The Smugglers Rest. I have stayed there myself on a few occasions. Good food, comfy beds and glorious views over the ocean. You will be catching the 7.30 from Paddington tomorrow morning, which gives you the remainder of the day to catch up with any outstanding paperwork and to tidy up your messy desks."

"But we never tidy up our desks," pleads Head.

"You will today as the new Chief Constable is coming around for an inspection tomorrow, and he is a stickler for order. Order equals discipline and efficiency, so he says. Right, bugger off so I can have a fart, a cigar and a scotch in peace."

We get to our feet and I pick up the folder. Just as we reach the door, Clump says, "One more thing. This coming Friday, which is four days hence, Mrs Clump and I shall arrive at Bullington Castle to stay for the weekend. It is Miss Matilda Bullingtons twenty first birthday along with her engagement to Lord Jeremy Trout. But do not worry 'lads' I will be in holiday mode and will not encroach upon your investigations. Besides you may well have solved the case and headed back home before I even get there. So, good luck and see you both soon."

"Thank you, sir," we chorus.

"Bloody Cornwall," groans Head slamming our office door the second we are inside. "I can't go, Gerald. Why it's practically at the end of the world and further away than France. I can't be that far away from Chloe at this critical stage in her bump."

"To be honest, Richard I think Clump's being very unreasonable about this because he doesn't want to lose his face. He's more concerned about his relative's welfare than ours, while winning himself massive trollop points by sending us there, in the certain knowledge, we'll solve the case and prove that Scotland Yard is the penultimate crime fighting force in the entire world, while we, trained of course by him, are two of its best detectives."

"We're not that good, are we?" says Head plonking himself down beside his desk.

"Compared to most of the idiots in the force we are. Why are we so good? I will tell you; we think for ourselves, act on our decisions and say bollocks to convention. But to be effective we cannot operate efficiently if we are burdened with personal problems that causes conflict between us. Are you with me so far?"

"No."

"Good. Let me enlighten you," says I sitting down on Heads desk and accidently pushing off a pile of papers in the process. "I can't have you moaning and groaning throughout the trip because you are worrying about Chloe. Therefore, I suggest we take the girls with us."

"How can we? Clump will crucify us should he find out."

"He won't find out, trust me."

"But what about Chloe's job?"

"To hell with it. She'll have to give it up shortly anyway." Leaning closer to Head I lower my voice in case someone is earwigging at the door. "I still have most of the money we made from the Blue Diamond case and you must have as well."

"The wedding cost a fare bit and things for the baby made a small hole, plus a few little luxuries. But yes, I've still got seventy pounds hidden away, which is more than enough to put down on our own little place in a decent area."

"Which you can't do without attracting attention to yourself."

"I know that, Gerald. Trust me when I say I'm not so stupid as to go throwing money about."

"Of course, you wouldn't. Even so we must continue to be careful and not allow ourselves to get too cocky. Right, that's enough of that, let's get on."

Head lets out a groan, "I can't bear the thought of Chloe suffering on a train all the way down to Cornwall, Gerald. All that swaying about and bumpety bumps. Constant clickity clacks and squealing brakes..."

"She'll be fine. What do you want to do? Leave Chloe here and drive yourself mad worrying about her? Or perhaps you should consider going sick to get out of it, or leave the force and take your chances. Or, as I suggest, we take the girls with us. It is early June, Richard. Summer is here, so let's enjoy it for a while away from the big smoke. We shall be working but not all the time, while the girls can just enjoy. Betty needs a holiday and Chloe could certainly do with a change of scenery, and all she has to do is put up with the journey there and back."

"Chloe's never seen the sea let alone walked on a beach."

"There you are then. It is settled. We shall all go."

"What if Chloe doesn't think she's up to it?"

"Well that will be that I suppose and we'll have to go back to plan A. Chloe will move in with Betty until our return and I will have to suffer your constant moaning and groaning, your sour face, bad tempers and lack of concentration regarding the case."

"I'm not that bad, surely?"

"Yes, you are. Now until we put it to the girls, let us get on."

Gazing around the room I admit that it is in a bit of a mess. My desk is piled high with files and rubbish of all sorts, including a plate with left over mouldy bread, cheese and a giant dead slug on it. There are piles of documents stacked up against the filing cabinets that are themselves stuffed to over flowing. The floor looks like a communal rubbish dump, and there must be at least half a dozen mugs laying around half full with stagnant green coloured liquid of various sorts. But at least they act as effective insect collectors.

"Why don't we just set fire to the office?" says Head dead pan. "We could accidently knock over a lamp or something."

"Clump would want to know why we lit a lamp when the sun is shining through our little window. A fire is a good idea, Richard but out of the question. We need a proper plan."

"Why don't we go to the store room, grab a few packing cases, chuck everything in and then take it around back and set fire to it there?"

"And have half the Yard descend on us complaining about the smoke. I think, Richard we should do as you suggest, but instead of setting fire to everything we'll just find somewhere to hide it all until we return from Cornwall, and then burn it."

"Brilliant," smiles Head getting to his feet. "We could hide it all behind the old stables. No one goes there much because they're due to be demolished."

"An excellent idea. Let's get to it and pray that no one sees us."

It takes us two hours of hard graft to clear the office, sweep the floor and polish up the furniture. Standing back to admire our work we both agree it looks good. The little added touches set it all off. The vase of flowers on Heads desk, stolen from the canteen, are very beautiful, and complement the pair of small rural panoramas in oils nailed on the wall that we pinched from the 'unclaimed stolen property cupboard'. But my favourite is the small bronze nude of Aphrodite we also found in the cupboard; that now sits on the window sill.

"That statue won't be there long," warns Head. "Once the Chief Constable sees it, he'll have it removed while extolling the virtues of virtue, and then what? We'll get in trouble, Gerald that's what."

I shake my head. "Richard, the Chief Constable is a hypocrite of the highest order. He may sprout the bible and harp on about chastity and moral ethics, when in truth he's a secret collector of filth and a notorious wanker."

Head appears amazed at this revelation. "Really? How do you know that?"

"Let's just say I have done my homework. Not only is the Chief Constable a collector of dirty printed works he is also a collector of, shall we say, erotic art. He'll certainly remove the statue, but rest assured it will end up in his collection. In short he will steal it."

"The cheeky bastard. Is nothing safe from the thieving morons in this place."

"In short, no." I rub my hands together. "I think, Sergeant it is time for a pie and a pint at the Dirty Duck, don't you?"

"What about our promise to ourselves not to drink before and during lunch?"

"We could try adhering to it again tomorrow."

"Alright then, let's go."

Westward Ho

The station at Bullington is small but very pretty. Red brick walls and grey slate tiles. Hanging baskets full of budding geraniums, and several cut in half old beer barrels full of small rose bushes that are breaking out in flower. Stepping down on the platform, I set our bags down and turn to offer Betty my hand.

"Oh, isn't it lovely," smiles Betty. "I could live here, Detective Inspector."

"Until you get covered in smoke," says I as the train puffs out a cloud of smut, that luckily, fans over our heads.

I help Head with his suitcase while he assists a somewhat exhausted Chloe out of the train. She has not had a comfortable ride over the last two hours of the journey and is suffering from back ache, but to her credit she has made little complaint, and is so excited about the trip she is a joy to have on board.

There doesn't appear to be anyone around so we pick up our luggage, step into the station and go up to the ticket office, which seems to be manned by a large ginger cat that hisses at us through the wire grille.

"I feel a little sick and dizzy," says Chloe placing a trembling hand over her forehead.

"Let's get you out into the air," says Betty wrapping an arm around Chloe's back to steady her.

I take charge of the luggage while Head assists Betty in gently steering Chloe through the station and out back into the sunshine, where they sit her down on a park bench that looks over towards rolling meadows full of sheep and nothing much else. Setting the luggage down I quickly note there are no cabs waiting. The place is completely deserted.

"There's no cabs," grates Head, "and we need to get Chloe to the inn as quickly as possible."

"She needs to lay down," adds Betty. "Why isn't there any cabs, Detective Inspector?"

"I have no idea," says I in all honesty. "It said in our itinerary that all transport has been arranged, so perhaps a cab will turn up shortly."

"There must be someone about," grates Head sitting down beside Chloe and taking her hand. "I'll bet that's the Station Masters house over there behind those thick bushes," he points. "Perhaps we should go and knock on the door."

"I'll look around inside first," says I on hearing what sounded like a door slamming. Back inside I go up to the ticket office again and place a hand too close to the gap under the grille, the cat suddenly pounces forward, shoots out a paw and tries to scratch me, but I am too quick for the spitting lump and swiftly retract my hand as its claws dig into the wooden counter instead of my flesh. I follow that action on with a clenched fist banging down on its paw. Belting out a screeching wail it jumps backwards, flies off the counter and tears out the office and disappears.

"Did yer just hurt my little Pussy?" sounds a rough voice from behind me.

Spinning around reveals a hairy faced giant of a railway man in full uniform with Station Master emblazoned on his hat. He is also doing up his fly buttons, so I assume he's just been in the toilet.

"No," lies I. "It took one look at me and fled."

"Ah… That's because he don't know yer from Eric. Once he gets to know yer he'll be a purrin' and a snugglin' up to yer. Now, what can I do for yer?"

"We need transport to the local police station and then on to the Smugglers Rest."

"Ah… Yer'll be the famous detectives from London then, I take it."

"You take it right."

Making a show of taking out his fob watch from inside his waistcoat he gazes officiously at it before clicking the cover shut and putting it away. "It's 4.30. Ol' Seb' will be here in about half an hour with a load of sheep to be loaded on the next train. He'll take yer wherever yer want ter go for a few pennies."

"We have two ladies with us who couldn't possibly travel in a sheep wagon. They'll require something more comfortable."

He scratches at his scruffy beard, "Can they ride bicycles?"

"One is with child," grates I.

"Well it ain't my fault. Tell yer what me handsome, Doctor Brent will be a comin' here ter see to my wife's gout about six. He'll give them ladies of yers a lift to the Smugglers once he's done with the ol' woman. Goes right past the Smugglers on his way home, he does."

"Thank you."

"Yer welcome. Now then, do yer folks want refreshments while yer wait?"

"That would be nice."

"I'll get the wife to make a pot of tea and plate up a few scones. Come with me an' yer can all wait in the waitin' room."

The waiting room we find is very small but the bench seating along one wall is padded and comfortable. Chloe feels a little better, which instantly cheers up Head and Betty.

Snuggling up to me she whispers in my ear, "Do you think we may have a four-poster bed to sleep on, Detective Inspector?"

"No idea my little fantasist. So long as it is comfortable that is all that matters."

"And doesn't squeak too much," she grins saucily.

We chat on until the Station Master returns carrying a large tray with our refreshments on. Dragging over a heavy looking round table with one hand he sets the tray down onto it.

"That'll be five shillings," smiles he.

"How much!" gasps Head.

"Alright, four shillings."

"How about one shilling?" frowns I.

"'Ow about two and six?"

"How about a poke in the eye?" warns Head.

"Alright, my final offer, or I'll take the tray away, one and six."

"Done," says I. Fishing around in my 'new' coins only purse, that Betty bought me for Christmas, I hand the money over.

"Lovely," grins he while starring at Betty's bust. "Anything yer want just ask."

"We will," says I glaring at the man. How dare he gawp so brazenly at my Betty's bust?

Betty stirs the pot before straining the tea into very clean white cups on saucers.

"Those four scones look nice, Detective Inspector," smiles she. "As does the jam and clotted cream."

"That equates to one each," says I watching Head like a hawk as he swiftly grabs the biggest scone to place triumphantly onto his plate.

The scones turn out to be as delicious as they looked, and after a couple of cups of tea each, we are all in good spirits.

"I'm really enjoying myself," coos Betty.

"So am I," smiles Chloe, the colour having returned to her cheeks. "I've never been on holiday before. It's wonderful."

Head puts an arm over her shoulders and hugs her to him as I stand up for a good stretch.

"I'd love to paddle my feet in the sea," says Chloe. "Do you think we can all do that later?"

"You and Betty can," says I. "Tonight, Richard and I will be going through the local forces reports to find out what's what, so that we are fully prepared when we meet the Bullingtons tomorrow. It says in our itinerary that we will have a liveryman and a coach at our disposal throughout our stay, and we'll be picked up at nine-thirty tomorrow outside the Inn."

"Cor, a lay-in, what luxury," beams Head. "Why so late, Gerald?"

"I assume, Richard it is so our visit doesn't encroach on their personal routines. You know what these aristocrats are like, sticklers for routine and etiquette. Meals at an exact time. Everyone and everything in its place. Strict dress codes, especially for the ladies who will change clothes several times throughout the day to comply with convention. They'll change for lunch, change for dinner, change to walk in the garden, change for a shit…"

"What a load of old tripe," says Betty. "I couldn't be bothered to change clothes umpteen times a day even if I were a queen. Goodness me, they must spend half their lives changing."

"Well what else do they have to do except for crocheting?"

"Have sex with the gamekeepers behind the sheds," grins Head.

"I'm sure they do lots of things," grates Betty giving Head one of her admonishing glares. "It isn't their fault they're seen as secondary beings only capable of having sex and giving birth. I'm sure they play musical instruments, read and write, and are very learned."

"We shall see, Betty," says I. "Anyway, their world is far removed from the real world and in truth what do the men do when not going off to war?"

Head gives out a yawn, "Boring stuff like playing billiards and shooting millions of birds, that is when they're not with their mistresses shooting other stuff."

"You seem to know a lot about it, Richard," says Chloe.

"I read a book about them once. It was called: The English Aristocracy Stripped Bare."

"Never heard of it," says I.

"You may well not have," grins Head. "It was printed by an underground press and is currently banned for being too graphic. The book exposed several aristocrats, some still living, for their debauchery, their eccentricities and the madness that is inherent within them because of too much inbreeding. According to the book, your average aristocrat, whether male or female, are as mad as monks."

Fortunately, Heads ramblings are interrupted by the sound of bleating sheep and a wagon pulling up outside. The Station Master sticks his head in.

"Ol' Seb's here. He's only got a few sheep. He'll put 'em into a pen ready ter be loaded on the train when it arrives. Give him ten minutes an' he'll give yer a knock. Have yer finished eating and drinking?"

"Yes, thank you."

"The scones were delicious," says Betty.

"Thank yer, madam," says he to her bust.

"I think he's become quite sweet on me," says Betty once he'd gone.

"Indeed," frowns I. "Especially between your stomach and neck."

"Don't be coarse, Detective Inspector. The man's simply too shy to look me directly in the eyes that's all."

"If you say so." I sit down again. In truth I am itching to eventually get to the inn and settle in once Head and I have visited the local police station. A few beers and a good meal while we ponder over the case files thus far, followed by an early night in a comfortable bed, that hopefully doesn't squeak too much, sounds marvellous.

A scruffy hairy face wearing a floppy felt hat pokes itself around the door.

"Who's wantin' a lift to thee police station?"

"We is. I mean we are," says I pointing to Head.

"Right then, come yer along with me." He touches his hat with dirty gnarled fingers and disgustingly long nails. "Welcome to Bullington ladies. I hope yer enjoy yer stay."

"We will," they beam.

"Lovely too," smiles he, his eyes twinkling all over Betty's bust before he disappears.

I told her that red dress was too risqué for the back and beyond. She should have worn something more fitting, but she wouldn't listen, and now she has to suffer every yokel she meets gawping at her cleavage. "Are you sure you'll both be alright until this Doctor Brent turns up?"

"Of course, we will, Detective Inspector. Do not worry we shall be fine." Betty pats Chloe's hand. "Won't we Chloe?"

"We will indeed."

"Well don't go giving birth early unless I'm with you," warns Head.

Chloe shoots him a confused look, "Why? What do you know about delivering a baby, Richard? Especially if it comes early."

"I read this book…"

"Let us get on, Sergeant," orders I grabbing mine and Betty's bags. We kiss the girl's goodbye and head out into the sunshine. It is surprisingly warm for early June and it seems as if summer started a month or more back. Flora and fauna are all ahead of themselves and the air rings with life. Hopefully it will last and we'll enjoy a long hot summer.

Having unloaded his sheep, Seb' is waiting for us along with a scruffy sheep dog beside a cart with huge wheels that is pulled by a bay coloured heavy horse. In full view, Seb' is a thick set, short man with bandy legs covered with tatty corduroy trousers that are tied with string around the ankles just above manure covered leather work boots. He's wearing a grubby smock with a red neckerchief tied around his thick neck. A long smoking clay pipe hangs precariously from the corner of his mouth and he exudes an aura of 'I have all the time in the world so take your time'.

"Come yer over," says he, and we do so, which is when my nose is assaulted by the stench of sheep shit steaming up from the waggon.

Seb' climbs up onto the waggon, "Pass me up yer bags."

I pass up my first bag which is wrenched away from my grasp and then tossed carelessly into the back of the waggon. For some reason, known only to God, I pass him my other bag which again is snatched away and tossed into the back. Head steps forwards and passes up his suitcase, Seb' grabs hold of it by the handle, mumbles that it's, "friggin' heavy," before hurling it, with a grunt, into the back. Now our luggage is undoubtably soaking in sheep's piss and covered in shit, that's covered in little muck flies, that have appeared in little clouds and seem to be attacking everything even remotely alive.

"Come yer up," says Seb' offering me a dirty smelly hand which I take hold of despite myself. Seb's grip is so powerful, I fear it will break my bones as he practically hauls me up while nearly wrenching my shoulder from its socket.

I help haul Head up as Seb' takes up the reins and pats the wooden board beside him.

"Sit yer down beside ol' Seb', me handsome," says he.

I sit down and Head squashes up beside me. Glancing behind me I look down into the waggon, relieved to find that our luggage has been dumped on top of clean straw in a fenced off space separate from where the sheep were.

Seb' pats me on the thigh and says, "Yer ready my lovers?"

I nod before meeting Heads questioning gaze as he mouths, 'My lovers?'

'No idea,' mouths back I.

The dog leaps up into the back of the cart. Seb' slaps the reins and the horse moves off while I wonder what Seb' is wondering. I know that Head is wondering if Seb' might be a bit strange, while I'm also wondering if the Station Master is also a bit strange as he also called me his handsome? Either way I'm not about to take the chance of Seb' being a bit strange and say to Head, "Do you want to change places, Sergeant?"

"What for?"

"You don't like sitting on the edge, do you?"

"I don't mind. Actually, I have never minded."

"Are you sure? I seem to recall you prefer being in the middle."

"No, I don't…"

"Now, now my lovers," says Seb' slapping the reins again. "Yer can take turns sittin' on the edge if yer want. Perhaps yer'd like ter change round at the station so the sergeant can sit beside me for a while."

"How about I sit in the back," suggests I.

"What and get all straw on yer arse. No, yer stay put me handsome while ol' Seb' sings yer a song. Here, hold my pipe, but don't smoke it cause I'm near out of baccy."

He gives me his pipe, takes a deep breath and starts to sing so loudly I reason the seagulls soaring high in the sky can hear him.

"My lover an' me went down to thee brook and stripped off all our gear.

Oh, he cried, I ain't never seen one so big, I fear.

No, my handsome laughed I so. It takes a while for such a whopper ter grow.

But don't you worry, we're in no hurry, yer'll soon have yer hands on he.

Yer'll soon have yer hands on he.

Cause he marvelled at its shape and size, for he couldn't believe his eyes.

Cor, he cried with glee, I'll soon have that bugger in me gob yer'll see.

I'll soon have that bugger in me gob yer'll see.

I said he would, but if he could, leave a little for his mother and me.

Leave a little for his mother… and me…"

I am speechless and contemplate pushing Head off the waggon so I can edge away from Seb' who is obviously seriously strange. However, Head doesn't move an inch when I try to cagily shoulder him off the waggon.

"What kind of fish was it, Seb'?" laughs Head.

Seb' takes back his pipe, sticks it in his mouth and takes a draw, "A trout. The biggest me an' my boy had ever seen. Cause we ain't never seen it since."

"Why's that?" says I sighing with relief.

He throws back his head and laughs, "Cause, we caught the bugger an' ate it. We often go down ter the brook on a nice day, me an' the boy. Takes us a bar of soap an' has a good scrub. Nothin' like bathin' in pure clean water."

"You have just the one boy?" asks I.

"No… By heaven I got six boys an' two girls. My oldest boy works with me while the other boys work on other farms as I ain't got enough land an' sheep ter employ 'em all. One of me girls is still at home while the other lives and works up at the castle doin' chamber maidin'."

To confirm to myself that Seb' isn't funny I ask, "So, you and your wife have eight children?"

"Nope."

"You just said you did."

"I said I had eight children, but I didn't say who with. Me an' Mary got four between us an' I got three with Angela an' one with Beryl."

"Are Angela and Beryl your previous wife's?" says I while wondering if the poor man may have twice been a widower.

"No…" he drawls. "They're me girlfriends of course."

"Girlfriends? Don't you mean mistresses?"

"Same thing."

"Well I wouldn't want to be in your shoes when your wife finds out."

"She found out years ago, when I told her."

"But surely she can't be happy with the situation?"

"She don't mind so long as I don't bring 'em home ter stay thee night. Mary don't mind seein' 'em in church though. An' we all gets together at Christmas an' Easter."

"That must be nice and interesting," says Head.

I'm not sure if he's being sarcastic or not, either way I settle back a bit and relax, as the waggon heads upwards towards the top of a hill flanked on both sides by low stone walls.

A light salty breeze kisses our faces so the sea can't be far away. Skylarks sing above our heads in a bright blue sky dotted with puffs of snow-white cloud. It is truly wonderful just plodding along and enjoying the scenery. Coming over the hill we are looking down towards a valley where nestles a small hamlet of painted white stone cottages with grey tiled rooves, as a cloud covers the sun and a shadow sweeps over the hamlet to accentuate the magic of the moment. This is all a dream, so different from the noise, hustle and bustle of London that I am lost in the euphoria of the moment, until Head grates, "Bet nothing much goes on down there. It looks deader than a dried-up old toad that was run over by a traction engine."

"Thank you, Sergeant for that stirring rendition," grates I. "Remind me to destroy your euphoria someday."

"What euphoria was that, sir?"

"Never mind."

"Bullington Village down there in thee valley," says Seb'. "An' believe it or not, Sergeant, yer'd be surprised what can go on in a small place like that. 'Specially when yer got buggers like that Percy Bullington livin' up thee road. Cor he's a sod he is."

Now, this could be interesting, "In what way is he a sod?"

"Can't say me handsome. Too bloody risky what with me bein' a tenant farmer in dept to the buggers. I'll just say watch how yer go when dealin' with 'em."

I attempt to get more out of Seb' but he's clamped his mouth so tightly shut it would require the services of a crow bar to force it open.

At last we reach the edge of the village. It is so quiet there doesn't appear to be a soul around. Undaunted the horse trundles on. We pass a rustic old thatched inn called the Rams Head, the village school, a tiny slate roofed post office and a more modern general stores, until we come to a halt outside a small thatched cottage with tiny latticed windows and a wisteria covering half the frontage.

"Here thee be," says Seb'. "Thee, police house."

"Are you sure?" says I thinking I have never seen a police house looking like something off a chocolate box.

"Sure, as me balls only itch on Fridays."

Head makes the mistake of asking, "Why only on Fridays?"

"Cause me drawers have been on all week an' tend ter get a bit crabby by then."

"How much do we owe you, Seb'?"

"Square me up later. How long shall thee be?"

"Hopefully not long. We shall go through the evidence gathered thus far on the case with whoever has been in charge of the investigation…"

"That'll be Constable Burroughs," cuts in Seb'. If he ain't in he'll be down the pub. I'll be goin' there me self an' will send him over to yer if he's there. Come an' get me when yer ready."

"Will do," says I. "Can we leave our bags with you?"

"Yer can. They'll be safe with me."

Head and I jump down as Seb' clicks the horse on. Steering it around in the narrow street he heads back towards the Rams Head. Head and I walk up a flag stone path to the house where we find the door wide open.

"Hello," calls I knocking on the door frame while nosing inside. "Anyone in?"

"Probably up the pub like Seb' said," says Head. "Let's just go in."

Stepping inside we find ourselves in a very neat and tidy small parlour with a pair of armchairs, a sideboard and an ingle nook fireplace. The heavily beamed ceiling is so low we have to remove our bowlers.

"It's all very cosy," says Head looking around. "Smells of lavender and roses."

And exudes a strong sense of wellbeing as well, thinks I calling out again, "Is anyone there?"

There's a planked door one side of the fireplace that probably leads upstairs while a similar door on the opposite side undoubtably leads outback, the latch on this door suddenly clicks up, and ducking his head in walks a twenty something policeman in uniformed trousers and dusty boots, with braces over a white flannel shirt with sleeves rolled up.

Broad shouldered, with a weathered handsome face and thick bushy moustache, he looks every inch the village copper as he straightens up so his hair just brushes the beam above him.

"Sorry gentlemen, I was out back digging up a few potatoes for dinner."

He is lying, his hair appears ruffled and his fly buttons aren't all done up while his cheeks are somewhat red. "Are you not on duty then, Constable?" remonstrates I.

"Oh, yes of course I am, sir. But then I'm always on duty. Seven days a week and twenty-four hours a day."

"I see," says I even though I don't. I introduce myself and Head.

"I am Constable Burroughs," says he fidgeting from one foot to the other. "Shall we go into the office and look over the case files, or would you care for a pot of tea first?"

"Why not both at the same time?" smiles I.

"Right sir. If you'll kindly follow me."

And we do so into a reasonable size kitchen, where we sit at a table with four chairs centre of the room, while he puts the kettle on the blackened range.

Neatly stacked police material covers half the table from wanted posters to pamphlets, case files and regulation manuals. Around the walls are more posters such as: Have you seen this chicken? Do you know who stole this ewe? Have you seen this man who was last seen riding a stolen bicycle through the village on April Fool's Day while dressed as a nun? Below the heading is a rough sketch of someone in a nun's habit, and the only way you could reasonably assume it's a man, as its face is mostly covered by a wimple, is because the hem of the habit is around his waist to expose seriously hairy legs. But then it might actually be a nun on the bicycle who just happens to have seriously hairy legs.

"I can see you are a busy man, Constable," says I to his back while reasoning that nothing much beyond petty theft rarely occurs around the area, leaving our constable with not a lot to do except get up to mischief. To confirm my suspicions I ask, "Do you mind if I visit your privy, Constable?"

Spinning around with a look of abject horror on his face he stutters, "N-n-no of c-c-course not, sir. It's out back down the bottom of the g-garden."

"Thank you." Getting to my feet I throw Head a wink and take myself outback into the garden, where I find a well tendered vegetable patch and a wall of in flower, runner beans that heralds a narrow gravel path down towards a wooden shed beside a red brick privy with a green painted door. Behind the privy, running right across the garden there's a low-cut hedge with a thoroughbred horse tethered on the other side, who gazes curiously at me before letting out a nodding neigh. The horse is wearing a side saddle, which tells me that its female rider is probably close by and even more probably in the shed. I go and peep through the sheds little window to see a firm young cleavage being hastily covered up by a white blouse. Things are looking up. Taking a few steps back I wait.

Three minutes pass by before the shed door opens and a petite, hatless dark-haired beauty steps out with her head down while trying to do up a final button on her blouse.

"Good afternoon, madam," says I.

"Oh bugger," she startles instantly fixing me with scathing hazel eyes. "Who the hell are you?"

"I am Detective Inspector Potter from Scotland Yard. Who the hell are you?"

Tossing back her head she sneers, "I am Matilda Bullington."

"How do you do, madam? Do you often get dressed in sheds at the bottom of gardens?"

"If you must know I was galloping across the meadow when one of my buttons popped off my blouse. On spying Constable Burroughs out in his little garden, I rode over and asked him for needle and thread so I might stitch the button back on for proprieties sake. I simply popped into his shed, removed my blouse and did the deed. I mean, stitched on the button. Anything else you wish to know?"

"Not just now thank you."

"Good. Then I shall be on my way."

I watch her flounce off towards a little gate central of the hedge, her dark velvet skirt swaying to the rhythm of her curvaceous hips. She truly is a very beautiful young woman. Having gone through the gate she is out of view for a few moments before she mounts the horse and settles herself down. She now has a fashionable women's riding hat on, a stylish short jacket over her blouse and a crop in her hand. She waves the crop in the air and calls out, "I trust you will keep this to yourself."

"Of course, madam."

"Good. No doubt I will see you before too long at the castle."

"Tomorrow."

Without another word she yanks on the reins to pull the horse's head around, I hear the slap of the crop on the saddle and Matilda Bullington is swiftly carried away across the meadow.

After a urination, I go back into the cottage to find Constable Burroughs has made tea and is stirring the pot while sat at the table opposite Head. Burroughs gazes up at me with guilt and trepidation etched across his face.

"Did you find the privy to your satisfaction, Inspector?"

"Yes, thank you," smiles I deciding not to mention my confrontation with Matilda. It has nothing to do with me unless it is linked to the attempted murders on Lord Percival. But Constable Burroughs is playing a very dangerous game messing around with an aristocrat who is expected to become engaged to another aristocrat this very weekend. What the hell he and Matilda think they are playing at I have no idea, unless they are in love? I take a seat beside Head and we start going through the constable's files on the case, where it soon becomes apparent that the constable does not have enough experience to conduct an attempted murder on a chicken, let alone on a man. It also becomes apparent that he hasn't the mental capacity to deal with anything above petty theft or sorting out the odd drunk. However, he is a very amiable young man who wants to do his best. In truth the lad is stuck in a veritable crime free area, leaving him nothing much to do except attend to his garden and roger the local posh girl while getting payed for it. The lucky sod.

An hour and a half later Head and I take what files we need and say goodbye to Burroughs. We make our way towards the Rams Head to find Seb'.

"I think old Seb's sweet on you, sir," teases Head. "He keeps calling you his lover."

"On reflection, Sergeant I vaguely recall they are common phrases in these parts that mean nothing more than, say… a Londoner addressing you as mate or governor, or an eastern counties farm labourer calling you, me ol' beauty."

"I'm not so sure, sir," says Head gazing askance at me.

"Let us leave it for now," warns I. "I need a pint."

"That sounds like a bloody good idea my lover."

Ignoring his attempts to wind me up I walk on with a song in my heart. It truly is glorious; the sun is still shining; the birds are singing and the peace and quiet lull you into euphoric ecstasy.

"Christ, does anyone actually live here?" grates Head. "It's so bloody quiet, apart from the twittering birds, you'd think everyone's buggered off to the moon."

I am about to go for him again when the sound of ribald laughter echoes down the street.

"Sounds like humans ahead," grins Head. "There is life after all."

"Coming from the Rams Head no doubt," says I.

"It's only seven, sir I reckon we've got time for a few pints before we head off to the Smugglers Rest."

"A quick one will suffice, Sergeant. The girls will be expecting to have dinner with us before it gets too late. Plus, they can't change until we get there because we have their bags with us. But worse, do you really want to antagonise them on the first night of their holiday by turning up half drunk?"

"I suppose not," whines Head.

As the Rams Head comes into view, we find there are several locals sat outside on benches while swilling cider, judging by the strong aroma of fermented apples. Seb' is sat amongst them and appears well gone already. They are a jolly, noisy group, most have bushy beards and floppy hats over longish scruffy hair, and are wearing smocks or flannel shirts.

"Here they be," cries Seb'," raising a pewter tankard. "My lovers, meet Detective Inspector Potter an' his partner in crime, Detective Sergeant Head."

They all raise their various drinking vessels in unison to greet us as one bellows out, "Beth, get yer lovely self out here, there's gentlemen from London want servin'."

A well-rounded busty barmaid appears from the pub's open doorway and saunters over to the fellow who bellowed out, hands on hips she says, "Jim Thatcher, you got a gob on you like a fog horn an' you'd be best served using it on a foggy night to keep ships from crashing onto the rocks." Everyone laughs as she turns her attention to me and Head. "What would you gentlemen like to partake of?"

"A piece of yer," says Jim with a wink. "Like us all."

"Ignore the old sod, gentlemen. If I gave him a piece of me it'd kill him."

"Two pints of your best bitter please," says I.

"You want ter get a man's drink into yer," laughs Seb'. Get 'em a jug of scrumpy, Beth."

"They won't be used to such shit," says she. "If you aren't on that stuff from birth it'll go through you like a bowl of prunes."

"I'd like to try it," says Head.

"Be it on your own head," warns Beth.

"I'll take the risk."

"I'll stick with the bitter," says I.

"Sensible man," says she giving me, for a change, a saucy wink before sauntering off.

One hour later we are back on the waggon and heading away to cheers of farewell from the locals. Seb' is well drunk, but surprisingly coherent as he chats away nine to the dozen while offering us his opinion on who would want to try and kill Lord Percival Bullington. Which is practically everyone. The man isn't the least bit liked so it seems. The information gathered from Seb' and the locals about the Bullington's was interesting but obviously guarded as everyone, one way or another, can't afford to fall out with the local gentry, especially the Bullington's.

Once at the top of the hill we've been climbing the sea comes into view a good hundred or so feet below us, and it's barely twenty feet to the edge of the cliffs from the winding track we are on. In the far distance ominous rolling black clouds seem to be sitting on the horizon, while closer to the shore navy blue waves, topped with brilliant white foam, gently curl onto a sandy beach that stretches for miles.

"Storm a brewin' up," says Seb' matter of fact. "Be rough later on."

"This is heaven," burps Head. "Like that scrumpy, you can't get enough of it."

At last we reach the Smugglers Rest. Standing alone and barely yards from the cliff edge it is a rambling stone building with a slate roof. Isolated though it is, it appears well frequented as there are several horses tied up outside, a couple of posh carriages and a hansom. I pay Seb' two shillings which he kisses before putting the coins in his pocket. Head and I jump down while Seb' climbs into the back of the waggon and starts throwing our bags out over the rails. "That's that then," says he as he retakes his seat with the dog cosying up to him. Seb' clicks the horse on and they trundle away.

After shoving the case files in one of the bags we carry our luggage into the inn, where we encounter more low beams and walls covered with photographs of the area, paintings and general memorabilia. Over a dozen well healed gentry are enjoying meals, drinks and conversation. They greet us amiably as we make our way towards where Betty and Chloe are sat at a round table in front of a tiny latticed window that looks out over the sea.

"At last," giggles Betty. "We were wondering when you'd turn up."

"Did you miss us then?" says I.

"No," she grins through twinkling eyes.

Head bends down and kisses Chloe on the cheek.

"You smell like a rotting apple," says she.

"You smell of the sea."

"We went down the steps to the beach and had a paddle. It was wonderful."

"Wonderful," choruses Betty. "Oh…, Detective Inspector it is heaven. And our room is huge," she cries spreading her arms wide. "And it has a four-poster bed that doesn't squeak."

"Marvellous," smiles I, while noting that the wiped clean plates in front of them states they have already eaten and thoroughly enjoyed it along with a bottle of claret.

Dumping the luggage against the wall I take a seat opposite Betty and ask, "Do we need to check in?"

She shakes her head. "All done, Detective Inspector. But if you want food, you'd best order now as they stop taking orders in fifteen minutes."

I raise a hand to attract the attention of a very young-looking waiter who's smartly dressed in a dark suit, white shirt and bow tie. He comes right over.

"Good evening, sir and welcome to the Smugglers Rest. How may I serve you?"

Not having seen the menu, but as the Yard are picking up the bill, I order a medium rare sirloin steak with new potatoes and seasonal vegetables along with a pint of bitter, a bottle of claret and a bowl of nuts.

"And you, sir?" says the waiter turning his attention to Head.

"I'll have the same please, but leave the steak alive."

"I don't understand, sir," says the waiter shooting me a confused look.

"He likes his steak rare," smiles I. "Can you put everything on our rooms but ensure all alcoholic drinks are invoiced separately."

"Why's that?" says Head.

"As you well know the Yard won't pay for alcoholic drinks, Richard. Tea, coffee and non-alcoholic drinks only."

"Really! The miserable bastards. You'd think as we've come all this way, they might make an exemption and at least pay for our beer."

"Well they won't, so get used to it."

"I still think it's mean."

"Ask the girls if they want anything," says I to get him off the subject.

"We're alright for now," smiles Betty.

"That is all for now, thank you," says I to the waiter.

"Thank you, sir. I will give the chef your orders and then bring your drinks over."

"Isn't he lovely?" says Betty as I note her eyes following the waiter as he heads away.

"Just because he's tall, dark and handsome, well spoken, polite and helpful doesn't mean he is nice," says I. "For all you know he could be a nasty piece of work with a tiny winkle."

"Do I detect a little bit of jealousy, Detective Inspector?" teases Betty.

"Not in the least. As if I would be jealous of a mere boy," lies I. In truth I am a realising that Betty has captivated every Cornishman she has come into contact with since we arrived, and even now, I can sense the men in the room casting fervent glances her way to the chagrin of the females they are with. Betty is vibrantly friendly and exudes an aura of worldly sophistication and sexuality that demands attention. To the locals she an exotic enigma that they can't help being drawn to, the moth to the flame. And it doesn't help matters her wearing that dress. It may be suitable in fashionable London, but it isn't suitable in the back and beyond, especially as her tits look as if they might pop right out at any second. Time to cool things down a little. "Betty, do you wish to go and change now your luggage has arrived?"

"No thank you, Detective Inspector. Chloe and I both freshened up in our shared bathroom once we'd checked in and been shown our bedrooms. Ours clothes have kept clean and as neither of us smells, despite our walk down to the beach, I see no need to change just now."

"As you wish," grates I while contemplating ordering her to go and change. Only Betty isn't a woman of her time, she is her own person, she believes women should be equal to men, and in truth will never allow any man to dominate her. Besides I adore her just as she is.

"I could stay here for ever," smiles Chloe through misty eyes.

"So, could I," says Betty. "What about you, Detective Inspector?"

I shrug, "I haven't been here long enough to form a true opinion. All appears wonderful, but we are in essence on a working holiday which isn't reality. Who knows how your feelings about Cornwall may change once you actually live here? What about you, Richard?"

"I agree it's a beautiful county. The people seem very friendly and the air is invigorating. But in truth I'd be bored to bleedin' death staying around here. I'm used to the chaos of the big smoke, the madness and the excitement. No, I can't imagine laying around sucking on a piece of straw while waiting for something exciting to happen, like the local pervert getting caught rogering a sheep."

The waiter returns with our drinks and places them down on the table, and I note he leans way too far over while doing so in order to take a sneaky gawp down Betty's cleavage. Worse than that, Betty lifts her eyes to fleetingly meet his as he straightens up and smiles down at her, even worse, neither has noticed that I am flicking admonishing glances from one to the other because they are fixated in mutual admiration of each other.

"I feel a storm brewing," warns I as the waiter walks away with Betty's eyes following him. "A storm so violent it may well destroy an awful lot more than just property."

"Whatever are you going on about, Detective Inspector?" grates Betty.

It would be foolish to go too far with this too early so I opt for the easy way out. "Look behind you, Betty." She looks behind her out of the window and gives an expressive gasp.

"Oh, my goodness, Detective Inspector! It looks like hell is heading our way."

Dinner was served during one of the most ferocious storms I have ever witnessed. The wind howled like a demon, rattling the tiles on the roof and hurling clouds of dust and grass at the windows. Thunder boomed so loud it felt as if it was inside the inn, the lighting was so violent it caused more than a few females to scream out as it lit up the bar and shook the window panes. Torrential rain hammered the roof and tortured your hearing for nearly an hour before the storm passed and the setting sun returned, where upon, almost everyone in the inn rushed outside to view the majesty of a shimmering orange orb sinking below the horizon. Marvellous.

After a delicious sweet of chocolate cake washed down with the Claret and a further study of the case files, Betty and I say good night to Head and Chloe. Head throws me a sulky look because he's not going to get what I'm hoping to get because of Chloe's bump. Never mind, such is life. Leaving Head to mull over his wine. Betty and I head upstairs to unpack and get ready for bed.

"What do you think, Detective Inspector?" says Betty once we're inside the bedroom and she'd closed the door.

There's no gas lighting here and the sweeping room is lit by two large oil lamps, each on its own tiny table. The furniture is quality along with a rug that covers the centre of the oak floor boards. Several landscape watercolours adorn the ochre walls. But most impressive is the four poster that has a deep sprung mattress that promises a good night's sleep. I give it a test by bouncing my backside up and down on it. "Marvellous," smiles I patting the embroidered quilt to entice Betty over.

"Sorry, Detective Inspector. You've been running around all day long getting all hot and sticky. It's been absolutely hours since you washed, so I think a bath is in order, don't you?"

"A bath for two sounds wonderful."

"One."

"One what?"

"One in the bath at a time, it isn't big enough for two."

"Really? Why isn't it big enough for two?"

"Because it isn't. Now let's get in the bathroom before, Richard and Chloe do. Grab your towel and follow me."

Grabbing a big fluffy towel from a rack on the wall I follow Betty out, across the landing and into the bathroom, Betty locks the door behind us. Lit by a pair of wall mounted oil lamps the bathroom is very posh with its porcelain sink, blue flower-patterned flushing toilet bowl and little boat pictures on the wall. There is also a full-sized stand-alone mirror to admire your nakedness in. The only downer is the bath.

"It's half the size of a decent sized tin bath!" grates I. "If I get in there, I'll probably get stuck and have to be pulled out by a cart horse."

Ignoring my outburst Betty bends over, puts the plug in and turns the taps on as it hits me that the bath is plumbed up for hot and cold.

"You're only allowed two inches of hot water," says Betty. "According to the hotels information guide; if you hog any more than that others will not get hot water because the boiler can't cope."

"Two inches is barely enough to cover your manhood"

"That's the beauty of a small bath, Detective Inspector. Two inches of hot with an inch or so of cold is more than enough once you get in and the water is pushed up to your belly button. How clever is that? So, stop moaning and get stripped off."

I do as I'm told. In no time the water has reached the required depth, Betty tests the heat with her hand, declares it safe and in I get. It is a squash to sit right down, my knees are up to my chin and I can barely move. How the hell I am expected to wash myself I have no idea, but at least the water feels unusually soft and delightfully warm. Rolling up her sleeves Betty sets to washing my face, neck and shoulders with soap on a flannel. After a rinse off she goes for my back, chest and arms.

"Right. Stand up, Detective Inspector."

I do so and Betty sets to washing the best bits without the flannel. It is heaven.

"What a good little soldier you are," teases Betty. "Standing to attention like that."

"I won't be for long if you keep soaping it up so vigorously."

"I just want to make sure it's nice and clean."

"It's probably the cleanest knob the worlds ever seen."

She stops soaping and pulls out the plug, "Right, bob down a bit."

"What for?"

"So, I can rinse the soap off with cold water. I may like the scent of carbolic soap, Detective Inspector, but I can't bear the taste of it."

Not wanting to disobey orders I bob down to receive surprisingly cold water all over my bits, killing my ardour dead, which is good as I was very close to decorating Betty's hair.

After a dry off I slip the towel around me, grab my clothes and make for the bedroom.

Betty closes the door, "Turn the lamps down, Detective Inspector, but don't draw the curtains, I want the rising moon to cast it's light over us while you're slowly undressing me."

Bullington Castle

Breakfast was a wide choice from tinned fruits to good old kippers, kedgeree, toast, marmalade, tea, coffee and of course full English, all served in the main bar.

At exactly nine twenty-five, Head and I head outside to wait for our pickup. At exactly nine thirty a gleaming black carriage arrives pulled by a pair of black horses and driven by a liveryman in top hat, black jacket, white breeches and knee-high black boots.

Pulling up beside us he jumps down, drops the step and bids us good morning. We introduce ourselves and he informs us his name is Simmons, and he is at our disposal. We climb aboard, Simmons snaps up the step, climbs up and takes the reins. Clicking the horses on he turns them around and we head off back towards the village.

"It's a lovely day, Simmons," says I as we trot along.

"It is indeed, sir," says he. "Blue skies all day, so I believe."

"Where are we going?" asks Head.

"To the castle, sir. I assumed you would want to meet the Bullingtons first thing."

"We do indeed, Simmons," says I. Settling back I open the case file and flicking through it I find Simmons name. Interviewed by Constable Burroughs it seems that Simmons had no information to give regarding the attempted murders on Lord Percival. According to the constable's records nearly everyone in the household also knew nothing about nothing. Well we shall see once Head and I have grilled them all again.

The carriage turns off the lane and heads down a hill towards a wooded area and shortly we are flanked by trees full of twittering birds. After a while the wood ends and we are afforded our first view of Bullington Castle. Expecting to see a Norman castle I am surprised to find the castle appears relatively new despite recessed parapet and towers at each end.

As if picking up on my thoughts, Simmons says, "The original Norman castle fell into virtual ruin about two hundred years ago, but the Bullingtons continued to live in it. Poor as church mice they were until the Tenth Earl restored the family fortunes in the early eighteen- hundreds. In the twenties he had the castle flattened and this one built in its place."

"Out with the old and in with the new," says Head.

"So, they say, sir. Except not all the old has gone. The original dungeons remain along with the ghost of the Fifth Earl who still walks the battlements…"

"I don't do ghosts," says Head. "What time does this ghost walk about?"

"Around midnight, sir. Especially on stormy nights."

"What every night!"

"Only now and again, apparently."

"And has anyone ever seen this ghost?" says I.

"No one except for the current earl who sees it regularly."

I'll bet, thinks I. According to the locals the Twelfth Earl is absolutely nuts and imagines all sorts. This is going to be a very entertaining investigation.

"If this ghost comes near me, I'll shoot the bastard," snarls Head slipping a hand under his jacket where his revolver usually sits, only it's not there because Clump ordered us not to go armed while on this case. 'You will not carry your revolvers at any time during your stay in Cornwall, as I cannot risk you shooting Cornwallians willy 'bloody' nilly. Is that clear?'

The carriage comes to a stop in front of a pair of studded oak doors. Simmonds jumps down, drops the step and informs us that he has a few errands to run but will be back at our disposal within the hour, should we need him. He also advises us to beware of the dogs.

"What dogs?" demands Head as we alight.

"Six white highland terriers, sir."

"Are they vicious?"

"No, sir. But they are a nuisance because they are undisciplined and allowed to do what they please. Beware of shit everywhere and try to avoid petting them."

"Why? Do they bite?"

"No, sir. But any sign of affection and they will try to mate with you."

"Well they won't be mating with me the dirty bastards," snarls Head pulling a face. "If they try it on me, I'll wring their bloody necks!"

"I would not advice that, sir. Her ladyship adores her little 'bubbly boos' and anyone being unkind to them will find themselves on her wrong side. Which isn't good."

"We shall bear it in mind, Simmonds," smiles I.

"Thank you, sir. Welcome to Bullington Castle."

Snapping the steps up he climbs back on the carriage and drives it away.

"You seem somewhat grumpy this morning, Sergeant," says I as we go up to the oak doors. "Did you not sleep well?"

"No, I didn't. The bed was too comfortable."

"And Chloe, how did she sleep?"

"Like a pig. She snored all bloody night."

"So, it was she who kept you awake and not the comfortable bed."

"It's not her fault she snores. She can't get comfy because of her bump unless she lays on her back, but in doing so she snores. Normally, I would prefer her on her back…"

"Let us get on," warns I before the conversation gets very rude. Rolling up the case files I shove them in my waistband and cover them with my jacket. On pulling the bell cord a resounding clang-clang comes from inside the castle. Almost immediately one of the doors is violently opened inwardly and we are confronted by a wide eyed, tall skinny man with a big nose, a stubbly face and receding starchy grey hair. He is wearing a striped shirt, a pair of black socks held up by sock garters and sports a pair of seriously knobbly knees.

"I only requested one batman," frowns he. "But never mind, two is preferable to none. Thank God you are here at last. Quick, there is no time to lose. This is life or death."

Spinning around he runs off and we follow, across a chequered tiled floor, past an open-mouthed footman and up curving stone ballasted stairs, along a hallway and into an open door where we are confronted with a huge bedroom that appears to have been ransacked. There are clothes, shoes and all sorts scattered all over the bed, the teak furniture and the wooden floor.

Panting hard the skinny man gasps out, "Right men. Get to it, I have less than two hours until tee off for the most prestigious golf match of the year. Dress me."

I quickly ascertain where he is coming from, "I am sorry, sir, we are detectives, not valets."

"Really? Are you sure?"

"We are certain."

"You don't look like batmen, but you do look like valets."

"We are definitely detectives from Scotland Yard, sir."

"What do you detect? Can you detect where my favourite golfing tiepin is? You know it, the one with the gold golf club and little pearl golf ball."

"We are here to investigate the attempts on Lord Percival Bullingtons life…"

"That's my son, though that is open to scrutiny and something else you might care to investigate. Anyway, fuck him the turd. Look here detective chappies, can't you just find it in your hearts to help an old soldier get kitted up for his golf?"

"May I be of assistance?" asks a tall, posh looking middle-aged man with grey flecked black hair as he steps into the room.

"Are you a valet?" asks Skinny.

"No, Major. I am your butler."

"Well I don't require a bally butler. I have no need of a shitty stuck up butler, so gather your stuff together and bugger off. You are fired."

"Thank you, Major. I take it gentlemen you are the detectives from Scotland Yard."

"We are, sir. I am Detective Inspector Potter and this my colleague, Detective Sergeant Head."

"I am Ronald Smithers, head butler. The Countess is expecting you. Please follow me."

"Oh no you don't," snaps the Major stabbing out a finger. "She doesn't need any valets she's got hundreds of lady's maids, the greedy old trollop."

"I shall escort the detectives down to her ladyship, Major. Then I will return in a short while to assist you in dressing."

"Why don't you speak English man. Damn foreigners. Bally nuisances they are, detectives. Take my advice and don't employ the buggers. You'd be better off with a teapot."

"If you will kindly follow me, gentlemen," gestures Smithers.

"That's it, desert me in my hour of need, you bastards. You haven't heard the last of this."

"Ignore him, gentlemen," says Smithers closing the door once we are in the hallway. "Once I have assisted him in being suitably attired, I shall pack him off to his golf club and we shall not have to worry about him until dinner time."

"I assume he is the Twelfth Earl of Bullington," says I as we head down the stairs.

"He is indeed. However, do not ever address him as earl. My lord or just, sir will suffice. At present he is convinced he is back in the army and home on leave. Addressing him as major confuses him less and helps to keep him moderately in line."

"Is he dangerous?" asks Head on reaching the bottom of the stairs.

"To himself, sir. Not usually to others, but he is becoming more troublesome…"

"I won't forget this!" yells out the major from the top of the stairs. Having removed his shirt, he is now naked apart from his socks while waving a sabre around.

"If you do not return to your room immediately, Major," warns Smithers. "I shall call the cook."

The major rattles his sabre at Smithers. "You rotten swine. How dare you threaten me with that old witch. I'll cut her damn head off and feed it to the porkers. You see if I don't," says he before spinning around and affording us a view of a skinny rump before he disappears. The violent slamming of a door then echoes all around the hall.

"Is the earless mad as well?" asks Head as we pass by a suit of armour at the bottom of the stairs.

"Only when there's a full moon," grins Smithers. "Or when the earl winds her up too much. There is no such title as an earless, sir, simply address the countess as my lady or ma'am. She likes ma'am, it makes her feel more royal, like a queen."

"How do we address the rest of the family?" asks I as we head down a long oak panelled corridor with the odd medieval weapon hanging off the walls.

"Lord Percival, when it suits him likes to be called just, Percy. Lord or sir otherwise. Robert and Algernon are honourable but never address them as honourable. Master, sir or even Mr will suffice. As in Mr Robert. Both daughters should be addressed as my lady or mistress, but miss will suffice, they much prefer it to too much stuffiness."

We come to a halt at a wide mahogany door. "The drawing room, gentlemen."

"Will there be dogs in there?" asks Head.

"They're out on their walk, Sergeant, but should be back shortly. Do you like dogs?"

Head screws up his face. "Not much," he growls.

"Oh… dear," says Smithers. He opens the door and we follow him in.

Sat on a wide green velvet sofa sits an elegant slender woman wearing a dark blue dress, she has her grey flecked auburn hair piled up, around her long swan neck sparkles a serious looking neckless that would look even better on Betty. Not to say that the lady before us isn't attractive because she is, but she appears very aloof as she gazes at us with indifference.

"The detectives have arrived, ma'am," announces Smithers stepping forwards. "May I introduce Detective Inspector Potter and Detective Sergeant Head."

"You may, Smithers."

Smithers gestures towards me, "This is Detective Inspector Potter, ma'am, and his colleague, Detective Sergeant Head. Gentlemen, may I introduce my Lady?"

Head gives me the eye; he is as confused with all this bullshit as I am. Why don't these people just get on with it? "You may, Mr Smithers."

"Thank you, Inspector. Gentlemen this is my Lady: Countess Constance Louise Bullington."

"Thank you, Smithers. Gentlemen, please hand Smithers your hats and take a seat."

Smithers takes our bowlers and we plonk ourselves down on a matching sofa opposite the countess, between us is a very long ornate coffee table with armchairs at either end. Flicking a glance around the huge room I see it is well furnished in the French style. Large mullion windows look out over a croquet lawn and beneath our feet lies an exquisite thick green rug. Over by one of the sideboards is a young and pretty, busty maid who shoots me a saucy smile, before going quickly back to polishing one of the several Chinese looking vases sat here there and everywhere.

"Would you gentlemen care for refreshments?" asks Smithers.

"Coffee would be appreciated," says I.

"With a few biscuits," says Head.

"Any particular choice of biscuit, Sergeant?"

Head shrugs, "I don't mind. But I do love chocolate ones the best. Thank you."

"I will relay your wishes to the kitchen," smiles Smithers. "I have a few tasks to perform and then I shall be assisting the earl in preparing for his golf match. Following that, gentlemen, I shall be at your disposal for most of the time you are here."

"Thank you, Smithers," says the Countess.

Smithers clicks his fingers, "Mary," he says to the maid, "leave that and come with me, I have other tasks for you elsewhere."

I'll bet, thinks I. Judging by the look in Heads eyes he's also thinking on the same lines.

The Countess smiles at me and I am realising she isn't as aloof as I first thought she was.

"Gentlemen, first I must apologise for my husband, who, judging by the commotion, you have already had the misfortune to encounter. I'm afraid sound travels around the castle and is akin to the whispering gallery in Saint Pauls Cathedral, so, be careful of eavesdroppers while you are here. My husband is quite mad but he is also quite harmless. Most of the time he is fairly coherent and you must deal with him as you think best. Should he become too unruly then we lock him in his bedroom until he calms down. On rare occasions he can turn a little nasty, that's when we threaten him with the cook."

"The cook," echoes Head.

"The current cook, Mrs Kemp, is the granddaughter of Mrs Porter who was the cook when my husband was a child. Mrs Porter was the only person in this establishment for whom my husband was afraid of. When he was naughty, everyone indulged him rather than set him off on one of his tirades, except for Mrs Porter that is, who would lock him in a kitchen cupboard until he had calmed down. Mrs Kemp is strikingly similar in appearance to her grandmother and my husband believes they are one and the same, and that Mrs Kemp is in fact Mrs Porter reincarnated. Just another of his delusions. I must warn you that my husband's delusions can be very trying and he will rant on with the most fanciful of tales."

We are interrupted by a footman entering carrying a large silver tray with china coffee pot, milk and sugar jug, and of course a plate of biscuits. Setting the tray down on the coffee table he says, "Would you like me to pour, ma'am?"

"No thank you Jackson. You may go. Now, detectives, I would like to know what you already know about the dreadful incidents that have occurred of late."

Taking out the files for reference I recant all we have learnt from Constable Burroughs' investigations. She listens patiently, and is about to speak when the door is slammed open with such force one of the Chinese vases falls off a sideboard and smashes on the floor. The earl marches in and plonks himself down beside the countess. Thankfully he is now wearing a black silk dressing gown.

He stares at me and Head through suspicious eyes, "They're the ones my dove," he hisses. "Entered on the pretext of being valets, but when I unveiled them, they changed their bally tunes and insisted they were bally detectives. The shit faces."

"They are detectives, Claude. Now, if you intend to remain here during my discussions with the detectives please keep quiet or I shall be forced to have you locked in your room. Do you understand me?"

"No!" he snaps folding his arms and going into a sulk.

"Good. I cannot stress the stress we have been going through, detectives. Our eldest son, Percival remains in fear of his life having narrowly avoided three assassination attempts. We have no idea who was behind those attempts on his life, but are terrified that if the culprit isn't caught before he tries again then he may well succeed in his efforts."

"Let's bally well hope so," mumbles Claude. "Teach the lazy blob a lesson, what."

"Shut up Claude! I give you my last warning, either you shut up or I'll have you removed."

Claude sinks down in the sofa as he sticks his tongue out at Constance.

With a defeatist sigh, Constance says, "Help yourselves gentlemen, please do not stand on ceremony."

Heads hand flies out like a striking cobra to grab, not one but two coconut biscuits covered in chocolate, the greedy pig, leaving me with the choice of plain digestives or plain oatmeal. I pour the coffee as there are only two cups, I assume the countess didn't want any.

"Feel free to ask me anything you want, detectives."

"And then bugger off," warns Claude. "Bally free loaders."

I ask, "It states in the reports that you have five children, ma'am, but it doesn't state who comes after Mr Percival. Can you give me that information, please?"

"Of course. After Percival comes Robert, followed by Elizabeth, followed by Algernon, followed by Matilda. Algernon and Elizabeth live away and will not be here until tomorrow."

"Thank you for that, ma'am. How do they get on together?"

"Abysmally. Their sibling rivalry is notorious. In short they hate each other's guts."

"And what stinking guts they have," puts in Claude. "Especially that Algernon. Too much meat, sir, that's his problem. Feed the bugger on nothing but seaweed, that'll sort him out."

"I thought you were off to your golf, Claude," sighs Constance.

"I am! I'm just waiting for that idiot valet to turn up. Where is the fool?"

"You turfed him out two days ago."

"Did I?"

"You did indeed."

"Oh, yes, I remember. He committed a gross act of licentious behaviour while he was pulling my drawers up." He points at me. "You should investigate, detective whatever your name is. The filthy swine touched my manhood, don't you know."

Constance glares at him," Shut up, Claude. Your stupid ramblings are ringing in my head. Shut up right now or I shall call for the cook."

"Yes, my dove."

"I am thinking," sighs Constance, "that you are wondering whether the attempts on Percival's life may have been made by one of his siblings in order to climb up the inheritance ladder."

I swallow the biscuit in my mouth and take a sip of coffee before answering, "It certainly wouldn't be a first, ma'am."

"I'm sure it wouldn't," she frowns. "Up until now no one has questioned my children in any depth, Inspector. Constable Burroughs was too intimidated by their status to go beyond asking them trivial things, but I suspect you will not be so lenient."

"If we are to catch the culprit and save lives, ma'am, I assure you I will not be intimidated by anyone's status. Better that then a body on our hands."

"Meanwhile," cuts in Claude sitting bolt upright. "It's about time you dropped me a couple of more sons my dove in case they start getting killed off."

"My days of 'dropping' children have long since passed, thank you, Claude."

"Why so old duck. You can pop 'em out like corks from a Champagne bottle."

"Percival may well have popped out like a Champagne cork as you so eloquently put it, Claude, but no one else did. Being pregnant and giving birth can vary considerably from one child to the next. It can range from being comfortable to hell on earth and I have no wish to even contemplate going down that avenue again. No woman has it easy, Claude. Unlike a man, especially a man like you. You, sir have had the easiest of times bringing up your children, because in truth you have never ever done a thing for them."

"I bally have! You need to appreciate my part in their conception old dear. Without my athletic prowess and not inconsiderable virility where on earth would you be?"

"The conception was the entirety of your efforts, Claude. Let's see, ten seconds for each child multiplied by five equals fifty seconds. Your input over the years amounts to less than one minute. Now go away or I shall be forced to call for the cook."

"Damn the witch!" he yells jumping to his feet. "I shall have her head chopped off."

The door opens again and in strides Smithers."

"Excuse me, ma'am I am ready to assist the major in readiness for his golf match."

"About bally time to. Where the hell have you been, what's your name?"

"Thank, God he's gone," sighs Constance. "I really cannot suffer his madness for more than a few minutes."

Nor can we, thinks I meeting Heads look of what the hell have we let ourselves in for?

The door opens again and in hobbles an old prune dressed all in black, she is held up by a walking stick along with a young maid supporting her other arm.

"It gets worse," cries Constance burying her head in her hands before wiping her face in utter despair. "Mamma," sighs she as the old prune is dumped down beside her. "These are the detectives from London."

Prune face fixes us with watery hawk eyes over her pince-nez. Screwing up her wrinkles she says, "Defectives, are they? "Where have they defected from?"

"Not defectives, Mamma, detectives."

The old prune cups a hand to her ear, "Speak up wretched girl."

"Where…is…your… ear…trumpet?"

"I didn't trump. It was that defective," she grates pointing at me. "You can see the guilty smirk in his eyes."

Constance addresses the maid, "Janet, where is Mamma's ear trumpet?"

"I don't know me Lady," says she turning scarlet.

"Mamma, where is your bloody trumpet?" shouts Constance.

"I have said. I did not bloody trump. It was that defective. Who are they really? I think they're tax collectors not defectives. Shifty and piggy eyed tax collectors."

The door opens and in walks Jackson carrying a silver tray with an ear trumpet on it.

"Heaven be praised," cries Constance as Jackson hands Prune her trumpet which she promptly pushes into her ear.

"Right," says Prune glaring at me, "Let's have it. Who are you really?"

"They are detectives from Scotland Yard, Mamma. They are here to investigate the attempted assassination of your grandson, Percival."

"Good. It's about time he was arrested and thrown into prison."

"Mamma, it's time for your nap," sighs Constance.

"But I've only just got up! I haven't even had breakfast yet."

"You did Mamma. You had boiled eggs and little bread soldiers."

"Oh… Did I? I've had a few soldiers in my time but never for breakfast. Are you sure I had soldiers for breakfast?"

"Yes, I am sure, Mamma. So, go and have your nap and come back later for lunch."

"When's that?"

"At lunch time."

"Jolly good show. The best time to have lunch is at lunch time. It isn't the same at other times," says Prune as Janet reaches over to help the old girl up onto her feet.

The second Prune has gone, Constance exhales dramatically, "If anyone should be committing murder detectives it is I. Would I not be justified in doing away with my entire family? Now, where on earth were, we?"

Having lost the plot, I have no idea and ask Head.

"We were considering possible motives, sir."

"And the possibility of Mr Percival's younger siblings being behind the attempted assassinations in order to climb the inheritance ladder, which we shall look into later. Also, ma'am, do you know of anyone else who might desire to see Mr Percival dead?"

"Yes, I do."

This comes as a surprise, "May I ask who?"

"One moment please." She fiddles around her dress, finds a small pocket and extracts a folded-up piece of paper. "I have written you a list, Inspector."

"A list?"

"Yes. There's about twenty people on it from here to eternity."

"He's not much liked then?" says Head.

"He has made a good many enemy's," frowns she passing me the paper.

Unfolding the paper, I am astounded at who is top of her list. "Your husband is top of your list, ma'am. Can you explain why?"

"I'm afraid my husband's paranoia over who is really Percival's father puts him in the frame. Claude's madness encompasses many illusions, suspicions and conjecture. A few months ago, he got it into his head that Percival is really the son of our new vicar, the Reverend Albert Hardpuzzle, simply because the reverend is tall and thin and looks a little like Percival. Apparently, I committed adultery on our wedding night with the Reverend Hardpuzzle before Claude, as he put it, had picked the cherry himself. Bearing in mind that the reverend was not only not at our wedding he would also have been about ten years old at the time. Plus, Percival is the utter image of Claude. Neither of which has had the slightest effect on Claude's determination to root out a confession from that 'dirty vicar' and make him and Percival pay for their crimes." She puts a hand to her forehead and sighs. "I am sorry, gentlemen, I feel a severe headache coming on and a fervent desire to go and lay down for a while."

She gets shakily to her feet and we do so as well but without the shake.

"We can continue when you feel up to it, ma'am," soothes I.

"Thank you, Inspector. Anything you require please ask Smithers; you will find him an absolute rock. When you desire sustenance please make your way to the kitchen where Mrs Kemp will see to your every need. Good day for now."

We watch her leave and then sit down again.

"More coffee, sir?"

"Fill them up, Sergeant," says I extracting a hip flask from my jacket pocket. "And top up with a drop of this. Bugger the not drinking before lunch, I feel in dire need of fortification."

I scan through Constance's list of possible suspects while reading them out to Head, who by now has polished off the rest of the biscuits and is dibbing in a licked finger to hoover up the remaining crumbs.

"Everyone on this list, according to Constance, has a motive for wanting to kill Percival, Sergeant. However, she does not say what those motives are."

"I suppose she would have said if her headache hadn't have come on. Bloody hell, sir, she's just given us how many possible suspects?"

"Twenty-two in all. No wonder Constable Burroughs failed to get anywhere. This case is going to be like looking for a pimple on a pineapple."

"What next then, sir?" says Head before gulping down his fortified coffee.

"We'll interview Percival next and take it from there." Going over to the bell cord by the window I pull it and then sit back down to drink my coffee.

"Play it by the ears," says Head.

"Indeed."

Meeting Percy Bullington

While we wait, I ponder over what little I learnt from the villagers, what Burroughs wrote down and Constance's list of suspects which includes several females. One thing above all links all three; Percival is a rake, a womaniser with no scruples who would seduce any female he can get his hands on. Reading between the lines I note Janet the maid's, father: one Samuel Jenson, the head gamekeeper, appears on Constance's list and is mentioned by Burroughs along with a mention from the villagers. Percival, I conclude messed about with Janet, her father found out and was overheard one night in the Rams Head threatening to, 'Do that filthy bit of 'orse shit in good an' proper.'

Smithers appears, "You rang, sir?"

"I did, Mr Smithers. We would like to interview Mr Percival if you would kindly take us to him."

"Follow me gentlemen."

Smithers leads the way towards the rear of the castle, around corners and finally down a flight of stone steps to the dungeon, where we come to a halt in front of a very heavy looking cell door with a small grille at eye height. He thumps the door three times, the grille flies open and we are confronted with a younger version of Claude, only with a thick black beard and scurrilous eyes.

"Who the devil is it?" demands he.

"It is I, sir. Ronald Smithers the butler."

"Who are those buggers with you?"

"They are the detectives from Scotland Yard."

"About bloody time to," snarls he.

The sound of a rusty lock being unlocked with a key, grates your ears before the squealing door is opened and we file into a windowless cell lit by a pair of oil lamps. The inside of the cell isn't what I had expected to see, there's no sign of rats, chains hanging

off damp grey walls or that nauseous smell that such places always seem to have. Inside is more akin to a Parisian brothel, not that I've ever been to a Parisian brothel but I have seen pictures. Decadent French furnishings include a fancy bed covered by a red velvet quilt, nude pictures of French looking women cover the walls and there is even a small wine rack tucked in one corner beside an opium pipe.

Percy complements his surroundings, he is wearing a deep green smoking jacket, fancy brogues and white flannel trousers. He goes and sits by a small round table and gestures for us to also sit. As there is only one other chair and as I am the senior officer, I take it, Head pulls up a milking stool and Smithers goes and sits on the bed. I introduce myself and Head.

"You may call me Percy, dear boy."

"How do you do, Percy dear boy?"

"Just Percy will suffice," says he staring directly in my eyes as a sneer forms on his mouth.

I had already formed an opinion of Lord Percy and it wasn't good, the way he is eyeballing me now tells me exactly the type of person he is. I go straight for the throat, "Percy, according to Constable Burroughs' report you are not a well-liked man. Our investigations thus far confirm that theory. Even your own mother has set out a list of people who, quite simply, hate your guts. Which leaves us with a mind-numbing number of possible suspects who would love to bump you off at the first given opportunity, and that's just those we know of."

"Mother has drawn up a list," guffaws he tossing back his head to display a large green bogey, hanging off his nose. "Discount her silly ramblings, Potter, she is so ill-informed her list will be nothing more than a load of old piffle. Hand it over and I shall peruse it."

Ignoring his out stretched hand and the disparaging use of my name and not my title, I continue, "Who do you suspect may have tried to kill you?"

He sits bolt upright, "There is no, may, in it, Potter. Why do you think I have shut myself away for the past three weeks or more if I wasn't certain someone is trying to kill me? Who that someone is, is yet to be revealed? Let us hope that you have more success than that imbecile Burroughs who got nowhere with the case because he was far too busy sniffing around my sister, Matilda. I warn you, as I have warned Burroughs, do not think your position gives you cart blanche to try and wheedle your way into the bed of an aristocrat. Know your places officers, just as Smithers knows his place. And don't forget who my Uncle is."

"I'll try not to forget a single word you said, Percy. Now, who do you think hates you enough to try and kill you?"

Settling back in his chair he puts his hands behind his neck and stretches his back, "No one hates me that much, Potter. In truth I am more adored than hated. I brighten up everyone's miserable little lives. Wherever Percy goes, joy, excitement, intrigue and downright jolly japes follow. I am an enigma, the quintessential extrovert, a pioneer of expressionist ideals. If I had my way every good looking young being on this earth would be as rich and privileged as I am, so we might all party together forever. While being waited on by endless minions of course."

"That you can use and abuse," says Head with a very odd look in his eye.

"That's what they are there for, Constable. The minions of this world were put there by God Almighty to serve their betters, it is as simple as that."

"You, sir," begins I, "have an appalling opinion of those less fortunate then yourself. Like those of your ilk you believe it is your God given right to use and abuse your 'subjects' howsoever you please, but heaven forbid those lesser beings should get above themselves for even an instance. Your 'type' goes around taking full advantage of your position to seduce young women of lesser status, get them pregnant and them throw them out of their position to be left destitute, with no other option but to fall on the workhouse where they'll be abused all over again."

He shrugs, "And? Look here Potter, this is the way of the world as you should well know working in your trade. Besides, can I help it if women fall at my feet and can't wait to feel me inside them?"

Heads eyes have gone deathly blank and I'm thinking he is taking Percy's ramblings too personally. He is thinking about

Chloe, and the dreadful life she had to suffer because of pathetic, vile creatures, like Percy. It is time to leave before Head does something Percy will bitterly regret, and no doubt, Head and I will also regret. Betty and Chloe will regret and no doubt, Clump will regret. Not to mention, Percy's mother.

"Besides," sneers Percy, "If I was that bad don't you think someone would have shot me dead years ago?"

Standing up I say, "We will leave this for now but be assured we will return. Take that time to seriously ponder over the situation you find yourself in and how much you yourself are to blame for it. Next time I talk to you be sure you adopt a better attitude or you will find my Sergeants boot up your arse. And ponder also on the fact that should there really be someone out there just waiting to top you, the only people standing in his way are my Sergeant and I. Good day to you, sir."

"Where do you think you are going, Smithers?" snarls Percy as Smithers follows us out.

"I have been ordered by her ladyship to assist the detectives at all times until they no longer require my services, sir."

"I am over riding those orders, Smithers. My shit bucket requires emptying, now. And is it not time you brought me something to eat you, lazy bugger! I am bloody starving here."

"How about chewing on this bastard then," grates Head barging past Smithers, stepping back in the cell and shaking his clenched fist right in Percy's face.

"You wouldn't fucking dare!" goads Percy.

Normally, such a challenge would have been swiftly met, but oddly, Head just grins and lowers his arm before he gives Percy a wink, turns on his heals and walks out.

"With us, Mr Smithers, if you please," demands I.

"But, Mr Percy…"

"Can empty his own bucket or I shall empty it myself over his arrogant head."

The second we are out of the door it is slammed shut and locked. Percy can be clearly heard screaming out a string of obscenities before throwing things about while ranting and raving. Most of what he's going on about is incoherent but the F and C words are very clear.

"He's nothing but a spoilt upper-class nincompoop who needs a good slap," grates Head.

"To whom would you like to speak to now, Inspector?" sighs Smithers.

I place a friendly hand on his shoulder. "Do not allow the fool to get to you, Mr Smithers. I had expected Percy to accompany us to the scenes of the supposed attempts on his life, but I am glad he is not as I fear I might kill the fool myself. Can you take us around to where the incidents occurred while I refer to Constable Burroughs' notes?"

"I can, Inspector. But I will need to change first as I can't go outside in my butler's uniform."

"Very well, Mr Smithers. Shall we wait here?"

"No. Please follow me."

We follow him to the servant's hall, a long room with a long table, benches down the sides and ladder-back chairs at each end. One wall is covered in framed photographs of the family, plus staff, posing out front of the castle. They probably go back many years. Through a half-closed door wafts the aroma of roasting beef and boiling stock along with the sounds of several chattering females. Head and I take seats at one end of the table.

"Do you require refreshments while you wait?" asks Smithers.

We decline his offer and he march's away.

"Bloody huge room, sir," says Head gazing all around him.

"Indeed. Big enough to house a regiment of sailors. The entire castle is huge and I'll bet we haven't seen half of it as yet. I'll also bet there's lots of little nooks and cranny's as well."

"With secret doors, secret rooms and secret tunnels."

"Quite possibly, Sergeant. Plenty of places for a ghost to hide I shouldn't wonder."

Heads jaw drops as his face drains of colour, "Perhaps we could wait outside in the fresh air," says he wide eyed.

"I am quite happy here. Let us just relax for a while, and fear not, Sergeant, apparently ghosts do not come out in the daytime."

Smithers returns fifteen minutes later having changed into a green tweed suit with socks up to his knees, highly polished brown footwear and sporting a deer stalker hat.

"This is the outfit I wear when attending to the earl on shooting parties," he announces.

"And very fetching it is, Mr Smithers. Is the earl a good shot?"

"An excellent shot. But then, apparently, he's been shooting since he was a small boy."

"Will we require a carriage to take us to wherever we are going?"

He shakes his head, "All is in easy walking distance, Inspector."

An hour later, we relieve Smithers so he can go back to his duties. Head and I walk back to the scene of attempted murder number one, a thigh high field of already ripening barley.

"So, Lord Percy, or should I say, Dishonourable Percy? was alone enjoying the peace and quiet as he 'floated' around in a dream state while reciting Wordsworth, which is something he often does to release his inner spirit from the trials and tribulations of his stressful position in life."

"The poor bastard," snarls Head.

Ignoring Heads comment I step into the field and conjure up the scene in my mind's eye. "Percy is in another world when suddenly up pops a shadowy figure who takes a pot shot at him, but misses spectacularly."

"Are you talking to yourself, sir, or to me?"

We face each other, "Um… I'm not sure, Sergeant. Perhaps a bit of both. What do you think about murder attempt number one?"

"Well, sir, Percy's statement said he didn't recognise whoever took a shot at him because he was wearing a paper bag over his head, and when he took it off the would-be assassin had fled."

"That being the case how could he be sure that the shot was aimed at him and not at, say, for instance a pigeon or a crow?"

"Because, according to Percy, the bang from the gun sounded very close and he felt the brush of death whiz by him, and when he whipped the bag off his head it had a few pellet holes in it."

"The would-be assassin fired a shotgun at close range. That being the case, Percy's head would have been blown off, bag and all. For our assassin to have missed so spectacularly means either he, or she, was a rotten shot or they never intended actually killing Percy."

"Or more likely the incident never happened."

Stepping further into the field we cross over it and come out to stand on a narrow bridleway.

"Attempt number two. Percy was out on his horse collecting rent from the tenants on this estate. All was well with the world, but as he made his way back to the castle while coming down this very track alongside that bubbling brook," I point, "a figure jumps out from behind a hedge and fires off an arrow from a long bow that misses Percy by a mile…"

"But, was close enough to spook the horse which reared up and threw Percy from his saddle and into the brook."

"Soaked to the skin he dragged himself back up the bank, where upon he found his horse had run off and the would-be assassin had also run off, taking the rent money with him."

"Or more likely none of it happened."

"Because?"

"Because Percy told a pack of lies about both murder attempts so he could steal the rent money to cover his gambling depts, while hoping to get away with it."

"Exactly. Which is the same conclusion, Burroughs came up with. However, murder number three is a very different kettle of soup."

"Fish."

"Yes, it is fishy, Sergeant. Very fishy, and it was this incident that convinced a good many people that it really was an attempt on Percy's life."

"Thus, exonerating him from lying about the other attempts."

"Let's go over it again. Percy was going out of the front door intent on climbing into a carriage that had been sent from a neighbouring estate to pick him up and convey him back, so that he could join in with alike fellows in getting drunk, playing cards and gambling away the family fortunes. The driver of the carriage was one, Alfred Carter, not a servant but one of Percy's acquittances. Behind Percy, as he was stepping outside; was Smithers. Back from Smithers and standing at the foot of the stairs was a footman named John Chambers. So, there were three witnesses to the incident."

"Carter stated: 'That something moving caught my eye up on the parapet above the door. It looked like a pair of hands were about to push a big block of stone off. I shouted out to Percy. I shouted out: Get back you, cunt!'"

"We'll omit that word, Sergeant and replace it with another, like clot."

"But it's not what Carter said, sir. If we change the wording in Burroughs' report it will look odd."

"All I'm saying is, if we have to give evidence in court it might be prudent to change the rude c word to a more agreeable c word, rather than embarrass the court."

"As you wish. Shall I continue?"

"Please do."

"Where was I? Oh… yes. Omitting the word cunt for clot. Carter then saw the huge stone block was being wobbled right to the very edge of the parapet and was about to topple over."

"Exactly so. Meanwhile, Percy, being oblivious to anything whatsoever merely called out, 'What was that Carter old chap?'"

"To which Carter replied, while frantically waving his arms about, 'Watch out you, clot!' Only he didn't actually say clot he said cun'…"

"I know what he really said, Sergeant," snaps I. "But are we or are we not trying to avoid having to use that disgusting word?"

"No. You are but I ain't."

"Am not."

"Not what?"

"Never mind. What happened next?"

"A huge stone came down and thumped into the ground right in front of Percy's feet."

"Clearly witnessed by Carter and Smithers, with the footman stating that he heard everything but didn't actually see much because Smithers was blocking his view."

"Smithers then charged upstairs and out onto the roof intent on confronting whoever was up there. But there was no one to be seen. Despite his terrifying ordeal, Percy still climbed up into the carriage and went off to his card game as if nothing had happened."

"Only to return later that evening drunk as a skunk while demanding that the dungeon be furnished out immediately, so he could take up residence for the duration until the would-be assassin was caught and safely locked away."

"Which leads us to wonder if attempt number three was genuine or a set up."

"But it happened, that much is certain and we have to assume it was genuine because if we don't and it was, then we'll look a right pair of cun'… clots if we don't treat it seriously."

"Um…" ums I scratching my chin. "The other thing is, we went up on the roof with Smithers, where we were informed that parts of the top tier on the parapet were loose and had been reported by the estate maintenance men, who were in the process of taking them down before re-cementing them. So, whoever pushed the block over the edge must have known it was loose and also knew when Percy was about to step into the line of fire. It is certainly feasible that by the time Smithers got up on the roof, whoever had been up there had gone and no one saw who he or she was. But?"

"A chambermaid called Rose Bush, who was cleaning the hallway at the time, didn't see anyone come down from the roof, but did state that she saw Smithers when he flew past her and went up the stairs and out onto the roof. She saw him also on his way back and Chambers saw him when he came back down stairs. Problem, on Monday night both Rose Bush and Chambers disappeared."

"Having apparently eloped together. According to Smithers they had been indiscreet about their relationship and everyone knew what was going on between them, but no one dreamed they would run off together. But?"

"If Bush and Chambers had both lied about not seeing someone else other than Smithers going up or coming down at that time, we have to ask why they lied and whether they are covering for someone. I'm thinking that the moment they knew we were on our way they panicked and fled, rather than be questioned again about the incident."

"My thoughts exactly, Sergeant. Meaning they are at least guilty of something."

"Smithers said, he didn't inform Constable Burroughs that Bush and Chambers had disappeared until after the storm last night in the hope they might return."

"Which gave the 'elopers' close on an entire day to put a good amount of distance between themselves and the estate before anyone actually went looking for them."

"So, were do we go from here?"

"Let us head back to the castle, have some lunch and consider our options."

Crossing back over the field we step onto the drive leading to the castle where I spy Matilda on her horse and heading our way. Coming to a halt a good hundred yards back she sits bolt upright and glares at us, or is she glaring only at me?"

"Who's that?" asks Head.

"Miss Matilda Bullington."

"Why is she stopped there staring at us?"

"Not us, Sergeant, just me."

"Why? And how do you know who she is anyway?"

"I'll tell you later." Raising my arm, I beckon her to come.

Matilda walks the horse on but as she nears us, I have an inner ear message that tells me she is about to do something very, very, stupid. "Be prepared to jump for your life, Sergeant!"

"Yah!" yells Matilda as her crop cracks on the horse's flank causing it to rear up, snort and then charge straight at us. We jump back onto the grass verge as the wild-eyed beast thunders past us, pelting us with kicked up stones and debris as we turn our backs and cover our faces.

"The bitch," snarls Head. "What the hell was that about?"

"What do you think, Sergeant?" muses I as I watch the horse slow to a trot, while Matilda dares to throw back a taunting contemptuous glare aimed directly at me.

"I would say, sir, she's just given you a threatening reminder to keep quiet. But quiet about what exactly?"

I relate my earlier encounter with Matilda.

"The little hussy," grins Head as we walk on. "She's getting engaged this coming Saturday to some nob while carrying on with the village bobby. It's madness."

"It certainly beggars' belief, Sergeant. Surely the stupid girl must know that if she is exposed, she'll not only not be getting engaged, the scandal will see her excommunicated from the family and thrown out with the garbage."

"Losing all her privileges and at the mercy of the real world."

"Let us not dwell on her act of folly for now. We'll sort her out later."

"She shouldn't get away with it, Gerald. What with her and that twat Percy. Who the hell do they think they are?"

"Rich, privileged and powerful. Fear not, Richard, I'm sure we shall get an opportunity to teach them both a lesson in propriety and manners before we leave Bullington Castle."

Meeting Mrs Kemp

We reach the castle and clang the bell. The door is opened by Jackson who waves us in. I ask him if he has any idea where Chambers and Bush may have run off to. He shakes his head before offering to take our hats and jackets. We decline, thank him and then head off towards the kitchen. On entering the servant's hall, we find six maids and a goblin faced young lad sat at the long table tucking into pork, potatoes and cabbage. They all stand and gaze at us with trepidation.

"Please do not let us disturb you," says I.

"You're them detectives," says the lad pointing at us.

"Be quiet, Billy Roper," growls a deep voice, as appearing from the kitchen door steps a short, nicely rounded, red cheeked middle-aged woman wearing a crinkled white cotton hat. "Speak when you are spoken to. All of you sit down and eat your meal. I want you back in the kitchen in ten minutes flat." She turns her attention to me and Head. "You must be the policemen from London," she smiles wiping her hands on her well-floured apron. "Please follow me."

We do so into the biggest kitchen I have ever seen. Two large ovens, a huge spit where a huge joint of beef is being basted and turned over the flames by a young girl. Ham and ox tongue are boiling away on the hot plates while that wonderful aroma of bread baking in the oven just swamps your happy senses. Wonderful.

"Marvellous," sighs Head.

"Welcome to my domain," says she spreading her arms wide. "I am Mrs Gloria Kemp the best cook in all of Cornwall."

"I am Detective Inspector Gerald Potter and this is my colleague, Detective Sergeant Richard Head and we are the worst, I mean, best detectives in all of London."

"So, I have heard. Her ladyship has instructed me to feed and water you well. How does hot beef sandwiches in freshly baked crusty bread with home churned butter and lashings of horseradish sound? All washed down with a pint of Cornish light ale."

"It sounds wonderful," says I.

She excitedly claps her hands together, "The proof is in the eating, gentlemen. Now, so you don't have to suffer the slurping of the lower staff please sit at the kitchen table," she points.

It's hot in here even with the windows open, so we dump our hats and jackets on a chair and take another chair each at a huge table that enables us to see what's going on, and away from four young maids peeling vegetables. One dares to look up and smile furtively at Head and he gives her a wink, she goes bright red, drops her head and whispers something to the others who all start giggling.

"Stop that silliness right now. Especially you, Rosy Roper," warns Gloria waving a carving knife around. Gloria takes a meat plate over to the spit and expertly slices off some of the nicely blackened beef. Setting that down opposite us on the table she fetches a bread board, a well fired loaf, a bread knife and cuts off four thick wedges. Butter is spread thickly onto the bread, the beef is layered, horseradish spread over, sandwiched and squashed down with podgy hands before being cut in half. The sandwiches are then plated up and pushed over to us.

"Tuck in gentlemen. After that, I shall serve you the best scones in all of England. Rosy," she barks. "Fetch the gentlemen a pint of Cornwall's best."

"Yes, Mrs Kemp," she curtsies before hurrying away to disappear into a larder at the end of the kitchen.

Gloria stands hands on hips looking over to us with a beaming smile on her face, as lifting the thick sandwich to my mouth I take a bite. Butter, horseradish and beef fat run down my chin as pure ecstasy invades my taste buds.

"Beyond delicious," praises Head as he chomps away.

I swallow first, "It doesn't come any better than this, Mrs Kemp."

"Good," she smiles as Rosy comes hurrying back and sets down a pint of beer for Head.

"What is that you, silly girl?" demands Gloria pointing at the pint.

"What yer ordered Mrs Kemp. A pint of beer."

"Do you expect the gentlemen to share that one pint?"

"Rosy shrugs and goes bright red again, "Um…""

"Go and fetch another one."

Rosy hurries off again.

"Stupid girl," grates Gloria. "You see what I have to put up with gentlemen. If I do not give the lower staff exact orders at all times, heaven knows what might happen, for they do not have the ability to think for themselves. Two gentlemen. One pint. God help me!"

A flustered, Rosy returns and sets down a pint beside my plate, she curtsies before hurrying back to her place at the vegetable peeling.

"Martha," barks Gloria. "Baste all of the beef and turn the spit a bit faster. Ethel, top up the water in the saucepans and then start getting the cold meats out, we have the family lunch to serve up in less than an hour."

Billy Roper sticks his head in the door, "Please Mrs Kemp, we've finished."

"Good boy. Clear the table, wash up and then fill the wood baskets."

"Yes Mrs Kemp."

It is fascinating watching how Gloria runs her kitchen and the toing and froing of her staff, along with their general banter while vying to keep in the cook's good books. Gloria strictly maintains order and discipline, but you can sense her staff feel secure and are happy to follow her instructions.

Once we've polished off our sandwiches, Rosy removes our plates and replaces them with clean ones. Gloria sets down another plate with two large scones on it, a pot of clotted cream and a jar of strawberry jam. "Help yourselves, gentlemen," says she spinning away.

I manage to grab the biggest scone before Head does, but he counteracts that piece of niftiness by splitting his scone and spooning on two thirds of the cream before I can blink.

"You appear to have more than your fair share of the cream, Sergeant," remonstrates I pointing at his scone.

He gives me the innocent look, "Do I? Sorry I didn't realise."

"I think you did realise."

"Are you accusing me of being greedy?"

"Yes."

He leans his face closer to mine. "So, what? You grabbed the biggest scone."

"No, I did not. I merely reached out and took the one nearest me."

"The biggest one."

"I never meant to."

"Yes, you did."

I straighten up and fix him with an accusing glare, "Are you calling me a liar?"

Gloria picks up on the quarrel and comes over, "Everything alright, gentlemen?"

"Beyond the dreams of avarice," smiles I gazing up into her brown eyes.

She giggles, turns away and goes over to the spit. Snapping out a hand I grab Head by the wrist in an iron grip before he can spoon most of the jam onto his clotted cream.

"Let go, sir," warns he.

"Or what?"

"Or I might just forget we are friends as well as colleagues."

"We are indeed friends as well as colleagues, Richard, but that doesn't give you the right to take more than your fair share of cream and jam."

"I'll try not to in future," hisses he. "Now, let go of my wrist."

"Do you promise to share evenly from now on?"

"I promise," he grates trying to twist his wrist free.

I release my grip and Heads arm shoots up into the air like a siege catapult, the remaining jam on the spoon shoots off, flies across the kitchen and splats onto Gloria's hat. Spinning around she glares at her staff in turn before gazing up at the ceiling and then shrugging.

"Bloody hell," says Head. "That was a close shave."

I spoon most of what's left of the jam onto my scone and the rest onto Heads scone. He peruses both scones.

"Satisfied?" says I.

He nods. I cap the jam pot and we tuck in.

Gloria comes up and says, "Good?"

I take a swig of my beer to clear my mouth, "Exceptional. Thank you, Mrs Kemp."

"Marvellous," grins Head before ramming the remainder of his scone into his gaping orifice.

"Would you care for anything else, gentlemen?"

"Not for me, thank you," says I.

Head holds up a hand and mumbles something similar.

"Gentlemen, I must get on. If you wish to question me please do so around three o'clock when I shall be on my break."

"Very well, Mrs Kemp. Just one question for now. Have you any idea why Chambers and Bush disappeared and where they might have gone?"

She shakes her head, "No idea at all, Inspector. All I can tell you is; that on Monday afternoon all the staff were informed of your intended arrival yesterday to take over the case. John Chambers and Rose Bush both disappeared sometime after eleven o'clock on Monday night, while the vast majority of the staff and the family were in their beds."

"And no one saw them leave?"

"Chambers was rostered for night watchman duty on Monday and could have slipped away at any time he chose without the likelihood of anyone seeing him. Rosy Roper shares a room with Rose Bush and she told me Rose was in bed reading a book by candle light the last time she saw her. Rosy dropped off but when she awoke next morning, Rose was gone."

"Do you know if Chambers and Bush were in a relationship?"

"They were sweet on each other, Inspector, that much I am certain of. The other thing I am certain of is that they would not have run off together unless it was for a very serious reason."

"Such as?"

"Well she wasn't pregnant that's for certain. If she had been pregnant, she would have come to see me, she trusted me implicitly you see. Besides, John Chambers wasn't the sort to take advantage of a girl anyway. I am very worried for them, Inspector. Very worried."

"I can see that by the look in your eyes, Mrs Kemp. Thank you, that's all for now."

She smiles wanly and steps away. We finish off our beers, wipe our mouths on our sleeves, grab our stuff and leave.

"What now?" asks Head as we head back up the corridor.

"Let us take a look at Chambers and Bush's rooms and take it from there."

As we pass by the drawing room Smithers comes out carrying an empty silver tray, behind him follows a chorus of yapping dogs. Obviously the 'bubbly boo' pack has returned.

"Gentlemen. I trust Mrs kemp looked after you well," says he shutting the door.

"She did indeed, Mr Smithers. The woman's an absolute jewel."

"My sentiments entirely, Inspector. I have to supervise the setting out of lunch and can only spare you a few minutes or so until after two o'clock."

"If you or someone else can show us to John Chambers and Rose Bush's rooms we can be left to our own devices."

"I can take you there right now, if you please,"

"Lead on please, Mr Smithers."

We traipse back the way we just came, past the servant's hall and right to the very end where we follow Smithers up a narrow flight of stairs, and out onto a longish hallway that heralds the servant's bedrooms.

"Females only this side of the castle, Inspector," says Smithers. "The male quarters are reached by following the corridor the other side of the stairs at the main entrance. Once you have finished here, if you make your way to the main entrance you will find Jackson on duty. He will show you to Chambers' room. After that Jackson will escort you to Mr Robert's bedroom. Mr Robert has requested you go and see him before two o'clock as he wishes to speak with you."

"Will he not be at lunch by one o'clock?"

"Mr Robert rarely joins the family for lunch, Inspector, preferring to have something in his bedroom, come office." Stepping up to the third door along Smithers opens it and waves us in. "I will see you later this afternoon then, gentlemen," smiles he.

"Thank you, Mr Smithers," says I.

"What do you think of, Smithers, sir?" says Head the second we close the door.

"He seems to be a rock, just like the countess said he was."

"Agreed, honest, trustworthy, and commands respect."

"My thoughts exactly, Sergeant."

The room is small, two single beds, one bedside cabinet between the beds with a candle in a holder upon it. A small wardrobe and a tiny chest of drawers. A cross on the wall, a couple of framed photos on the chest of drawers with a posy of lavender in a jar between them.

"Not a lot to get excited about here," says Head yanking open the wardrobe door.

"But at least it's clean, tidy and smells pleasant," says I.

I go through the draws in the chest of draws, two are empty and the other two are full. The full ones obviously contain Rosy Ropers things, what little she has. Head goes through the wardrobe and announces that as there is only one each of what little there is, he is of course assuming that everything in the wardrobe belongs to Rosy. The bedside cabinet has a small draw which I open to find a few pots of various ladies' face and hand creams, a few pieces of cheap but bright jewellery, and, a diary.

"Ah…" says Head watching closely as I open the diary.

"This belongs to Rosy," says I. "It may be a bit naughty to read a ladies personal diary without her permission, Sergeant, but needs must."

"I won't tell if you don't," grins he.

We sit down side by side on a bed and begin reading from the date when the first attempted murder took place. Rosy has religiously entered something for every day, but most days very little has been putdown other than a brief overview of her day. There's no mention of the business with Percy. As we fan through the pages, we finally arrive at yesterday's entry which makes for interesting reading. I read aloud, "Rosy weren't 'ear when I got up. All her stuff 'ad gone. But the silly cow took my bag an' not her own bag. Don't know why she left?"

"Perhaps in the dark she mistook Rosie's bag for her own," offers Head.

I raise my eyebrows for effect, "Or perhaps someone else packed her bag for her and just assumed they'd got the right bag."

"Which opens all kinds of cans," frowns Head.

"It does indeed, Sergeant." Putting the diary back in the draw, I then get down on my knees and look under Rosie's bed, I know it's hers because her names above it on a small plaque nailed to the wall, reading: 'God Bless Rosy Roper.' Beneath the bed is a flower-patterned valise which I pull out and put on the bed. Embroidered inside is Rose Bush's name. The bag is empty. I look under Rose's bed, nothing. "Darkness or not, why on earth would Rose take Rosie's bag when her own was almost certainly under her own bed?"

"Perhaps Rosie's bag was more desirable. Or more likely it was bigger, so Rose stole it because her own bag wasn't big enough to cram all her stuff into."

"That's just what I was thinking," lies I. "We shall ask Miss Roper what she thinks about it when we see her."

"But then she'll know you read her diary," says Head all smugly.

"So, did you."

"Only because you were reading it."

"Whatever," grates I. "Let us get on."

Meeting Robert Bullington

We find Jackson looking suitably bored by the front door, he is only too pleased to escort us to Chambers room, where after a quick search we find nothing to further our investigations. Following that, Jackson escorts us to Robert Bullingtons bedroom come office. Jackson knocks on the door.

"Come," calls a voice and we enter to find Robert Bullington sat behind a small knee hole desk piled up with neatly stacked papers. The room again is huge and furnished in the same style as the earls. There is the distinct smell of pipe tobacco.

"The detectives from Scotland Yard to see you Mr Robert."

"Thank you, Jackson. Would you mind bringing up a pot of tea for three?"

"Right away, sir," says he, turning and leaving he shuts the door behind him.

"Gentlemen," says Robert rising from his chair and coming around to meet us, he holds out his hand, "I am Robert Bullington."

We shake hands and I introduce us. Although tall and thin like his father, Robert has his mother's looks. Robert waves us to seats across from his desk and retakes his own seat.

"Thank you for coming to see me on such short notice, officers. I have so much still to do in preparation for Matilda's big day I feared that if I did not see you know, I never would."

We make small talk for a while and I realise that Robert is a very intelligent level-headed young man who does not take his position in life lightly. Having taken over the task of estate manager he is passionate about moving it into the fast approaching twentieth century. The only thing I find odd about him is why he has his office in his bedroom. So, I ask him.

"Convenience, Inspector. Should I awake in the night with an idea, or have remembered something I should have done I have everything on hand, which is preferable to tramping down to the main office at the rear of the castle."

There's a knock on the door and Jackson enters. He sets the tea stuff down, asks if there's anything else, is told 'No thank you, Jackson' and he leaves.

"To the matter in hand, gentlemen," says Robert gravely. "The attempts on Percy's life. I did not witness a single thing, but knowing my fool of a brother as I do, I would say that incidents one and two were entirely fictitious. And do you know why?"

"Because Percy wanted to steal the tenants rent money while hoping his charade would ensure he got away with it," says I.

"Exactly, Inspector. Just another of his 'jolly japes' I'm afraid, and there has been an awful lot of them over the years." He pauses to pour the teas into china cups, partly I suspect to calm his rising temper over his brother and to gather his thoughts. "My brother is a lazy, womanising, drunken, drugged up, gambling waste of a life. Misguided beyond belief he actually believes everyone adores him, because he sees himself as a lovable rogue who has been sent by God Almighty to cheer up everyone's miserable existence. He is also, in his own eyes, generous to a fault. 'Just ask Percy and he will deliver.' The only people he delivers to are his hangers on and those that constantly flatter his ego to ensure he continues to hand them his money, for whatever the reason: The inn keepers, the gamblers, the doxies and the sycophants and those who are just like him; over privileged idiotic buffoons who call themselves aristocrats. If I had my way, gentlemen, I would see the damn lot of them put on to a tramp steamer and never allowed to set foot on solid ground ever again."

"You don't care for him much then?" says Head pausing from his notes to sip at his tea.

"He is a disgrace to the family name and the reincarnation of the Eighth Earl who was as debauched as the Marque de Sade."

To keep us on course, I ask, "What's your opinion of murder attempt number three, sir?"

"I believe it was a genuine attempt to kill Percy. It's just a pity it did not succeed."

"What if it was just another 'jolly jape' to add credence to the first two 'jolly japes?' After all it seems no one believed him over the first two, so perhaps he ensured the next one was much more believable by orchestrating it in front of witnesses. One of which was an associate of his, one Alfred Carter, who Percy still went off with for a night of gambling, despite just missing having a huge lump of stone hit him on the head."

"I saw the state Percy was in when he returned that night, Inspector. I have no doubt attempt three was genuine and that whoever was behind it will try again, once the opportunity arises."

"Your mother seems to believe that all three attempts on Percy were for real."

"She would say that to you, Inspector, but she knows full well that the first two were simply Percy's way of trying to cover up his theft. After I had uncovered the evidence from his secret hiding place under the floorboards in his bedroom, I went and accosted him with the rent book and the missing rent money, while he, was trying to convince mamma of his innocence. She continued to listen to his lying prattle and still she forgave him."

"His secret hiding place wasn't that secret then, sir," says Head.

"Not to me, Sergeant. Very little Percy does is a secret to me."

"What else leads you to believe attempt three was genuine?" ask I.

"Percy was unfazed by attempts one and two. He carried on as normal, but once it had sunk into his pea sized brain that the third attempt was genuine, he shut himself away and refused to come out while allowing no one near him other than Smithers."

"Why only Smithers, sir?"

"Smithers is the most trust worthy employee to have ever walked within these walls. He is as solid as a rock. He doesn't like Percy, but that will not stop him from serving him in exactly the same way as he serves the rest of the family. Stalwart, honest and a true professional. That is Mr Ronald Smithers in a nut shell, Inspector."

I swallow my tea in one go, you don't get much in fancy little cups. "I find it hard to believe nearly three weeks have gone by without another attempt on Percy's life, sir. He may be incarcerated in a dungeon, but a determined assassin would at least try to get at him. If I wanted to kill Percy I'd simply knock on his door, and the second he opened the grille I would shoot him in the head."

"Or put some poison in his food," puts in Head. "That way Smithers would get the blame, wouldn't he? Failing that you could pile up a load of logs, soak them in paraffine and set…"

"Thank you, Sergeant. I think Mr Robert gets the picture. Now, sir. Have you any idea who might be behind attempt number three."

His gaze is unwavering as he says "No, Inspector. I realise that I have an excellent motive for wanting to kill my brother being next in line for the earldom. However, I do not want it that much to have to kill for it. Besides, I already run this estate and have done so for the past two years since father's illness deteriorated. Percy will inherit the title but he will never run the estate, nor less, have access to its wealth other than his allowance. Which brings me to another point. Before incarcerating himself in the dungeon, Percy had been spending more money than usual. Usually he has gambled or frittered away his monthly allowance within a week of receiving it. He then goes begging to mamma or one of his siblings. He hadn't been begging money anywhere near as often. Therefore, I just know he had been getting money from somewhere else."

"Perhaps he had won at cards or something?"

Sitting right back Robert shakes his head, "The whole world knows when Percy has won at cards, Inspector. No, I believe Percy has been up to his old tricks. As stupid as my brother is, he is also a master at finding out people's secrets, those kinds of secrets those people would rather no one knows about."

"Are we talking blackmail, sir?"

"We are indeed, Inspector."

"What do you think of Robert Bullington, Sergeant?" says I as we head towards the kitchen intent on talking to Rosy Roper before we tackle Percy again.

"I think he is genuine, sir."

"So, do I. He obviously hates his brother, but he loves this estate so much he will not take the risk of trying to kill Percy, possibly getting caught and losing everything."

"And ending up swinging from a rope," grimaces Head.

I check my fob watch, one fifty-five. "The Bullingtons will be coming back from lunch very shortly, Sergeant. I'm wondering if we should perhaps talk to the countess and Matilda before we see Percy. Who knows we may learn something to be better prepared to grill Percy?"

"I think the sooner we go for Percy the better, sir. Especially if Smithers isn't there to witness our interrogation of the arrogant cu…"

"Do not say that word, Sergeant," snaps I. "In fact, I order you not to say it ever again."

"Sorry, sir. I'll try not to, but it isn't easy when referring to cu… idiots like Percy."

"Agreed, Sergeant. And I sympathise with you."

Turning into the servant's hall I stick my head into the kitchen and call out to Gloria.

"What is it, Inspector?" frowns she, "I'm still too busy to stop right now."

"Sorry, Mrs Kemp. Can we speak to Rosy Roper for a few minutes?"

"Whatever for?"

"We need to ask her a few questions about Rose Bush's disappearance."

"Very well. But please be quick about it." Swinging around she bellows out, "Rosy Roper, the Inspector wishes to speak with you for a few minutes."

Turning instantly white, Rosy jumps away from the butler sink where she was washing up, to stare in horror at me, "'Ave I done something wrong?"

"Of course, you haven't, you, silly girl," snaps Gloria. "Now hurry up we haven't got all day and I suspect neither have the policemen."

Drying her hands on her apron, Rosy hurries over and follows me into the hall. "You are not in any trouble, Rosy," confirms I. "Please take a seat while we ask you a few questions about Rose's disappearance."

She sits down while nervously wringing her hands. Head gives me a sneaky grin which tells me he can't wait for me to confess to Rosy that I read her diary without permission.

"Relax, Rosy," smiles I, sitting down beside her. "Did you witness Rose packing her bag with all she owned and then leaving on Monday night?"

"No, sir. Rose was readin' her book by the candle light. She likes to read in bed. I dropped off but when I woke up in the mornin', she was gone."

"My, Sergeant and I went and searched your room earlier on and we found a valise beneath your bed which had Rose's name on it. Can you explain why she obviously took your bag and not her own?"

She shakes her head and swallows hard as if she is hiding some terrible secret.

"I will ask you again, Rosy. Why did Rose take your bag and not her own?"

"I don't know," she pleads. "It didn't make no sense."

"Was your bag bigger than hers?"

"No, it were smaller an' it was older an' more scruffy. I didn't mean to keep 'er bag, sir. I just did because I didn't 'ave a bag once Rose took mine."

"Can I assume you haven't told anyone about Rose taking your bag instead of her own?"

She shakes her head and looks about to cry, "I just told Mr Robert, when he questioned me, that I didn't know anything about anything."

"You should have told him about the bag, Rosy. One more question. Apart from Mr Robert, has anyone else spoken to you about Rose's disappearance?"

"Yes."

"Who?"

"Everyone in the kitchen."

"Thank you Rosy, you may go."

"What about the bag?"

"Keep it, but don't tell anyone I said so."

At last a smile spreads across her lips and she practically skips away into the kitchen.

"I noted how you sneakily avoided owning up to reading Rosie's diary," says Head somewhat perplexed. "I hadn't thought of handling it like that."

"Nor had I until the last moment," grins I. "Let's go and tackle Percy if he'll open the door. We'll leave the countess and Matilda until later."

"How far are we going to go, sir?" asks Head as we pause at the top of the steps leading down to the dungeon. "Can I have permission to knee him in the roundies a few times if he plays up?"

"Absolutely not, Sergeant. If he turns violent then we will restrain him according to the manual."

"What if he accidently bangs his head on the wall during that restraining?"

"Then I'd say it was just one of those unavoidable accidents that often occur when whoever you are trying to restrain turns violent."

"Excellent," grins he.

We go down and I give the door a few kicks.

"Who is it?" demands Percy through the closed grille.

"It is I, Inspector Potter."

"Is Smithers with you?"

"No."

"Well bugger off and don't come back until he is with you. I will not open this door to anyone except Smithers."

"I am ordering you to open this door right now, Percy, or suffer the consequences."

"What would those consequences be?"

"I'm not sure as yet. But, be assured they will be dire."

"Oh… just clear off Potter you bloody baboon and leave me in peace."

"If that's the way you want it. Right, Sergeant, start pouring the paraffin all over the door."

The grill is snapped open and Percy's glaring eyes clash with mine, "Your bluffing."

"I'm not."

"All right. What do you want?"

"Let us in first."

"So, you can give me a good roasting. Absolutely not, Potter. Say what you want through this grille or piss off and take your gorilla with you."

"We have information that leads us to suspect you are blackmailing someone. Who is that someone?"

"I will bet this information comes from that bastard who calls himself my brother."

"What bastard brother is that?"

"Robert the bastard, as you well know, Potter. Now, I am telling you he should be at the top of your suspect list because he hates me, and because I know he is only half a Bullington. The other half coming from God knows who. I know it probably hasn't entered your thick head, but if I die who do you think will then get the bloody lot? Why it would be Robert the bastard no less, would it not? Wakeup you fool! Smell the dog shit! He's taking you for the proverbial, he knows he's a bastard and he knows I know he's a bastard. And once the old fool dies and I take over, Robert the bastard also knows I will excommunicate him from the family and have him thrown back to the common scum where he truly belongs."

"What makes you think he's only half a Bullington?" puts in Head. "He's got the Bullington statue and the looks of your mother."

"Ah… But you haven't seen his dong, have you?"

"What's a dong?" puzzles I.

"His cock you fool. Look, the Bullington men have always sported long thin dongs. But him, that bastard, has a short one as thick as a donkey. Mother obviously gave birth to him, so why don't you pop upstairs and ask the dirty cow who she did it with thirty years ago, because it certainly wasn't with the old boy. Now, fuck off." With that he slams the grille shut.

"That Percy is just about the biggest turd I've ever met," grates Head as we tramp back towards the main entrance only to bump into Robert coming the other way.

I block his way, "Can you spare us a moment, sir?"

"If it is only a moment, Inspector," gasps he.

"Your brother would not admit to blackmailing anyone. But he gave us the impression he may be blackmailing you…"

"You are referring to his lies concerning my parentage. Mere jealousy, Inspector. Percy has been obsessed by the size of my manhood since we shared baths as children. He tried to blackmail me years ago, unless I agreed to his demand for a monthly payment of a third of my allowance, he threatened to spread it around that I couldn't possibly be a Bullington. I told him then he could go and boil his head. I will never hand over one penny to that self-serving nincompoop. No, Inspector, you will have to look elsewhere for his victims."

"Any ideas who those victims might be?"

"My other siblings would be a good place to start. Percy always goes for those he knows the most about. However, no one is safe from his skulduggery. Who knows, even mamma might be a victim. Now, if you'll excuse me, I must get on."

I move to the side and let him pass.

"Perhaps," says Head as we walk on, "Percy knows about Matilda and the clotstable."

I stop and face him, "What the devil is a clostable, Sergeant?"

"An unranked policeman without the rude word at the begging of his title," grins he.

"Very droll, Sergeant. We shall have to put your theory to Matilda and see how she reacts. And I think we should do that right now."

As we near the drawing room who should come out but Smithers with yapping dogs on his heals, which he has to push back with his foot so he can shut the door.

"Little devils," laughs he when he'd obviously rather have said: little bastards. "I was just coming to find you gentlemen. The countess would like to continue with the discussion you began before her headache came on."

"What, right now?"

"If you don't mind, Inspector."

"What about those dogs?" asks Head. "We can't have them yapping away like that when we're trying to talk."

"They'll calm down once they get to know you, Sergeant. Would you care for any refreshments?"

"Not right now, thank you. Sergeant?"

"I wouldn't mind a few biscuits, Mr Smithers."

"Ah… That could create problems for you, Sergeant. If you are the only one with biscuits you will subsequently become the only one the 'bubbly boos' will fuss over, until you give them something. Which may become something of an ordeal for you."

"I'll risk it," smiles he patting his stomach. "Besides, I have a way with animals, Mr Smithers. Trust me, once I've finished with them, they'll be eating out of my hand."

More likely eating your hand, thinks I on seeing several sniffing noses and snarling teeth being pushed as far under the door's bottom gap as is possible. This is going to be hell!

Smithers opens the door a crack, the dogs immediately go for the crack and try to force their way through. "Good boys. Good boys," coos Smithers. "Make way for Uncle Ronald and the nice policemen."

Clapping hands coming from inside draws the dogs away and Smithers opens the door, hustles us in and then shuts it, cleverly leaving himself on the other side.

Leaning back against the door, Head and I survey the scene. Sat side by side are seven white Highland terriers all watching us intently through questioning eyes, but at least they are quiet. Constance is sat on the sofa with Prune on one side of her and Matilda on the other side. Matilda has a patronising smile on her lips while her mocking eyes sparkle with spiteful intent.

"Come over, gentlemen and take a seat," smiles Constance.

"Oh… yes, please do…," smirks Matilda.

Head marches forwards and I trail behind. Two of the dogs get to their feet and start wagging their stumpy tails. We sit down opposite the women. The standing dogs' edge closer towards us, the rest get to their feet and also edge closer.

"Good after noon, gentlemen," says Constance. "I must apologise for deserting you earlier on. It was somewhat rude of me I know, but I am afraid once my head bangs, I need to rest."

"We understand, ma'am," says I, aware that my shoes are getting the sniffing treatment.

"How are you getting on with your investigations, Inspector?"

"It is early days, ma'am," says I, aware that my shoes are now being licked, while another 'bubbly boo' is trying to sniff at my crotch.

"Henry likes you, Sergeant," says Matilda as one of the dogs is now sat at Heads feet while gazing mesmerised up at him. "Why don't you pet him?"

"Best not to," says Constance worriedly. "He may…um… bite you."

"No, he won't, Mamma," giggles Matilda. "Henry never bites."

"I have a way with animals," boasts Head. "Watch this."

With that Head leans forwards and ruffles Henry's wiry hair, which is a big mistake as the dog is on him like a demented leech. Clamping itself to Head's leg, Henry goes at it as if his life depends on it. Head shakes his leg in an attempt to disengage the pervert which only serves to increase Henry's excitement. He doubles his efforts.

It is embarrassing beyond belief and I just pray Head won't lose it, grab the dog by the scruff of its neck and hurl it across the room.

"Oh…, look, Mamma, Grandmamma, Henry has become enraptured with the policeman. How sweet…, hugging his leg like that," says Matilda, oh, so, innocently.

"I wouldn't mind hugging his leg like that," puts in Prune.

Constance claps her hands together, Henry releases Heads leg and the dogs all go back to milling around mine and Heads feet. Three of them are so close to my legs I can feel their hot breath through my trousers. But Head is faring much worse as one dog is sat on his foot, another is rubbing its arse on his other foot, Henry is staring up at him with rapists' eyes while the fourth one is licking its lips as if contemplating having Head for dinner.

I hear the door open and shoot a glance behind me to see Smithers coming over carrying a small silver tray with a variety of biscuits on it.

"Biscuits, Smithers?" questions Constance, her eyebrows going up to the ceiling.

"The, Sergeant requested them, ma'am."

"Oh, dear," sighs she.

"Biscuits," cries Matilda. "How I love a nice sweet biscuit. But I fear I must refrain. I do not want to look a podge for my birthday and engagement, now do I? I am afraid the good Sergeant will have to eat them all himself. Hand them to him, Smithers."

Smithers steps right up to the coffee table and hovers the tray over it, seemingly reluctant to set it down. All the dogs have now forgotten about Head and I as their eyes are riveted on the tray. Head reaches out and takes hold of the tray before setting it down on his lap. The dogs' edge towards him, sniffing and lolling out their tongues. The second Head takes just one bite of a biscuit I fear all hell will be let loose. One dog starts barking at Head, another whimpers, while the rest sit up and beg. Suddenly they look really cute, well behaved and well trained. Panic over. Head takes a bite from a ginger nut, the dogs' squash together and come right up to him. One jumps up, rests its paws on his knee and licks it lips.

"Get back," demands Head. "All of you get back and go and sit down. Sit I say."

We all watch in amazement as the dogs' back up a foot, and all, except for Henry, sit.

"Would you believe it," sneers Matilda.

"You certainly do have a way with animals, Sergeant," beams Constance.

"He'll have them doing tricks next," grates Prune.

A big grin crosses Heads mouth as he picks up another biscuit, a digestive, and takes a bite. Henry moves forwards, the other dogs' rise and begin sniffing, and it crosses my mind that as I could smell the ginger biscuits so could the dogs, and may not have cared for that smell. But a digestive?

Crumbs fall onto Heads chin. Henry starts wagging his tail. Constance appears apprehensive and then Head makes mistake number two, he offers Henry a piece of biscuit. Henry snatches the treat; the rest of the dogs' leap forwards and Head is suddenly covered with dogs, with one licking furiously at his chin. Head lets go of the tray and jumps to his feet as Henry clamps himself back onto his leg. Constance jumps up and furiously claps her hands, but to no avail, the dogs' have one thought only, pushing, scrapping and snarling at each other they vie for the biscuits now on the floor. Head tries to make a run for it, and heads for the door with Henry still hanging on, while Matilda shrieks with laughter.

Enough is enough, jumping to my feet I bellow out, "STOP!"

"Good grief," amazes Smithers as Henry lets go and the remaining 'bubbly boos' instantly go quiet, sit up and adopt looks of total innocence.

"Perhaps, ma'am," says I with authority. "It would be prudent to have the dogs' removed elsewhere so we might talk in piece."

She flops back onto the sofa, "I agree, Inspector. And I must apologise for my boys, they're not normally so naughty. Smithers, be so kind as to see the boys outside and have someone play ball with them or something."

"Very well, ma'am," says he slapping his thigh. "Come on boys. Come to Uncle Ronald."

They throw Smithers a puzzled look but then continue to fix their eyes on me.

"They're waiting for your command, Inspector," taunts Matilda.

I have no idea how to handle dogs and play it by intuition, clicking my fingers I bark out, "Off with the lot of you. Go on, follow Uncle Ronald or you'll be trouble."

To open mouthed amazement by everyone, the dogs trot off in an orderly fashion behind Smithers as he makes for the door.

"I am impressed, Inspector," says Constance. "If I had not witnessed that with my own eyes, I would never have believed it. You, sir, are a natural and must have extensive experience in controlling our beloved canine friends."

"Thank you, ma'am. Now, perhaps we can continue where we left off earlier."

Head retakes his seat while appearing somewhat strained and stained with a creamy coloured wet patch on his trouser leg.

Matilda gets to her feet, "I must get back to the stables, Mamma."

"We would like to speak to you, Miss," says I.

"I don't know why, Inspector, because I do not wish to speak to you."

"That was rather rude of you, Matilda," remonstrates Constance. "The detectives have a job to do and we must all do our best to accommodate them in their investigations. Do I make myself clear?"

"Yes, Mamma," she sulks. "Perhaps we could talk tomorrow, Inspector. I have a very busy schedule today and really must get on."

"We shall make every effort to accommodate your wishes, Miss," smiles I.

"Thank you," sneers she before flouncing off.

"Please excuse my youngest child, gentlemen," says Constance. "She is such an innocent, so naive, so gullible, she cannot grasp even the fundamentals of acceptable proprieties."

Head shoots me a 'what the hell is she on about look?' I have no idea other than to think that Constance can see nothing bad in any of her children, she's that enthralled with them. Matilda is a class A snob and a spoilt little madam, while Percy is an absolute piece of shit. I can only imagine what I'll come up against when I meet the other two tomorrow. But at least Robert is a level-headed gentleman.

The door is suddenly and ear shatteringly thrown open and in walks Claude swinging around a golf club with no head on the end.

"You're back early, Claude," grates Constance. "Why are you back early?"

"This!" barks he. "The bally head flew off, the rotten bastard, on hole eight. Damn it all old duck, I was par three up on old Turnbull." He flops down beside Constance. "You detective chaps need to investigate this. I want you to find out who made this club and have them arrested for selling ineffectual golf equipment. By God, it cost me the match. For the first time in years I'm ahead of the field when this happens." He waves the club in my face. "So, Inspector Who, can you get to it immediately or what?"

"Not," snaps Constance. "Please find a modicum of sanity in your muddled brain, Claude. Someone out there is trying to kill your eldest son and all you care about is a stupid stick that is older than this building. Now, please go away."

"Yes," puts in Prune. "Shove it up your backside and clear off you annoying tick."

"That's enough, Mamma," warns Constance. "Isn't it time for your nap?"

The old girl takes off her glasses and fixes Constance with a suspicious glare. "I've only just got up. Or did I?"

"Bugger off you, old trollop," demands Claude waving his stick in Prune's face.

Constance pushes it away as her face screws up in frustration, "Do not talk to your mamma like that, Claude."

"She's not my mamma the old trollop. She's yours."

She is yours, Claude. Now please shut up or go away,"

"What about my golf club?"

"We shall look into it as soon as possible, Major," lies I.

"Good man, Inspector Who. Now, to show the old duck I do care about what's his name, has there been any developments in your investigations thus far?"

"We are considering the possibility that blackmail may be involved, Major."

Sitting bolt upright he appears somewhat horrified, "Blackmail, hey? Damned business that, Inspector Who. Apart from that has there been any more attempts to kill the turd?"

"No, Major. Not since Mr Percival has been ensconced in the dungeon…"

"Got the blighter locked up have you! Damn good show, Who. Best place for him. Let's put him aside for now and get down to more important issues. When can you start investigating the case of the broken golf club? Oh, yes, any progress in finding my golfing tiepin?"

Constance covers her face with her hands and I feel her headache coming on again. She draws her hands down over her eyes and suddenly looks as if she's aged ten years, "The detectives do not have time to investigate your stupid golf problems, Claude. Why don't you go upstairs to your bedroom and search for your silly tiepin yourself?"

"But that's not my job, is it? It's Inspector Who and his merry men's job. Why I'll bet that bastard Sheriff of Notre dame has stolen it and given it to his doxy, that Maid in Marion woman."

"What was that?" demands Prune shoving her trumpet even further into her ear. "Who mated with my sister Marion and gave her the pox?"

Constance is on her feet to storm over to the bell pull where she furiously yanks it up and down several times. Within seconds,

Smithers comes hurrying in followed by Jackson, followed by Mary the maid.

"Jackson, please escort the earl up to his bedroom and lock him in. Mary, help Mamma up to her bedroom and read her a story until she drops off. Smithers, I feel a headache coming on and must go and lay down for a while. Please bring me up something to soothe my jangled nerves."

"Very good, ma'am," says he flicking a glance of alarm my way that says it all. Smithers is rogering his boss. And I don't mean Claude.

"Well, here we are, sir," says Head gazing around the drawing room. "Just the two of us."

"And what have we learnt from this meeting with the countess, Sergeant?"

"Sod all really."

"Well I learnt that Smithers is almost certainly poking Constance."

He gives me the disbelieving look, "Really, how did you deduce that?"

"From the look Smithers gave me when Constance ordered him upstairs."

"I missed that one. But I'll tell you this, I don't think the major is anyway near as mad as he's making out."

"Neither do I. And I'm also thinking, Sergeant, this case is going to be like trying to crack a coconut with a headbutt. The more you go at it the bigger the headache you'll get."

"Where to now?"

"Let's help ourselves to a scotch or two from that drinks cabinet and then we shall go and torment that snotty little cow, Matilda."

"The scotch sounds a good idea, but didn't we promise to go see Matilda tomorrow?"

"We didn't promise her anything. And I would like to get her out of the way before we go and see the cook at three.

Interviewing Matilda Bullington

After a couple of fortifiers, we head further down the corridor where we bump into a maid hurrying along with a basket full of bedlinen. We ask her which way to the stables and she tells us if we go to the end of the corridor, we'll find a door to the rear of the castle.

Once outside we gaze over a huge lawn complete with tennis courts, beyond that there stands a line of brick and pantile stables with a clock tower in the centre. Beyond the stables rolling meadows with cattle and grazing horses roll up to a horizon devoid of a single cloud. Following a gravelled path around the tennis courts we head for the stables. A young lad in a flat cap leading a bay thoroughbred stops to ask us if he can help us.

"Is Miss Matilda about?" asks I.

"Yes, sir. Go through the arch way an' you'll find her in there."

Going through the arch way we find the stables form a square, there are several stable hands busying themselves, horse's heads are sticking out everywhere and over in one corner, Matilda's back is to us, while a tall muscular fellow with his sleeves rolled up is grooming her horse. Matilda is so engrossed in watching the tall muscular fellow she fails to realise we are approaching her.

"Get right down to his fetlocks, Taylor," orders she. "I want to see them shine like silk."

Taylor turns his back to her and bends right down, as he does so, Matilda tilts her head to the side to ogle his buttocks.

"Good afternoon, Miss," says I breaking into her erotic fantasy.

Spinning around and raising the crop she's holding she looks about to swipe me.

"Not you again! Why don't you leave me alone, I have no wish to converse with you today or with that object beside you."

"Object!" grates Head.

"Madam," says I narrowing my eyes for effect. "I will not tolerate your rudeness for a second longer. Who the hell do you think you are?"

"I am your bosses' favourite niece, don't you know?" she sneers hands on hips.

"Your Queen Vic's favourite niece?" amazes Head.

"No! I am Uncle Arthurs favourite niece, you bone head."

"We couldn't care less whose niece you are." grates I. "Could we, Sergeant?"

"No, sir. We certainly couldn't."

"But you must."

"Why?"

"Because… because, if you upset me any further, I shall tell Uncle Arthur and he will ensure you are suitably punished."

"No, he won't," scoffs Head.

"Yes, he will."

"No, he will not," snaps I. "Now, either you start acting like a lady or you will suffer the consequences."

"Which are?" sneers she.

"Arrest and incarceration in the nearest cell for being aggressive, obstructing a police officer in his sworn duty and being a right little madam."

Matilda turns to Taylor, who, mouth agape is obviously lost for words. He is a handsome chap, fair and clean shaven.

"Taylor, kindly escort these baboons from the premises, they are trespassing."

"Do so at your peril, Taylor," warns I.

Matilda glares into my eyes, "Look at Taylors physique, Inspector Baboon. Do you think you dare to tangle with such hard muscle?"

"Easily. Taylor, do you wish to try and escort us from the premises?"

"Not really, sir. I just want to get on with me groomin' an' be left alone."

"Why you utter weakling!" gasps Matilda shaking her crop in his face. "Are you scared of a pair of baboons?"

"I am knowing them Scotland Yard detectives carry bloody great big revolvers on 'em."

"Oh… Really?" scoffs she. "That's because they are cowards, Taylor. In a real fight with a beast of your stature I'm sure they would wilt and run away."

"No, we wouldn't," says Head, matter of fact. "Would we, sir?"

"Indeed not, Sergeant. In truth, madam, apart from small truncheons, we are unarmed on this occasion, and even when we are fully armed it is rare for us to use our revolvers. We use our fists and our short truncheons and have thumped and bludgeoned so many thugs over the years we have lost count. We are often outnumbered and when needs must, we are quite content to shoot someone dead to save ourselves. If I were you, I would stop your silliness and answer our questions as quickly as possible so that we can leave you alone. How would that suit you?"

"It does not suit me in the least. But, needs must. Follow me."

Turning away, she stomps off to where a pair of lads are sat outside the tack room vigorously polishing up bridles.

"Go and work elsewhere," demands Matilda. "In here, detectives."

The lads clear off and we follow her into a tack room stuffed full with gleaming saddles and tack. That heady scent of leather and polish pleasantly assaults your nostrils. Rosettes hang everywhere alongside pictures of magnificent, seriously expensive horses. On a wall, opposite a rough-hewn desk strewn with papers, there's a large photograph of a man's head with so many darts stuck in his face he is unrecognisable. My inner ear tells me who he might be.

Matilda slaps her crop down on the desk and sits down on a chair, leaving us to sit opposite her on a bench.

"This is my office," she sulks. "I run the stables, and as you can see, I have a mountain of paperwork to catch up on. So, hurry up and conduct your silly interview and then clear off."

"The fellow with the darts in his face. I take it he is to become your faience this coming Saturday."

She sits bolt upright, thrusts her chest out and looks about to explode, "What on earth has that got to do with you?"

"Perhaps nothing. Perhaps everything. You are getting engaged to someone you obviously detest. Why?"

Her anger instantly subsides and she fixes me with a very odd look that defies explanation.

"Why? Because mamma decrees it and what mamma wants, mamma gets."

"But surely she wouldn't make you marry someone you have no feelings for?"

"Oh yes she would. Lord Jeremy Stanford Bridlington Trout is heir apparent to a massive chunk of Kent. I do not wish to marry the demented imbecile, but I have no choice."

"Are you up the dumpling without a paddle?" says Head.

"Dumpling? Oh… no I'm not pregnant."

"Are you sure?" asks I.

"Absolutely. Look, this is how it is. Mamma is so envious of my youth and beauty she cannot bear the competition any longer and has decided, once and for all, to get rid of me by forcing me to marry Jeremy the drip on pain of stopping my allowance, taking away my horses and sending me off to Africa to become a missionary. There is no way out other than suicide."

"You could just say no," offers Head amiably. "Tell your mother how unhappy you are about having to marry Jeremy. Dig your heals in and play to her better nature."

"I have tried everything. Look, Sergeant, whatever your name is …"

"Head. Sergeant Richard Head."

"Sergeant Head, I have managed to avoid marriage since mamma first tried to get rid of me on my sixteenth by pairing me up with an old goat…"

"A goat!" gasps Head. "That's illegal isn't it?"

For the first time since meeting Matilda a beautiful smile crosses her ruby lips and lights up her entire being, "No, silly boy, not a real goat, he just looked like an old goat. By my seventeenth she tried marrying me off to another, even older old goat who was a professor of philosophy. By the time I reached eighteen she was presenting me with old goats and young goats at the rate of two a month. A few were suitable I suppose, but most were not. To be honest I prefer my men earthy in comparison to most of the pompous, weedy specimens she presented to me. I prefer less complicated men who are attentive without being condescending or treat you as if you are some silly little thing; who requires nothing more from a man except ridiculous complements and babies."

"Safe to say then that Constable Burroughs fits your expectations in the man department."

"He does, Sergeant. If Albert was acceptable to mamma, I would marry him tomorrow."

"Why not marry him anyway and say to hell with convention, wealth and status," says I.

"I may adore Albert, Inspector, but unfortunately I adore wealth and privilege more."

"So, why risk losing it all by sleeping with a commoner?"

"I am not sleeping with him, I just… um, cuddle him a bit."

"While in a state of undress?"

"He likes to check my heart is ticking on time," she grins.

I can tell Head is warming to her as am I. However, we have gone off tangent and need to get back to the real matter in hand. Just one more question on this subject.

"Why are you risking all for this clandestine relationship with Constable Burroughs?"

"I couldn't bear to have a child by Jeremy in fear that it would turn out to be as stupid as he is. If I am to have children, I want the girls to be at least pretty and the boys to be handsome, stalwart and have a modicum of intelligence. When the time is right, Albert and I will, um… How shall I put this?"

"Get shagging," blurts out Head. "And start just before your wedding to Jeremy to hopefully be already pregnant before the honeymoon."

She goes bright red and I'm wishing Head could have chosen his words with more decorum.

"Something on those lines."

"The problem is, Miss," cuts in I. "Your plan is deeply floored even if you did get away with it. You are your father's daughter, and not being rude, he isn't much in the looks department. You could choose whomsoever you wish to father your children, but no matter how handsome, bright and manly they are you could still give birth to a child who's the spitting image of your father, with say the character of your brother."

"God! If I popped out a Percy, I would drown the little rat."

"You don't care much for your brother?"

"I hate his chicken guts. I hate his face. I hate his voice. His lying, cheating manipulative ways. Most of all I hate his stupidity. You know he faked those attempts on his life just to steal the rent money, don't you?"

"We have serious reservations over attempts one and two, Miss. But not on attempt three. We are of the strong opinion that attempt three was genuine and whoever was behind it will almost certainly try again."

Her eyes light up, "Really? Oh, how glorious. Let's hope the next time will be a success."

"Your brother Robert was of the self-same opinion, Miss."

"I knew he would be. You have cheered me up no end, Inspector. What else do you wish to know?"

"Where were you when the third attempt on Percy's life was made?"

"Gosh. That was weeks ago. I can't recall exactly. Certainly, I wasn't anywhere near the front door when that block of stone was pushed from the roof. I'll have a think... but..."

"No matter. Do you know anyone who would want to kill Percy?"

"Yes, lots. I'd have to write you a list."

"Whenever will suffice. Do you want to see your brother dead?"

"Of course. Well, not really," she frowns. "I'd like to see him kidnapped by pirates, transported across the oceans to some far-flung country and dumped, never to return. That would teach the swine for…" she pauses and drops her gaze.

"Blackmailing you over your 'friendship' with Constable Burroughs," puts in I.

She meets my steady gaze and I see a tear in her eye, "Who told you? Was it, Robert?"

"A simple seduction, Miss."

"Seduction? Do you not mean deduction, Inspector?"

"Of course, I do," lies I aware that Matilda is growing on me to the extent I really wouldn't mind seducing her if given half a chance. Not that I would anyway even if the chance did arise, which it won't…"

Matilda cuts into my inner ramblings, "Torments me and ridicules me, that's what my rotten brother does. He messes with your mind to the extent you cannot think straight, and then before you know it, you have given him enough insight into your affairs to allow him to blackmail you. But of course, it's all just a jolly jape to him. It's a good thing Albert doesn't know Percy's blackmailing me or he'd go for the pig."

The interview drags on for another thirty minutes, with Matilda almost apologising for nearly running us down just for the hell of it, before Head and I finally take our leave and head back to the castle to interview Gloria Kemp and hopefully have a beer and a piece of cake. In truth, I could have carried on talking to Matilda all afternoon her having dropped her snotty cow attitude a tad. I've also realised that her life isn't anywhere near as closeted as I'd thought it was. Considering her position, she was also incredibly candid about her life.

"What do you think of Matilda now she's pulled her neck in a bit, Richard?" says I as we cross the lawn to the rear entrance.

"Do you want the clean version, or the dirty version?"

"I'll settle for the clean one."

"I wish I was a bar of her favourite soap and she was about to have a long hot bath."

I contemplate asking him what his dirty version is, but think better of it and take out my fob watch to check the time. "It's three minutes past three" announces I. "Wherever has the time gone?"

"It flew past ogling Matilda," grins Head as he pushes open the door and we step inside to be accosted by a short, evil eyed old fellow with a mass of thick curly greying black hair on his face and head, and huge dirty hands, one of which is holding a dripping with blood chopper.

"Who be you fellows then?" demands he raising his chopper and taking a threatening step closer towards us.

Heads reaction is both incredibly fast and brutal; his short truncheon is out in a flash and then cracked on the chopper wielder's head before you can blink. Said fellow collapses in a heap onto the flag stone floor with his eyes revolving in their sockets.

"Well done, Sergeant," says I kicking the chopper away. "Let's handcuff the devil before he comes around."

"I reason we have the would-be assassin in our hands," says Head wrestling the man's hands behind his back and slapping on the cuffs. "Case solved."

"Brilliant," praises I. "What luck we turned up when we did. But?"

"What poor sod's blood is on that chopper? If it's the cook's blood we might not get a piece of cake and a beer."

"Well let's hope it's someone else's, like Percy's."

Grabbing the groaning would be assassin by an arm each we drag him along the corridor and into the servant's hall, where we haul him onto a chair ready for interrogation. He starts to come around and snarls as he glares with evil intent into my eyes. Head cracks his head again.

"Brilliant, Sergeant. Stay here and guard him while I go and see what's what in the kitchen."

I find the cook all alone and sat at the table spooning what smells like oxtail soup into her mouth. Looking up she says, "Goodness, Inspector, you appear somewhat stressed. Is everything alright?"

"No, Mrs Kemp, it is not. We have just caught a mad man running around with his bloody chopper in his hand."

"That'll be Sam' Jenson the head gamekeeper. He just killed a couple of geese for me to cook for the family's dinner tomorrow. Mr Algernon's favourite is roast goose."

I spy the headless geese hanging from a beam and dripping blood into a bucket.

"Ah… So, the blood on this Sam's chopper is from those geese?"

She fixes me with a puzzled look, "Indeed it is."

"Has this Sam' ever been known to behead people?"

Breaking into ribald laughter she wipes her sleeve over her mouth, "Good God no. Sam' hasn't got it in him to behead people."

"It didn't stop him beheading those geese, so he might be capable of beheading people."

"I suppose, Inspector, but I really wouldn't think so."

"Right, thank you, Mrs Kemp. I shall return presently."

Hurrying back into the hall I find Sam' is coming around again, "We've cocked up, Sergeant. The man is innocent. Quick, let's get those cuffs off him and get him onto his feet."

"And then what?"

"We'll dump him out back and hope he doesn't remember what happened to him."

"What the bloody 'ell 'appened?" groans Sam' as we drag him towards the back door.

"You fell over and banged you head," says Head.

"Bloody let go of me will yer," snaps Sam' wrestling his arms free, falling back on the wall and rubbing the bumps on his head. "Sweet Jesus, it feels like I've been banged on me bonce with a 'ammer." Stabbing a finger at Head he growls, "'ang on 'ear. It was yer 'it me on thee 'ead, yer bloody thug!"

"Sorry," says Head sounding sorry. "We mistook you for a madman who'd just killed someone."

"Well I ain't no mad man. I just brought in an' killed a couple of gooses for thee cook."

"Geese," corrects I.

"I 'spect yer're them fancy coppers down from London. I'm goin' ter do yer for brutality."

I have never been called fancy before and cannot say I like the term, "Look here my good man. You waved a bloody chopper at as, what did you expect, a handshake?"

"You could've asked why I was carrying a bloody chopper before yer 'it me on the bonce."

"Mister," growls Head. "We can't take the risk of asking anyone why they are swinging their bloody great choppers around, we just drop them before they drop us. Any other way would be tantamount to committing suicide. I just acted instinctively that's all."

"What's that mean?"

"I dropped you before you stuck your chopper in my skull."

"But I weren't about ter stuck my chop… cleaver in yer bonce."

"I didn't know that," grates Head. "See it from our point of view."

He scratches at his bumps, "What's that mean?"

"We misinterpreted the situation, "groans I. "Now, kindly clear off before you receive a few more cracks on your head."

"Where's my cleaver?"

"Near the back door."

"Alright, I'll be off. But don't think yer've 'eard thee last of this. I want me compensation."

"You'll be lucky," scoffs Head.

"I will an' all. My brother sleeps with the local magistrate, yer see 'ow yer like a comin' up against 'im."

I cave in, "How much do you want?"

His eyes go all shrewd, "I'd say ten shillin' for each bump. That's a pound."

"One shilling per bump. That's two shillings. Take it or leave it."

With a derisive shaking of his head he says, "Eight shillin' fer each bump. That's sixteen shillin' altogether. Pay up or yer'll be seein' thee magistrate."

"Alright, sixteen shillings it is. Sergeant, pay the man."

"Why me?"

"You were the one who hit him."

"I know that. But I was protecting the both of us you know."

"That may well be so, but in a court of law you would be convicted for assault as I did not order you to hit him."

"You and I could fall out over this, sir."

"We could but we won't," smiles I as a stroke of genius comes into my head. "Sam,' you say your brother sleeps with the local magistrate?"

"That's what I said."

"Therefore, as they are both men, they are breaking the law. Perhaps we should go and arrest them right now. What say you, Sergeant?"

"Sounds like a plan to me, sir. Perhaps we should also arrest Sam' for threatening to 'sort out Mr Percy' as witnessed by several locals in the Rams Head a few days ago."

"Brilliant, Sergeant. What's it to be, Sam'? Sixteen shillings compensation along with a trip down the nick, for you, your brother and the local magistrate?"

"Alright yer bleeders," snarls he clenching his fists. "But yer ought ter give me somethin'"

Fetching out my purse I find a shilling and hand it over, "One more thing before you skip merrily off, Sam'. What did Percy do to upset you so much that you want to do him harm?"

"I don't like ter say, but I will. That bastard grabbed my girl from behind while she was plucking a duck in the kitchen an' he felt up her woman's parts. She was very upset about it."

"I see. Just you keep out of it, Sam' and leave Percy to us. Now, off you go."

"Can you believe that cheeky sod?" grates Head. "He honestly thought he could get compensation from us for just doing our job."

"Incredible, Sergeant. Can you imagine what a policeman's lot would be if everyone we brained thought he could get compensation for his suffering."

"It would be dreadful. We could find ourselves up in court being charged with assault just for booting some mad bastard in the roundies to stop him from say, stabbing us."

"Exactly so. Imagine the scene; the prosecution demanding to know why, when there was two of us, we didn't try to restrain his client before kicking him in the balls?"

"I'd say because he came at us with a knife in one hand and a chopper in the other with a lump of someone's flesh hanging off it, so we dropped him before he could kill us. The case would be laughed out of the court."

"But what if the prosecution then demanded to know what led us to believe his client would actually use his weapons?"

"I would say; as he'd already stabbed and chopped up six people, including his own mother, there was a good chance he'd do the same to us."

"Ah… but was it not a fact at the time that my client hadn't been charged with a single murder? Therefore, you acted in haste without sufficient evidence that my client was in fact guilty of anything at all, and you kicked him in the balls out of sheer malice, while arrogantly believing you would get away with it simply because you are policemen. And so, it would go on, Sergeant. Ridiculous. What's more important, the wellbeing of a mass murderer or that of the law enforcers?"

"Us and the mass murderers' potential victims are the most important."

"Agreed," agrees I. "Compensation for scum bags! It will never happen."

Stepping into the kitchen we find a tankard of ale waiting for each of us on the table alongside two large wedges of jam sponge that actually has jam in it.

"Did Sam get off alright?" asks Gloria as we sit down opposite her.

"Yes, he did," smiles I.

"Good. Well tuck in gentlemen and fire away with your questions. I can spare you a good fifteen minutes before bedlam returns to the kitchen. I sent everyone out for a walk to get some fresh air into them, and to give me a bit of peace for a while, so we can talk freely without those silly girls listening in and then spreading highly embellished gossip all over the place."

"What's your honest opinion of Percy?"

"Will this be in confidence?"

"It will."

"I don't get on with him. I have a constant battle to keep him out of my kitchen and away from the girls."

I take a long swallow of my ale while shooting Head an admonishing glare, he's tucking into his cake as if it's the last supper and not taking notes like he should be. Catching my eye, he pushes his plate away and gets out his note pad and pencil.

"Percy is an absolute swine," continues Gloria chewing her bottom lip.

"Agreed," smiles I. "What's your opinion on the attempts on his life?"

"Hogwash! He set them up himself so he could steal the rent money. An absolute farce. But surely you have ascertained as much yourself?"

"We have, Mrs Kemp. Except we are of the firm conviction that attempt number three was genuine."

There's a flicker in Gloria's eyes that tells me she didn't like that comment, and it's enough for me to suspect she knows something.

"Where were you, Mrs Kemp when attempt number three was made on Percy's life?"

"I would have been in here at that time of the day. Ask any of the girls. Look, Inspector do you honestly think for a second, I could have ventured up on the roof and shoved off a block of stone at the exact moment Percy was leaving the castle, and then got back here without being seen or missed from the kitchen?"

"Of course, I don't," smiles I.

"Then why even ask?"

"Because Mrs Kemp, anyone who has a motive to want to see Percy dead is a suspect. Even you, and we will not be able to rule anyone out unless they are open and honest with us."

"I am being honest and will also be open with you providing it is strictly between us."

"You have my word."

"What exactly do you want to know?"

"You more or less said it yourself earlier. You are like a mother to the staff below you. You are also in contact with the entire household one way or another. Those that serve the Bullington's meals would drip back information about what is being said between the family. Parlour maids, chamber maids, footmen and so on would tell your kitchen staff things that will eventually come to your attention. You're accessible, easy to talk to and despite your strict demeaner you are obviously loved by your staff. So, what do you know about Rose Bush and John Chambers that you haven't told us?"

She drops her eyes and begins wringing her hands together, "They were worried about something and I suspect it was to do with the roof top incident. I believe Rose lied to Constable Burroughs about not seeing anyone come down from the roof. I also believe that Chambers also lied about not seeing anyone except Mr Smithers go up or come down the stairs. The trouble is I don't know why they lied, but I could make a guess."

"So, could I, Mrs Kemp. Rose did see someone come down from the roof. Someone she knew who would have a great deal of influence over her and she lied to protect that person. I'm also wondering if that person was Chambers himself…"

"Alright, Inspector," cuts in Gloria. "I see where you are going with this. That beast Percy cornered Rose when she was alone in one of the bedrooms while changing sheets. Percy forced her onto the bed, put a hand over her mouth while his other hand forced its way up her dress. The attack lasted barely a minute before he calmly walked out of the room leaving the poor child in a state of absolute shock. The housekeeper heard her sobbing on passing the bedroom and after comforting her, took her to her office where she comforted her further until Rose had calmed down and regained her demeanour."

"The housekeeper in question at the time, according to Constable Burroughs' notes, was a, Miss Juliet Saunders who left her employment the day before the roof top incident. Can I assume she left because of the incident between Rose and Percy?"

"That and other reasons. The assault on Rose took place three days before the rooftop incident. I know Juliet confronted Percy over it, only to have him laugh in her face and accuse her of just being jealous. She just had enough and left. Since then no one suitable has, as yet, been found to replace her."

"And was it, Juliet who told you about the assault on Rose?"

She nods and then gets to her feet, "I could do with a brandy. Will you gentlemen join me?"

"We certainly will," says Head.

"What are you thinking, Sergeant," asks I once Gloria is out of ear shot.

"Rose told Chambers she'd been assaulted by Percy and Chambers decided to get even, but failed. After that he didn't get another opportunity because Percy had fled to the sanctuary of the dungeon. So, Rose and Chambers concocted a story to cover their tracks when questioned by Burroughs, but when they heard we were on our way they panicked and fled. Therefore, Chambers has now become suspect number one."

"My thoughts exactly. But if that is the case then Smithers has also lied, because he said, Chambers was standing right behind him in the hallway when the stone fell and narrowly missed Percy. I do not believe Smithers lied in his statement."

"Which means it was more likely that Rose pushed the stone off the roof. She had the opportunity with no one to witness her going up or coming down from the roof."

"Exactly. Therefore, Rose Bush becomes suspect number one."

Gloria returns with three half full tumblers of brandy and sets them down. Sitting down she fixes me with eyes full of trepidation. "I honestly don't know if it was John Chambers or even Rose who tried to kill that swine, Inspector, but I'm afraid to say I believe it was one or the other. The trouble is I'm also afraid that I cannot condemn them for it and I hope they get away with it forever."

"So, do we," says Head raising his tumbler. "A toast to justice, and death to Percy."

"Death to Percy," choruses I and Gloria.

"Do you know, Inspector? I am the longest serving member of the household. I have been cooking for the Bullingtons for over twenty-five years. Before taking over here, from my grandmother on her retirement, I had learnt to cook under my mother at the Finchley household near Truro. I love it here and it would be perfect if my Jim were still alive and that bastard Percy was dead instead." Tears well up in her eyes, she downs her brandy with a shudder and then says. "Is there anything else for now, Inspector?"

"No thank you, Mrs Kemp."

"Then I shall go outside and round up my staff. Leave the little devils too long and they'll be taking advantage."

Head scoffs the rest of his cake and hoovers up the crumbs in the usual manner. He really is a gannet at times. "Feel free to lick the plate, Sergeant."

And he does, picking it up and running his tongue all around until it's spotless.

"Lovely," he grins, banging it down and picking up his brandy he downs it in one swallow. After a belch he picks up his ale, gulps it down and then bangs the tankard down. A quick run of his jacket sleeve over his mouth and he is obviously ready to go. "What now, sir?"

"We could start interviewing the staff and try and find out if anyone has any idea where Rose and her boyfriend may have gone. But I'm thinking it will take up too much time, and may well be a waste of that time as the couple left in such haste it's unlikely, they told anyone where they were going, if they even knew where they were going. We need to find Rose and her boyfriend, but I am at a loss how to go about it."

"I am thinking on the same lines. They've had a long time to put a lot of distance between themselves and the castle."

"Perhaps the constable may have gotten somewhere. Let's go and visit him if he's about."

"And if he isn't?"

"Then we'll interview the locals in the village. Post offices and general stores are always great places to gather information."

"Followed by the pub," grins Head.

As we step into the servant's hall Gloria comes in behind her chatting and giggling girls, the girls pass by us but I stop Gloria for a moment. "Can you point out Bush and Chambers from any of these photographs on the wall?" asks I.

"Oh, yes," she smiles. Stepping over she points to the one on the end. "Taken a few weeks back. That's Rose, and behind her with the men, is John Chambers."

I take a look; Rose appears quite small and fair with a chubby pretty face, while Chambers is tall and lean with dark hair and a thin pencil moustache. Head takes a look and nods. He's thinking the same as me, they're of good character and have probably not committed an evil act in their entire lives. But then you never know.

Gloria moves down the line, "That's me in this picture taken in eighteen seventy-three when I first joined. And there's Mr Smithers in this picture when he first joined us back in seventy-five. He'd have been about thirty then. Handsome chap. All the ladies fancied him back then. He could have had his pick but he never did pick a one. Single to this day."

We thank Gloria and head off. On reaching the hallway the open front door is suddenly invaded by the 'bubbly boos', barking and yapping and tearing all over the place with a stressed looking Jackson on their heels.

The second Henry goes for Head's leg, Head takes a swipe at him with his boot but misses, allowing the demented hound to latch on. Heads truncheon appears in his hand but I cover it with mine. "Don't do it, Sergeant."

He puts the truncheon away and settles for clipping Henry around the ear, which has the effect of increasing Henry's assault.

"Bastard mutt," hisses Head trying to shake the dog off by jockeying his leg back and forwards.

Jackson steps forwards and grabs Henry by the scruff of his neck and is met by a warning snarl and bared teeth. Henry has no intention of letting go of Heads leg until he's sated. I contemplate barking out a STOP! The trouble is I'm finding it very difficult not to laugh out loud at Heads discomfort. At last, with a howl of pleasure, Henry falls off Heads leg to lay panting on his side.

"I'll do for that bastard," growls Head shaking his fist. "The things a filthy rapist."

"He's merely showing you his love, Sergeant," goads I.

Giving me the 'get stuffed' look Head stomps out the door into the air, immediately followed by Henry who clamps himself onto Heads other leg. This could be the end for Henry. He really is pushing his luck. Head is obviously in a beyond furious mood as he hops off on one leg while dragging the dog along on his other leg.

"I am so sorry, sir," pleads Jackson. "I dare not hit the dog in case I get into trouble."

"Fear not, Jackson. I'm sure the Sergeant will survive."

"But where is he taking him? The countess will be very, very, upset if anything happens to Henry."

It strikes me then that Head will almost certainly have his razor-sharp flick knife on him, and that Henry is going to be taken out of sight and gelded, or worse have his throat cut. Time to act, "HENRY! Get back here this instant."

"I don't think he heard you, sir."

"He heard, but he's so enamoured with my Sergeant's leg he is refusing to listen. Has he always been like this?"

"He does have a penchant for people's legs, but I've never before seen him this obsessed with one person's leg. Anyway, usually it's female legs he goes for."

"How strange," ponders I. "Let us hope Henry soon gets tired of unrequited love and for his own sake moves on to someone else less dangerous."

At last Henry falls off Heads leg to roll over on the ground for a back scratch. Talk about being in doggy bliss. What more do you want? For his part Head keeps walking and I'm thinking it might take a little while for him to calm down, so it's best to leave him be.

"Do you know where Simmonds is?" asks I of Jackson, as Henry comes charging over and into the hall to join in with his fellows who have all decided to piss up the suit of armour's legs.

"He's over at the stables having a loose shoe secured."

"What's up with his shoe?"

Jackson grins, "Not his shoe, sir, one of his horses."

"Thank you, Jackson," says I before hurrying to catch up with Head.

"I'll swing for that bloody dog next time he comes near me," snarls Head.

"Perhaps you should try a little phycology, Sergeant. You know, appeal to Henry's better nature."

Head fixes me with scathing eyes, "He's a bloody dog! He wouldn't understand a thing I say. No, there's only one way to deal with this," hisses he running a finger across his throat.

Dropping the subject, we head over to the stables where we find Simmonds has had his horses shoe fixed and is ready to go.

"To the village police station, please, Simmons," says I.

Apart from the noise coming from the school playground and an old lady hobbling into the post office you'd think the village was deserted. We alight at the police station, send Simmons on his way and head down the path and bang on the door. No answer.

"We could try around back," says Head.

Following a narrow path, we go around back to find the constable sat on a chair while sipping tea from an enamel mug as he surveys his vegetable plot. Braces hanging down and his shirt sleeves rolled up he is lost in his euphoria but jumps when I call out, "Good afternoon, Constable Burroughs."

"And to you, sir," says he standing up and turning to face us. "I wasn't expecting you. Sorry, I was just having a cuppa. Would you care for some tea?"

"No thank you, Constable. We have come for an update on your search for the runaways."

"Right, sir. Shall we go inside?"

"Out here will do."

"I'll fetch a couple more chairs from the kitchen."

"Alright for some," says Head as Burroughs hurries off. "It doesn't look like he's done much searching for anything except caterpillars in his beans."

"Perhaps," says I noticing a slimy lump of squashed green caterpillars at my feet.

Returning with the chairs, Burroughs sets them down on the grass and we sit facing each other. There are bags under his eyes, he looks tired and weary.

"Excuse me, sir," yawns he. "I've been up most of the night. I didn't get the message that Rose and John had run off until sunset last night. It would have been fruitless chasing after them with no idea where they may have gone, so I got on my bicycle and went around to everyone I thought may have had an idea where they'd gone."

"Family and friends?"

"Exactly, I went to see the Bush's first, Seb' is Rose's father."

"Are we talking Seb' the sheep farmer?"

"Yes, sir. Anyway, Seb' wasn't best pleased to know they'd run off together. He wished they'd have come to him first. Anyway, apart from giving me an address of a relative in Truro, where Rose had been to stay a few years back, none of the Bush's had any idea where they might be heading."

"Did you think they may have been hiding something from you?"

He shakes his head, "They're honest people, sir. They wouldn't lie in a situation like this. After Seb' I went to see three of Rose's older married brothers who have tied cottages on the estate. By now it was dark and I had to knock two of the brothers up, they go to bed early because they get up at four to go and do the milking. Anyway, they knew nothing as to where the couple might have gone, as did the third brother. Another two of her unmarried brothers live in and work on the Carter's estate. I went there first thing this morning and it was Billy Bush, Seb's youngest, who reckoned Rose had always wanted to go to Lands' End, so she may have gone there."

"When someone suddenly runs, Constable, their priority is to get as far away from whoever they're running from. Once they feel safer and have caught their breath, they will then try to decide where best to go and invariably go where they believe no one would think they'd go, or where it would be difficult for a pursuer to find them."

"Like a large town or a city where no one knows them, so they can hide amongst the mayhem," puts in Head.

"Ah…" sighs Burroughs. "I'm not that good at detective work am I, sir?"

"You could be, with the right training and experience," says I. "After seeing the brothers what did you do then?"

"Well I didn't worry about questioning anyone at the castle as I thought you'd be doing that, so I went home for a short sleep. At first light I set off to cycle around neighbouring villages asking anyone I met if they'd seen Rose and or John."

"That sounds like it would have been a complete waste of your time, Constable."

"It was, sir. I gained nothing bar a saddle-sore rump and a sunburnt nose."

"No wonder you look so knackered," grins Head.

"Where do I go from here, sir?" asks Burroughs sounding thoroughly dejected.

"Right. Get your head down for an hour or so and then go to the castle and see if you can pick up the runaway's trail to see what direction they went. They may have gone across the fields rather than kept to the lanes. Less likely to be spotted and possibly a shorter route to wherever? Try a circumference of, say, three hundred yards around the castle. It's a lot of plod work and only an outside chance, but who knows? It may just be worth the effort."

"Thank you, sir. Is there anything else I can help you with?"

"You can, Constable. How much in love are you with Matilda Bullington and how badly do you want to see her brother Percy, dead?"

"Did you believe him?" ponders Head as we walk towards the general stores.

"I'll give him the benefit of the doubt for now. He was very candid about his relationship with Matilda and about how much he'd like to attend Percy's funeral, hopefully in the very near future. But I don't believe he'd go so far as to try and kill Percy."

"Nor I. Matilda though, lied to us when she said, 'It's a good thing Albert doesn't know Percy's blackmailing me or he'd go for the pig.'"

"And who could blame him? Matilda was just trying to protect Burroughs by leading us to believe he knew nothing about the blackmail."

"Do we cross Burroughs off the suspect list just because we think he wouldn't try and kill Percy, even though he has one hell of a motive? He's in love with Matilda and is fully aware of the consequences of their actions should it come to light. It would destroy the pair of them.

"We'll cross him off for now, but we won't cross Matilda off." We pause to face each other. "This investigation could drag on for weeks, Sergeant. The more we question people the more suspects will materialise. The more lies we'll have to unravel and the deeper into the mire we will find ourselves. We could do with some help, because while we waste time on the remote chance someone who's not really connected to the castle will tell us something of importance, the less chance we'll have of cracking through the shells of those who might be more likely to further our investigations. Are you with me so far?"

"No."

"Allow me to put it another way. The answer lays within the castle and we must concentrate our efforts there. We need another trained detective to do more of the donkey work for us. Perhaps we could find someone from a neighbouring town or village."

"I've got a better idea. Why not telegraph Clump and request he comes down earlier than he intended to, so he can help? Afterall it's his bloody family we're dealing with."

"Brilliant. He'd also get more out of Percy then we would unless we torture the bastard."

"Exactly. If he could get here by tomorrow, he'd have all Friday to question suspects before Saturday's big event, by which time, with luck, we could be heading home with him none the wiser about our wives being here."

"I like it. If I take the post office and send the gram, you can take the general store. After that we'll leave the door to door for now in exchange for the Rams Head where we'll conduct further, more serious interviews with the locals once we've encouraged them to have a few too many. Are you with me?"

"Well I am standing here looking at you so I suspect I am with you."

I look up to the sky, it is still blue, devoid of cloud with seagulls soaring majestically. A slight breeze tickles my face and the scent of lavender flowering close by caresses my nose buds. The laughter of children from the school lifts my heart. All is well with the world. But sometimes, I really do wonder if D. S. Head may be suffering from being punch drunk from all the rucks, he's been in over the years

Back to the Smugglers Rest

"Sending Simmons off earlier wasn't such a good idea, Gerald," moans Head as we tramp ever uphill towards the Smugglers Rest.

"Was it my fault that no one would give us a lift, or were too drunk to drive?"

"Yes. On top of that it cost us a bomb getting the buggers drunk in the first place only to learn no more than we learnt yesterday."

"I did."

Head comes to a stop to position himself facing the stone wall beside the lane, "I need a pee, Gerald."

"Good idea, Richard. So do I." Facing the wall on the opposite side of the lane for decorum's sake, I relieve myself and manage to squirt a rough picture of a sheep on the wall, drawing inspiration from the sheep and lambs grazing and gambolling in the meadow.

"Ah that's better," sighs Head. As we turn around to face each other I can't help but notice the pig image he's squirted on the wall is more accomplished than my sheep.

"What did you learn then, Gerald?" smiles Head while smugly perusing my sheep.

"When I went around back for a pee, I heard a couple of locals in the toilet talking about the landlord. Holding back from going in, I listened. 'Now them their policemen int no fools my lover,' said one. 'That's fer sure. Ol' landlord oughta leave off the smugglin' while they're about, I reckon,' said the other. 'Not unless he want's ter end up in thee dock.' That was that, they were coming out so I slipped around the side of the toilet and waited until they'd gone before going in."

"Smuggling hey?" says Head. "What's that got to do with us, Gerald?"

"Nothing really. We've got enough to get on with without becoming involved with smugglers. I was just thinking before we go back home, we should tap the landlord up and ensure, for turning a blind eye, we go home with a few bottles of whiskey at an extra cheap price to put away for Christmas."

"Good idea. Why not get a few dozen bottles of extra cheap brandy to sell on as well?"

"An excellent idea, Richard."

We trudge on in silence. It is so warm we remove our jackets and sling them over our shoulders. I loosen my tie and undo my top button. Head takes off his bowler and wipes his sweating brow with his shirt sleeve, which is sods law as a low soaring seagull decides at that very moment to drop its guts onto his head. Not realising, Head puts his bowler back on. Now he's got both trouser legs stained with Henry's secretions plus a sizeable splodge of grey white mess in his hair. If that wasn't enough to contend with, he walks straight through a pile of horse dollop without even noticing, and I realise he is miles away.

"Do you have something on your mind, Richard?"

He looks me in the eye, "I was just imagining what life will be like once the little one is born. Our lives will never be the same again I shouldn't wonder."

"Indeed not, Richard. Do you have reservations about the intended arrival?"

"Not really, Gerald. But I am worried about Chloe. It's dangerous having babies, so many women suffer terribly and even die. Two of my mother's sisters died giving birth. Poor old Aunty Maud was worn out by the time she gave birth to her twelfth child and died of exhaustion."

"How old was she?"

"About thirty, I think."

"Oh…," I place a comforting hand on his shoulder, there isn't much I could say to ease his fears. No wonder he's been so distracted of late. "All will turn out fine, Richard. Chloe is young, fit and strong. All will be well, trust me."

At last the Smugglers Rest comes into view. As we near the hotel I advise Head to clean up a bit before we go in. He scrapes his shoes on the shoe scraper and finishes off with the stiff brush left out for such a reason. I then use the brush to comb out as much of the seagull shit from his hair as I can.

"You'll need a hair wash, bath and change of clothes before dinner," says I.

"I will. Do they have a laundry service here?"

"They do, but it isn't cheap."

"Better that then having trousers stinking of dog semen," sighs he.

We go inside and into the bar to find the girls are not there. Perhaps they are out somewhere? I go up to the unmanned bar and ting the bell. A middle-aged barman quickly appears. I ask does he know where our wives are and he informs me they are up in their rooms resting before dinner. He then hands me a telegraph that was delivered by a postman. Clump will arrive tomorrow, sometime late afternoon.

Head and I head upstairs with me leading the way. Once on the landing I pause as the sound of Betty giggling, and a man laughing, floats out from the open door of my bedroom. Betty is in there with someone and it isn't Chloe, unless her voice has turned masculine. I put a finger to my lips and Head nods his understanding before quietly opening his bedroom door and stepping inside.

I edge my way closer to hear all the better.

"Oh… Andrew, you are such a cheeky young man," coos Betty. "What shall I do with you?"

"I don't know, Mrs Potter. Anyway, I must get on or I shall be in trouble."

"I shall see you at dinner, Andrew."

"I shall look forward to it, Mrs Potter."

Stepping quickly back, to give the impression I had just stepped up onto the landing, I pause until 'Andrew' comes into view. Andrew is the young waiter from last night, the one who kept ogling Betty's breasts. He is carrying a tray with two empty coffee cups on it, a big smile on his lips and an unmistakable bulge in his trousers. The randy swine!

"Good evening, sir," says he nervously meeting my furious glare.

"Is it?" hisses I clenching my fists.

Stepping around me he hurries down stairs with the cups chinking away on their saucers. I walk into the bedroom and close the door. Betty is sat by the window and gazes up at me with a look that says it all. She is as guilty as hell. But of what exactly?

"Your back much earlier than I expected, Detective Inspector. Have you had a good day?"

"So, so," replies I. "And you?"

"We had a lovely day," says she narrowing her eyes in defiance. "We went to Truro and did a little sightseeing."

Throwing my jacket and hat onto the bed I pull a chair over and sit opposite Betty across a small round table. "Good. I am pleased that you had a good day."

"Obviously you didn't, judging by your grumpy face, Detective Inspector."

"I wasn't grumpy until I saw that smarmy waiter leaving the room, Betty. Whatever did you think you were doing by entertaining a young man in your bedroom while on your own?"

She sits up straight as a flash of anger glints from her eyes, "I was not entertaining a young man on my own as you so accusingly put it. Besides which I left the door open for proprieties sake."

"If you weren't entertaining him why did he have two cups on his tray and not one? And who knows if he'd only just opened the door in order to leave."

"So, it's the detective talking and not the husband, is it? Very well officer! I shall come clean and own up. I am enraptured by that young man. I think he is charming, very polite and, oh, yes, oh so handsome. Arrest me, for I am as guilty as sin of wanting something so much it is heart breaking. What do you think of that confession, officer?"

"Not much," snarls I. "How far have you gone with that boy?"

"I went all the way to Truro with him. What say you to that little snippet?"

I'm not sure what she means by this? Perhaps it is a Cornish saying that simply means all the way sexually, God forbid. "Well from now on you are forbidden to talk to him, forbidden to be alone with him at any time, and forbidden to wear any item of clothing that may give him the impression that you are enticing him to flirt with you. Is that clear?"

"It is. What shall I wear for dinner tonight then, officer? Would an old sack do? And shall I converse through you when ordering my meal or would it be better if I wrote it down?

"There is no need to be sarcastic, Betty. I have informed you of my wishes so let us leave it like that. Unless you desire for this to turn really horrible."

She gets to her feet and throws down the most furious glare any women could throw at her man. "I feel sick to my stomach," pleads she as tears fill her eyes. "Go to hell! Detective Inspector and do not return until you have regained your sanity."

With that she flies out of the room into the bathroom, slamming the door so hard the walls shake. Time for a drink. It would be fruitless to try and reconcile with her at this moment. I will allow her the time to calm down and consider how foolish she has been.

Taking myself off to the bar I find it is fairly quiet, a pair of elderly gentlemen with dog collars on are supping sherry and gazing lovingly into each other's eyes, while a middle-aged couple of ample proportions are sat in one corner shovelling food into their mouths. Andrew the waiter, is standing to attention in another corner awaiting the call to serve and doesn't appear that happy to see me as I take a seat by the window. He comes over anyway. "What would, sir care for?" asks he in a voice that trembles ever so slightly.

Your balls on the end of my boot, thinks I. "A pint of best bitter," says I noting he is avoiding meeting my eyes. He is as guilty as sin, that much is certain. But again, of what exactly? How far has their relationship gone? Has he been intimate with my Betty? Or has it merely been mutual flirting? I don't know, but I will find out.

As he hurries off to get my order, I ponder over how Betty has conducted herself ever since we have been here. She has been flirtatious with practically every man who has come within a sniff of her perfume. Part of the reason is the sheer excitement of being here, but mostly I believe she is revelling in the attention, especially from that horny bloody waiter, the slippery toad! The thing is how can I keep an eye on Betty when I'm out and about investigating? I can't, but perhaps Chloe can? I'll talk to Head on the quiet about it the first chance I get. The waiter returns, he appears somewhat breathless and increasingly nervous.

"One pint of best bitter, sir," says he. Hands trembling, he sets it down on the table while spilling some of the beer. "Sorry, sir. I'll fetch a cloth."

"How old are you lad?" demands I.

"Fifteen, sir," says he straightening up and looking over my head to avoid my eyes.

"Have you ever killed anyone?"

He shakes his head, turns deathly white and looks about to fill his drawers. Good. Hopefully he has got the message. "Thank you. I will call you should I require anything else."

He sorts of wobbles away back to his corner and suddenly I feel rather guilty and not a little foolish. Did I have to ask him such a ridiculous question just to scare him? In the rough areas of London, such a question to most of the boys his age would be answered with an indifferent shrug, but here, in this peaceful enclave the underlying menace from that question was utterly misplaced. Rubbing my eyes, I suddenly feel very tired. I have never spoken to my lovely Betty in such a way before. I need to get a grip of my faculties having allowed suspicion and jealousy to cloud my judgement. Betty would never cheat on me. Or would she?

Sipping at my beer I note it is now six o'clock and I should be getting ready for dinner. But I would not be welcome upstairs for some time until Betty has calmed down. Waving the waiter back over I order a double scotch and a glass of water in a more amiable tone of voice. Softening my approach would be the best way to get the boy on side so he might open up to me and answer my questions truthfully. I will work on him over the next couple of days until I've gained his trust. Leaving it there for now, I relax a little while pondering how I am going to creep back into Betty's good books.

Half an hour later, by which time the couple of gannets have left, Head comes in and sits down opposite me. He appears well scrubbed and smells of roses.

"How is Chloe?" asks I.

"Weary and increasingly uncomfortable, but in good spirits. She's having the time of her life, bless her. She's in with Betty at the moment having a woman to woman talk."

"Ah… So, you know we had a row?"

"We heard a door violently slammed. But until a very tearful Betty knocked on our door a few minutes after that we had no idea about anything. I left them to it and taking a change of clothes I went and got cleaned up for dinner. Do you want to talk about it?"

"I do. I must. I have to."

The waiter comes over and asks Head if he wants anything. He orders a pint and a plate of biscuits. "What was the row about then, Gerald?"

"I think, Betty's having it off with that waiter," says I pointing to Andrews back.

"Really! How do you know that?"

"I just do. Men know when their partners are messing around."

"I didn't."

"Didn't what?"

"Know Clarissa was getting rogered by someone else."

"Why didn't you know?"

"Because she seemed normal."

"Clarissa was never normal. What eventually led you to believe she was getting it elsewhere?"

"Firstly, she wasn't as keen in bed as she'd been before."

"And secondly?"

"There wasn't a secondly. She just left me a note saying she was off as she'd found someone else who really appreciated her and wasn't more interested in his job than his woman."

"Interesting. What was his job?"

"A sewage maintenance inspector."

I scratch my head in confusion, "A sewage maintenance inspector? Anyone who messes around in sewers for a living, has to be more interested in anything other than ensuring that the shit keeps floating down the pipes and out to sea. Couldn't she see that?"

"Apparently not. Anyway, I don't care, her buggering off left me free to find my Chloe. And look at us now."

Rubbing my eyes again I say tersely, "I can't believe that Betty would betray me so."

He reaches across the table and pats me on the shoulder, "Nor I, Gerald. Look, I'll bet you're not reading this right. Betty would no more go behind your back to shag a waiter than I would, regardless of how good looking he was. I mean she was."

We are interrupted by the surprising arrival of Simmonds coming into the bar with his top hat tucked under his arm. He steps up to our table and says, "I am sorry to interrupt gentlemen, but I have been sent by Constable Burroughs to inform you that John Chambers has turned up."

"Dead or alive?" asks I.

"Dead, sir. Very dead indeed. Murdered apparently."

Downing my scotch, I get to my feet and head upstairs to get my jacket and bowler. Head follows me up. Betty isn't in and is obviously still in with Chloe. Slipping on my jacket I step out on the landing just as Head comes out of his room, where upon the door is shut behind him and the sound of it being locked tells me Betty doesn't want to see me right now.

"Betty," calls I through the door. "It is I, your devoted and loving husband. Please allow me in to talk for a moment or two."

"Go away, Detective Inspector."

"I could be out for hours, Betty. Please give me a minute…"

"Stay out all night for all I care. Should you return before morning; no doubt you'll find room to lay your rotten head in the stables, as there won't be room for you in my bed."

"You don't mean that, Betty."

"I do. Let me put it another way, Detective Inspector. Fuck off and don't come back."

Head grabs my arm, "We must go, Gerald."

"I know. Duty first, hey?"

A Brutal Killing

As the horses' fast trot towards the castle, I ask Simmonds what he knows about Chambers turning up.

"Not much, sir," shouts back he. "Samuel Jenson came to the castle and informed Mr Smithers that Constable Burroughs came to his house and told Samuel to go and fetch the detectives. Then I was sent out to fetch you. John Chambers body was found by the constable about a half mile from the castle in a small wood. Samuel said he would wait for our return and then he will take you to the murder site. That's all I know."

"Any mention of Rose Bush?"

"No, sir."

"Do you have anything with you which would be suitable to bring the body back in?"

"Yes, sir. I have a thick tarpaulin under your seat."

We settle back, nothing to do until we arrive at the scene of the crime unless your name is Richard Head, who somehow must have grabbed hold of a handful of biscuits on our way out, as he's now munching away as if nothing else on earth matters.

Arriving at the castle we find Jenson and a very worried looking Smithers waiting outside. Smithers is dressed in his country attire while Jenson has a shotgun tucked under one arm.

Jumping down Simmonds drops the steps and Smithers and Jenson climb aboard to sit opposite us.

"A damnable business," says Smithers exhaling dramatically. "I cannot believe it."

"Well it's true, me handsome," says Jenson fixing stark eyes onto me. "Shot in thee back with a bleedin' arrow, no less. Now we can get half way before we'll 'ave ter get off an' walk. Then I'll lead thee way as I know where ter go."

We trot on and I am feeling somewhat intimidated by the way Jenson keeps staring at me while fiddling with his triggers. "Is that gun loaded?" asks I.

"Be no use if it weren't," sneers he.

"Kindly break it and remove the cartridges for safeties sake, Mr Jenson."

"Or what," says he pulling off his felt hat and dropping his head. "So, yer can give me a few more lumps on me 'ead likes these ones?"

"I advise you to do as I ask," says I returning his glare even more glaringly.

He breaks his gun, removes the cartridges and slips them in his scruffy jacket pocket.

Following a narrow bumpy track, we go past the stables and out into open country side with low rolling meadows full of sheep on both sides. Apart from the sound of the horse's clip clopping, Heads munching away and the sound of sea gulls high in the blue sky, it is strangely quiet, until at last Simmonds reigns the horse's up.

"Can't get no closer than this," says Jenson. "Best get out an' follow me."

We pile out and leaving Simmonds with the carriage we follow Jenson, with Head carrying the tarpaulin, over a stile into a meadow full of buttercups and nothing much else. Sloping gently upwards it is a comfortable walk, the ground is hard and there's no animal droppings to avoid. Half way up we come upon a stream where there are two chest height sticks sticking up in a muddy patch of ground.

Coming to a stop, Jenson points down, "Constable said for yer ter look at this."

"Footprints," says Smithers.

"Indeed," says I crouching down to take a look. One large set and one smaller set.

"A man and a woman," says Head.

"They be John an' Roses prints," says Jenson. "So, thee constable says."

I look around to see if there are any other prints. Nothing other than a heal print, where it appears someone may have jumped over the stream intent on clearing the muddy edges, but didn't quite make it. However, it isn't enough of a print to get too excited about.

"That's definitely someone else's heal print," says Head.

"Someone who perhaps was following the couple. We'll need plaster casts of these, Sergeant. Right, please continue, Mr Jenson."

At the top of the hill the ground levels out, and a couple of hundred yards or so ahead the edge of a small wood comes into view.

On reaching the wood, Jenson ventures inside and we follow, there's no path and we weave around a mix of trees until at last we come to a dappled clearing, where Constable Burroughs is standing on guard beside a face down body with a big arrow sticking out from its back.

"Evening, sir," says he. "Sorry to drag you out at this time of the day."

"You did right, Constable," says I bobbing down to peruse the body and waving away blue bottles buzzing around the victim's head. His face has turned grey and there's a strong smell of decay but no sign of maggots as yet. This tells me, through experience, that death occurred, roughly, over thirty hours ago and most certainly on the Monday night into Tuesday morning when they ran. From the outset someone followed them on that fateful night intent on killing them in this wood, where it was hoped they wouldn't be found for a long time. But where is Rose?

"Well he didn't get far," puts in Head as he dumps the tarpaulin on the ground.

Standing up I say to Burroughs, "How on earth did you find him?"

"I did as you suggested, sir and did a wide circle of the castle. But ventured a lot further afield until by chance I came upon this." Taking out a small piece of torn blue material from his trouser pocket he hands it over. "Found it on the stile where you would have come over. It obviously got snagged on the rail and I thought it might belong to one of them. I then headed up the hill and found the footprints by the stream. I headed into the wood and stumbled upon the body. Then I hurried over to Sam's place to ask him for his help."

"How far away is your place, Mr Jenson?" asks I.

"Just a couple of 'undred yards thee other side of the wood."

"Forensics, Constable. Where would we find a forensics team?"

"You'd have to get someone from Truro, sir. I can take photographs and Dr Brent can tell you a lot about a crime scene, but other than that…" he shrugs.

"Your first murder, Constable?" says Head.

Burroughs glumly nods.

"Right. Mr Jenson," says I, "as your home is close by, any chance of a hot drink?"

"Why not," sneers he. "Would yer care for a nice hot pasty as well?"

"Sounds lovely," smiles Head.

"It'll cost yer."

"That won't be a problem," says I. "Mr Smithers, will you go with him? I wish to speak with the constable alone."

"Of course, Inspector."

I wait until they've gone before speaking to Burroughs. "Who do you know is an expert shot with a bow and arrow, Constable?"

"Sam' is undoubtedly the best around here. But he isn't the only one. Except for Matilda the Bullington children are all good with a bow and arrow. Sam' taught them as youngsters. Percy is particularly good and won a contest held in the village a few years back. The earl can fire a half decent arrow as can a few of the locals…"

"Which gives us several suspects," sighs I. "That arrow is dead centre of the victim's back. I'm no expert, but judging by how far it's imbedded I'd say that either the shooter lacked the strength to pull the bow far enough back to achieve maximum power, or he or she, fired from way back. If the latter is true, we are looking for a killer who is an expert shot to be able to shoot through these trees, in the dead of night, and hit their victim. Leaving, Jenson at the top of the list, with a very questionable Percy behind him. As far as we know."

"And if the former is true," puts in Head. "The field opens up considerably."

"And if our killer is that good why isn't Rose's body laying here as well. Have you ventured away from here to search further, Constable?"

"I did, sir." He points behind him. "Fifty yards or so further in, the ground is softer and I found more footprints to match the small ones by the stream, but no others. I didn't follow them too far as I didn't want to be too far away from the body."

"Assuming it was Monday night into Tuesday morning when they came this way, I'm wondering why last night's torrential downpour didn't wash away those footprints, Constable."

"That's because the storm ran more along the coast. We're a good mile in land here, sir. The storm would have just missed the wood."

"Hopefully, Rose got away." Rubbing at my chin I ponder over why Rose got away with obviously such a ruthless killer on her trail. Unless? "I think, Sergeant we had best track Roses footprints until we can track them no further."

"What about our pasties?"

"Perhaps Jenson can tuck them under his armpits to keep warm until our return," frowns I. Good God the man is turning into a gannet. Food, food, food, that's all he seems to think about. He'll be getting as fat as butter the way he's carrying on. "Perhaps, Constable you will remain here and when Jenson returns you can blow your whistle to let us know." In truth I am famished not having had any dinner. Taking out my watch I see it is now seven forty. We have just over an hour of full sunlight left.

"Is it me, sir or is it turning decidedly colder?" says Head as we go deeper into the wood.

A shiver runs through me, "It has definitely turned chilly, Sergeant."

"And got darker," says he turning up the collar on his jacket. "In fact, it's a bit creepy. You don't think this wood is haunted, do you?"

"No," says I with finality. We find the footprints Burroughs told us about and track them easily for several minutes until they come to a stop and disappear.

"Fuck this, Gerald," says Head. "Look at that! She just vanished into thin air. I reckon she got taken by an evil spirit that lives in this very wood."

Bobbing down I see the footsteps carry on but are very faint. "She took her shoes off, Richard."

"Of course, she did. Harder to follow and quieter. Less likely to snap twigs and stuff."

"So, no ghosts here," says I getting to my feet. "Let's continue."

Five minutes later we come out of the wood to face a wall of fog that appears to be edging towards us.

"I didn't think they'd get smog out here," says Head.

"I think it's called a sea mist, Richard. Its blotted out most of the sun to take away its heat and light. Hopefully, it will blow over in a little while."

"And if it doesn't?"

Just then a whistle sounds long and hard.

"Lovely," smiles Head rubbing his hands together. "Pasties are served."

"Let's just see if we can find anything of worth by heading back on the outskirts of the wood, Richard. I am thinking our killer had to also kill Rose and may have gone around the wood instead of through it, as no doubt it would have been just as quick, possibly even quicker. He may well have been waiting for her once she came out. If our killer is that good a shot, he may well have hidden behind a tree and waited until Rose was a fair way across this meadow before letting fly and killing her."

"You're saying her body could be out there?"

"I am. The trouble is it would be pointless to conduct a search in this thick mist. You go left and I'll go right. Unless you prefer going right."

"I don't care, I just want to get to the pasties before they're all gone."

"Have you got your whistle on you?"

"No. Have you?"

"No. Let us hope the constable blasts away now and then so we can find him, because if this mist gets any worse, we'll find ourselves disorientated with not knowing where the devil we are. If the worse comes to the worst we'll have to abandon the search until tomorrow."

Turning right I skirt around the wood while looking for foot prints or signs that someone had come out through the wood. The air has turned even colder, the mist even thicker and the constables whistle suddenly sounding off makes me jump out of my skin. Now I start to believe someone may be following me; as the cracking sound from a twig being stood on seemed to come from behind me. Pausing, I listen intently. Nothing. It is eerily quiet. Then it hits me, Jenson is almost certainly our killer? Isn't it just too much of a coincidence that the couple ran this way so close to Jenson's home? Did he lure them this way intent on killing them, to cover up the fact that it was he on the castle roof that day when the attempt was made on Percy's life? Jenson comes and goes in the castle with impunity and could have easily gotten up on the roof unchallenged. Did Rose know Jenson was going to try and kill Percy and was she in on the plan? After all, she herself would want revenge for what Percy had done to her. Jenson certainly did for what Percy did to his daughter. Jenson, Rose and Chambers must have believed no suspicion was falling on them, but when they were told of our intended arrival, they all panicked. Did Jenson then convince the couple their best bet was to run, while ensuring they ran straight into his ambush? The sound of another cracking twig behind me sees me slipping into the wood and taking out my truncheon.

"Is that you there, Gerald?" sounds Heads voice.

I breathe a sigh of relief. "What the hell are you doing here? You're supposed to be going around the other way."

"Sorry. It was so bloody creepy I couldn't bear it. I couldn't see more than three feet in front of me, the mists that thick on the left side, so I thought I best come this way."

One thing Head definitely isn't is a coward, but he doesn't do ghosts, ghouls and things that go bump in the night.

The whistle sounds again, and I suggest we head into the wood, as visibility is a little better with the trees keeping back the worst of the mist. By now I am disorientated with no idea which way to go. Head is following in my footsteps and if he gets any closer, we may well appear to be too friendly. The bang from a shotgun makes us both, jump.

"Bloody hell!" yells Head.

"Constable!" shouts I.

"This way, sir," he shouts back.

"That way I think," points Head.

Quickening our pace, we stumble and trip towards where we think the shot rang out. The whistle keeps sounding and at last leads us back into the clearing where we find Burroughs, Smithers and Jenson all looking a bit sheepish. Jenson has hold of his shotgun but at least it is broken. "Who fired that shot?" demands I.

"No one did," says Jenson. "I stood thee gun up against a tree an' it fell over an' went off."

"Then you shouldn't have reloaded it before standing it up against a tree," snaps I.

"I know that now, don't I," growls he.

"No harm done," says Smithers patting his chest. "But my, did it give me a fright."

"Forget all that," says Head. "Where are the pasties?"

Half an hour later, having each tucked into a large pasty and shared a pot of tea poured into well chipped enamel mugs, I deem it is time to pack up and leave it for the night. The mist hasn't abated, it is very cold, damp and quite dark. We manage to lift the body onto the tarpaulin and wrap it up with the arrow still sticking out. Jenson tells us to leave the tea stuff where it is as he'll pick it up later. Between us we convey the body back and onto the coach. Do I now arrest Jenson on suspicion of murder, take him back to the castle and lock him in one of the dungeons? The trouble is I have no evidence against him, as yet. Tomorrow I will question him and search his property for that evidence. Perhaps I will find a bow with arrows that matches the one in Chambers' back? I hand over half a crown to Jenson for supplying the 'supper', thank him for his help and we set off for the castle. On arrival, Smithers suggests we put the body in the castle's ice cellar for the night. Burroughs will then convey it to Truro in the morning where they have suitable accommodation for bodies. Chambers came from Truro and his family will be able to view and identify his body there. Smithers shows me where the castle's bows and arrows are stored. I find then covered in dust and cobwebs, obviously they haven't been used in years, but the arrows are identical to the one in Chambers back. Having been summoned, Dr Brent arrives to view the body and write out a death certificate. It is now nine forty-five. Time to go back to the Smugglers and make it up to Betty.

The Hunt for Rose

Head and I are picked up by Simmonds at five thirty the following morning. Mist still hangs around, but is nowhere are thick as it was and is very likely to disappear as the sun heats up. The hotel packed us up a homemade pasty each for our breakfast, Head is already tucking into his and is likely to have scoffed it before we've covered a hundred yards.

"How did you get on with, Betty last night?" asks he licking his lips as the last morsel is gulped down.

"I didn't," groans I as my back jerks with pain. "She let me in, but only after a lot of persuasion and a promise that I would sleep on a chair instead of in the bed."

"Really? That must have been uncomfortable."

"It was torture. I've barely slept, Richard. I am tired, I ache all over and am thoroughly pissed off. Did you ask Chloe what she knows about Betty and that waiter?"

"I broached the subject only to get an ear full. She said you were wrong to accuse Betty of any impropriety with that Andrew fellow, and you should be ashamed of yourself."

"Was that it?"

"It was."

"So, they could be in conclusion with each other."

"Don't you mean collusion?"

"Probably. Do you think Chloe is covering up for Betty? You know, siding with her, turning a blind eye or something?"

"No, I don't. I think, Gerald that you over stepped the mark and have misread the signs. Betty was just being Betty and it's as simple as that."

"We shall see," grates I as I take my pasty from its cloth wrapping and start eating it.

"What's the plan for the day?" asks Head eyeing my pasty with ravenous intent.

"As I spent most of the night awake, I had plenty of time to think," says I quietly so Simmonds doesn't hear. "I think once we've conducted a search for Rose Bush, and assuming we find nothing, we'll search Jenson's place and grill him. After that, assuming we had also gotten nowhere with him, we'll go back to the castle and question Smithers."

"What makes you think he knows anything about anything?"

I give him my clever look. "The key to this entire sorry tale, Richard as always is motive. We know no one likes Percy much, but how many would be motivated enough to try and kill him? And to have already killed to cover themselves. I think if anyone knows the answer to that question, Smithers would. He was present at attempt number three. He didn't report the missing couple for hours while insisting he did so in the hope they might return, when in fact he may well have simply allowed them plenty of time to escape."

"Because?"

"I'm not sure as yet. Most of all he is the only person who the entire family is likely to have confided in, including Percy. They all trust him. They have respect for him and value his council. Smithers has been very helpful to us thus far, but I know he could be an awful lot more helpful if questioned the right way."

"I can't say I'd be that keen to give the man a few tongue loosening punches, Gerald."

"Nor I, Richard. We will have to convince Smithers that it is paramount to us solving the case by his opening up to us. Even by betraying confidences. Agreed?"

"Agreed. What happens when Clump arrives?"

"The usual. We update him and let him take over." I tuck into my pasty while arching my back to relieve the knots in the muscles.

On reaching the castle we find Smithers and Claude waiting outside along with a pair of black labaradors. Claude is carrying a shotgun and a pair of binoculars. For once he appears quite normal, his gun is open and not loaded. After greetings, Smithers, Claude and the dogs climb into the carriage.

"I thought you could do with some assistance," says Smithers as he settles back. "I have brought Roses maids cap that she wore on the day she went missing. It hasn't been in the laundry since then. I thought the dogs might pick up on her scent and lead us to where she might be."

"Thank you, Mr Smithers for your foresight. An excellent idea."

"And I'm here to control my boys," beams Claude. "Have no fear detective chappies, if my boys can't find the girl, no dog can. Or human for that matter. Now all that aside, how are you getting on with the investigations concerning my golf club and tiepin?"

"We are still searching, Major."

"Good show, Inspector Who." Leaning forward he whispers, "Have you thought that the turd might be behind the murder of my valet?"

The turd being Percy, ponders I, and the valet being Chambers. "No, Major, I had not considered that suggestion. But I will give it some thought." It strikes me then that Percy can leave his cell at any time he wishes, even to go outside and wander about. However, I cannot imagine why he would kill Chambers unless he was sure Chambers was behind the attempt on his life; or if he even had the guts to leave his cell let alone carry out such a heinous act. Most importantly, only Smithers could have told Percy about the couple running off for Percy to know when to go out and track them. Unless Percy communicates with someone else? Someone who was also prepared to kill for him. No, the idea is just too fanciful.

On reaching the stile we alight and climb over into the field. Simmonds is to return to the castle, leaving us to make our own way back. We head up hill with the tail wagging dogs leading the way having had a sniff at Rose's cap. The mist has cleared and it promises to be another warm day. On reaching the stream the dogs go right through and straight over the footprints while we go around, jump the stream and clear the mud. Looking behind me, I see Smithers do the same, but unfortunately Claude goes straight over behind the dogs. Stepping back to the stream, I swear inwardly, to see he has trampled right over the prints and messed them up, except for the heal print. I call back Head.

"Look at that, Sergeant," whispers I.

"At what, sir?" whispers back he.

"Claude's heal prints exactly match that one we spotted last night," points I.

"Bloody hell! We'll need plaster casts of those. And photographs."

"I told the constable to get those done once he returns from Truro. Until then let us hope the prints remain intact." Claude and Smithers have stopped to wait for us. Curiosity shows in Smithers eyes but Claude appears oblivious to anything.

"The major could be our killer, sir."

"He could indeed, Sergeant. For now, let us keep this to ourselves."

"Problems, gentlemen?" says Smithers as we step up to him.

"The major has just messed up the prints," sighs I.

"Oh… dear," grates he giving Claude an admonishing glare.

"What's up old chap?" smiles Claude.

"Nothing of importance," lies I.

Trudging on we enter the wood, go past where the body was found and pick up on the other side of the wood where we left it last night. The dogs keep working over the meadow, sniffing and weaving around while their tails keep wagging. Two miles on we come to a wide, fast flowing brook where the dogs come to a halt, lap up some water and then sit and wait.

"Get over," orders Claude throwing out his arm.

The dogs jump in, swim over and scramble up the bank. They sniff around for a while before sitting down and facing us.

"They've lost the scent," says Claude waving them back.

"Perhaps Rose went in but not out," says Head.

"If so then we had best follow the brook up stream and down. Sergeant, if you go with Mr Smithers I'll go with the major. We'll give it one hour and then meet back here. If you find anything blow your whistle. You did bring your whistle?"

"I did. Did you?"

"Of course, I did. Can you split the dogs Major so one goes with my Sergeant?"

"I can, Inspector Who. Which dog do you want?"

"The one easiest to control, please."

"Very good. Roger," he addresses one of the dogs. "Go with Sergeant What and do everything he tells you."

To my amazement the dog goes right up to Head and wags its tail. I just hope he doesn't clamp himself on Heads leg. Head and Smithers head off, while Claude, I and the other dog head off in the opposite direction.

"It's a lovely day, Inspector Who," says Claude as we walk along while scanning the brook and the surrounding area.

"It is indeed, Major. While we are alone, Major. Have you any thoughts on John Chambers murder?"

He gives me the confused look. "Who's he?"

"He was one of your household staff."

"Really? I know the one you mean. The valet chap, but not the one who fiddled with my diddle." He scratches at his head beneath his hat. "Or was he?"

Deciding to drop the subject for now I concentrate on the job in hand. The dog keeps working along the bank and intermittently Claude sends him over to the other side. A half hour passes and we have not found a single clue as to where, or even if, Rose came out of the water. Not a sign of someone clawing their way out of the water, or going in. Nothing. The brook narrowed on more than one occasion to a point where a body would have got stuck. Wherever Rose is I sense she isn't anywhere around this way. Then I hear Heads whistle sounding off. It is faint but clear enough and earnest enough to tell me to come back immediately.

Rose is wearing a pale blue dress, a white bonnet and brown ankle boots. She is floating face down in the water, one hand gripping hold of a bunch of reeds while the other is stretched out straight and bobbing eerily about in the current. There is an arrow in her back. My stomach kicks inwardly, I feel wretched and deeply affected by the scene. Smithers is sat away from the scene on the buttercups, head bowed with his hands covering his face, shaking and sobbing.

"Her bag and a shawl are on the other side, sir," says Head. Swallowing hard he looks away and up into the clear sky.

How strange it is that we are rarely affected by the sight of a body having seen so many, but occasionally even the hardest of hearts can melt. Rose and Chambers, both so young with so much living to do, executed by someone who can only be called a monster.

"A damnable act," growls Claude. "Whoever carried out such an act deserves to hang."

I meet his furrowed eyes that blaze in fury. Even Claude is affected. Or is he? Taking off my hat and jacket I sit down on the grassy bank. I need time to gather myself together. Head does the same and comes to sit beside me. Claude produces a hip flask from his tweed jacket and passes it to me before he also sits down beside Head. Both dogs lay down amongst the buttercups. They are so quiet I can only believe they know exactly what is going on.

With a lopsided smile, Claude says, "Drink up, Inspector and pass it around."

I take a long swallow from the flask and pass it to Head. He drinks and passes it to Claude who doesn't drink. Instead he goes over to Smithers, sits down beside him and places an arm over his shoulders. "Have a fortifier old chap."

Taking his hands from his face, Smithers takes the flask and drinks. "Thank you, Major," says he. "Such a lovely day. Such a lovely area. But from now on I will always think of this place as tainted and this day as being the worst I have ever experienced."

Claude starts taking off his walking boots. "These boots are too tight," grunts he. "Are you sure they're mine?"

"Absolutely sure, Major," returns Smithers. "I took them from your wardrobe this morning. Don't you remember?"

"Can't say I do." Throwing off his boots to reveal odd thick socks with holes in them, Claude sets to rubbing his feet. "But I suspect you must have given me the wrong boots."

"Perhaps," sighs Smithers. "Sorry, Major but you do have several pairs of the same boots."

"Why is that, whatever your name is?"

"It is because you refuse to give or throw anything away Major."

"Oh… I see. That must be the answer then. Perhaps I bought these boots years ago before my feet had fully grown." He gazes at me. "You need to investigate these boots, Inspector Who. Perhaps you can find out who I bought them from so I can return them and get my money back. Damn business selling a man boots that are too small for him."

Smithers holds out his arms in a gesture of 'I give up' and I can't blame him. Claude is hard work, but I'm wondering, if he is our killer why would he come on this trip wearing the same boots he wore when tracking Rose and Chambers? A clever killer would reason that he may well have left footprints all over the place, and would ensure that he got rid of the boots he wore and not use them again to possibly incriminate himself. Did our killer plant the boots he wore in Claude's wardrobe to incriminate Claude? Afterall, once we had plaster casts of the killer's prints, we would conduct a search to see if we could find a match. But again, this is all too fanciful. All we have is one heal print which wouldn't be enough to convict someone even if we could find a match. What we need is to find more complete prints.

"Right, gentlemen," says I. "Sergeant, you and I will wade over the brook and have a look around to see if Rose went into the water from that side. We know she went in further back but did she get out again and we missed it. Then, we'll fetch back Roses bag and shawl and then we'll haul her out. Mr Smithers can you go with the major and start looking for footprints." I point behind me. "The killer must have crossed the meadow by walking parallel to Rose, but far enough away for her not to see him, or her, clearly. Knowing she was being followed and in fear of her life; she took to the water in the vain hope she could confuse her pursuer by wading upstream and keeping her head low while praying he went downstream. If you both zigzag a couple of hundred yards or so across the meadow, hopefully you will find something."

Claude puts his boots back on while Head and I strip down to our drawers. As Claude and Smithers head off with the dogs, Head and I go into the cold water which comes up to the top of our thighs. Surprisingly the bottom is quite firm and we comfortably wade over.

"Claw marks," says Head, pointing to the muddy bank which rises up a good three feet above the water. "She tried to drag herself out of the water."

"She must have been exhausted, Richard. Rose clawed at the top of the bank and then slid back as obviously she hadn't the strength to get out. She then tried to haul herself out by way of the reeds. It was then that our killer struck."

Giving Head a leg up he easily gets onto the bank, but the fart he let off in my face as he went does nothing for me. Grabbing hands and wrists I am also easily hauled out. Sitting down I go through the bag and empty the contents on the grass.

"Didn't own much the poor cow," says Head sitting down.

"No," sighs I. There are enough clothes for one complete change. A few treasured little nick knacks and next out a small photograph of the Bush family, that of course includes Seb' Bush.

"I don't want to be the one who has to tell Seb' his daughters been murdered," says Head.

"It would be best if Constable Burroughs tells him." Next there is a pencil followed by a torn piece of paper that probably came from her diary?

"What's written on that bit of paper, Gerald?"

The inside of the bag is bone dry as is the note, somehow Rose must have held the bag aloft to stop it getting wet and tossed it onto the bank before trying to haul herself up. The writing is neat and tidy up to the last line when it is scribbled, hastily written but decipherable. I read the note aloud: "He told us we got to go before them coppers from London come. He said he'd help us get away but I don't trust him. I think he's evil. If someone finds this note please tell the police that the… That's it, Richard."

"She obviously wrote the tidy part on the Monday sometime after the staff were informed of our intended arrival. The last bit was obviously scribbled down while trying to escape from her pursuer."

"The killer must have searched the bag after killing Rose and found her diary, but missed this torn off piece which she tore out hoping it would later be found, but in her panic, she left the vital part, his name, still in her diary. Whoever he is, Rose and Chambers must have trusted him at first but then he did or said something to change at least Roses mind about him. I think he's evil."

"Meaning she thought at one time he was the opposite."

"Hence the reason they went along with whatever he told them, or asked them to do."

"That still doesn't tell us whether he tried to kill Percy, or was stringing Chambers and Rose along because he knew they were behind the attempt on Percy's life."

"Agreed. But at least we know we are looking for a man."

"Which narrows it down a bit," scoffs Head as he gets to his feet. "I'm getting cold."

"Let's check for footprints and then we'll get Rose out."

Replacing the items back into the bag along with the shawl, which is also dry, we search the bank for footprints, but find none and slip back into the water. Wading across I place the bag on the bank and go back to assist Head. Head pulls up the reeds Rose has hold of and we move her on top of the water to the bank, lift her up and push her onto the grass. Within seconds we are out ourselves. We turn our backs on each other, whip off our drawers and give them a thorough squeezing out, then use them to dry ourselves as best we can and then squeeze them out again. Then we get dressed. Time to look Rose over.

"Can't we remove that bloody arrow, Gerald? It's horrible seeing that stuck out of her back like that. Plus, we can't turn her over."

"Cut it off with your knife just above the end of the arrow head."

Head's flick knife is out in a second and he quickly cuts the arrow away and lays it down. We turn Rose over onto her back. Her face is all shrivelled up from being in the water too long, but even so you can tell she was a kindly sort.

"Bet she was a nice kid," croaks Head. "Kind and thoughtful. Until that Percy attacked her! Whichever way you look at this, Gerald, it's all down to that piece of shit. I really could kill the cu'-clot myself before going on to kill Rose's killer, whoever they are."

"Our biggest headache, Richard. So many suspects, so many avenues to explore as to who, what, where and why. Percy can go to hell for now. We have two murders on our hands and a killer so evil he will stop at nothing to achieve his ends."

"The trouble is what are those ends? Are the murders related to the attempt on Percy's life? Or nothing to do with it at all?

"Whatever, Richard. All I know is that I am thinking two young people have been murdered just to keep a secret. I don't know whether or not it is related to the attempt on Percy's life, but I sense that it is and that the killer is not going to stop until Percy is dead, assuming of course, that Percy isn't our killer. We have to narrow down the suspects and then get serious with each one in turn."

"Agreed. Once Clump gets here, I think he'll be able to help us narrow down a few suspects, he's good at that."

"The trouble is Richard he won't get away with booting aristocrats in the balls like he does the common riff raff. Let us get on."

After going through Roses dress pockets, we find only a small handkerchief with a single rose embroidery on it. Just down inside her cleavage Head pulls out a link broken, thin silver chain with a St Christopher on it. It is very poignant as we take turns holding it while gazing forlornly at it.

"Well the patron saint of travel didn't do our poor Rose much good," sighs Head.

"I think Rose took Rosie's bag because it has her name stitched inside. Perhaps Rose intended to pass herself off as Rosy to make it harder to trace her."

"Sounds feasible," sighs Head.

Smithers and Claude return with good news. They have found plenty of footprints for us to look at. At last we are getting somewhere.

Claude sits down and takes his boots and socks off and lets one of his dogs lick his toes. Unable to look at Rose, Smithers takes me aside away from Claude as he wishes to speak to me in confidence.

"The footprints we found exactly match's the majors, Inspector. I am sorry to say I believe the major is our killer."

"We have already considered that possibility," returns I. looking over at Claude I see he is lost in his own world having laid right back and closed his eyes. I grab one of his boots.

Smithers leads me over the meadow to where he found the killers prints.

Bobbing down I compare the two sets of prints. The similarities are striking. Depth of indents showing wear and tear on the soles. A grove in one heal, caused perhaps by the wearer having stood on a sharp object. However, the length of strides doesn't quite match, Claude's strides are just that little bit longer and he digs his heals in first, just the way a marching soldier would. Claude isn't our killer and I believe he was right to complain that the boots he's wearing aren't his. But for now, my inner ear is telling me to go along with Claude being our killer.

"The evidence is stark," says I standing up to look Smithers directly in the eyes.

"This all too much," says he looking away.

I place a comforting hand on his shoulder. "We must face up to it, Mr Smithers. The major is mentally unstable and we must have him committed as soon as is possible. Does he have cartridges on him for that shotgun?"

He shakes his head, "I only agreed to his bringing his shotgun on the condition he did not bring cartridges."

"Good. Say nothing and act normal. We need to take Rose's body back to the castle. It could take hours to get a team of forensics to come out here, and would almost certainly be a waste of time anyway. We have enough evidence already to arrest the major, but we will hold back on that until safely back at the castle. Will you go and find Jenson, if you can, as his place is the closest. Inform him of the situation and ask if he has a means of transporting Rose's body back to the castle…"

"He has an old carthorse which pulls the game waggon when a shoot is on."

"Good. Say nothing to anyone that we believe the major is our killer. It must be kept between us for now, Mr Smithers. And I mean strictly between us."

"Of course, Inspector."

"Right, Mr Smithers, off you go please."

An hour later Smithers returns with Jenson who is leading a cart horse pulling a small cart. We load Rose onto the cart, cover her face with her shawl and set off at a slow walk. Jenson takes us back the way he came and onto a track, that although a longer way around, will apparently take us back to the castle without any obstacles in our way. Any earlier thoughts that Jenson may have had something to do with the killings vanished on seeing Jenson's initial reactions on coming face to face with Rose's body. The man crumpled up and fell on her. Wretched beyond belief he wailed, sobbed and shook so violently I thought he was going to have a heart attack. Head and I had to physically drag him away from the body. Claude gave him the last of his brandy and it took over a half an hour to calm him down enough to get on.

Walking along side Jenson as he leads the horse, he hisses, "If yer don't catch thee killer, I swear I will, even if it takes me the rest of my life."

"We will catch him, Mr Jenson."

"Just pray yer get ter 'im before I do. Cause, I'll tell thee now, I'll skin the bastard alive!"

Silence reigns as we walk on. Head is walking with Smithers a good fifty yards in front of us while Claude, now limping, trails behind the cart with his dogs at heal. I go over several possibilities in my mind, but only one stands out. If Claude was to be convicted for the murders he would be stripped of his title, leaving Percy to be crowned the 13th Earl of Bullington. What if Percy is our killer? Someone would have had to inform him that Rose and Chambers were going to run. That someone was either Smithers, or most certainly, someone else in league with Percy. That someone else could be a man or a woman, but for now I'll say it is a man. Risky though it was, I am thinking the third attempt on Percy's life, was possibly, also set up by Percy and his accomplice, meaning no one is out to kill Percy. Did, Rose and Chambers trust this mystery accomplice enough, at the outset, to cover up for him having not connected him with Percy. Did Percy sneak out from his cell on Monday night to track and kill Rose and Chambers? Or did Percy's accomplice do the dirty work? The boots the killer wore were then planted in Claude's wardrobe, in the expectation that we would conduct a search for a pair of boots that matched the plaster casts, once we'd eventually taken some plaster casts. The only thing I'm certain of is that Rose knew who was on that roof and she told Chambers, thus putting both their lives in danger. Assuming the killer now has Rose's diary, I ask myself what if Rose told others who went up onto the roof, along with noting it in her diary. If she named names it would leave the killer with no other option but to kill again. Now it is imperative we question everyone in the castle

Return to Bullington

Barely a hundred yards from the castle stables we meet Matilda coming the opposite way on her horse. She reins up and gazes over into the rear of the cart.

"Dear, God," says she as her gloved hand goes to cover her mouth.

"Perhaps, Miss," says I looking up and meeting eyes filling with tears. "You might ride back to the castle and inform the countess of our arrival."

"Yes. Of course." Turning her horse, she trots off.

"There's definitely a heart inside that girl," says Head.

"Indeed, Sergeant."

On reaching the stables several of the hands have already formed a line. As we pass by caps and felt hats are removed and heads bowed in a show of respect. Chambers arrival the previous night did not attract anywhere near the attention, not that he didn't receive respect, it just feels that Rose was loved by everyone, including Matilda.

It appears that the entire household is standing outside the castle on our arrival. Even the outside staff are there; the gardeners and the groundsmen. Constance stands rigidly out in front with Robert and Matilda either side of her. Silence reigns except for the singing from a single robin. I realise that I haven't seen or even spoken to most of the people stood before me. Interviewing all of them will be daunting, but has to be done. I step up to Constance.

"You have brought our Rose back to us, Inspector," says she her voice trembling with emotion. "Thank you for being here."

"We do what we must, ma'am. We will require somewhere cool and private to lay Rose, so her family may come and visit her before I ask Constable Burroughs to take her to Truro."

"The family chapel would be the best place to lay her down, Inspector. Would it be alright for two of my eldest and most trusted ladies' maids to dress Rose appropriately so she may look her best? They are fully experienced in such sad matters."

"Thank you, ma'am. I see no reason why not."

"Can I take these bloody boots off, now?" says Claude having come up behind me.

Constance gazes down at his feet, "Compared to your usual walking boots, Claude they appear a half size too small for you. Go to the drawing room and take them off. Then kindly wait there until I come to you."

"I will, providing you don't bring that cook with you."

"I promise not to. Off you go. Has he been any trouble, Inspector?"

I shake my head. "Quite the opposite, ma'am. Without him and his dogs we may well not have found Rose so quickly."

"Allow me to oversee the moving of Rose into the chapel, Inspector. You and your fellows must be in dire need of fortifying. Mrs Kemp will see to your every need."

"Thank you, ma'am. Afterwards I would like to address your entire staff before we begin interviewing them. Would that be possible?"

"Of course. Once I have set everything in motion, I will gather everyone who is available into the great hall. Probably in about half an hour, if that suits?"

"Thank you," says I. "Please ensure Roses possessions are kept in a safe place…"

Surprisingly I feel Matilda's hand grip my arm, "If there's anything I can do, Inspector, please do not hesitate to ask."

I meet her eyes to see again that odd undefinable look in them that she gave me when interviewing her over at the stables. "Thank you, Miss."

"That goes for me also, Inspector," says Robert.

"Thank you, sir," says I. Time for a drink and something to eat.

Smithers and Jenson accompany us to the kitchen where we find Gloria sitting all alone at the table with her head in her hands. On hearing us enter she gets to her feet, brushes down her apron and greets us with a brief smile. She has been crying, her eyes are circled red while her face looks tired and drawn.

"I couldn't go out there," she says holding out her arms in despair. "It's all too much. Too terrible to comprehend. But life must go on. You must be hungry and thirsty."

"It seems that everyone loved Rose," says I.

"Everyone except thee bastard who killed 'er," growls Jenson.

"Rose was an absolute joy," says Gloria. "Always singing little ditties. Always smiling and never a cruel word for anyone. Now, what can I get you?"

"Have you got any horses?" grins Head to lighten the tone.

"Not cooked," smiles Gloria. "How about a big wedge of bacon and egg flan each and a pint of ale."

"Sounds wonderful, Mrs Kemp," says I.

"No ale for me, thank you Mrs kemp," says Smithers. "But a coffee would be welcome."

"Well sit you down while I get busy."

Removing hats, we all sit and I take the opportunity to thank Smithers and Jenson for their invaluable assistance.

"What now, Inspector?" asks Smithers.

"Mr Jenson has volunteered to go and see Seb' Bush and inform him of the terrible news. Will you do that after we've eaten, Mr Jenson?"

"I will. I'll uncouple thee 'orse and ride him over ter Seb's place. Seb' an' 'is missus will want ter come and see Rose right away. Is that alright?"

"Of course, it is. We owe you, Mr Jenson and once again I can't thank you enough. I also wish to apologise again for the injuries to your skull."

"They be alright. Just yer make sure when yer catch thee killer you crack 'im on thee bonce so bloody 'ard 'is brains shoot down to his guts."

"After I have addressed the staff, Mr Smithers, I would like to interview you first of all."

He appears somewhat agitated by this request, "Could you see me later, Inspector? I have an awful lot of pressing duties to catch up on, what with Miss Matilda's…"

"It is imperative I interview you first, Mr Smithers," says I with a touch of venom in my tone. Matilda's 'day' comes second to the murders and I am more than a little chagrined by Smithers, 'the family comes first' attitude. "Murder is always an inconvenience to someone, sir. But it must transcend everything else however important we might think it to be."

"Sorry, Inspector. I did not wish to cause offence. Sorry, I'm just tired and upset."

"We all are, Mr Smithers. Perhaps we shall feel much more awake and settled once we've had our lunch."

Smithers pecked at his food but drank all of his coffee, while the rest of us demolished two large wedges of flan and downed a couple of pints each. A footman I hadn't seen before comes in to announce that the staff are all in the hall waiting. Time to get on.

"May I ask why you did not lock the major up the moment we arrived?" asks Smithers as we head towards the great hall.

"We need more evidence of his guilt first. While I'm interviewing you, Sergeant Head will conduct a search of the major's room to see if he can find anything else that might incriminate the major further. Just ensure you say nothing about any of this to anyone. Is that clear to you?"

"It is, Inspector. Do you mind if I do not attend the meeting in the great hall? I have much to do."

"As you wish. Mr Jenson, you need not attend either. Please give Seb' our condolences and inform him that he may speak to us whenever he wishes."

"Will do, Inspector," sighs he.

The great hall is so huge the fifty or so people gathered beneath its heavily beamed, pitched ceiling, barely fill a quarter of it. Crystal Chandeliers hang down, the walls are covered with oil paintings and the floor is solid oak. There is a stage up one end complete with red velvet curtains. The Bullingtons stand in front of the staff, a bare foot Claude is staring up at the ceiling, while between them, Constance and Matilda hold Prune up. Robert steps forward to meet me.

"Rose is at rest in the chapel, Inspector. I left Jackson and mamma's ladies maids to watch over her. Her possessions and the arrow have been locked in my safe."

"Thank you, Mr Robert. I shall begin."

Robert steps back to his family. Slowly I run my eyes along the lines, except for Claude who's still staring up at the ceiling, I have their undivided attention. Head stands beside me.

"We have a murderer amongst us. A man who is almost certainly a man. This man will be known to each and every one of you in some capacity or another. He may work alongside you. You may serve him. He may well be your superior or your inferior. You may think him a wonderful person or even a lovable rogue. The problem is, it is unlikely that you will have any idea that he is indeed a monster of the highest order. To uncover and expose this monster we need evidence. I urge each and every one of you to rack your brains, search your memories and see what you can come up with. Do you have reasons to question someone's integrity? Have you witnessed or heard something that at the time you thought was suspicious, unusual or just plain odd? We believe Rose kept a diary. We, also believe the killer now has that diary and that in that diary Rose may have written down the name of someone who would turn out to be her killer. If Rose confided in any of you, then those people are now in mortal danger if Rose then entered into her diary exactly who she confided in. If those whom she confided in then went on to confide with others, it is very probable they may well have confided with the killer himself. Our killer is ruthless and merciless. He will stop at nothing to get what he wants and have no allusions; he will kill again if he has to. From now on, until we unmask our killer you will all ensure you keep in pairs. Do not work alone. If you are not resident in the castle do not go home alone. Be vigilant and be aware of your own mortality. My, Sergeant and I will be interviewing each and every one of you in turn. It is imperative that you are honest and open with us. Do not try and shield anyone that you suspect of doing or saying anything you felt was odd at the time. Most of all I want a name. If Rose, or John Chambers gave anyone of you even a hint who may have been responsible for the attempted murders of Lord Percival Bullington, you must tell me or my Sergeant when interviewed. Do not go and tittle tattle to your friends and colleagues first. Anything you say to us will be in the strictest confidence. Any questions?"

Billy Roper raises his hand, "What's imperi... imper...?"

"Imperative means vitally important, Billy."

"What's that mean?"

Rosy Roper gives him a clip around the ears and hisses, "Shut up Billy. I'll tell yer later."

"Do you know if the killer lives and works in the castle?" asks Robert Bullington.

I shake my head. "Our killer may live in or out of the castle. He may work in or out of the castle. He may well be someone who doesn't enter the castle much at all, but has easy access whenever he wants."

Matilda asks, "Why are you so sure the killer is a man?"

"We found a scrap of paper in Rose's bag that informed the reader that she was frightened of the very man who would go on to kill her. I believe that scrap of paper was torn from her diary so she might add to what she had previously written, by naming this man, in the hope that it would later be found. She was killed before she achieved this."

"What if it was the killer who wrote on that scrap of paper?" says Matilda oh so smugly. "And what if the killer did it just to bamboozle you into thinking the killer was a man, when it may well be a very clever woman."

Gasps of surprise echo around the hall. Matilda has a very good point. In truth it was odd to find just that scrap of paper. Odd and all a bit too convenient. I am lost for words.

"We have considered that notion, Miss," cuts in Head. "Now that you have mentioned it, we have no option but to admit we were not about to inform anyone of our suspicions that the killer could be a female, in order to allow our killer to relax and possibly make mistakes thinking they had indeed bamboozled us, when in fact the opposite is the truth."

Matilda smirks. "Liar," she mouths.

Wouldn't I just love to put her over my knee and give her a damn good hiding, thinks I as I meet her dancing, taunting eyes. Who the hell does she think she is? She has belittled us in front of everyone present, which in turn loses us respect while striking even more fear into everyone, thus making our task even more difficult. I must take her down a few notches. "To conclude, I will say this: my Sergeant and I have solved multitudes of murder cases over the years, some so brutal the details of which would make your hair fall out. We are professionals who leave no bones unturned in our quest to bring the guilty to justice. We have almost a sixth sense when it comes to tracking criminals. While I appreciate Miss Matilda's comments, she is in dire danger, like all amateur sleuths, of coming up with all kinds of theories, conjecture and ridiculous fantasies. In truth, I urge you all not to start unfounded rumours and speculation because of misplaced amateur detective work, as before you know it the ghost of the 5th Earl will become our main suspect."

Giggles, titters and one outward guffaw fills the room. Matilda, though, just stares at me in the same odd way she has done before. Rarely do I fail to read someone's eyes, but in her case I am flummoxed. "That is all for now. Will all senior staff relate what I have told you to those who aren't present? Interviewing everyone will of course be disruptive to your usual routines, I apologise for that but there is no other way. So please bear with us. Thank you all for your understanding. Over to you, ma'am."

Constance steps out to stand beside me, leaving Matilda to prop up Prune on her own.

"Thank you, Inspector. When interviewed by the police men," she barks out, "you will conduct yourselves appropriately. No lies or fantasies. Answer honestly the questions put before you and I will have no reason to discipline anyone, or worse have to consider the possibility of staff members losing their position within this household. In a quiet and orderly fashion, please return to your duties."

"And don't forget to keep a look out for my tiepin," shouts Claude as the staff file out.

"Do shut up about your stupid tiepin, Claude," grates Constance. "Can you not comprehend that we have more important issues to deal with. We have a murderer amongst us."

Claude sticks his chin out, "I know that. I helped to find the body of that girl do not forget. But she's gone now and won't return. But my tie…"

"Enough! Go and put something on your feet, Claude and then take yourself to the dining room ready for lunch."

"Where are the boots you were wearing, Major?" asks I.

"In the drawing room. But I'm not putting them back on, Who, they're too bally tight."

"Could you kindly fetch them, Mr Robert and place them in the safe with Rose's things?"

"At once, Inspector. May I ask why?"

"They are the same boots the killer wore when he killed Chambers and Rose."

Constance's hand goes to her mouth. "But…"

"They're not the majors' boots are they, ma'am?"

"No, Inspector. They are a half size too small for him." She points down at Claude's feet. "See, they have swollen his feet and given him blisters. He wears shoes with thin socks that size, but takes a half size bigger for walking boots so he can wear thick socks to keep his smelly feet warm."

"Who else wears such boots. Bearing in mind that such boots are way beyond the affordability of your staff."

"Not so, Inspector," says Robert. "We supply all our staff with good quality footwear along with appropriate uniforms. It is important to us that staff are comfortable when carrying out their duties. I'm afraid those boots could belong to anyone they might fit. Also, when someone leaves our employment, new staff may be given second hand boots, shoes and uniforms, provided they fit. In short, those boots could belong to a dozen or more staff who work on the estate. Not only that we donate similar to the poor in the village."

Making our task to unmask the killer even more difficult, thinks I.

"You should do a Cinderella trial," smiles Matilda. "See whose feet fits the boots. But what if it was a woman who wore those boots, even if they were too big for her? What then?"

"What then indeed, Miss?" grates I. "It would then put even you in the frame."

"And me," says Prune throwing Head a saucy look. "You better come up to my bedroom immediately, Sergeant and see if those boots fit me."

"Just bugger off you, old hag," snaps Claude. "You couldn't spread 'em even if you tried."

"You can hardly walk, Mamma," grates Constance, "let alone tramp across fields. You are above suspicion. Why don't you go and have a lay down before lunch?"

"What time is lunch?"

"At lunch time you, stupid old cow," grates Claude.

"Excellent. I do…"

"Claude, escort your mamma up to her room and then go and lay down yourself for a while, you are both bringing on one of my headaches."

"The only place I wish to escort her to is the graveyard," scoffs he. "I'm off to get my lunch. You take the old bag up there yourself. I've got fish to boil."

Claude marches off while Constance takes hold of Prune. Together she and Matilda half drag and half push the old girl towards the corridor.

"See you later, Inspector," grins Matilda throwing me a searching glance over her shoulder.

"I shall look forwards to it, Miss," grates I.

"Take no notice of my infantile sister, Inspector," says Robert. "She loves to torment. Everything is a game to her. It is her way of filling in the excessive amount of time she has on her hands. Once married with a husband and children, along with a country house to run, she will have to grow up and join the real world."

"At least she cared for Rose," puts in Head.

"She did indeed," sighs Robert. He claps his hands together. "Right, Inspector. You can use the main office to conduct your interviews. It is roomy and bright and looks out over the tennis courts. Last door on your left down the bottom of the corridor. Anything you require please ask Butler. Butler is one of our footmen that I believe you may not have met as yet. I am assigning him to you for as long as you need him. Nice fellow, been with us for over a year. I'll send him down to you."

"Thank you, sir. Could you also locate Mr Smithers and send him down to us immediately? We shall interview him first."

"Really? Is there any need to interview, Smithers, Inspector? The man is beyond reproach."

"Agreed, sir. However, when I said we intend interviewing everyone, I meant everyone."

Robert exhales dramatically. "It's just that with so much to organise for Saturday's events I really could do with Smithers help."

"We shall try and not keep him for too long. Under the circumstances you still have no wish to postpone Saturdays events?"

"Everything has gone too far for that, Inspector. However, I assure you that John and Rose will not be forgotten. We intend to hold a special service for them by the chapel before the start of events."

Once alone in the hall with Head I put it to him that Matilda might be linked to our killer. He looks at me askance and says, "Burroughs said that Matilda never learnt how to use a bow and arrow."

"I'm not saying she actually killed Rose and Chambers. But what if it was, she who pushed that lump of masonry from the roof? Wouldn't Rose and Chambers cover up for her? Of course, they would until panic set in over our impending arrival. Matilda would then panic and so would Burroughs. What if Burroughs is our killer?"

"He never said whether or not he was any use with a bow and arrow, so I suppose it is feasible. It makes sense, Gerald. If their secret got out the pair of them would be finished, so they had no option other than silence Rose and Chambers."

I run a weary hand over my brow. "The case is turning into a quagmire; take a wrong step and you'll sink without a trace. We shall have to interview Burroughs and Matilda while reasoning that they could both be a good deal more intelligent than we first thought. Burroughs may have deliberately not investigated properly to cover up his and Matilda's guilt."

"Perhaps," says Head dolefully. "Matilda is clever but I don't believe she's evil. Look how she reacted when she saw Rose lying dead in that cart. It isn't easy to fake such reactions…"

"Agreed. However, we shall interview them later on and see what comes up."

We head down the corridor where we find a tall, clean shaven young footman stood to attention outside the office door. I introduce us and he confirms his name is Butler. Which could be confusing having a Butler as a footman. Inside the office we find it is a large room with comfortable high back chairs, a large desk and lots of wooden filing cabinets lining the oak panelled walls.

"Mr Robert should have sent Mr Smithers to us, Butler," says I. "Can you go and find out where Mr Smithers is, and inform him we are waiting for him?"

"Very good, sir. Mr Smithers is overseeing lunch for the family at this moment. I shall relay your request to him and ascertain at what time he can attend."

"It is not a request. It is an order, Butler. Mr Smithers must leave whatever he is doing and attend immediately. After that can you please organise a large pot of coffee…"

"And a plate of biscuits," puts in Head.

"Very good, sir. Anything else?"

"Yes, take one of those chairs out into the hall so you may sit down while you wait."

"Her ladyship wouldn't like that, sir. I am expected to stand at all times."

"Not while you're under my charge, Butler. It is going to be a long drawn out process and you will need to take the weight off your feet from time to time. And bring enough cups so you can have a coffee as well."

A broad smile crosses his face, "Thank you kindly, sir."

"Clever," says Head, the second Butler had gone. "He'll tell everyone what lovely chaps we are and not to be frightened of us."

"Therefore, they will be much more likely to trust and confide in us."

The Interviews

Smithers is seated opposite us. He is obviously guarded, having made it very clear he will not be prepared to divulge embarrassing family secrets, as it would be a betrayal of trust and would cost him his position. I send Butler to ask Mr Robert to come and see me. Within five minutes Robert enters. Having stressed to him the importance of all staff answering our questions regardless of proprieties, he fully agrees and gives Smithers cart blanche to tell all. The second Robert has gone I get to it.

"God knows where our killer may strike next, Mr Smithers. Forearmed is forewarned. The more you tell us now the more likely we will be able to prevent further killings."

"Understood, Inspector. What do you wish to know?"

"We already know that Percy is black mailing Miss Matilda and the reason why. We want to know who else he is blackmailing."

Exhaling dramatically, he sits right back in his chair as a grimace tightens his features. "A good deal of what I am about to tell you would be conjecture, Inspector. In short, I do not have exact facts and figures, so to speak…"

"Just get on with it," grates Head. "Roll it off your tongue and say to hell with it. You could be saving lives, Mr Smithers. Is that not more important to you than anything else?"

"It is. So be it. To hell with it! Mr Percy spins so many tales the difficulty is knowing when he is telling the truth, blatantly lying or merely embellishing a tall tale that happened to someone else that he has decided to credit to himself. I am fairly confident that what I am about to tell you is as near to the truth as I believe it to be. In no particular order: Mr Algernon is a senior librarian at one of the colleges in Oxford. He is obsessed by written works on the ancients. So much so that the castles library has grown over the years with over thirty scholarly masterpieces that should be in libraries elsewhere, if you see what I mean.

Borrowed indefinitely, according to Mr Algernon. To keep the secret, Mr Percy receives one third of Mr Algernon's allowance on a monthly basis."

"Coffee, Mr Smithers?" asks Head.

"Oh. Yes. Thank you. Any biscuits?"

"No," grins Head. "The inspector ate them all."

"Please continue, Mr Smithers," grates I.

"Miss Elizabeth is actually Mrs Tremaine. Her husband is a Captain in the Royal Navy. Currently chasing pirates in the China seas, so I believe. She has two children, Rachel four and Thomas who is five. Miss Priscilla Thornberry is Miss Elizabeth's personal maid. She is also her lover. Mr Percy receives money from Miss Elizabeth on a monthly basis to keep her secret, but I do not know how much."

"Bloody roll on," gasps Head. "How the hell did Percy find out his sister was doing it with another woman?"

Smithers shrugs. "I have no idea. All I know is that Mr Percy is extremely good at finding out peoples darkest secrets."

Head pushes over a cup of coffee. Smithers takes a sip and appears to be relaxing a little.

"Mr Percy, to my knowledge, does not have anything on Mr Robert and even if he did, Mr Robert would almost certainly refuse to play Mr Percy's games. Because that is what they are, gentlemen, mere games to him. He has no empathy with anyone. He has no remorse for anything he does and is interested only in his own self."

"We are fully aware of Percy's faults, Mr Smithers," says I. "The man is a turd, full stop."

"Reginald Freeman," sighs Smithers.

"The landlord of the Rams Head," cuts in I. "Would I be right in saying that Percy knows the landlord is a smuggler and is also blackmailing him?"

"You have surprised me, Inspector," says Smithers. "You obviously go around with your eyes wide open."

"We do," smiles I. "The list continues to grow, Mr Smithers. Who is next?"

"Mrs Kemp."

"Mrs Kemp," repeats Head wide eyed.

"Mrs Kemp, shall we say, helps herself to the odd bottle of expensive red wine to drink in her room."

"How many odd bottles?" asks I.

"Two or three a week."

"And Percy is blackmailing her," puts in I. "But surely the poor woman doesn't earn enough for anyone to get more than mere pennies from her?"

"Money is not what Mr Percy wants from Mrs Kemp, Inspector."

"The dirty rotten bastard!" growls Head thumping the table. "I'll do…"

"Remain professional, Sergeant," orders I. "Do not allow your emotions to cloud your judgement. How often does Percy demand payment from Mrs kemp?"

"Once or twice a week I believe."

"The rotten bastard," snarls Head.

Taking out my fob-watch, I say, "It is one o'clock, Sergeant. The family should all be at lunch by now. Off you go."

Getting to his feet, Head gulps down the remainder of his coffee and leaves. Smithers watches him go before throwing me a questioning look.

"Is he off to search the major's room, Inspector? If so, what does he hope to find?"

"I have no doubt something incriminating such as a bow and arrows."

"Oh… So, you still suspect the major may well be our killer?"

I shake my head. "Someone is either trying to incriminate the major or simply muddying the water. The fresh blisters on the major's feet tell me there is no way he could possibly have tramped over the fields, that fateful night in pursuit of Rose and Chambers, while wearing boots a half size too small for him, even if he was wearing thin socks. The major definitely is not our killer. But that doesn't mean he isn't involved in some capacity." Taking hold of

Heads note book and pencil I ask, "Anyone else we need to know about?"

"The local vicar. The Reverend Albert Hardpuzzle used to visit the castle on a regular basis for the purpose of the staff's spiritual welfare. Interesting to note that the major banned him from the castle on the very day that Mr Percy was nearly killed."

"The major believing that the reverend is Percy's real father?"

"Which is of course utterly absurd. Again, you already seem well informed, Inspector."

"I am indeed." It strikes me then that Constance fully confides in Smithers, which in turn gives more credence to my suspicion that Smithers is giving her one. "For what reason is Percy blackmailing the vicar?"

"By threatening to spread rumours that the reverend has often taken advantage of some of the maids in the castle during his visits."

"How much truth is there in Percy's accusations?"

"Utterly unsubstantiated, Inspector. But mud sticks, doesn't it?"

"It certainly does. How much does Percy drain from the church funds?"

"No money. Information about his parishioners, that's what Mr Percy wants from the good reverend. Information that may lead to further Mr Percy's blackmailing business."

"Good grief man. Is there no end to Percy's skulduggery?"

"I fear there is not, Inspector."

"Is there more?"

"I do not know of anyone else who's being blackmailed, but I wouldn't be the least surprised if the numbers are far higher. Mr Percy is that prolific in his dirty doings."

"The earl and the countess. Are they being blackmailed?"

He shakes his head and pauses to drink down his coffee. "I believe he is behind the 'jolly jape' in the major believing that the reverend is Mr Percy's father. The countess is virtually untouched by Mr Percy's shenanigans and probably always will be. She is probably the only person on earth he has ever come close to loving.

Even so, he constantly lies to her about anything and everything while manipulating her into believing he is no more than a naughty boy. His hold over her affections is quite sickening. The countess is nobody's fool, Inspector, but when it comes to her children, I am afraid she wears blinkers."

It's my turn to exhale dramatically. We haven't even touched the surface yet, but already we have a list of more suspects with strong enough motives to want to see Percy dead than I could have imagined. The landlord and the vicar would not have enough access to the castle to be high on that list, but may well be involved in some way or another. But could they have been behind Rose and Chambers murders? I doubt it. With the possible exemption of Percy, I doubt any of the family would be our killer, but may have engaged someone else to do the deed for them. Now to move on to other reasons behind the attempt on Percy's life, if in fact there ever was any attempts on his life. "Have you any idea how many females on the estate have fallen foul to Percy's sexual attacks?"

"No, sir. Percy likes to brag about his sexual activities, but he never names-names or numbers. Besides, with the exception of Mrs Kemp, none of the females inside these walls would confide in me on such delicate matters. You would be better served to question Mrs Kemp on these matters. In doing so I trust you will keep my name out of it."

"Of course. Well thank you for your honesty Mr Smithers it is most appreciated. Before I allow you to return to your duties, I would again like you to take me through what happened on that day when someone tried to kill Percy."

"Are there disparities between the evidence I gave to Constable Burroughs and you?"

"No. It often staggers me what witnesses may recall at a later date, Mr Smithers. Sometimes a tiny piece of information missed earlier turns out later to be of vital importance. So, humour me, please. In your own words, right from the beginning."

Stretching out his arms he swings his head around a few times to obviously relieve the tension in his neck. "I was up on the landing about to go and knock on Mr Percy's door to inform him that Mr Carter had arrived. Rose was coming out of Miss Matilda's bedroom with a bundle of washing in her arms which she dropped into her basket."

"Matilda wasn't in her room and Rose was alone in her duties.?"

"Correct. Mr Percy came out of his room which is next to Miss Matilda's. I informed him that Mr Carter was waiting for him. He ignored me and proceeded to go downstairs with me behind him."

"Did you see anyone else while you were upstairs?"

"No, Inspector."

"Did you have reason to believe anyone else other than Rose was upstairs at that time."

"I believe the major was in his room. Otherwise no one else was upstairs at that time."

"How did Chambers seem to you at the time?"

"Somewhat anxious. His eyes blazed with fury on seeing Mr Percy. I could feel the hatred exuding from his very being."

"Percy must have also noticed this. What did he do?"

"He merely smirked right in Chambers face. Chambers stepped away and went to stand right back beside the knight."

"Could you see Carter clearly as Percy went to go out of the door?" This was a question he hadn't been asked before and I could see his mind ticking over before he answered.

"Do you know, Inspector, I really cannot recall. I think I could half see him."

"When you ran back upstairs who did you pass?"

"Only Rose who seemed very surprised to see me charging past her."

"Once on the roof you said you saw no one up there. You looked all around you and still you saw no one?"

"Correct."

"So, you did not search the entire roof. Was it not feasible that someone could have been hiding, or may have had access to one of the turrets on each corner?" Again, this was a new question.

Smithers hands go to the back of his neck, he stretches some more. "The turrets are false, Inspector, there purpose being only to hide the multitude of chimneys. In truth, if you had a key to any of the four small service doors you could have gone in there to hide, but I tried each one and each one was locked, as I have informed you and the constable before. Besides, only the head of maintenance holds those keys. Other than the turrets there is nowhere to hide."

"Agreed. Who did you see on your way down?"

"Again, only Rose who was standing at the bottom of the roof stairs while appearing very curious, and then Chambers who was at the bottom of the main stair."

"Did you notice if any bedroom doors other than Matilda's were open?"

"No."

"Who locks their doors when they are not in them?"

"No one that I am aware of so the chamber maids can go in.?"

"How often is the major locked in his room?"

He smiles, "Hardly ever. He definitely was not locked in his room on that day. The threat to lock him in his room is nothing more than the countess's way of getting rid of him when he tries her patience too much. Now, really Inspector, I must get on. Is that all?"

"Nearly all. You testified that once Percy had gone, you and Chambers went back onto the roof where you tried every service door in the turrets again and still found them locked?"

"Correct. We saw no one up on that roof, Inspector."

He is definitely becoming agitated. They often do when being questioned for long periods. It is then that if they are hiding something, they begin to trip themselves up. In Smithers case I feel his agitation is nothing more than a desire to get back to his duties. "Is it not feasible that someone was inside one of the turrets having locked themselves in?"

"I thought that well after the event. But it never crossed my mind at the time."

"Whoever was up there could have come down and then gone into any bedroom and then hidden until the coast was clear, with the only one seeing them being Rose."

"And she unfortunately has been killed because of it."
"Exactly. Thank you, Mr Smithers. That is all."

Once Smithers had gone, I ask Butler to fetch Rosy Roper just as Head returns carrying a bow and a bag of arrows. He appears somewhat stressed.

"What's up, Sergeant?"

"Up!" growls he dumping the bow and arrows onto the desk. "On my way back down the stairs that bastard mutt, Henry and the rest of his degenerate crew came flying into the hallway. Henry fixes me with wide open lustful eyes while his tongue lolls out all slavering and sloppy. Then he goes for my leg, the swine! But this time I'm ready for him, and grabbing him by the throat I held him up at arm's length and gave him a good talking to."

"A good talking to?" says I trying not to laugh.

"I told him: Look here Henry, your infatuation with my legs must come to an end. You are a dog and I am a man. Not only are we of different species but we are also of the same sex. If you do not cease these disgusting assaults on my person, I will be forced to take drastic action."

"Do you think he understood what you were telling him?" grins I.

Head fixes me with admonishing eyes. "This is no laughing matter, Gerald. That dog is a seriously demented pervert, but, yes, he understood all right. He's clever he is, he kept trying to gain my sympathy by pathetically paddling his feet while opening his eyes even wider."

Probably because he was being strangled, thinks I. "I hope you didn't hurt him too much or had anyone witness your assault on him."

"I did consider squeezing his neck until he was dead, but the second I increased the pressure he employed a defence mechanism."

"A defence mechanism?"

"He squirted his filthy fluid onto my jacket, causing me to instantly drop him. Whereupon he ran off, the coward, just as that Jackson fellow came into the hallway. Look at my lapels, Gerald," says he pointing at a creamy wet stain. "I'll smell of semen all bloody day thanks to that little shit."

"Did you find anything else?"

"Just this," smiles he taking something out of his jacket pocket.

"One golfing tiepin," smiles I. "The major will be pleased."

"It's a wonder I found it amongst all the mess in that room."

"Now, more important, where did you find the bow and arrows?"

"Under Claude's bed."

"Surprise, surprise. That must be one of the most pathetic plants ever."

"Agreed. I'm thinking our killer wants us to believe he isn't very bright, when in fact he's very clever and calculating. That pig Percy is our killer, Gerald. You mark my words."

"I hope so, Richard as I would be more than happy to attend his hanging. Now, take yourself off to the nearest wash room and clean that mess off your jacket."

There comes a knock on the door and Butler sticks his head in, "Miss Roper, sir."

"Thank you, Butler. Please send her in."

An, anxious looking Rosy steps in, as Head steps out. She gives him a backward glance that says she would like to follow him. Anywhere rather than be here. Good, the more nervous they are the more likely they will answer your questions correctly.

"Sit down Rosy and relax. I promise you I won't bite."

She sits down and folds her arms across her chest to obviously try and curb their trembling, that's her arms trembling and not her chest.

"Rosy, did Rose keep a diary?"

She nods as the colour drains from her cheeks.

"Did you have access to that diary?"

"I don't understand, sir."

"Did you ever read her diary without her knowledge?"

The colour returns to her cheeks, deep crimson and no doubt burning. She drops her face.

"Why did you read her diary?" No answer. "You must tell me, Rosy. Holding back information to a policeman is a criminal offence and can lead to you being arrested. Tell me the truth now and I promise you nothing bad will happen to you."

She meets my eyes, "I only did it cause, she did it first."

"How do you know she read you diary without your permission?"

"Rose read a lot of books. She always folded the top of the page when she stops readin' so's she knows where she is next time. I don't read books an' I don't fold pages. We don't always work at the same times. Them chamber maids don't start much before eight, but me, I 'ave ter start at six but get time off for an hour after the family 'ave 'ad breakfast. One day I go up to me room for a lay down, Rose ain't there. I gets me diary an' find a page had a turn at the top. Just like she does to 'er books."

"Which obviously made you angry enough to read her diary."

"It did. I was really riled, sir, we promised each other we'd never read each other's diary an' she broke that promise."

"Perhaps it was fate, Rosy. Now this is very important. Tell me every little detail that you can remember reading along with the entry dates."

"Can't remember dates, sir. I just opened it up anywhere. I was hoping to find if she'd said anything horrible about me."

"And had she?"

She shakes her head. "She was lovely was Rose. But I didn't know she could be nasty as well." Pausing she swallows hard before a very dry looking tongue flickers over her lips.

I pour her a coffee, it's nearly cold but it's wet. "Drink this Rosy," orders I passing her the cup. She takes a long swallow, coughs a bit and appears to relax as her blushing subsides.

"I read where that Mr Percy really felt her up bad, it were disgusting. Rose was so upset but she were angry as well. She'd writ' she was goin' ter get someone to make him pay. She writ' she wanted someone ter cut off his… his…"

"Penis?"

"What's that?"

"His manhood."

"Oh. Never 'eard it called no penis before."

"What else did you read? Did Rose name any names regarding who she hoped would help her to get revenge?"

"No. I was afraid Rose might come up an' catch me readin' her diary. So, I just rushed through it, but I did read the bit about when she saw who went up on the roof the day Mr Percy nearly got killed."

I sit bolt upright in expectation. "And who was that person who went up on the roof?"

She shrugs, "It didn't say. She writ': He went up and tried ter kill Percy by pushing down a lump of stone on his head. We know we must do exactly as he said so we don't get in trouble. He's a good man and he hates that bastard as much as me."

"But she didn't name this mystery man?" says I sinking down in my chair.

"No. Rose rarely put in names in her diary. She told me not to as well. She said if someone ever reads yer diary an' yer've put in nasty things about someone or yer want ter keep a secret, don't ever put their name down then they can't go at yer for it, or get upset about it."

Bloody marvellous, thinks I. A bleeding diary that doesn't name names. "Did Rose ever discuss with you the attack Mr Percival made on her?"

"No. But everyone knew. I never told no one except Miss Saunders about when I got touched inappropriately, but everyone knew. Yer can't keep much a secret in this place."

It strikes me then that Rosy might not be that bothered about having been assaulted by Percy. "How upset where you when Mr Percival assaulted you?"

"I was a bit at first. But later on, Mr Percy gave me a sixpence when no one was looking and said he was sorry an' he'd only done it because he was in love with me."

"Did he give you many sixpences after that?"

"Only every time he said sorry. But then he ran out of sixpences an' give me pennies instead. Only since he's been down in the dungeons, I haven't had any pennies."

I hate to ask, but can't help myself, "What exactly did you have to do for Mr Percival to give you pennies?"

"Just stand there while he examined my chest. He wants ter be a doctor doin' special things to ladies' chests, an' as I've got a very special chest, he's practicing on it. An' he loves me. But yer have to keep it a secret, sir. Please don't tell no one."

"I won't, Rosy. But believe me when I tell you that Mr Percival doesn't love you and he has no intention of ever becoming a doctor, he is merely taking advantage of your innocence."

"Oh…" says she looking crestfallen. "I did wonder cause Mary an' Ethel gets pennies as well as me from Mr Percival. An' Mrs Kemp said I shouldn't let him touch me anyway as it's not right."

"You must listen to Mrs Kemp in future and do what she tells you. One more thing before I let you return to your duties. Did Mr Percival ever ask you if you knew who might have tried to kill him?"

"No. We never talked much, he just examined me, made a few funny doctor noises an' then went off before anyone saw us."

"Thank you, Rosy. Do not discuss our conversation with anyone at all. Not even Mrs Kemp. Is that clear to you?"

"Yes, sir. If I think of anything else shall I come an' tell yer?"

"Please do. Off you go."

I follow her out and ask Butler to escort her back and tell Mrs Kemp I must interview her right now, and more coffee please."

Head returns. "Bloody job getting that muck off," he grates. "Have you ever tried removing that stuff, sir? It's worse than dog's shit to get off." He plonks himself down. "What did you learn from Rosy?"

In between yawning my head off, I'm that tired through being up half the night and out so early, I relate all that Rosy told me. He clucks his tongue a few times and snarls every time I mention Percy. "It gets worse," grates he. "That Percy is the devil incarnate. Dirty sod, tricking poor Rosy into believing he loves her."

"That man will stop at nothing to get what he wants. After we've seen Gloria, I think we'll pay Percy another visit, Richard."

"I thought you were going to leave him to Clump. Besides he won't let you in anyway."

"He won't have a choice. Smithers has a key. We shall demand that key, take ourselves down there and be in before the cunt has time to fart."

"The what has time to fart?"

"The rude word we're not saying."

"But you just said it!"

"No, I didn't, it just sounded like I did."

"Whatever. Why are we going anyway?"

"I intend searching the place and scaring the shit out of him by accusing him of murdering Rose and Chambers. Look, Richard, Percy could easily be our killer, or behind the killings. On top of that, what was stopping him from sneaking out of his room in the middle of the night and planting the boots and the bow and arrows in Claude's bedroom? Or getting his accomplice to do it for him?"

"Nothing. The trouble is before we've finished, we'll have so many suspects it'll spin our heads. Besides that, Percy isn't going to just wilt and own up to anything, no matter what. Unless we give him a really good going over. And I mean a good going over."

"He deserves a good kicking. But if we go too far, we are finished, Richard. Clump wouldn't sanction an aristocrat getting seriously beaten up anyway, even one as foul as Percy. But twisted balls don't show up like broken noses, do they?"

"They don't," grins Head. "But the other problem is Percy could be innocent. We want him to be guilty of the murders so we can enjoy seeing him hang. But what if he is innocent? Blackmail and assault aren't to be sniffed at, but they're still a long way from double murder."

I take a deep breath. I'm so fatigued I realise my brain isn't working properly. I should be questioning the head maintenance man as he could be the one behind the roof attempt on Percy's life. He undoubtably had the opportunity. He has keys for the roof and the turrets. But does he have a motive? On top of that would he go so far as to kill Rose and Chambers to cover up his attempt on Percy's life? Besides that, I haven't even met the man as yet.

"And what about Smithers?" says Head knowingly tapping his nose. "No one else is in a better position to be behind all of this. He could be Percy's accomplice. He could be the man responsible for the attempts on Percy's life. He could be the man who killed Rose and Chambers. He could easily have planted the boots in Claude's room while ensuring Claude wore them to incriminate him. He was keen to have Claude arrested. In fact, Gerald I'd say Smithers should be at the top of our suspect list and not at the bottom of it. Not only that his feet look like they'd fit comfortably in those boots. The trouble is what motive does he have?"

"Unless this is all about protecting the family, Richard. Percy is an embarrassment to the Bullington name. He may one day become the 13th Earl, but he will never as such inherit the estate. Above all else he has become a dangerous liability. He could ruin the family by just opening his mouth about what he knows. I'm thinking that possibly, and I mean possibly, Smithers may well be behind all this out of misplaced loyalty or by direct collusion with one or more of the family. Only it all began to go wrong once they knew we were coming."

"They could all be behind it. Matilda, Burroughs, Claude and no doubt the cleverest one of all, Robert."

"Um…" ums I. "Perhaps Algernon and Elizabeth also. And what about Constance? Maybe even she has had enough of her disgusting first child. Maybe the conspiracy goes even deeper and half the staff and villages are in on it. But I can't believe any of them would have sanctioned the killings of Rose and Chambers. Can you? There has to be more to this. Until the killings what harm had been done? Nothing that anyone could prove. Nothing that couldn't be covered up or gotten out of. The motive behind all this has to be a lot deeper. An awful lot for someone to gain or something even more serious to cover up. The murders of Rose and Chambers may not be connected to the attempts on Percy's life at all."

He dolefully shakes his head as the door receives a knock followed by Robert's face.

"I thought this may be of help to you, Inspector," says he handing me a large leather-bound book. "It contains a complete list of current staff inside and outside of the castle. Tenants who rent land and property and all businesses we trade with."

"Thank you, sir."

"There are personal details in there, Inspector that must be kept strictly between you, your sergeant and Uncle Arthur. I would not appreciate the local constabulary knowing such details."

"Understood," says I stifling a yawn. "We shall be concentrating our efforts on the men who work mostly inside the castle to begin with, sir. However, no one, male or female, whatever their position will, for now, be beyond suspicion."

"Fully understood. I shall leave you to it, Inspector."

"Thank you, sir," says I opening the book once he'd left. "Bloody hell, Richard. I didn't realise how many people worked here. There's the butler, the under butler, the trainee butler. Six footmen and two junior footmen. Four general labourers just for inside the castle. Kitchen lads. Maintenance men. Valets. The list goes on and on. Outside staff include a dozen or more gardeners and groundsmen. Eight stable lads. We'll be here for a month of Sundays interviewing this lot."

"And that's just the men," moans Head.

"The list includes staff ages, marital status, wages, previous employment and each person's previous serious offences, if any, down to their peccadillos."

"Peck a what's?"

"Minor indiscretions. Failure to behave appropriately. Reprimands for insubordination and so on."

"It's very detailed then?"

"It certainly is. But then, Robert is the meticulous kind. Everything has to be right; which means if he decided to bump off his brother, he'd do it properly and plan the perfect crime. He certainly wouldn't try killing Percy by pushing a block of masonry off a roof."

"Unless he wanted to allay suspicion?"

"Perhaps. But I doubt it."

There comes a knock on the door, Butler enters carrying a tray with more coffee and biscuits on it. "Mrs Kemp sends her apologises. Could you give her fifteen minutes?"

"Very well. But not a minute longer," yawns I.

"Thank you, sir." He places the tray down and takes away the other one.

"I'll just close my eyes for ten minutes, Richard. Wake me when Gloria arrives."

When I open my eyes again, I am somewhat perplexed to see Gloria isn't present, "Where's Gloria, Sergeant?"

"Been and gone."

"Why didn't you wake me?"

"I tried, but it was like trying to wake a punch-drunk boxer. Every time I gave you a shake you started throwing punches."

"Really?"

"Yes, really. You were dreaming and getting angry about whatever was on your mind."

Betty, sighs I to myself. Imagining her with that randy young waiter has been playing on my mind since last night. God knows what they've been up to when I'm not around. "What time is it?"

"Just gone four."

I snap myself upright, "Christ have I been asleep for two hours?"

"You have, so you must have needed it."

"Any cold coffee left in that pot?"

He shakes his head, "Butler will be here with a fresh pot in a minute or so."

"What have you been up to while I've been asleep?" Apart from scoffing all the biscuits thinks I, noting the plate looks as if it's been licked clean again.

"I've interviewed Gloria, four footmen, the under butler and head of maintenance."

"You have been busy," says I stretching out my arms and twisting my head to get the knots out. "What did you learn?"

"Gloria gave me six names of young females who Percy has preyed on of late. Plus, several more from the past including the former housekeeper, Juliet Saunders. Gloria admitted she helps herself to the odd bottle of wine and that Percy is blackmailing her because of it."

"For sexual favours?"

"She said at least it helps to keep him from pestering the girls as much."

"Well, one thing's for certain, Sergeant, once we've had words with Percy all this blackmail business will come to an abrupt halt. Unless he wants to suffer the consequences."

"Like a pair of nuts tied into a knot," grins Head. "Jeffrey Cornish, the head of maintenance, insisted that no one could have gotten into the turrets without his say so. He keeps a firm hold of the keys and on the day of the rooftop incident he and two of his men were over a mile away repairing the thrasher. Other than that, I learnt nothing of interest from anyone else. I've taken notes should you wish to read them."

"Thank you. Who's next?"

"No one for a bit. The countess has summoned us for a meeting in the drawing room for four thirty. I thought I'd wake you; we'd have a cuppa and then go see what she wants."

The knock on the door heralds Butlers arrival. He enters carrying another tray complete with even more biscuits. "Anything else, Sir?"

"Not just know, thank you."

"Has there been any sign of Constable Burroughs?" asks I once Butler had gone.

"Yes. He stuck his head in just as I was finishing with Gloria. He'd been consoling the Bush family. He said Sam' would show him where to take his plaster casts. They'll be no forensics coming from Truro until tomorrow if at all, as they're short staffed and really busy. And once every one has visited, Rose, he'd convey her to Truro."

"Truro's forensics sound useless anyway." I get to my feet. "Right, pour the coffee Richard. I shall be back in a minute once I've freshened up a bit."

Except for Percy and thankfully the 'Bubbly Boos', the entire family are in the drawing room. Claude is sat beside Constance with Prune beside her, Matilda is between Prune and Robert. Algernon and Elizabeth, at least I assume that's who they are, are sat on armchairs either side of the sofa. Two decanters of sherry and little crystal glasses sit on the coffee table.

"Inspector Potter. Sergeant Head," says Constance getting to her feet. "Thank you for joining us. I shall not detain you for long." She waves a hand. "May I introduce my eldest daughter, Elizabeth? Elizabeth this is Inspector Potter and Sergeant Head."

Elizabeth stands. Head and I give little bows, as she says, in a very posh voice, "How do you do, gentlemen?"

She is tall and elegant like her mother. We say our how do's then she sits back down.

We are then introduced to Algernon who steps forwards and shakes our hands. Coming only up to my shoulders, he is very rotund and sports a thick black curly beard with hair to match, and with his tiny glasses and dark staring eyes surrounded by hand bags, he looks every bit the mad professor. Algernon retakes his seat while Head and I sit down opposite the family. They all appear rather worried except for Claude and Matilda, who judging by her twinkling eyes is at least two parts pissed.

"What about me?" cries out Claude.

"What about you?" grates Constance.

"You haven't introduced me, have you?"

"You already know the policemen."

"I might. I might not. But I still…"

"Oh, do shut up, Claude, or go to your room."

"I won't. I can't stand that room. It's a veritable pigsty. It's about time someone cleaned the place up."

"Why don't you go and clean it up yourself you, lazy swine?" growls Prune.

"Enough!" snaps Robert. "Father. Grandmamma. Please be quiet or leave the room."

Claude sits back and folds his arms while Prune glares at him. Why they hate each other so much I have no idea and care even less.

"Will you join us for sherry?" asks Constance.

"Thank you, ma'am."

"Do the honours Matilda."

Matilda rises unsteadily onto her feet. She looks stunning in a cream crinoline heavily embodied dress buttoned up to her neck. Her hair is piled up and decorated with loops of thin silver chains dotted with tiny pearls. She over fills a couple of glasses, passes one to Head and the other to me. I meet her eyes; she throws me a saucy wink before wobbling back to her seat. I take a sip of the creamy sherry.

"We have received a telegram from Detective Chief Inspector Clump," says Constance. "Due to train hold ups he will not be arriving until after eight o'clock tonight. He has requested that you do not wait for him, he will see you tomorrow morning at ten o'clock sharp. Tomorrow gentlemen, we shall be invaded by a host of people intent on preparations for Matilda's big day on Saturday. A large marque is to be erected on the main lawn at the rear of the castle for the use of the estate workers, tenants and villagers. Everyone not required to serve the honoured guests inside the castle are invited. There will be music and dance. Spit roasts and beer by the barrel. All manner of jovialities including clowns and acrobats. The great hall is to host a lavish feast for up to one hundred quests followed of course with a grand masked ball. We have hired the services of a renowned French chef and his entourage to ensure the feast of all feasts. It would have been too much for Mrs Kemp to organise alone. You can see the amount of disruption it will cause having all these people coming and going. Therefore, I will liaison with the Chief Inspector to see if he will suspend investigations in and around the castle until Monday. I thought I would put this to you Inspector, before I speak to Chief Inspector Clump, as a matter of curtesy and to hear your views."

"Thank you, ma'am. I do not see a problem in suspending investigations until Monday. We can spend our time interviewing villagers, estate workers and tenants. You never know what might turn up. But ultimately we will do as instructed by the chief."

"Thank you, Inspector. You along with your partners will be welcome to join in the festivities in the marque on Saturday. We will commence the proceedings with a short service in remembrance of poor Rose Bush and John Chambers. It will do you both good to take a break from what must have been a very trying ordeal for you over the past two days."

"Thank you, ma'am. May I ask, how did you know our wives are here?"

"The chief inspector informed me by letter over a week ago, that you would be arriving with your wives, and were booked into the Smugglers Rest."

Head shoots me a confused look. So, Clump expected the girls would come, even if he refused to sanction it, hence the reason he booked us into double rooms each, when Head and I would have expected one cheap and cheerful room that hopefully had twin beds instead of a double. It's one thing having to listen to Heads snoring and farting all night, but it's one hell of a worse experience when your sharing the same bed.

"The Smugglers Inn will be packed to capacity on Friday and Saturday night," continues Constance. "While every spare bedroom in the castle will be taken along with every spare room at the Carter mansion. Lord Henry Carter having kindly offered room at the inn, so to speak. Even the Rams Head will probably be full with those from a lower station."

Alfred Carter, someone else I must interview thinks I. A phycological darkness suddenly descends on the meeting as I note nearly everyone suddenly looks very doleful indeed. I sip down the remainder of my sherry.

"On a much more dreadful note, Inspector, I understand that you have uncovered some rather unsavoury information regarding certain practices being carried out by my eldest son, Percival."

Matilda glares into my eyes, more beseeching than threatening. Algernon begins squirming in his seat, and Elizabeth's cheeks turn scarlet as she sits bolt upright and wriggles her bustle to the very edge of the seat. A broad smirk paints itself onto Prunes wrinkly mouth in obvious anticipation of what's to come. Robert looks embarrassed beyond belief, while Claude remains calm as he's more interested in a bogey up his nose than anything else. Constance has turned white and looks about to be sick. "We have reason to believe Mr Percival is blackmailing several persons in and around the castle and across the estate, ma'am."

"Will you elaborate on that statement, Inspector?"

Here's the predicament. Do I tell all and destroy the reputations of all who are being black mailed? Matilda and the constable will be finished. Algernon will never again be allowed into any place of learning and will probably have his library card revoked. Elizabeth won't go to prison, as despite Heads believing lesbianism is illegal, it isn't. Even so the scandal would destroy her and her family. As for Gloria, the landlord of the Rams Head and the local vicar, their lives will all be fucked right up. Scandals within the aristocracy are forever being covered up, but this family have far too many secrets to cover up should they all come out at once, with the scandal of Percy putting the icing on the cake. To torment her I meet Matilda's eyes and throw her a 'got you' smile. I look over the rest of the family before settling my eyes into Constance's. She knows or suspects I know about her and Smithers. They must be very close indeed for him to have told her about Percy's blackmailing shenanigans. Unless Robert told her, which I doubt. "Our investigations into the blackmailing accusations are still in their infancy, ma'am. However, even if they were advanced, we would not divulge anything to anyone except on a need to know basis, in case it jeopardises future possible legal action. The information we have received regarding this matter was given in the strictest confidence. With apologises, I must inform you that those confidences will not be broken, not even to you. We shall of course be pursuing the allegations to substantiate their credibility. In short, we cannot and will not tell you anything until we have all the facts along with cast iron evidence or a confession."

She looks relieved, you can hear the air imprisoned inside her escape through her mouth. The family relaxes, Matilda smiles at me while Algernon nods knowingly. They are for now, all off the hook.

"Thank you, Inspector. I fully understand that you must follow your protocol. Unless anyone has anything else to say I suggest we call this meeting to an end."

"I've got something to say," says Claude wiping his bogey on the chair. "Any luck with finding my tiepin, Inspector Who?"

"Oh God save me," sighs Constance burying her head in her hands.

"I have it, Major," beams Head hauling it from his pocket.

Claude jumps to his feet, "You do? Oh, bally good show, What, old chap. Wherever did you track it down to? A pawn-shop? On some bastards tie?"

"Neither, Major. I found it in your bedroom."

"Really? How on earth did it get there? Someone must have planted it."

"I fear it has been there all along."

"Amongst all your other crap," snarls Prune. "You couldn't find a dead elephant in that room it's so full of rubbish."

"Shut up, Mamma," snaps Constance. "Why don't you go off for your nap?"

"What was that?" says Prune poking her earpiece deeper into her ear. "I can't hear you because my trumpet has packed up, I think it's run out of gas."

"I wish you would," grins Matilda.

Claude edges closer to Head, "May I have it, Sergeant What?"

Head hands it over and Claude raises it to his lips and gives it a kiss before fixing me with guilty puppy dog eyes, "I suppose I'll owe the turd an apology now."

"For what reason will you owe Mr Percy an apology, Major?"

"I thought he'd taken it the bounder. Thought he'd pawned it the bugger. Never got no money has he the dogs mess. Always thieving and lying the bloody cheat. Damned disgrace to the family name, don't you know, Inspector Who?"

"Do shut up with your ramblings and disgusting language, Claude," snaps Constance.

He turns on her, "I will not shut up! Time you admitted to yourself what a devil we have spawned between us, old duck."

"Us! Don't you mean me and the Reverend Hardpuzzle have spawned a devil between us?"

"Cause not. That flowery fool couldn't father a pigeon. The turd spread those rumours just to cause trouble and torment me." He stabs an accusing finger at Constance. "He's trying to convince me I'm mad and off my rocket..."

"That's because you are," spits Prune.

"No, I'm not. I'm as sound as a block of fudge. All that aside I'm now rather pleased that block of stone didn't hit the turd on the head. But then I didn't quite judge it right. Given one more second or two and it would have knocked the buggers head right off. Now I can watch and smirk for a change while he gets his just deserts."

Back in the office, with Claude sat opposite me and Head, I start grilling Claude, "What just deserts do you believe will befall, Percy, Major?"

"Hopefully he'll be done for blackmail and get sent to the Tower for life and have to live on a diet of dish water and cockroach sandwiches. That'll sort the bugger out."

"Have you attempted to kill your son on any other occasions before or after the roof top incident?"

He shakes his head. "Spur of the moment that was. I came out of my room and saw the turd's back heading towards the stairs with that valet chappie. I heard the valet say the turds carriage was outside, so I thought here's a chance to get the swine and strike a blow for freedom from turds. I ran up on the roof, peered over and then selected a lump of masonry that was directly above the door. I heard someone shout out 'Get back you something or other' so I shoved the block off the roof and then leaned over to see it had missed the swine by inches. Then I hurried back to my room. And that's that, Inspector Who."

"Did anyone see you going up or coming back down from the roof?"

"I don't think they did," says he scratching his scalp.

"Did you see the chamber maid, Rose Bush?"

"No. Well not true, as I came out of my room, I saw her back going into Matilda's room. I suppose she might have seen me."

She certainly did, thinks I. "How did you know that some of the masonry was loose up on the parapet?"

"That fellow who repairs things had taken me up there earlier to show me. He said he was going to repair it the next day and that it wasn't dangerous unless someone shoved it hard, then it might tumble down and hurt someone. Which gave me the idea to try and kill the turd. He was always going out of that door, Inspector Who, galivanting off when he should be helping to run the estate, the lazy whelp."

The major's memory is much keener than I would have thought likely. Obviously, he isn't as mad as everyone believes.

"Are you going to arrest me, Inspector Who?"

"Not right now, Major. But I will if you do anything like that again."

"Good show old chap. Then I can go off and play golf after all. Talking about golf, any luck in finding those devils who sold me that useless club?"

"Not as yet, Major. Right off you go, and do try to behave yourself."

"One more thing, Major," pipes up Head. "Have you ever killed anyone?"

"Um… Shot a couple of bandits in India when I was serving out there, don't you know? Damned thing that was. The buggers went for me while I was out riding and tried to unhorse me. Out with the old revolver so I did and dropped them. Had the odd skirmish here and there with usurpers and shot one or two. Shot a punkah-wallah by mistake once. Thought he was going to attack the old duck with his big leaf when in fact he was only going to fan her. A bad business that, I had to pay the man's wife a heap of money in compensation."

"The countess was out in India with you?" asks I.

"Yes. She came out for a couple of years for a holiday, just after she'd given birth to the turd, in the hope that by the time she returned the turd would have been sent off to boarding school."

"Wouldn't he have been a bit young to send off to boarding school?" grins Head.

"Not in his case. The sooner the better. By God gentlemen, that boy was a nightmare from the day he was born and he's still a nightmare. Should have given him to the gypsies. Anyway, the old duck didn't like India, too hot and too many flies, so, after a couple of months she up and buggered off back home. Grabbed a passage back on a posh boat so she did. Good thing there were other women on board or she'd have had to stay in her cabin throughout the trip. But at least by then she was up the bally Khyber with Robert. Nice lad, one of my better ones is Robert. Anyway, I missed her so much I gave it a few more months and returned myself. Missed the birth of Robert of course. Been on leave ever since." He smiles broadly. "Golf time me thinks if that is all, Inspector Who."

"It is, Major. If you recall anything else please let us know immediately."

"I will, Who old chap. About what exactly?"

"What now?" asks Head the second the majors gone.

"God knows. We've concentrated our efforts on trying to link Rose and Chambers murders to the attempted murders on Percy. Now, Percy may well be behind those murders, but I'm now even more convinced that the murders may have had nothing whatsoever to do with Percy, and we need to start looking elsewhere."

"Like where?"

"I don't know. All we can do is carry on interviewing all and sundry while hoping something pops up out of the green and gives us our first lucky break."

"The green?"

"Yes. Like a snowdrop shooting up out of the grass to tell you spring is coming."

"Are we going to question Percy again? I'm still thinking he is behind the murders, and it has nothing to do with anything else other than he thinks Rose tried to kill him."

"Let's leave Percy to Clump, but I think it may be a good idea to find out who has visited Percy since he's been incarcerated. Ask Butler to go and find Smithers, I'd like a quick word with him."

Smithers was in and out in two minutes to inform us that: Constance visits Percy on a regular basis, at least once a week. Robert has visited him once. Matilda once. While Algernon and Elizabeth haven't visited him at all. Claude visited only to be told to 'clear off you, old prat.' The only outsider to visit regularly was Alfred Carter with over eight visits to date.

"Interesting to note that Carter stayed with Percy longer than anyone else who'd visited," says Head.

"Indeed, Sergeant. Perhaps to plot and plan together. Again, let's hear what Clump has to say before we go any further with this. Meanwhile, I think a beer's in order, don't you?"

"And a great big lump of Gloria's cake."

"You are getting fat, Richard."

He fixes me with a pained expression, "I'm eating for two don't forget."

"I thought Chloe was the one supposed to be eating for two."

"She is, I'm just joining her to get a taste of what it's like to be pregnant."

"I see. Hence the extra stone of stomach you're carrying around."

"Exactly. The more I eat the bigger my stomach gets, just like if a baby was growing inside me."

There is no answer to that one

Getting Nowhere

By seven o'clock we are on our way back to the Smugglers Rest, having interviewed nearly half the males who reside or work inside the castle. We learnt nothing of real worth, but did get Algernon to admit he's a book thief and is being blackmailed by Percy. I ask Simmonds to do a detour to Seb Bush's farm so we might pay our respects. After a couple of pints of cider with Seb' and most of his family, while sat outside on the patchy grass, we take our leave. Head and I come away feeling immensely sad for the Bush's, they are broken at losing Rose. We swore to them that we would catch Rose and Chambers killer. What we didn't say was that we are going around in circles at the moment and getting nowhere. Time to face Betty.

We're just about to step into the bar of the Smugglers, when I spot Betty and Chloe sat by the window being entertained by a pair of pompous looking, rakish young toffs. Grabbing Head by an arm I side track him into the snug.

"Our ladies are obviously enjoying themselves, Richard, judging by their laughter."

"Don't get upset, Gerald, it's just four people having a bit of fun. Those fellows are hardly likely to be trying to seduce the girls, are they? I mean, they can see the girls are wearing wedding rings and any prat can see Chloe's in the advanced stages of pregnancy."

Through the open hatch in the snug I can see through the bar to where Betty is sitting, and I don't like what I am seeing. One of the rakes is sat too close to Betty, so close their shoulders are barely an inch apart. And he's a handsome devil with his neatly trimmed thin black moustache, oh so neat sideburns and collar length hair. His friend is a bit tubby, with a round clean shaven face and large nose, even so I do not like the way he is looking at Betty as if he could eat her. It's not helping with her wearing that dress again.

"Good evening gentlemen," says the barmen stepping up and blocking my view.

"Double scotch with water and a pint of bitter," says I. "Richard?"

"Just a pint for now. We need to order our food, Gerald, or it will be too late."

"Two dinners," snaps I trying to look around the barman.

"What dinners do you want, sir? Steaks, roasts, fish and chips…?"

"Fish and chips with mushy peas and lots of thick cut buttered bread," says Head.

"And you…"

"I'll have the same," snaps I.

"Where will you be sitting, sir?"

I meet his eyes aware that I haven't seen this one before. "On a chair."

"Um…"

"We'll be sitting in the bar over by the window where those four are sat," says Head.

"The tables aren't big enough for six, sir."

"Those fellows will be leaving very shortly," growls I clenching my fist.

"I'm sorry gentlemen, but are you currently in residence here?"

"We are," says Head. "And those ladies sat by the window are our wives."

"You'll be the famous detectives from London then?"

"We are," snaps I. "Now please stop jabbering on and get our drinks."

"Very good, sir. Where would you like your drinks…"

"Down my bloody throat, where else!"

"In the main bar, please," says Head tugging me back from the hatch. "You need to calm down, Gerald. Whatever's got into you?"

"Her!" I point to the hatch. "Flirting with everything in trousers. God knows what she's been up to while I'm out? She could be doing it with half of Cornwall for all I know."

"You're getting this all wrong. Look, with Chloe by her side all the time I can't see when Betty would have had the chance to play around. Chloe doesn't miss a thing, Gerald. If Betty was up to no good, Chloe would have said something to me."

"Not if Betty told her to keep it quiet. You know what women are like."

"Come on, we'll go into the bar and introduce ourselves. The second they know who we are, you just watch, they'll be off like a pair of chickens that has just been confronted by a ravenous fox."

"They better, Richard or they'll be very sorry."

I follow Head into the bar aware that Betty is so engrossed with her 'company' she fails to see me coming. Over in a corner stands Andrew holding an empty tray. Judging by his sulky features, he's obviously jealous of Betty flirting with the toffs. The toff with the moustache clicks his fingers without even looking behind him. Andrew jumps forwards, but I grab his arm. "I'll serve," says I snatching his tray.

"But…"

"Just bugger off, Andrew. Go and powder your nose or something."

Head blocks my way, "Hold on, Gerald what the hell are you doing?"

"Sorting my wife out once and for all!"

We are now sat out front of the Smugglers on a bench at a table eating our dinners; having been asked to leave the bar by the manager. Birds twitter, gulls soar in a bright orange sky, the sun is going down but the air is stuffy, a storm is on its way.

"That didn't quite work, Gerald," says Head. "Mistake number two was hitting that toff on the head with that tray and telling him to F-off before he 'gets it'. Mistake number three was head butting him on the nose, just because, quite rightly, he jumped to his feet and punched you in the face. Mistake number four was thinking said toff would then run for it before he got any more…"

"His second punch was just pure luck," says I touching my swollen lip. "It's a good job the manager stepped in or I'd have done some serious damage to that smirking gits face."

"Sorry, Gerald, you made a right fool of yourself in there, and God only knows how on earth you'll make this one up to Betty."

"She threw a glass of wine in my face."

"It's a wonder she didn't throw a chair in your face. The other thing is you didn't even consider Chloe. What if you and the toff had have fallen onto her? You could have done her serious damage!"

"Sorry." Setting down my knife and fork I sit back and sigh. I really have done it this time. Betty ran crying from the bar and disappeared upstairs, where no doubt she's now locked in her room while being consoled by Chloe. Luckily there were only a few other diners in the bar, goodness knows what they thought? "I've embarrassed Betty beyond her wildest nightmare, Richard. No doubt about it, I have utterly fucked up this time."

"You have indeed. Mistake number one was not asking to be introduced to the toffs before losing it."

"How was I know the prat is no other than, Jeremy 'bleeding' Trout, Matilda's intended. You'd have thought he would be staying at the castle rather than at the local inn."

"Etiquette, Gerald. It's all about etiquette. God knows what Clumps going to say."

I pick up my fork and start pecking at my fish. I've no appetite and even the scotch tasted tasteless. "I'm going to have to crawl to Betty for a while, Richard."

"For the next year at least more likely. That's if she ever speaks to you again. You're also going to have to apologise to Trout and his friend, what's his name?"

"Lord Palmer, son of the Lord Chief justice of Kent."

"Let's hope they accept your apology and not charge you with assault."

Obviously leaving it there, Head goes back to shovelling chips down his throat. I get to my feet. "I'm going to see Betty before it gets any darker, Richard."

With a huge piece of fish perched on the end of his fork he looks up and gives me the don't do it look. "You should leave it until the morning, Gerald. Let her calm down first."

I shake my head, "The sooner the better." Walking away I straighten my jacket, check my tie is straight and wipe a hand across my mouth. Whatever Head thinks, I'm thinking Betty has allowed all the attention she's been getting, from every Tom and Dick who happens by, to go to her head. If nothing else she's thrown convention out of the window and flirted wantonly. The real question is; how far has she gone with her flirting? Going into the inn I find the way clear to sneak upstairs to our room, where to my surprise I find the door open and Betty sat by the window gazing out at the sunset over the sea. I enter and shut the door.

"It's me," squeaks I. "Can we please talk for a while?"

She turns her head and gazes up at me through wet eyes surrounded by red puffy skin. "Why not, Detective Inspector? Sit down. Would you like a glass of red wine? It's very nice, smooth and silky, unlike you. You really are as rough and coarse as a drunken lout, aren't you, Detective Inspector?"

Pulling back a chair I sit opposite her across the little table. She pours me a glass of wine and passes it over. Picking it up I take a sip, again it doesn't strike the taste buds. "I'm sorry, Betty, I allowed jealousy to cloud my common sense. Obviously, you were only chatting, mere friendly conversation, nothing untoward. I took it the wrong way. It's been a long hard emotional day. It was all so innocent, wasn't it? You had no thoughts of…"

"Leaping into to bed with him! Despite what you think, Detective Inspector, a woman's world doesn't revolve around a man's penis. She is quite capable of enjoying a man's company while having a civilised conversation. Thus far, you have hinted that I am 'over fond' of Andrew, which in its self was very silly and totally misjudged. What you did in that bar was way beyond what even I could believe you would do. I thought you had left all this silliness behind you years ago. Whatever has gotten into you?"

I shrug. In truth I believe I'm going through a funny stage and feeling insecure when it comes to Betty. I love her so much, she is my world, but of late I can't help getting jealous the second any man I don't know, so much as smiles at her. Perhaps I should tell her all this? But then perhaps it would be better to say nothing and hope she forgets about it all.

"I've packed our bags," says she glancing across the room.

Twisting my head around I see both carpet bags appear stuffed full. "We can't leave, Betty. We haven't solved the case as yet. Are you forgetting we have two murders on our hands?"

"No, I haven't. I shall be leaving for home on the first train tomorrow, but for tonight I do not wish to see or be near you, so please piss off somewhere else for the night. Why don't you go and see if that Matilda girl will let you share her bed? I'm sure she would the way you keep going on about her. You must have become very close."

"I've barely mentioned Matilda, there is absolutely nothing between me and her, and you're just saying that to ease your own conscience because of what you've been up to. Flirting so outrageously with a mere boy in front of other people. What were you thinking of?"

"Nothing that your stupid brain could possibly comprehend. So, what if I do find Andrew sweet, polite, friendly and attentive? Or have they brought out a law saying it's illegal to like someone just because they're a likable member of the opposite sex?"

"There's nothing wrong in being friendly with members of the opposite sex, Betty, but a woman has to be careful those actions aren't misinterpreted by others. The way you were with that snotty, Trout bloke, was way beyond how a married woman should have been behaving."

"He was amusing, I won't deny it, but he was also very much the upper-class twit..."

"Who just happened to be bloody good looking and no doubt bloody charming to boot."

"He had all the charm of a typical man who thinks he's irresistible, Detective Inspector. At least he has some charm, unlike you who has all the charm of an un-kissed frog and is easily resisted. Now please, just go!"

"Not until I've finished. What about Chloe? She's never been so happy. It's not fair, you're forcing her to cut short her holiday, and besides that, we have all been invited to the big do at the castle on Saturday."

"Chloe won't go back without Richard. She's staying. As for Matilda's big day, I couldn't care less if I miss it. I'm sure she won't be missing me so long as you are there."

I have had enough of this. Its, obvious Betty is so full of guilt she's trying to twist things around as if it's all my fault. "As your husband, I am ordering you not to leave for home tomorrow. You will attend the do on Saturday. Clump knows you are here and he will expect you to attend. Meanwhile, I will expect you to conduct yourself with more decorum while we remain here. You will dress more appropriately for the area. You will refrain from engaging in ribald conversation with members of the opposite sex, and you will go nowhere unless chaperoned by Chloe. Is that all clear to you?"

"It is."

"Have you anything to say?"

"Yes. Fuck off Gerald!"

"It didn't go so well then?" says Head on my return.

Dumping my bag on the table, I note his plate has been wiped clean along with mine, despite my having left half my dinner on it. "I just wasted my breath, Richard."

"What's with the bag?"

"You're supposed to be a detective, work it out for yourself," grates I sitting down.

"She's either thrown you out or you've walked out."

"She told me to go and see if Matilda would let me share her bed for the night."

"Really! What on earth made her think Matilda would want to share her bed with you?"

"Apparently I keep going on about her. Utter rot, I've barely mentioned the woman. All I told her about was when I met her in Burroughs's garden."

"Did you mention peering into the shed and seeing her doing up her blouse? Followed by whatever did the silly girl think she was doing?"

"I may have mentioned it once. Well twice."

"There you are then. It's your fault."

"How the hell is it my fault?"

"Simple. You must have come across as fancying Matilda like a rampant rabbit. Not only that, you probably sounded rather jealous about her cosying up to Burroughs. I rest my case."

"If I did all you say then I suppose I am partly to blame, Richard. But quite honestly, can you honestly say, in all honesty, that you hadn't honestly noticed just how flirtatious Betty has been since we've been here with every man who so much as smiled at her?"

"That's a lot of honesties, Gerald. I don't believe Betty was so much flirting as being over excited and over friendly. You know what Betty's like? She just loves friendly people."

I take a deep breath, maybe I have been misreading things, but then maybe not. Either way I think Betty has gone bonkers! How dare she tell me to 'fuck off Gerald?' "I'm going back up those stairs to tell my wife that if she doesn't welcome me back into the marital bed tonight, our marriage will be over."

"Take my advice this time, Gerald. Leave it until tomorrow night, she'd have calmed down by then."

"Betty won't be here, according to her she's leaving in the morning to go back home."

"What did Chloe have to say about that?"

"Nothing, she wasn't there."

"Oh… She must be in her room. I best go up and see her. She'll be wondering where I am. I only kept away because I thought she was in with Betty. Well, one thing's for certain, Chloe will not be going home without me, nor will she be left here all on her own if Betty goes."

"That's two things, Richard."

"What is two things?"

"Never mind. I've suddenly decided to go to the castle and see if I can bed down there for the night. While there I better go and see Matilda and explain what happened with Trout."

"Clump will be there, Gerald, and he won't be happy to hear you've been head butting aristocrats."

"I'll try and avoid him. I'll see you at the castle in the morning."

Deciding to walk to the castle to clear my head, I set off. It is a glorious evening, birds singing, fresh air and a light breeze to tickle your cheeks. I estimate it will take me half an hour to get there.

All is well with the world until half way there a wind picks up, black clouds appear on the horizon, lightning flashes and all the birds seemed to have disappeared. I quicken my pace; it would be just my luck to get caught in a storm.

By the time I arrive at the castle I am drenched, shivering, thoroughly miserable, hungry and thirsty. It's so dark it could be the middle of the night instead of just gone nine. I pull the bell cord; one door is quickly opened by Jackson.

"Oh… It's you, sir," says he looking me up and down. "You are soaked."

"I know that. Can I come in?"

He stands aside and slams the door behind me. "How can I be of assistance, sir?"

"I need somewhere to kip down for the night, Jackson."

"Um… I will fetch Mr Smithers. Can I take your bag, hat and jacket?"

"I'll let them drip for a bit."

"As you wish," says he before hurrying off.

Already there's a pool of water around my feet, I really am drenched right through.

Jackson returns a few minutes later with none other than Matilda.

"Good evening, Inspector," grins she. "Have you been swimming in your clothes?"

"No, but it feels like I have." I meet her patronising eyes; she'd love to laugh out loud. In all fairness I must look a right sod so I can't blame her.

"Come with me, Inspector. You can have Percy's room for the night."

Squelching along behind her my eyes are glued to the sway of her hips as we climb the stairs and head down the hallway. Matilda comes to a stop outside Percy's room. She opens the door and waves me in and then shuts it behind us, which breaks etiquette. Lamps have been lit and curtains drawn.

"The bathroom," smiles she opening a door. "Get those wet things off and put them in the basket. The room has been prepared for whoever's staying in it tomorrow, so you'll find all you need. Then you can have a nice hot bath, followed by a good stiff drink."

"Thank you, Miss. Where is the chief at this moment?"

"Don't worry, Inspector. They're still dining. Then for the men: it'll be smelly cigars, stinky cheese, port and rotten fart time followed by boring billiards until gone midnight."

"Would it not be more appropriate if say, Jackson were here instead of you?"

"It would. But then it wouldn't be half the fun, would it? Besides, I want to know why you've turned up here at this time in search of a bed for the night, when you should be cosied up in the Smugglers with your beautiful wife."

"Ah... Several reasons, Miss. Perhaps I'll get changed before I tell you."

"You do that, Inspector. I'll leave you to it."

With that she goes out of the room and I sigh with relief.

The bathroom is huge and very posh. Full size bath with gleaming brass taps, sink and toilet, teak cupboards, full size mirror, blue tiled floor, lots of little bottles containing everything you could possibly need. Thick fluffy towels over a wooden rack and white dressing gowns on hooks on the door. I strip off, throw everything into the basket and open my bag. Wet on the outside, but inside all is dry. At least I have a complete change of clothes plus shoes. I run a bath and pour in half a bottle of scented, soapy looking stuff.

Lovely. The water's hot, soft and silky. Within five minutes I'm laid back surrounded by bubbles and sighing in ecstasy. The door opens and to my surprise in steps a young maid!

"'Scuse me, sir," giggles she grabbing the laundry basket. "My lady said I 'ad ter get yer clothes right away so they can be dried."

"Thank you. Please knock in future."

She goes off and I settle back down just as the door opens again and Jackson sticks his face in. "Do you want anything, sir? Hot beverage, something to eat?"

"Coffee and a hot pasty if there's any going, please." Plus, a little privacy thinks I. "And a scotch would be appreciated."

"There's alcoholic drinks in the drinks cabinet, sir. Please help yourself."

Settling down again I close my eyes while wondering what Betty is doing now. One thing's for certain she won't be missing me any more than I am missing her. I'm so bloody angry with her I feel like tramping back to the inn and having another go at her. What if she's cosying up to that Andrew or that drippy, Trout fellow? Touching my lip, I find the swelling has gone down. Trout might be an upper-class twit but he packed one devil of a punch, plus he took a headbutt but still managed to throw another punch. The trouble is, it is I who is to blame for the short but shoddy fracas, and it is I who will have to bear the consequences.

When I open my eyes again, I find Matilda sat on the edge of the bath just gazing at me. No, she's not there, I am dreaming. I'm also dreaming that the sleeves on her blouse are rolled up to her elbows, her hands and forearms are wet and it's not one of my big toes sticking up out of the water. All the bubbles have vanished and I am utterly exposed.

"You have a real man's body," says she all dreamily. "And a really beautiful…"

"What the hell do you think you are doing?" demands I covering my manhood. "Get out of this bathroom immediately!"

"Why?"

"Because you're not a dream! You're bloody here in real life!"

"I have been sitting here for ten minutes or so…"

"Doing what?"

"Just watching you. Why, what did you think I've been doing?"

I can't answer that one as I see her sleeves aren't rolled up, her arms are dry and the bubbles still cover my modesty. Not only that she is sat on a chair a good two feet away.

"You were dreaming, Inspector. Goodness knows what about, but whatever it was it caused you to cry out. Well more of a throaty groan to be exact."

"Even so, what on earth did you think you were doing coming in here, sitting down and watching me while I'm naked in my bath?"

"I brought you your coffee and pasty. Then I heard you cry out, and putting prudence aside I ventured in merely to check that you were alright. Which obviously you are. I'll leave you to get decent while I go and pour us a nice stiff drink. And hurry before your pasty gets cold."

I pull the plug and get out. Then I put the chair up against the door as there is no lock. Something I should have done earlier, but then I didn't think I was going to be invaded. Going over to the mirror and gazing into it I find bright red lipstick covers my mouth. Picking up a towel I can clearly see a damp patch where someone probably dried their hands? I've been sexually abused while asleep! What now? Pretend I have no recollection of anything because I was fast asleep and not in this world? Challenge her and demand an apology? Or go into the bedroom naked and ask her if she wants anymore? I plumb for dumb, because it rhymes. Washing the lipstick off, I dry off, get dressed and gingerly go into the bedroom.

Matilda, drink in hand, is calmly sat on a swivel chair by the dressing table gazing into the mirror. On a plate on a small table sits a sizable steaming pasty beside a pot of coffee. Beside that a tumbler of scotch. I pick up the scotch and take a chair by the writing desk to be as far away from her as possible. Spinning around she meets my eyes. Hers are full of mischief while I know mine are full of trepidation. This entire scenario is so ridiculously dangerous and thwart with dreadful repercussions it defies reasoning. I am lost for words.

"I'll bet you feel utterly free of stress right now, don't you Inspector?"

"I am dry, warm and content to drink my scotch, eat my pasty and then turn in, madam. Thank you for your kindness, but please leave right now while ensuring no one sees you."

"But you haven't explained yourself as yet. Why are you here when you should be elsewhere? You can talk to me in the strictest confidence, Inspector."

"Very well, but you are not going to like this."

Like it, she loved it. I had to put a hand over her mouth to stop her screaming out loud with laughter. She expressed her sorrow that Betty and I have fallen out, but my head-butting Trout filled her with glee. An hour later, and a few scotches too many, I finally persuade her to leave. By now I am not the least bit certain what happened while I was asleep. Perhaps all she did was give me a friendly peck on my lips?

"It has been delightful, Gerald," says she turning at the door to face me. "We must do it again soon."

I shake my head, "That wouldn't be a good idea, Miss."

"Why? Are you worried about getting too close to me because of my status?"

This brings a smile to my face, "No. Not in the least."

"What does worry you about our relationship?"

"We don't have a relationship, Miss. I am here to investigate crime and you are still a suspect. And I believe that what you are really doing is trying to win me over and take the heat off you and the constable."

She moves closer to me, tilting up her face, pouting her lips and challenging me with her dancing eyes. I should back away, but I can't move. "Please go, Miss."

"Kiss me."

"No."

"Hold me for a moment."

"No. Go!"

"Not until you kiss me." A finger traces my bottom lip, pausing at the still tender part. "At least allow me to kiss you better. Such a kiss that a sister might give to a loving brother. Or a daughter to a caring father. A mere peck and I shall be gone."

"Do you promise afterwards to go immediately?"

"I promise."

"Quickly then," says I pointing to the part to be kissed.

Clump Takes Over

Percy's bed was luxuriously comfortable, and I should have slept like a baby if it wasn't for thoughts of Matilda and Betty going around and around in my head. Matilda didn't plant her lips on mine, she glued them on and I struggled to get them unglued. The trouble was I enjoyed it far too much; feeling her body pressed up to mine, her arms so tight around my waste, the fervour of her endless kiss, so forceful, so demanding, until at last she broke away, turned and was gone.

Betty's accusing eyes haunted me throughout the night, despite telling myself I wouldn't have strayed if she hadn't have made it clear I wasn't wanted. I know I'm using this as an excuse to try and exonerate myself, just as I know that if this gets out my marriage is over along with my career. Whatever had possessed me?

I am up and dressed by eight o'clock. The sun is shining and the birds are singing. Percy's room looks out over the driveway. Gazing out I see Constable Burroughs cycling towards the castle. Picking up my bag, which has dried out, I step out into the hallway to come face to face with Smithers.

"Good morning, sir," says he. "Did you sleep well?"

"I did, Mr Smithers," lies I.

"The sleep of the innocent?" says he through judgemental eyes.

He knows! But will he keep it to himself?

"Chief Inspector Clump will see you in Mr Roberts office for ten o'clock, Inspector. Mrs Kemp will serve you breakfast in the servant's hall, if you so wish."

"Thank you, Mr Smithers. I must say I am famished."

"Your wet clothes have been fully laundered. You may pick them up from the laundry room at your convenience."

"Thank you."

A pair of chamber maids pushing a big square wicker basket on squeaking wheels head towards us.

"Marion and Sally will clean Lord Percy's room ready for the arrival of Lord Edward Marble and his wife Lady Claribel. Should you require a bed for tonight we can find you one in the servant's quarters, if that will suffice?" smiles Smithers.

"It would indeed, Mr Smithers." Despite himself, Smithers has made it clear that he would not have allowed me to stay above my station in an aristocrat's room had he gotten to me first. Making my way downstairs, I greet Jackson and Butler and then head down towards the servant's hall. The drawing room opens and out spills the 'bubbly-boos'. Yapping and tearing around they charge towards me followed by a miserable looking footman. Except for Henry, they go around me. Henry pauses, sniffs the air, disappointedly looks me up and down and then charges after the rest of the little brutes, who have already disappeared outside.

"Good morning, sir," sulks the footman.

"Good morning. Nice day for a walk."

"I have to pick up their droppings," winces he coming to a halt and holding up a hand that has hold of a small trowel and a small cloth bag. "We can't have the upper classes standing in shit, now can we, sir?"

"God forbids. At least you won't have to wipe their bottoms."

From the bag he pulls out a piece of cloth, pulls a face and walks off. I carry on to the kitchen and stick my head inside to find it buzzing. Mrs Kemp looks flustered as she catches my eye, but still she manages a smile before wiping a hand across her sweating brow.

"Ham, eggs and crusty bread, Inspector?"

"Sounds lovely."

"Tea, coffee, fruit juice?"

"Coffee please."

"Take a seat in the hall. Ten minutes."

I thank her and go into the empty hall where I take the opportunity to look at more of the photographs on the wall. Rose and Chambers killer will almost certainly be somewhere amongst them. They say the camera never lies. I know that if you cover up one eye on someone's portrait, and then change to the other you will see a different perspective of that person's inner traits. You may be surprised, even horrified at what doing this will reveal. Certainly, it is a window into the soul. It is not infallible, but from past experience of covering the eyes in turn from the mug shots of violent criminals, it really can help you to understand what kind of person you are dealing with. Someone appears nice and ordinary, until you look into their eyes one at a time and begin to question just exactly who you are dealing with.

"Breakfast, sir," calls a voice.

Turning I find Rosy Roper holding a tray with all I require on it. I take a seat where I can see anyone who comes in or goes out.

Rosy sets the tray down in front of me, "Anything else, sir?"

"Not just yet, thank you, Rosy. Have you remembered anything else since we last spoke? Anything at all?"

"Nothing, sir," says she blushing.

"Out with it, Rosy."

She starts wringing her hands and then leans closer to me, "I don't know nuthin' for true, sir, but it came to mind that Rose had said she'd got a secret to keep. A scandalous secret, but she wouldn't say what it was as she'd promised."

"Promised who?"

She shrugs, "She wouldn't say."

"When was this?"

"Up in our room the night she run off."

"Did she seem worried or upset about having to keep this secret?"

"Not really. She seemed to think it was a giggle."

"And she'd never mentioned this before that night?

Rosy shakes her head.

Mrs Kemps voice bellows out, "Rosy Roper, where are you?"

"I must go, sir."

"Thank you, Rosy. In future come and see me immediately should you remember anything else. Is that understood?"

Tucking into my breakfast I ponder over this new piece of evidence. A scandalous secret? Being a chamber maid, Rose would witness all sorts while going about her business. The wrong person going in or coming out of the wrong room. Finding something that belonged to someone other than the person whose room it was. She giggled about it so it's probably a sex secret. What did she witness and did it lead to her death? Trouble is it might be related to servants with nothing to do with the family and subsequently has no relevance to the case. But then?

I'm just running my bread around the plate when Head walks in.

"Good morning, Gerald," says he sitting down across from me.

"Morning, Richard. How is everything?"

"All is fine. Chloe's relaxed and comfortable."

"And Betty, has she left yet?"

"No. She's staying for Chloe's sake."

"Good."

"But did you know we've only got the room for tonight? We have to leave by nine in the morning as it was fully booked for this weekend before we even arrived."

"I didn't know that. We'll have to find alternative accommodation. We could try the Rams Head."

"Also fully booked according to the landlord at the Smugglers."

"Well we'll have to find somewhere. Perhaps they'll put us up here in the stables."

Mrs Kemp sticks her head in, "Oh… Good morning, Sergeant. Do you require anything?"

"Good morning, Mrs Kemp. Coffee and a …"

"Plate of biscuits," grins she. "Anything more for you, Inspector?"

"No thank you, Mrs Kemp. That was delicious."

"I like a man who appreciates his food," smiles she. "Must get on."

"This place smells like heaven," slavers Head sniffing the air. "Roast beef on the spit. Ham boiling…"

"Did Betty say anything about our row?" cuts in I.

"She spoke a lot to Chloe. They stayed up late while I went up early as I had a lot of farting to do."

"I'm not surprised the amount of food you've been stuffing down you of late. Anyway, what did you find out?"

"About what?"

"Me and Betty!"

"Um… Nothing much. Chloe wouldn't tell me much. She said the conversation was between her and Betty and in the strictest confidence, and if Gerald asks, I'm to tell you to go and talk to Betty or to go boil your head."

"That's it? Didn't you grill her?"

"Cause, I bloody didn't. Look, Gerald, whatever's going on between you and Betty you'd best try and sort it out yourselves. I don't want me and Chloe ending up porkers in the middle."

"Pigs!"

"No need to be rude."

"No. it's piggy's in the middle not porkers."

"Whatever," sighs he. "How did you get on last night?"

"Fine. I ended up in Percy's room."

"Of course, you did," scoffs he. "And no doubt Matilda payed you a visit in the middle of the night and jumped into bed with you."

"Actually, she turned up earlier than that."

"And then you woke up."

"Something like that. Honestly, I did sleep in Percy's bed."

"Well I never."

Rosy comes in with a tray and sets it down in front of Head and then hurries away.

"To the business in hand," says I watching Head shovelling biscuits down his throat.

He swallows hard, "What business?"

"The murders!"

"Yes of course. The murders."

"Any new thoughts on the case, Richard?"

He shakes his head. "None. I've gone over everything we've learnt ready for Clumps grilling but can't think of anything new. What about you?"

I relate what Rosy told me but he's too busy hoovering up his biscuits and chucking down his coffee to listen.

"Did you see that Trout bloke at breakfast this morning?"

"I did."

"Did he try and flirt with Betty?"

"No. He stayed well away from her as did that sulky young waiter. Trout was sporting a bruised nose and two not so black eyes. He looked a right sod."

"I should have butted him a lot harder."

"You shouldn't have butted him at all, Gerald. It'll come back on you; you know that."

"I do," sighs I. "Anyway, finish up it's time to meet Clump."

Clump is sat behind Robert's desk with Constable Burroughs sat opposite.

"Ten minutes early," says Clump. "Good men. Take a seat."

We exchange pleasantries before Clump hands over to Burroughs.

"Inquest on Monday," says Burroughs. "Ten o'clock in the village hall. The coroner will be from Truro. I will inform everyone who must attend. John Chambers funeral is on Tuesday in Truro. Details." He hands me a small envelope. "Rose's funeral on Wednesday at two thirty, at the village church."

"Thank you, Constable," sighs Clump. "We shall of course attend the inquest and both funerals. Let us hope we have netted our killer before the first funeral so we can have something more joyous to look forward to. Namely a hanging. Right. Any questions about anything at all before we continue?"

I put up my hand, "We have nowhere to stay after tonight, Chief."

"You do now. You will be staying in the castle tomorrow night, because a few quests have sent telegrams to say they won't be attending festivities due to sickness and diarrhoea. Which is a load of old crap, if you'll excuse the pun. It is obvious that as we have a killer amongst us the cowards have jumped overboard. Smithers has been informed and you are both to have lesser rooms on the main floor where the more important guests will be staying. Everyone will feel much more secure knowing three of the Yards finest are amongst them. Anything else?"

We shake our heads.

"Good. Firstly, the constable and I have had a heart to heart. His relationship with my niece is over and from now on he will not meet with her anywhere, or at any time unless someone else is present, on pain of receiving my boot up his backside, and the loss of his position. Everything we say between us will be kept strictly between us unless I sanction it first. Is that clear to you?"

We nod.

"Good. I want the constable in on this meeting because he may have valuable information that he hasn't as yet realised may be of importance. Not only that," he shoots Burroughs an accusing glare, "He is still very much in the frame until we can prove for certain he had nothing whatsoever to do with the killings. Now to Percy. He will be attending the celebrations…"

"Percy won't leave his cell, sir," says I.

"He will once I've had a word with him and stuck my boot up his rotten arse, the blackmailing snake. Lady Constance wants him to attend, and attend he shall, unless we find out something that leads us to believe he had something to do with the killings. Right. Let's have a drink. Robert has slipped a fine large bottle of scotch in the draw for us to keep our spirits up." He grins broadly. "Keep our spirits up. Do you get it?"

We all laugh, but not too much.

"Or are you two still abstaining before lunch?"

Head and I shake our heads, but I note Burroughs doesn't appear too happy at the thought of drinking so early. But then he's probably only ever drunk cider.

A single malt appears along with four tumblers, "Like old times," says Clump as if we hadn't met up for years.

Over the next three hours, Burroughs, Head and I relate all we have learnt to Clump. Chalking up suspects along with motives onto a large blackboard helped us to see the picture more clearly, and made it easier to link whatever, with whoever and whenever.

Sandwiches and coffee are delivered dead on one and we take a break. Having emptied the scotch between us, I for one am feeling rather tired, while Head is unusually happy and Burroughs can barely put a sentence together, while Clump is still very much in charge of his faculties, if a little slurred in his speech.

"Right, lads. Once we have finished eating, we'll go for a nice little walk to clear our heads and give ourselves time to stink, or even think. I am convinced that our killer is on that blackboard, and we need to eliminate as many of the suspects as we can to enable us to concentrate on whoever is left in the frame."

Lunch over we follow Clump out into the corridor to find the place deserted. So much for all the coming and going. Just as we near the drawing room the door fly's open and out charge the 'bubbly boos' with Henry out in front. On seeing Head approaching, Henry lets out a yelp of joy and goes for it, clamping himself onto Heads leg before you can spit.

"What on earth?" growls Clump. "Sergeant, get that hound off your leg immediately."

"I can't, sir short of killing the bastard!"

Clump takes a small bottle of something from his jacket pocket. He unscrews the top and chucks whatever's inside onto Henry's nose. Henry jumps backwards off Heads leg with an ear shattering yelp, then rolls and twists all over the floor like a demented snake while furiously scrabbling at his nose with his paws. Then he's up on his feet and tearing off as if his balls are on fire.

"Pepper," winks Clump screwing the top back on the bottle before putting it away. "Always carry a small amount of pepper with you, gentlemen, it will subdue even the most vicious cur or violent criminal when thrown in their faces. Had pepper thrown into my face a while back. Evil it was. Incapable of even farting for at least ten minutes."

I pray my face hasn't turned red. Heads has, but he can put it down to embarrassment.

"Onwards, men," says Clump with a forward wave.

It has clouded over but very warm as we follow Clump around to the rear of the castle. Passing the dining room, I spy the family inside enjoying lunch. Matilda waves at me, I smile back not daring to wave. Clump throws her a nod, a wobbling on his feet Burroughs doesn't notice and Head farts. Luckily, he's bringing up the rear.

Around back there are all kind of carts and delivery waggons parked up and a good many people milling or rushing around. A huge marque is in the process of being erected on the lawn along with a few fairground rides and stalls. Clump swings away and heads towards the stalls.

"Bloody charlatans," growls he. "Well I'll not have them cheating the poor folk around here and marring my niece's big day. Follow me men."

We were anyway, even so we mutter out a, 'Right, sir'. Clump marches over to a stocky, short bruiser who's busy putting coconuts into cups on chest height spikes.

"A word my good man," slurs Clump.

Spinning around the bruiser fixes Clump with hard eyes, "Do what, me handsome?"

"Pass me a coconut," demands Clump.

"What for?"

"Never mind what for. Hand one over."

"Look, Mr whoever yer are, I'm not open 'till tomorrow so bugger off and leave me ter get on."

"I am a Detective Chief Inspector and these are my junior officers. I intend to ensure that you stall people are genuine and not charlatans. Now if you wish to ply your trade here you will comply with my wishes, or you can clear up and clear off. Do you understand me?"

"No. But, I aren't about ter argue with no coppers, 'specially when I'm out numbered."

He passes Clump a coconut. Clump shakes it against his ear and then nods before dropping it on the ground and violently stamping his foot down onto it, causing it to shoot out and fly several feet away. "All good," says he through gritted teeth before limping to the next stall and demanding to no one. "Who's in charge of this darts stall?"

"I am," grates the bruiser appearing behind the frontage. "What now?"

Picking up a dart Clump waves it around in our faces. "You couldn't stick a fairground dart into a cow pat most times, they're that blunt. Hence the reason they're forever hitting the target and falling out."

Burroughs chooses this moment to make the mistake of sort of bending over, and then attempting to place a hand on the grass to stop himself falling on his face, thus presenting his rear end to Clump.

"Ah… Well volunteered, Constable," beams Clump before stabbing the dart into Burroughs' left buttock.

"Fuck was that," slurs Burroughs before collapsing on the grass and rolling over onto his back. "I've been stabbed in the arse."

"Good," says Clump. "Nice and sharp. Right, what's next?" He casts a beady eye along to the next stall which has western style Winchester rifles laid on the frontage. "Ah… The inevitable wild west shooting range. Who's in charge here?"

"I am," grates the bruiser. "But yer not firin' no rifles today 'cause I left the bullets at 'ome. Come back tomorrow."

"Load one up or else," says Clump picking up one of the very short barrelled rifles to find it is chained down, and won't allow you to swing it further than a foot in any direction. "Safety procedures in place. Good man. Hurry up with that bullet, I haven't got all bloody day."

"Yer a bloody sodden nuisance," growls Bruiser. "An' yer bloody drunk! Right, I'll give yer one bullet if yer promise to piss off an' leave me be."

"I promise," smiles Clump.

Bruiser slips a very small calibre bullet into the rifle. "Just yer aim at them little metal indjuns only, don't yer dare aim for them prizes. Do yer understand me?"

"Man talk through him arse," chuckles Clump before taking up a new kind of shooting position that's probably never been seen before in the annals of any military training academy anywhere in the civilised world. He's kneeling down with one arm flopped over the frontage while the other wrestles the rifle into his shoulder. "Inspector, remove my hat."

I whip off his hat and hold on to it.

"Right. Aim. Gently squeeze the trigger and FIRE…"

"A brilliant shot, sir" grins Head as the bullet hits a wooden dolly right between the eyes and splits her head in half.

"Yer prat!" snaps Bruiser. "Yer can't shoot fer bleedin' toffee apples."

Clump struggles up to his feet and sets the rifle down. He is definitely pissed. "I would say that was an excellent shot, wouldn't you, Inspector?"

"I would indeed, sir," lies I.

"Pass me my prize, my good man," says he to Bruiser.

"Yer ain't won nuffin'. Yer owe me for that dolly. They don't grow on ruddy trees them wooden dolly's yer know. Some poor sod 'as ter buy 'em."

Clump rummages around in his trouser pockets and takes out a handful of loose change, "How would a nice shiny new sixpence do you?"

"Alright I suppose," sulks Bruiser snatching the coin. "Now piss off an' leave me be."

"Right men, help the constable up on his feet it's time to get back to work."

Settling back in the office, with coffee delivered by Butler, the first question Clump asks is addressed to Burroughs, "Why are you sat with just one bum cheek on that chair, Constable? Sit on it properly."

"My left buttock hurts too much, sir. I think I've been stung by a giant bee or something."

"Never mind, Constable. At least it sobered you up. Sergeant, pour the coffee and let's get on. Rose and Chambers were killed because Rose knew something about the killer. If so, then that something must have been one devil of a secret, that obviously, had to be covered up at all costs. But we don't know what that secret was or who it concerned, thus leaving us nowhere. Plus of course, the secret might not be connected to the family and is merely a concern for some servant or other who Rose caught doing something untoward. Your thoughts?"

"I agree, sir," says I. "But should Rose have found out about any of Percy's blackmailing activities, anyone of the family, servants or outsiders, like the landlord of The Rams Head, could have orchestrated the killings to keep their secret. Smuggling can carry a long jail sentence."

"Agreed," says Clump pausing to light up a cigar. "However, I do not believe anyone we know of, who's being blackmailed by Percy, would go to such extreme lengths to have their secret kept hidden."

"I still think, sir," cuts in Head, "that the answer to the killings lays within these four walls and no one from outside has anything to do with it. It stands to reason that there's no way the landlord from The Rams Head could have lured Rose and Chambers out into the country side, and then topped them so expertly, because he's usually too bleedin' drunk to stand up properly, let alone fire arrows in the dark."

"And he's got big feet," says Burroughs. "he couldn't have worn those size nine and a halves the killer wore."

"So, for now we'll put aside the conjecture regarding, Rose's secret," says Clump. "I also believe we should, for now, put aside the blackmailing theories and look for another reason for the killings. Like…?"

"I ask myself, sir," says I. "Why do people kill? For money, for love, hate, power, jealousy or to save themselves. If I thought someone was trying to kill me then I'd make damn sure I got to them first."

"Which brings us back to my reprobate of a nephew. Before Claude confessed to shoving that block of stone off the roof the finger of suspicion pointed at Rose. She was the only one, or so it seemed, who had a golden unwitnessed opportunity to try and kill Percy."

"And if we could reason that Rose was the number one suspect, then slippery Percy would easily come up with the same, providing someone was keeping him updated on events."

"Having nearly lost his life Percy was going to make certain Rose didn't get another chance. Either he carried out the killings or he had someone else do his dirty work. Boots?"

I take a sip of my coffee. "Boots. Percy could probably fit in the boots worn by the killer."

"Bows and arrows?"

"Percy's an expert shot," says Burroughs.

"Opportunity," says Clump blowing smoke in Heads face.

"He can let himself out of his cell whenever he wants and go off and do whatever he wants."

"To even commit murder" sighs Clump. "And then to plant evidence to lay suspicion on his own father. Claude gets done for the killings and even if he escapes the rope, he won't escape the looney bin and losing his title. Percy becomes the new earl. And if the boots don't fit Percy, then perhaps he did have an accomplice."

"I think he must have had an accomplice anyway, sir, "says I. "Someone knew Rose and Chambers intended running. Maybe that someone even orchestrated their running by scaring them into believing that once we arrived, we'd quickly believe the only person who could have tried to kill Percy was Rose, and that Rose would then find herself up on an attempted murder charge with Chambers up on an aiding and abetting."

Clump downs his coffee, dumps his butt in the cup and gets to his feet. "Constable, stay here and write up notes on what's been said while we go and pay my nephew a long overdue visit."

"I would like to come if I can, sir."

"No. You are too prejudiced towards my nephew, Constable and may not maintain your professional standards as a result of that prejudice. Besides, I don't know you well enough to trust that you'll keep your trap shut should you witness anything untoward. Whereas with these buggers," he waves a hand across our chests, "can be relied upon to keep shut and lie through there anuses should the need arise. Right, Sergeant, grab a chair and let's go."

"A word, sir," says I once we are out in the corridor.

"What is it, Inspector?"

"Smithers."

"What about him?"

"I think he is rogering the countess. Every time she gets a bit stressed, she and Smithers disappear up to her bedroom for an obvious quickie. I also think that Rose found out and it was Smithers who scared Rose and Chambers into running for it. Maybe he even manipulated Percy into tracking and killing the couple. Smithers then set about trying to frame Claude…"

Clump doesn't look too happy as he stares goggle eyed at me, "Evidence?"

"Roses part note: I think he's evil, suggests she previously thought he was the opposite. Someone she could trust. Just as Percy and everyone else who knows Smithers trusts him implicitly. The man's just too good to be true, sir."

"I agree," puts in Head.

"Well I don't!" snaps Clump. "Ronald Smithers has an impeccable record. Not a stain upon his character, ever. He can be a bit up himself at times but other than that the man is an absolute jewel. However, everyone has secrets. Smithers has never married and I'll give you one guess as to the why?"

"He's got a wonky willy," says Head deadpan.

"One day, Sergeant you will push me too far!" snaps Clump shaking a fist in Heads face. "Smithers will never look at any woman the way you, randy sods would, and has had no thoughts of ever marrying since he lost his one and only true love over thirty years ago."

"What happened to her?" asks Head.

"All anyone knows is that he lost her, so shut up asking. You, Inspector are misplaced as to the reason Smithers goes upstairs with the countess, every time she has a headache. Smithers used to be in the merchant navy many years back. He travelled the world, but unlike the usual sailor, instead of spending his hard-earned money on booze and brothel creeping he spent his on learning about the cultures and mysteries of those foreign lands. In Asia he leant the soothing art of head massage."

"What, how to kill nits?"

"Bugger off, Sergeant and wait for us at the top of the dungeon stairs," growls Clump.

"Ah… but," says I. "Don't you think Smithers is just too perfect, sir?"

"At times, yes. Look, Inspector, this has been Smithers home for over twenty years. He has progressed from a trainee footman to the most important servant in the castle. He's well payed and enjoys a good many privileges other servants can only dream of. The man is besotted with his life and would probably kill himself should he lose his position. Not only that, I do not believe Rose would have giggled about this secret if it concerned Smithers and the countess. No, sir! She would have been horrified by it all. I knew Rose, she was fairly level headed for a girl. Trust me on this, you are on the wrong track. Let's get on.

Torturing Percy

Head is waiting at the top of the stairs, "All's quiet, sir," whispers he to Clump.

"It won't be for long," hisses Clump. "Allow me to do the talking and institute the rough stuff, lads. That way nothing can come back on you. Follow me."

Like a trio of cats on the hunt we descend the stairs. Clump goes up to the cell door while Head and I stand to the side out of site of the grille. Clump raps on the door.

"Is that you, Smithers?" sounds Percy.

"No, dear nephew. It is I, your Uncle Arthur."

"Are you alone?"

"I am."

"Is that the honest truth?"

"Would I lie to you?"

The door is unlocked and slowly opened. "At last," says Percy. "I thought you'd never get here, Uncle Arthur."

"You'll wish I hadn't by the time I finish with you!" growls Clump.

Percy doesn't answer and it's easy to see why as we come out from hiding, one handed Clump has Percy by the throat and is forcing him back into the room. Percy's eyes are wide open in terror and he is completed subdued. Head and I follow on in. Clump shoves Percy backwards so hard he lands on his bed. I close the door.

"What's this, Uncle?" pleads Percy "Why have you brought your dogs with you?"

"In case I run out of energy and need someone to take over. On your feet, Percy. Face me like a real man or I'll beat the guts out of you where you lay."

Percy scrambles to his feet, he is visibly shaking but his eyes are furiously defiant. "A sneaky act even for you, Uncle. How dare you trick your way into my home and start throwing your weight about? Have you forgotten that I am a peer of the fucking realm?"

"I have," grins Clump. "And for now, I am also forgetting that you and I are related. We can do this any way you want, Percy. Answer my questions with honesty and civility or answer them screaming. Which do you prefer?"

"I haven't heard the questions yet so I can't answer that one," sneers he.

Clump sticks his chin out, "Do not play your childish games with me, you piece of shit. We know all about your blackmailing activities. We also have good reason to suspect you are behind Rose Bush and John Chamber's murders. What say you to all this?"

"I deny everything! So, clear off before you find yourself excommunicated from this family and cast out amongst the swine. Oh… and take this pair of prats with you."

"It's to be the hard way then," mocks Clump. "Lord Percy refuses to cooperate while daring to threaten me with his exalted position. Pop that in your notes, Sergeant."

"As a no comment from the suspect?"

"Exactly. Last chance, Percy. Easy or hard? Take your pick."

Backing up a foot Percy scowls, "It's Lord Percy to you. Now I warn you, Arthur Clump for the last time, fuck off with your monkey's or face the inevitable consequences."

Clump's fist flies out and punches Percy right between the eyes, but knowing Clump as I do it was barely half the power of his usual. Still it is enough to knock Percy off his feet and send him crashing back onto the little table before he rolls off onto the floor. Clump leaps forwards, grabs Percy by his poncey smoking jacket, hauls him half way up onto his feet and then slams him back onto a chair.

Percy's hands cover his nose as blood seeps through his fingers, "You've broke my dose," splutters he.

"Start answering my questions or I'll break your fucking neck as well," snarls Clump. "Sergeant, open up a bottle of wine."

"Any preference, sir?"

"The cheapest. Inspector, find something to tie this piece of shit to the chair."

Looking around I spy a dressing gown cord and hand it over.

"Right, wrench his hands behind his back and cuff him."

I do so as Clump ties the cord around Percy's stomach and the chair. Percy glares up at his uncle then spits out blood at him only to receive a slap across his face.

"The wine, Chief," says Head. "How many glasses do you want?"

Clump shoots him the, don't be stupid look, and Head hands him the bottle.

"What are you going to do, Uncle?" implores Percy.

"We are going to get you drunk, Nephew. Pull his head back."

Grabbing him by his mop and scruffy beard, I wrench his head back. Head steps forward and pinches Percy's nose shut. Percy tries to put up a fight, kicking his legs about, twisting his body and trying to shake off my hold on his head. His mouth opens and he gasps for air which allows Head to grab his jaws and force them wide open. Clump raises the bottle and begins to pour the wine slowly down Percy's throat. Percy's, Adams apple is going up and down like a yoyo, he chokes a bit, snorts blood from his nose but easily swallows. Clump ups the torture by pinching Percy's nose shut and then increasing the amount of wine poured down his throat. Unable to breathe through his nose, Percy's eyes say it all, he is now terrified as he struggles to swallow and take in air. He starts to choke and has gone rigid, unable to move, his eyes tell me he feels as if he's drowning. At last Clump stops. Head and I release our holds.

"I will ask you again, Percy," says Clump. "Do you wish to answer my questions the hard…?"

"Alright!" chokes Percy. "I will answer the easy way. But damn you, you bastards. You have tortured me and shall pay dearly for it. You are nothing but a common thug, Uncle. You belong in the gutter with your…"

We wrench his head back again, "Alright! I yield."

"Good," smiles Clump. "Sergeant open a bottle of the good stuff and get four glasses."

"I've had enough," hiccups Percy.

"No… you haven't. Well not until I say so. Untie him and take off the cuffs, Inspector."

I do so. Percy rubs his wrists and stretches his back. He is as a white as a sheet, blood is splattered all around his nose and down to his hairy chin. Other than that, he doesn't look too bad all things considered. Head opens the bottle and we gather around the table.

"A toast," says Clump, raising his glass. "To Rose and John. May justice be served."

"Rose and John," toasts Head and I.

"I didn't have anything to do with their murders," says Percy. "As God is my witness."

"We'll come to that later," frowns Clump. "Sergeant, open the door and let some air into this shit hole. It smells like a sewer."

"That's because Smithers hasn't been around today to empty the shit bucket," says Percy.

"He's too busy ensuring everything's being done properly for tomorrow," says Clump. "Now be a good boy, Percy and answer my questions honestly or we'll be emptying your bucket down your throat. Do you understand me?"

"Yes, Uncle."

"Good lad. Let's start at the attempted murders. Attempts one and two were a load of old rubbish so that you could steal the rent money, correct?"

He nods, "Just jolly japes. A bit of fun. But attempt three was genuine. I nearly got killed! And now that I know it was that old fool who was behind it, I shall be getting even with him. What a rotten swine to try and kill his own son."

"Can't say I blame him," grates Head. "If I was your father, I'd have drowned you at birth."

"Enough!" snaps Clump. "Sergeant, take your chair over by the door, take notes and keep lookout. We don't want any earwigs sneaking around and listening in."

"Earwigs?" puzzles Head.

"You know what I mean. Percy, let us talk first about your blackmailing endeavours. Mrs Kemp, explain yourself."

"I caught her swilling down wine from our cellar one night in the kitchen some months ago. I said she better watch out or she'd lose her position and could be up on a charge of theft."

"So, you began blackmailing her for sex?"

"Not exactly. Look here, Uncle, do you think a man in my position would even contemplate blackmailing a mere servant for sex, nor less a woman old enough to be my mother? Of course, I wouldn't. Besides I wanted money, but she wouldn't give me any. Instead she offered me sex on a regular basis. And as nothing else was forthcoming, I took her up on her offer."

"Your trying to tell us Mrs kemp is happy with this disgusting arrangement?" grates I.

He nods, "Why else would she sneak down here two or three times a week in the middle of the night? Not to bring me ruddy cakes either, I might add."

"Good grief," says Clump. "Rest assured I shall ask her whether or not you are telling me lies, Percy…"

"Do so, Uncle."

Clump shakes his head in amazement, "Reginald Freeman from The Rams Head."

"Everyone knows, Regi' is a smuggler, Uncle. Truth be told we all love him for it. Top chap is Regi'"

"Top chap or not you are still blackmailing him."

"Not exactly. Regi' started blackmailing me. I hadn't paid my bar bill…"

"I find it hard to believe you'd drink in a peasants pub," says I.

"Why ever not. I love it there and they love me."

"I doubt that," growls Clump. "Continue."

"Regi' said he'd forget about my bar bill, and would supply me with a few bottles of wine every week, providing I got the castle to purchase their wines and spirits from him. He wanted to up his quota from the froggies, as he needed to make more money because he was drinking away the profits himself. Ask him if you don't believe me."

"We shall," groans Clump. He empties his glass and refills it. "Drink up lads there's plenty more on offer. Elizabeth. How on earth could anyone blackmail their own sister, Percy?"

"I have no idea, Uncle."

"But you must have you bastard. We have it on good authority that you are blackmailing her."

"Not exactly. Lizzy as you no doubt know, as you seem to know every bloody thing, is rubbing bodies with her personal maid, that Thornberry gal. They are in love or so she says. They would like to have a baby, but as everyone knows a hen needs a cock to get pregnant. Guess who's cock my sister wanted?"

"Stop!" yells Clump. "Good God man are there no bottoms to your depths of depravity? Do you honestly think we would believe that your sister wanted you to give her a baby?"

For the first time since we've been here, Percy appears utterly flummoxed.

"I think, sir that Miss Elizabeth wanted Percy to mate with Miss Thornberry."

"I fucking hope so!"

"I say, Uncle," titters Percy. "Dear God you got that bugger wrong. I may be a cad, sir, but even I wouldn't commit incest. Well I might do if I had a sister who looked like that actress, what's her name?"

"Fuck the what's her name actress. Continue."

"Anyway, Lizzy offered me money to shag Thornberry until she was pregnant. Normally I would carry out such tasks free of charge, but in Thornberry's case I would have declined unless I was paid serious compensation for my efforts."

"Why so?" pipes up Head. "Doesn't a man like you happily help himself for no payment?"

"Open up another bottle, Sergeant," orders Clump. "Then get on with your notes. You are not helping. Percy, continue. What is wrong with Miss Thornberry apart from being built like a battle ship?"

"Thornberry is more man then most men I know, Uncle. She can fell an ox with one punch, and it's rumoured she once entered the caber tossing while on holiday up in Scotland and beat all comers. Apparently, one instantly love-struck Jock begged her to marry him, only to receive such a kick beneath his sporran, his haggis' shot out of his mouth and ended up hanging on top of a Scot's pine like some kind of strange fairy on a Christmas tree!"

"Heaven help us," grins Clump obviously trying not to laugh.

Percy, if nothing else is hugely entertaining, but how much truth is in anything he says is seriously open to debate.

"So," grins Clump. "Did you or did you not take up Elizabeth's offer?"

"I had to. A man with my reputation for being a serious shagger could do nothing less. The plan was set. I was to go to Thornberry's room every night for one week and do the business. On entering her room, I found Thornberry attired in a pure white lacy nightdress while laid back on her bed like a hog in mud. Her eyes were closed, her arms crooked, hands behind her head and her trunky legs spread wide. I tried to make small talk by saying: 'Good evening, madam, how goes it?' Opening her eyes, she said: 'Get on with it, you maggot or I'll twist your winkle until the blood in it spurts onto the ceiling.' 'You are not into this arrangement, are you?' said I. 'I hate men!' spat she. 'But unfortunately, they are required in the breeding process. Rest assured, could I have done it with a beautiful stallion in place of a maggot like you, I would have done so. Now, get it over with as quickly as possible.' 'I fear, madam,' said I. 'The moment is lost and I shall have to return at a later date.' Thus, I escaped only to be forced to return the next night. But, by then I had hit on a plan so deviously clever it would have had an archbishop bowing before me. Having taken myself in hand, so to speak, before the intended breeding session, I had said necessary fluid in a syringe, ask not how I got it in there. I found Thornberry exactly as I had found her the night before. With the speed of a flash of lightning I squirted said fluid up her orifice, and then went to beat a hasty retreat. 'Is that it?' demanded she. 'It is,' returned I. 'Knew it,' scoffed she. 'When having sex with men do not blink or you will miss it.' I continued with this method until the week was up. Lizzy paid me and three months on I am pleased to say Thornberry is well and truly up the pudding. However, whether it is mine, a stallion's or a pig's will be open to conjecture until the little brute arrives."

"Let us take a break," puffs out Clump as he gets to his feet. "Percy, stay sat. Detectives, outside please."

We trail out and stand out of earshot of Percy.

"Is he lying or telling the truth, Sergeant?"

"Most of what he's said, sir, came straight out of his arse."

"Inspector?"

I shrug, "I'm not convinced either way, sir."

Clump scratches at his beard and appears very pensive. "Nor I, Inspector. Go and see Gloria. Quiz her and see if she'll corroborate Percy's story."

"I could do that, sir," says Head.

"Obviously you are not getting your oats at the moment, Sergeant. And you won't be getting any through Glory. Besides you'd no doubt be as subtle as a rampaging bull chasing a cow. Off you go, Inspector. The sergeant and I will make small talk with Percy until your return."

Finding the noisy kitchen in chaos, I do my best to skirt around dozens of flustered, rushing around servants in my search for Gloria, only she's nowhere to be seen.

Billy Roper suddenly comes into view carrying a huge leg of pork. I grab him by the shoulder, "Where's, Mrs Kemp?"

"She went off ter the wine cellar wiv that French chef," pants he.

"What for?"

He looks at me askance, "Don't know."

His reddening cheeks say different. "I think you do, Billy."

"Alright, I do. But I ain't sayin' because it's a secret."

"Tuppence says you will tell me."

"He's probably givin' her one over the wine tasting table. That's all I got ter say."

Fishing out a couple of pennies I hand them over, Billy grabs them and runs off. I make my way to the wine cellar just as Gloria and a tall thin fellow, wearing a ridiculously high chef's hat, are coming up the stone steps. Gloria is straightening up her piny while the chef is smugly curling his thin waxed moustache. Nether notice me until they reach the top. Gloria jumps with surprise.

"Oh… Inspector. I was showing Pierre our stock of wine so he knows what's on offer."

"Que, Mrs kemp is very good at showing me what's on offer," says he with a grin.

"No doubt," grates I. "Can I have a quick word with you, Mrs Kemp?"

"I'm very busy. Can't it wait until later?"

I shake my head and give Pierre the piss off look.

"How often do you go and visit Percy down in the dungeon?"

Her cheeks have turned so red they look as if they'll burst into flames.

"A woman has her needs, Inspector. I just need more than most as I often get very lonely now my Jim has gone."

"I thought you hated Percy?"

She drops her head for a second before facing me with defiance in her eyes. "I do hate him. He's the nastiest most useless man I've ever known. But, everyone's good at something, if you get what I'm saying. I go and see him two to three times a week at around midnight when no one's likely to see me."

"Thank you for your honesty, Mrs Kemp. That's all for now."

"Will you keep this to yourself, Inspector?"

"As much as I possibly can."

"I suppose you think I'm a terrible tart?"

"Mrs Kemp, I am not here to judge you. Let those who are without guilt throw the first rock cake."

"I must get on, Inspector."

"And I also." I watch her hurry away and ponder on the certainty that if Head had been here in place of me, Gloria would have been back down in the cellar and on the table before she'd even had time to say au revoir to Pierre. Which leads me to wonder if Clump already knew that Gloria was a woman of certain needs. I head back to the dungeon.

Ribald laughter fills the air as I descend the steps to Percy's cell. Even, Head is laughing. Percy truly is an entertainer.

"Ah… Inspector," says Clump. "We've just opened another bottle of red. Grab a seat and let us get on. Any luck with, Gloria?"

"She admitted to voluntarily coming to see Percy two or three times a week for sex in the middle of the night."

"There you are, Uncle, I told you the truth."

"You did indeed, Percy. But that doesn't mean I am about to believe everything you say, however entertaining it might be. Algernon. Are you or are you not blackmailing him because you found out he has been stealing valuable books from various libraries?"

"Not exactly. Believe it or not I enjoy a good read, particularly if it is racy. Therefore, I often poke around in the castle book store in my quest for erotic enlightenment. Often, I have come across certain books on the ancient scholars that weren't there previously. Inside those books they usually bear a stamp saying to which library they belong, and it isn't ours. Obviously, Algernon had snaffled the buggers from elsewhere. I confronted him with my findings a few years back. He went into a panic and offered to make me a deal should I turn the proverbial blind eye. In short he also pinches really dirty books for yours truly to keep me compliant and on side."

"He's supplying you with dirty books?" amazes Head. "How dirty is dirty?"

"Pretty damn dirty," says Percy nodding with enthusiasm. "You wouldn't want your granny to see them, it might give the old duck a heart attack."

"Any pictures?" asks Head in hope.

"Enough," snaps Clump. "May I remind you, Sergeant we are conducting a serious interview here and not on a self-titillation bloody exercise that could end up turning you blind. Percy, do you ever demand money from Algernon to keep quiet about his book crimes?"

Percy shakes his head, "The bugger wouldn't hand it over anyway. He's so bloody tight he never farts because he can't bear giving away free gas."

Clump roars with laughter, throwing back his head and pushing the chair back onto its hind legs he looks about to topple over. Which he does with a crash, but still he keeps laughing. Head is grinning and I must admit I'm struggling not to laugh. I help Clump back up onto his chair.

"Fill my glass," chuckles Clump. "Fill them all up."

Head does the honours, only he's a bit sloshed and the wine flows over the top which sets everyone off. Now things are getting really serious because we are all becoming rather endeared to Percy, while realizing his jolly japes might not be so sinister after all.

"The Reverend Hardpuzzle," says Clump before he splutters and then breaks into hiccupping laughter.

"The, the, Reverend Hardpizzle," giggles Head.

"Pizzle!" roars Percy. "Only God knows why a bull has a cock as long and thick as a fence post, while us mere mortals are lucky if we get one as big as a butcher's banger."

That's it for me, I'm up on my feet and heading for the exit before I choke to death or collapse from a heart attack, I'm laughing that much.

Ten minutes later, having all calmed down and returned to reality, Clump resumes the interview. We are obviously no longer so much as torturing Percy, as asking him questions as if he was an old friend who'd found himself in a compromising situation that wasn't entirely his fault.

"For what reason are you blackmailing the, the, the?" goes on Clump as obviously he can't bear to the say the vicar's stupid name without pissing himself.

"I'm not exactly blackmailing him," frowns Percy. "It's more of a mutual agreement to ensure the continued purity and Godliness within the church and the village. Between us we strive to unmask the unholy while championing the good."

"Enlighten me,' grins Clump.

"Some time back the vicar approached me and demanded that I never set foot in his church again, so as not to contaminate his flock. He accused me of being a: 'Fornicating, drunken, gambling reprobate who was destined for the sin bin and then onwards to hell.' I fired back, accusing him of being a dirty devil more interested in saving women's underwear then saving their souls. Thus, ensured a slanderous exchange that would have made the average solicitor rub his balls with glee at the thought of all the money he'd make, should the details of this confrontation, between two pillars of society, get to court. However, once I'd punched the bastard on the nose and calmed him down, we talked more amiably. In short, we reached an agreement. I would not attend Church for any reason, including my own demise, and in return he would inform me of all the sinners in the parish, so I might add them to my list of possible future allies against my war on poverty."

"Namely the money you require to keep up with your decadent lifestyle," says Clump.

"The thing is, Uncle. A man in my position cannot live on the meagre allowance metered out by the old man. I have debts to pay, palms to grease, places to go and tons of cash to hand out to good causes."

"What good causes would that be, Percy?" asks I.

"The ensuring the welfare of the lower classes, good cause."

Clump eyes turn very dark. "In short the money you pay out to ensure the female servants you abuse keep quiet about it. Am I right?"

"Usually they're more than happy to accommodate me. I look upon what I give them as more of a reward then hush money."

"And, Rose Bush?" demands Clump. "From what we've been told, Rose was anything but happy to accommodate you."

"Ah… I misread the signals she sent me, Uncle." Pausing he takes a long swallow of wine while flicking his eyes from Clump to me and back again. Putting down his glass he wipes his hairy mouth and sighs. "Rose was all alone in one of the bedrooms when I happened by. The door being open, and feeling somewhat curious as to why she was alone, it being the rule that chamber maids should work in pairs for proprieties sake, I stepped in and bade her good morning. She curtsied, then said, 'Good morning my Lord. Is there anything I can do for you?'

"There's nothing dear girl," said I. "Unless you're up to laying on the bed for me."

She smiled, 'As you wish my Lord.'

"I closed the door. She lay on the bed. I went to her and slipped my hand up her skirt. The next thing I knew she started screaming, which ensured a mumbled apology, followed by a very hasty exit by yours truly. Honestly, Uncle I had no idea the girl was such an innocent. There's me thinking she was up for it when in fact she was merely doing as I requested."

Clear to see by the look in Clump's and Head's eyes neither fully believe, Percy. For myself nor do I, but Percy admitted to assaulting Rose when he could have lied.

We are interrupted by the sound of Butlers voice echoing down the steps, "I have brought refreshments gentlemen."

"Come down," bellows Clump.

"Lovely," beams Head on seeing a large tray with hot steaming pasties on it, scones with accompaniments and a pot of coffee.

"Such wonderous delights," says Percy. "Aromas to please the Gods no less."

"Complements of Mrs Kemp," says Butler as we clear the table to accommodate the tray. "Anything else, gentlemen?"

"Yes," says Percy. "Can you take my bucket away and empty it?"

Butlers face screws up, "Very good my Lord."

Once we'd had a belly full of Gloria's delicious pastries and scones, and drunk the coffee pot dry, we took turns peeing in Percy's bucket, once a luckless lad had returned it all nice and clean, then we continued with the interview.

"Matilda," says Clump to Percy. "Are you or are you not…?"

"Not exactly, Uncle. One of my village informants, informed me some time back, for a whole shilling I might add, that Matilda was having secret trysts with that bastard Burroughs, in his bloody shed no less. Of course, I hit the roof and confronted her about it, while not so much as blackmailing her as threatening that I'd tell mother what the little trollop had been up to. Matilda went into a panic and offered me money to keep her secret whilst promising to end her attachment to Burroughs forthwith. I gave her a week to do so. Unfortunately, the next thing I knew I was down here and have no idea whether or not she has kept her promise."

"Their relationship is over," says Clump. "I have seen to that. Let us move on to Robert. I understand that you tried to blackmail him by threatening to spread rumours that he must be a bastard because he has a big penis. Explain yourself."

"I say, don't you think it's jolly unfair he's built like a stallion? But doesn't do anything with it because he's in love with Lady Clara Forbs Hamilton, and is saving himself until their wedding night next bloody year. What a waste of a weapon. If it were mine, why I'd have made use of it by now a thousand times over."

"So, this is all about jealousy?"

"It is. By God you'd be jealous if you saw the size of his weapon."

"I shall ask him," drawls Clump. "I will say: Robert, dear nephew, please show me your manhood so I might understand why your brother Percy is so jealous of you. Let us move on to more serious matters. If you killed Rose Bush and John Chambers, I ask myself why? I can only imagine they must have had something on you that was so serious it could have destroyed you."

"I swear I didn't kill them. I'm not a killer and had no reason to kill them anyway."

"You assaulted, Rose. Rather than allow her to spread that around the castle and the village, I would say you had a very good reason to want to see Rose dead."

"Not so. Even if I'd found myself confronted with mother's inquisitional nature and had confessed to touching up Rose, I would still vehemently plead my case. Rose spread it around that I fiddled with her secret bits while in fact I did not get above her knees. No, sir! I maybe a womanising scamp but to kill two young servants over a misunderstanding. Why would I? The fall back from the incident would have been negligible. Rose would have cracked under questioning from mother, and as a consequence would have been sacked for lying and all would have been forgotten in no time." A broad triumphant smile crosses his mouth. "Besides, I was incarcerated here at the time of the murders."

"But with the freedom to sneak out at any time you wished," puts in I. "Not only that, apparently you are one of the best bowmen around. A local champion in fact."

Percy leans across the little table and fixes me with an unblinking stare. "There's better bowmen around here than me, Inspector. If you want my opinion, I'd say try questioning that mad head game keeper of ours, Samuel 'bloody' Jenson. The mans a thug with a history of violent affray and has been known to threaten me in public. Jenson hates me so much he'd do anything to destroy me, even to go as far as murder in order to put suspicion on me. And why? Because he found out I cuddled his daughter Janet. How pathetic is that?"

"I am led to believe," says Clump as he sticks a cigar in his mouth and offers one to Percy. "That it was much more than a cuddle."

Percy takes the cigar and sits back, "Alright. I admit to squeezing her buttocks while we were kissing. I mean how can you resist fondling a nice round pair of buttocks unhampered by stupid bustles."

"That's the trouble with bustles," puts in Head while being stared at by an open-mouthed Clump. "They are a sexless instrument of torture designed to make women look like dollies while denying men a good grab of a nice bum."

"Exactly," says Percy. "And that is the beauty of servant girls, they wear a lot fewer constricting clothes, unlike the upper classes…"

"Shut up the pair of you!" snaps Clump. He lights his cigar and then holds the match out to Percy.

"Anyway," says Percy as he blows smoke in my face. "I gave Janet a few pennies so she might buy herself something. Only she went home and foolishly gave her mother half the money. Her mother told Jenson and he, forever not looking the proverbial gift horse in the mouth, demanded to know where Janet had got the money from. Of course, she wasn't about to tell him the truth, now was she? Apparently, she told Jenson I'd attacked her and felt her up and then given her the money to shut her up. It came back to me, that on the night Jenson threatened to do me in, he'd been stirred up by a couple of drunken locals to the point where he believed I'd actually raped Janet over a kitchen table, and then given her a few pence as if she were nothing but a cheap tart. And that's why I'd say Jenson should be your number one suspect for the killings, and he did it just to frame me. And if he could get at me, I've no doubt that he'll try to kill me as well. Followed by Seb' Bush; who wanted to 'geld' me because he had also been stirred up because of Rose's heavy embellishment over the incident on the bed. Can you imagine what he would like to do to me now if he believes I killed his daughter. Hence the reason I am staying put in fear of my life until the killer, or killers, have been caught. And…"

Clump holds up a hand to silence Percy. "Inspector, what's your opinion on Percy's accusations that Jenson could be our killer?"

"I doubt it, sir but I certainly wouldn't rule it out."

"Sergeant?"

"Much the same, sir."

"Then we must question Jenson once we have finished here, and if he is plotting to kill Percy he will almost certainly try tomorrow."

"Why tomorrow?" asks a horrified Percy.

"Because tomorrow everyone will be upstairs attending the celebrations thus leaving any potential killers free rein to come down here and bump you off."

"But they can't get into my cell."

"Inspector."

"They won't have to get in, Percy. There's a hundred and one ways anyone with a modicum of initiative could get to you. You'd be safer upstairs than down here."

"Especially if you have an armed escort at all times," says Clump pointing his cigar at Percy. "One of us will be with you from the moment you leave this cell and throughout the day, until you are safely tucked up in your own little bed. If needs be, we'll even hold your hand while you have a shit and read you a bed time story."

"While I'm having a shit?"

"You know what I mean. Anyway, you will be as safe as a rat in a sewer."

"All being well, Jenson and Bush will be outside throughout the jollities while I shall be inside," says Percy looking very doubtful. "But what about my maniac of a father? Will you lock him up so he can't get at me? By God and Jerusalem, the old prats already tried to kill me once, what's to stop him from walking up to me and sticking a dirty great knife in my guts and then pleading insanity, the rotten old swine?"

"He won't," says Clump. "Look here Percy, its time you took responsibility for your own actions. You may have thought it all a jolly jape to fill your fathers muddled mind with thoughts of your mother having committed adultery and becoming pregnant by a mere boy, but he actually believed you for a while. Now he knows you were just playing silly games, he is not only thankful that he didn't kill you, he is ecstatic about it."

Percy lets out a deep sigh of capitulation, puffs hard on his cigar and downs his wine, "Very well, Uncle. I'll accept I have been a bit of a nit in tormenting the old boy, but even so, don't you think he just might be unhinged enough to do something just as stupid again?"

"No, I do not. However, we shall err on the side of caution by ensuring that your father is watched at all times by someone he likes and trusts."

"Such as whom?"

"My wife, your aunty. You know full well that despite his oft ramblings and slips into nut world your aunt can still get through to him like no one else can, and as such he will do whatever she wants him to do. Agreed?"

Percy drops his head and nods, "Agreed. Thank you, Uncle."

"So, no more negativity, Percy. You will attend tomorrow and you will also have a jolly good time. Right, we need to wind this up. Inspector, do you have any more questions to ask?"

"Yes sir. Percy, since you have been down here who keeps you informed on what's happening in the big wide world?"

"Mother, mostly."

"And Smithers, does he add to what the Countess tells you?"

He shakes his head, "He does not. Smithers wouldn't tell you anything about anything if he could get away with it. That is why he's so trustworthy, Inspector. Why the man would rather cut his own throat then be forced to divulge a family secret. Though mind you, he's very good at keeping us informed of the servant's shenanigans."

"Trustworthy to the bitter end," says Clump shooting me a 'I told you so' look.

I am pondering on all that Smithers had told us about Percy. Smithers may have been boxed into a corner but he didn't put up much of a fight, and once his tongue was loosened, he was only too happy to use it to carve Percy's poor reputation into even finer shreds, with the information he gave being very questionable. I move on.

"Apart from Mrs kemp and of course, Smithers, Alfred Carter has been your most oft visitor. What are the primary reasons for his visits?"

"Alfie is my best friend. Well, only friend in fact. He picks up my wine from Regi' along with a few of my other pleasures. He collects any money that's owed to me and places bets for me."

"What bets?"

He shrugs, "Whatever the latest craze might be."

"Does he supply you with opium?"

"Yes. We play a game or two of chess, get inebriated and then relax while having a pipe. That's it really."

"Can he shoot a good arrow?" puts in Head.

Percy laughs, "Obviously you haven't met him, have you?"

Head shakes his head.

"Carter has a deformed right hand," says Clump impatiently. "He couldn't even pull his foreskin back with it let alone a bloody bow string. You are running down the wrong track, Sergeant. Anything else?"

Head and I shake our heads.

"Good. I would like a quiet word with my nephew, so if you pair don't mind waiting for me upstairs."

We take our leave. As we climb the steps, I'm feeling somewhat crestfallen. Having been so sure Percy was our man he has now plummeted to the bottom of my suspects list, with Sam' Jenson shooting up to the top. Yet I was so certain of Jenson's innocence by the way he reacted on seeing poor Rose's body. And now I must question everything I've been told by everyone. If Percy is to be believed then even Matilda has lied to me about his blackmailing her for money. I can't believe I've been so stupid and gullible.

"Where the fuck, do we go from here?" says Head as if reading my mind, the second we reach the top of the steps.

"Gods knows," sighs I. "I'm now thinking that we should start having a real go at everyone in the family, including the countess. Take the gloves off, Richard and grill them until they start cooking."

"Agreed. We've barely had a word with any of the buggers apart from Matilda and Percy. Robert's a nice fellow but we both know that once you really go for it even the nice ones can turn nasty and really surprise you. After all, if Percy was out of the equation it leaves Robert next in line for the earldom."

"Get rid of Robert as well and that leaves Algernon. Algernon is already a thief and a liar, nice as he is. Not only that, have you noticed the similarities in his features with a certain man who works on the estate?"

"Sam' Jenson?"

"Exactly. What if Rose found out that Algernon is Jenson's son and subsequently spread it around, thus giving Jenson one devil of a motive to want Rose out of the way as quickly as possible." I bury my head in my hands. "This entire investigation continues to drag us into a quagmire of ifs, buts and maybes, Richard."

"With too many possible suspects with too many possible motives. And now you're obviously still thinking that Smithers may well be involved. The trouble is, Clump doesn't want to know. As far as he and everyone else is concerned, Smithers walks on water."

"Doesn't he just. But, no one is perfect, not even the Queen."

"Not even the Queen," echoes he as Clump comes thumping up the stairs.

"Right men," puffs Clump while appearing all shifty. "We'll need a lift to Jenson's place. You two go off and second someone to convey us there while I pop upstairs to my room. Back in a bit."

He hurries off while Head and I give each other the knowing nod.

"The bloody old hypocrite," grates Head. "He had something stuffed under his jacket and I wouldn't be surprised if it was a book of a certain kind."

"We'll know by tomorrow if his eye sight seems to be impaired," grins I.

We are now heading for Jenson's place in a small cart meant to carry animals, you can tell this because it has four feet high boards all around it and smells of manure. Head and I are sat on a bum pricking straw bale, while Clump's sat up on the buck board beside Matilda, who's expertly controlling the black and white heavy horse that's pulling the creaking and groaning cart. Matilda volunteered to take us as no one else was available, the livery men having been sent to the station to wait for the train to arrive with expected guests.

Clump peers over the top of the boards, "You men alright back there?"

"Fine, thank you, sir," lies I wiping sweat from my brow with a handkerchief.

"Its bloody hot sat here," moans Head swotting flies away from his face. "And it smells of shit."

Wicked though it is I'm not about to tell Head that the fresh seagull shit on his bowler is what's attracting the flies, because it's keeping them off me. The sun is still high enough to beat down on us, trapped as we are in this wooden box with not a breath of the breeze Clump and Matilda are enjoying. I take off my jacket and bowler.

"Trees up ahead," says Head.

The cart trundles on, bumping and banging over ruts on the rough track. Clump lights up a cigar and for once the aromatic clouds of smoke drifting over us are a welcome respite from the stench of the cart. Seagulls soaring up high in a clear sky while hoovering up insects fill me with wonder. How on earth one of them managed to drop its guts from such a height to splatter dead centre onto Heads bowler I'll never know? The miracle of nature no less. Head sniffs at his arm pits before swotting away even more fly's while giving me the evil eye as if it's my fault he's under attack. However, I am more interested in Matilda's long silky hair fanning out behind her, and the sight of her bare skin where perspiration has stuck her white blouse to her curvaceous loins.

"You should keep your eyes off her, Gerald," whispers Head. "You're making it far too obvious you fancy her something rotten."

"I do not fancy Matilda," hisses I.

"Do so."

"Do not, Sergeant. Now drop the subject if you please."

At last we reach a dappled clearing where I stand up for a better view of what I assume is Sam' Jenson's place. A white stone walled, slate roofed cottage with pink dog roses growing all around the front porch. The frontage is weedy grass full of flowering orange dandelions and bright buttercups. Sat outside sits a dumpling of a woman peeling potatoes in an enamel bowl on a small table. She lifts her rosy cheeked face to gaze at us as a pair of black labaradors get to their feet and set off a bark before coming to meet us while wagging their tails.

"They look like the major's dogs," calls out I to Matilda.

"They are indeed," says she flicking me back a smile. "They stay here with Sam' as they don't get on with the 'bubbly boos', but they're still very much, father's boys."

"I wondered why I hadn't seen them around the castle," says I more to myself than anyone else.

Dumpling lady gets to her feet, dry's her hands on her flower patterned piny and walks towards us as the cart comes to a halt. Trepidation shows in her eyes and her rosy cheeks seem to be burning. She is not happy to see us. Clump jumps down, goes around to help Matilda down while Head and I wrestle down the back board before climbing out.

"Oh… my Lady," curtsies Dumpling. "Please excuse my untidy appearance. If I'd known yer was comin'."

"Our apologies, Doris," says Matilda. "Please excuse this unheralded intrusion. This is Detective Inspector Potter and Sergeant Head. You know my uncle, the Chief Inspector?"

"I do me Lady. Welcome to yer all."

"Gentlemen, this is Mrs Doris Jenson."

We greet the woman and then Clump says to Head, "If you clean that seagulls mess off your hat, Sergeant, you might find the fly's will leave you alone."

Head whips off his bowler. Peruses the grey white drying slop, gives me another evil glare and then bobs down to wipe his bowler clean on the grass.

"It's considered good luck 'round these parts, sir," says Doris trying to force a smile.

Matilda says, as the dogs' fuss around her and she fondly ruffles their heads, "Doris, the detectives wish to speak to Sam. Is he about?"

Appearing crest fallen she drops her gaze, "Yer haven't heard then my Lady. He's… he's in jail again."

"Ah… For what reason?"

Doris lifts her head, "Yer best come inside out of the sun, my Lady. I don't want the neighbours to hear."

What neighbours amuses I? The nearest must be at least a mile away. We follow Doris, she's so short she doesn't have to duck under the low beamed entrance, nor does Matilda. Clump has to duck as do I. Glancing back I see Head hurrying over, he doesn't duck and cracks his head, curses the f word through gritted teeth and follows us in. The kitchen is large, airy and welcoming, if a bit dark. There's a large pine table and a well blackened stove with a pot of what smells like rabbit bubbling away. Drying herbs and a variety of copper pots and pans hang from a thick oak beam that spans the centre of the room. The dogs have wandered in to sit quietly by the stove while licking their lips.

"Please sit," says Doris. "Would my Lady care for refreshments? Tea or lemonade?"

"Lemonade would be nice," says Matilda as she sits down.

"Any coffee?" asks Clump.

Doris appears even more crest fallen, "Sorry, sir we don't drink it much, so we don't buy it. I've got tea or there's a fresh jug of Sam's homemade scrumpy."

"We'll all have lemonade," says Matilda with finality.

"Lemonade!" growls Clump.

"Very well, sir," says Doris before hurry away and disappearing into a pantry.

"Well," hisses Clump once we've sat down opposite Matilda. "Our suspects in clink, again is he? No doubt for violence I shouldn't wonder."

"No doubt," frowns Matilda. "Well we'll soon find out."

Doris returns carry a small tray with four glasses and a pitcher of lemonade. She sets the tray onto the table with trembling hands before sitting down next to Matilda. Filling the glasses, she passes them around while avoiding eye contact.

"So, what's up with, Sam?" asks Clump.

"He set off to commiserate with the Chamber's family in Truro two nights back. He's been so upset over Roses death he just had to get away for a bit. I know he should 'ave asked permission first my Lady, but he just went."

"Never mind that, Doris," says Matilda. "Just tell us what happened."

"My two boys went with him but they come back yesterday. Sam' got into a fight in the Queens Head over something and nothin', he where drunk and still brooding over Rose. Anyway, the constable was called and arrested Sam' for startin' it all. They locked him up and fined him and he's due out first thing tomorrow."

"If he's being let out tomorrow with a fine it couldn't have been that bad," says Matilda placing a comforting hand over Doris's.

"Perhaps not," sighs Doris. "When will you be evictin' us, my Lady?"

"For what?"

"For Sam' goin' off his head again. The countess warned Sam' some time back, that if he got into any more trouble, he'd find himself out of work and evicted."

"The countess has more important matters on her mind right now, Doris. Let us say this is Sam's final warning. You will not be evicted, so please do not worry yourself."

Doris smiles as her eyes well up, "Oh... thank you my Lady."

"May I ask, Doris," says I. "Why is Sam' still so upset by Roses murder?"

"I don't suppose yer know or yer wouldn't be askin'. Rose was Sam's own."

Clump chokes on his lemonade. This revelation has obviously astounded all of us.

"Sam' was Roses father?" says I.

"He were. He had her with Mary Barber afore she married Seb."

"Does Seb' know this?"

"'Cause he do. When Seb' married Mary, Rose was already about three-year-old. Seb' brought her up like his own and she looked on him as her real dad. It's destroyed them both yer know poor Rose gettin' murdered like that."

Clump cuts in, "This is very important, Doris. Have you any idea who Sam' thinks might have murdered Rose and John Chambers?"

She shakes her head while pulling her hand free of Matilda's, "He don't know for sure an' its drivin' him mad."

"Because he wants to get even?" asks Clump.

"He do, sir. Why I believe he'd kill them if he found out, and even be happy to hang for it. That's how angry and upset he is about it."

"How does Sam' feel about Lord Percival Bullington?" asks I.

"I can't say, sir. I don't run down my masters."

Matilda places her hand back over Doris's, "You can in this instance, Doris. In fact, I insist upon it. It is very important that you tell us exactly how Sam' feels regarding Lord Percival."

Doris meets Matilda's sympathetic gaze, "I'm sorry, my Lady, but Sam' hates my Lord Percival and thinks he may be behind Roses death. But he won't do nothin' about it until he gets some proof."

"Thank you, Doris," says Clump. "Right, drink up everyone we must get on." He gets to his feet, noisily scraping back his chair. "Doris, when Sam' gets home you tell him that he is under threat of being arrested by me if he turns up at the castle tomorrow. Everyone else in your family will be welcome, but he must stay away from the castle until I have been to see him, which will probably be on Sunday. Do I make myself clear?"

"Yer do, sir."

"Good. The lemonade was… um… different, thank you. Let us get on."

Back at the castle I pick up my overnight bag, and with orders from Clump to go and see Seb' Bush on the way back to the Smugglers, Head and I set off in the luxury of a coach with Simmonds driving. A breeze has picked up while it has turned decidedly stuffy.

"Storm's brewing up," says Head.

If so, thinks I, then I shall call it Storm Betty.

Twenty minutes later, Seb's little farm comes into view with its collection of ramshackle 'sheds' for his variety of stock animals, rickety wind mill on a pole that pumps up water from underground and his home; a pair of old railway carriages joined together. Simmonds reins in the horses and I jump down to be greeted by a big ginger sow with five piglets in tow. Raising its snotty snout at me, the sow eyes me with indifference, sniffs the air and then waddles off with its piglets trotting after it. Which is good, as I wasn't sure if it intended eating me. I go and clang the bell hanging beside the entrance. Mary Bush, nee Barber, answers my clang.

"Inspector Potter. It's nice to see you again. Will you come in for tea?"

"That's very kind of you Mrs Bush but I can't stay. I just need a quick word with Seb' if I may."

"He's down at the brook after a trout or two for dinner." She points to a narrow track that runs between stone walls with meadows of ewes and lambs one side and a few bony milking cows the other side. "Follow that track an' it'll take you right to him."

I thank her, going on my own I follow the track and within ten minutes Seb' comes into view. He is sat on a grassy bank by a bubbling winding brook, holding a fishing rod and flicking a fly line into the sparkling water. Seb's sheep dog sets up a bark and a furious tail wag before running to meet me and jumping up. After a head ruffle he runs back to Seb'

"Well my handsome," says Seb' patting the ground beside him. "Sit yer down."

"Any luck?"

"Got one in thee bag. Be a couple more before long, they feed better when they know a storm is on its way. Now then, this here brook is the same brook that flows right beyond Sam's place. The same waters where yer found our poor Rose."

"How are you coping, Seb'?"

The eyes that gaze into mine are deep with sadness, "Not so bad. Be better once we see Rose off ter heaven. Mary's holdin' up well but she's on the edge of despair. Ain't we all. Anyway, I hope yer here ter tell me yer've caught thee bastard."

I shake my head and breathe in deep, "I believe it won't be long before we arrest the culprit, Seb'. Until then we have to keep some sense of order. In short; I've been ordered by my chief to try and find out if you have any intentions of taking the law into your own hands."

"I see. Yer've come here to warn me off. Is that it?"

"It is, and I apologise for it."

"Just doin' yer job. Can't hold that against a man. No, sir I don't have no notion of takin' the law into me own hands, just now. But I will, and so will others if we think the killer's goin' ter get away with it just because of who he is."

"Understood, Seb'. Trust me, whoever he is, whatever his position is, he will be facing the rope once we catch him."

"I trust yer and so does Sam', but we won't wait fer ever. Did yer know that Sam' be Roses real father?"

"I did. She was lucky to have had two good fathers."

He drops his head and I see a tear plink down onto his lap, "Not good enough ter keep her safe though." He meets my eyes. "Now, I'll ask yer straight. Do yer think that bastard Percy were behind my gal's murder?"

I hold out my hands, "I can't say, Seb'. All I'll say is this: we have more than one suspect and Percy's not currently at the top of my list."

"Meanin' he's still at the top of someone's?"

I get to my feet. "I have to go, Seb'. One last thing, do you intend going to the celebrations at the castle tomorrow?"

"No. The whole lot of us will be stayin' away. I ain't got nothin' against Lady Matilda but we're all too upset ter go."

"I understand." We shake hands and I set off back to the farm. Glancing back, I see Seb' with his head in his hands silently sobbing while the dog's licking at his neck. Suddenly I feel wretched and extremely tired.

Storm Betty

We arrive at The Smugglers Rest dead on six o'clock and it looks very busy. There's several carriages and horses out front with servants unloading bags and lugging them into the inn. Head and I step down onto the ground, say goodbye to Simmonds and take ourselves inside, where I hand a porter my bag and ask him to take it up to my room.

"I need a pint and a dinner," says Head.

"I think we've had enough booze this day, Richard. Why don't we make it a tea total night?"

"Why not forget dinner and go straight to bed as well?" says he sarcastically.

"One pint it is then."

"Good evening, gentlemen," says the bar man as we step up. "What would you like?"

"Two pints of best bitter, please," says I gazing around the bar to see if Betty's about. Which she isn't, probably because there doesn't appear to be a vacant seat anywhere. However, I do spot Trout and his friend sat in a corner staring over at us. Perhaps I should go over and apologise to the man, thus getting into Betty's good books.

"You should go over to Trout and apologise while you've got the chance," says Head. "Then you might get back into Betty's good books."

"Thank you, Richard," says I with a touch of sarcasm. "I hadn't thought of that."

"Two pints of best bitter," says the barman. "Your good ladies are in the snug, gentlemen. Would you like me to pass your drinks through into there?"

"We would," says Head. "And we shall be there in a moment once my college has completed a small errand. Off you go, Gerald."

"I do not need you to push me, Richard. I shall go and apologise once I've said hello to my wife."

He shrugs, "It's your funeral."

Stepping into the snug we find it half full, with Betty and Chloe sat by a tiny window and giggling over something.

"We're back," says Head as we step up. "What's so funny?"

I note on the little round table in front of them, sits two not quite empty whisky tumblers, along with a glass of red, Betty's, while Chloe is nursing a glass of 'milk'.

"Had company, have we?" grates I taking a seat opposite Betty.

Betty's eyebrows go up. "I'm well thank you, Detective Inspector. I am also in good spirits, unlike you."

Through the little window I can see the forecourt. Betty would have seen us arrive, and no doubt warned Trout and his poncey friend to hop it before we came in.

"Lord Trout and his companion are in the main bar," says Betty. "Why don't you act the gentleman and go and apologise to him?"

"For what?"

"For being a pig, a bully and a fool."

"Shall we take our drinks upstairs, Chloe?" says Head. "I've got a lot to tell you."

"I think it would be prudent, Richard," says she giving me the, 'you're a prat' look.

Head takes her milk as Chloe struggles to her feet. Her hands hold her stomach which looks as if it's sagged a bit since I last saw her. I wait until they've gone before saying to Betty, "Shall we go upstairs and have a talk?"

"No. I wouldn't go up a step ladder with you, the mood you're in."

She shoots a glare over my shoulder and I turn my head to see a beaky old bird, wearing half a flower garden on her bonnet, is obviously straining her lugs to hear a bit of scandal.

"Let's go and sit out back then," suggests I.

Betty nods and gets to her feet. We take our drinks and tramp around back to find most of the benches have been taken. And no wonder, it is a glorious evening and the perfect place to just sit and gaze over a mill pool sea; to a crimson horizon where dark clouds are slowly heading towards us. We find an empty bench away from the rest and sit down side by side, but with a good two feet between us.

Betty opens the conversation, "Just after, Richard left this morning while Chloe and I were finishing off our breakfasts, a very pretty young woman flounced in and headed straight over to Lord Trout. Of course, I guessed she was his intended, Lady Matilda Bullington. They went off together, returning about ten minutes later and coming over. Lord Trout introduced her to us and us to her. Chloe then excused herself as she was feeling uncomfortable, she can't sit down for too long on a hard chair. Lord Trout kindly assisted Chloe up to her room while Matilda sat down opposite me and struck up a conversation. Her conversation centred mostly around you and how fortuitous it was for me to have married a real man. And so, on and so forth, while all the time her mocking eyes were telling me that she could take you from me whenever she so wished. What do you think of that revelation, Detective Inspector?"

"I think it's a load of rubbish, Betty. You obviously misread the signs. Why on earth would Matilda want to take me away from you?"

"I'll come to that in a moment. She fancy's you. The question is do you fancy her?"

Who wouldn't? thinks I but dare not say so, "Why would I when I'm not even in her class?"

"Don't be flippant, Gerald. Just answer the question honestly."

"Alright! Can I help it if she fancy's me? Can I help it if half the males in Cornwall fancy you, including the juveniles?"

"You're evading the question again. Do you fancy her or not?"

"I admit that she is a very beautiful young lady. Not only that she is engaging, kindly and has a zest for life that is somewhat endearing…"

"That's a yes, then."

I take a long swallow of beer to play for time. Betty is at her most dangerous when she's calm and collected, one wrong word and I'll find myself psychologically castrated.

"Have you kissed her yet?"

That one rocks me, how the hell did she guess? Or is she just fishing? Technically she kissed me, which gives me my answer. "No, I have not kissed her."

Betty takes a sip of her wine then fixes me with her 'you're a liar' look. "You know she's just playing games with you, don't you?"

"Playing what games?"

"She doesn't want to marry Lord Trout. That spoilt little madam doesn't want to marry anyone and wants to stay just as she is. She's using you to stir up trouble so she gets what she wants. She was trying to make me jealous by oh so cleverly, not actually saying it, but implying that you and she had been intimate. Not only that, when Lord…"

"Why don't you just say, Jeremy? As I've not doubt that your friendship has progressed well beyond the strict codes of practice that is expected between casual acquaintances from different classes."

"My, what a mouthful," mocks she. "I shall continue, and you'd be wise to listen instead of again accusing me of being the one who's not acting with propriety. Jeremy returned and sat down beside Matilda. Matilda then changed tack by asking us how we were getting along, as if Jeremy and I had become more than just casual acquaintances, having bridged the class divide. Jeremy blushed and then made his excuses that he had to change as he was going riding with Lord Palmer. Once he'd gone, I said to Matilda: 'You must be so excited about getting engaged tomorrow, Lady Matilda?' She momentarily forgot herself and pulled a sour face before quickly regaining her composure to gush out: 'I can't wait, Mrs Potter. Jeremy's such a wonderful man. So handsome, so debonair, so thoughtful and so kind.' Then she smirked, 'Not to mention being fabulously wealthy and well educated.' I then said to her: 'But you don't love him, do you?'"

"You had no right to ask her such an impertinent question."

"She didn't answer anyway, she just stormed off and that was that."

"I'm not surprised. You had just insulted her in the most obnoxious way any woman…"

"Oh… just shut up and listen, Gerald."

"Alright! I'm listening."

"Steer well clear of that little vixen if you value your marriage, your reputation and your position. If you don't, you'll not only lose everything, you'll end up looking a complete fool."

"Huh!" scoffs I. "I could say the same to you regarding bloody Trout. Steer clear Betty, the mans a womanising rake, an upper-class twat and a sop of the highest order."

"Actually, he is a gentleman, unlike Matilda who is anything but a lady. Do not make a fool of yourself by falling for her charms."

"You, madam, are the one making a fool of yourself, and in public. First you flirt with a mere boy waiter who gets dumped the second Jeremy the jerk swans in and smiles at you." She goes to say something but I give her the pointed finger, warning her not to interrupt. "Ever since we've been in Cornwall you've been batting your eyelashes at everything in trousers. You have behaved disgracefully while even in my presence, and now you have the iron nerve to again try and turn it all around as if it were I who is at fault, just to cover up whatever it is you are trying to cover up. I'd say heaven and Chloe only knows what you've been up to behind my back. There now, what do you say to that?"

"That you are far more guilty of improprieties with Matilda then I have been with either Andrew, or Jeremy, or half the men in Cornwall. I swear to you that I have nothing to be ashamed of and have done nothing to feel guilty about. Stick that in your pipe and smoke it."

"I don't smoke."

"Well stick elsewhere!"

"So, you're denying any involvement with Trout?"

"Other than innocent conversation, yes I am."

"Such conversations throughout the day, no doubt, while I was out of sight and out of mind. And you were still all snug in the snug with him barely minutes ago. God knows what Chloe thinks about your antics."

"There were no antics. Jeremy popped into the snug with Hugo…"

"Who the hell is Hugo?"

"His associate Lord Palmer. Jeremy told me that he won't be pressing charges against you, providing you apologise, because he has no desire to mar tomorrows celebrations."

"Rubbish! The man's a spider and it's all nothing more than a ruse to endear himself deeper into your affections and lure you into his web. All he's trying to do is to get you beneath his sheets. One last conquest before he gets engaged to Matilda."

"What utter rot! I repeat, Jeremy is a gentleman while Matilda is a conniving little vixen, and the sooner you realise that the better you will be." She gets up on her feet. "Anyway, I've had enough of this, I'm going to my room."

"Our room."

"No, mine. You can go sleep with the horses and with luck one will stomp on your thick head and straighten out your befuddled brain."

I grab her wrist before she's gone a foot, spilling wine on her sleeve.

"Let go, Gerald."

"You listen to me, Betty and listen well. I will be sleeping in our room tonight and you will be sleeping beside me. We are man and wife and I demand my conjuring rights."

"In other words, you're desperate for your conjugal rights while no doubt imagining you're doing it with Matilda."

"Don't be so stupid," snaps I noticing that everyone has forgotten about the beautiful scene over the sea in place of the free entertainment on offer. "Everyone's looking at us, Betty. We must continue this upstairs in our room."

"Very well," she spits wrenching away her wrist and spilling the rest of the wine over her chest. She thrusts her glass at me. "Take the glasses back. I'll see you upstairs."

Doing as I'm told while ignoring the gawping eyes upon me, I march off to the bar, down the rest of my beer and bang down the glasses, before marching back and up the stairs to our room, only to find the door is locked. "Betty! Open the bloody door!"

"Go away, Gerald. Come back in the morning and pick up your things. I'll leave them outside the door for you."

"You'll do no such thing. Open this door or I'll bust it open.

"I'll throw all your things out the window if you don't go away, right this second."

"I am sorry, sir," comes a stern voice from behind me. Spinning around I find myself facing the landlord. "I will not have a repeat of the other night, sir. Please leave now, or, policeman or no policeman, I will have you physically removed from the premises."

"You just try it you puffed up old pudding."

I am now around back picking my clothes up off the ground and stuffing them back into the bag. The sky has clouded right over with ominous black clouds, the wind has picked up enough to force everyone, except me, inside, and the sounds of thunder and flashes of lightning are heading towards me at a phenomenal speed. I head back into the inn and go up to the bar and come face to face with the landlord again.

"I would like a double scotch," smiles I.

"Sir, I have asked you to leave. I have threatened you with physical expulsion and carried out that threat…"

"With the help of three bruisers I might add."

"Please leave the premises now, or else."

"Look here my good man. I have nowhere to go and it is about to dump an ocean down on us out there. I do apologise for my behaviour and promise that there will be no repeat of said bad behaviour. All that aside I am still a paying guest. If you press ahead with your threats, I will not only refuse to settle my bar bill, I will also instigate a search of your cellars to ascertain whether or not you are harbouring goods smuggled in from the continent. Do I make myself clear?"

His mouth opens wide and I notice he has several molars that require urgent attention from a dentist. I raise my eyebrows for effect and shoot him the 'well?' look.

"Perhaps, sir I have been a trifle hasty. Would sir like me to go upstairs and have a word with Mrs Potter to see if we might resolve the situation?"

"A capital idea, sir," smiles I.

He pours me a double scotch, "On the house sir," grimaces he before stomping off.

Lovely thinks I as I take a sip just as Jeremy 'bloody' Trout comes over.

"Potter," says he squaring up to me. "I wish to put the other evenings events behind us so as not to mar tomorrows celebrations. Providing of course, that you apologise first."

"And if I don't?"

"Then, sir I will be compelled to take you outside for a damn good thrashing."

Normally anyone speaking to me like that would be on the floor nursing a broken nose. But I really don't need any more trouble right now and gritting my teeth I say, "Sir, I apologise unreservedly for my stupidity the other evening and would also like to put it behind us."

He holds out his hand, "I accept your apology, Inspector Potter. We shall say no more about it."

I shake his hand despite a fervent desire to crush it. Even so I am surprised by the strength in his grip as he gives me the crush effect. Which I return only for him to crush even harder. Time to bite the bullet and end this, but just as I'm about to nut Jeremy, the landlord returns.

"Ah… Gentlemen so glad you have resolved your differences."

"We have indeed," smiles Trout releasing my hand. "Well must get on."

He marches away and I face the landlord.

"I am sorry, Inspector, Mrs Potter refuses to open the door which leaves us with a conundrum. Where do I put you for the night?"

"If you don't know neither do I," says I amazed that he should ask me such a silly question. How the hell do I know where he might put me? "How about in a bedroom?"

"There lays the problem, Inspector. I do not have a single room available unless you do not mind sharing with a complete stranger."

"What type of complete stranger."

"An elderly gentleman."

"How many beds in the room?"

"Two singles."

"On suite?"

"It is where the budget rooms for the upper-class guests, servants stay. You will share a bathroom…"

"Between how many rooms?"

"Six."

"Is this elderly gentleman a funny?"

He scratches his balding grey pallet. "He has a wry sense of humour if that's what you mean," says he obviously getting somewhat annoyed and giving me the impatient, 'beggars can't be' and all that.

"I'll take it," smiles I before he changes his mind and offers me the stables or a cupboard.

"Good." He reaches over the bar and tings a bell, two seconds later Andrew the waiter comes running into the bar. "Watch the bar, Andrew while I show Inspector Potter up to his room."

"Very well, Father," says he avoiding my eyes, the little shit is as guilty as sin, and given the opportunity later tonight I shall find out exactly what he's been up to with my Betty.

Carrying my own bag, I follow the landlord outside and around to a door on the side of the inn, he opens it and we ascend steep narrow stairs to the landing which leads down to the bedrooms, at number six, the end one, he knocks on the door.

"Come," says a gravelled voice.

"This is Inspector Potter, Mr Samuels. He will be sharing with you, for tonight only."

The old boy is sat writing at a small desk, he's about a hundred, with thin white hair and sagging red cheeks reminiscent of a beagle. He gazes with curiosity at me over his pince-nez and simply nods his approval.

"I shall leave you to settle in, Inspector," smiles the landlord.

The room is small and very basic, but smells and looks clean. As the old boy has gone back to his writing, as if I wasn't there, I unpack, hanging and pushing my clothes into the single wardrobe besides his. A small chest of drawers has one empty draw where I cram everything else in, except for my footwear, which I shove under the made-up bed along with my bag.

"There's a storm closing in," says I looking out of the only tiny window in the room.

Taking off his glasses he looks up at me with disinterest, "Yes, I had realised that." Putting his glasses back on he goes back to his writing.

"I'm going to freshen up and then go down for dinner, thus leaving you in peace."

Taking his glasses off again he gives me the 'shut up and piss off' look. "Good." The glasses go back on and he goes back to his writing.

Still, thinks I once I had freshened up, put on a fresh shirt and wandered down to the packed bar, at least I should have a quiet night with the old boy as I certainly could do with a good night's sleep. Betty has a table with Head and Chloe right at the back of the room, but I don't bother going over. There would no point, Betty would tell me to go away, I would get angry and the whole thing would start up again. Best to find a table out of sight of anyone I know. The trouble is every seat except the one beside Betty is taken. I settle for sitting up by the bar on a stool where I order a scotch and a steak dinner.

"Sorry, sir," says the barman. "We cannot serve dinner at the bar. But we can serve sandwiches of your choice."

"I'll think about it," says I. Now I'm really pissed off. Steak with mushrooms, onion, peas and buttered and minted new potatoes was top of my list, and I'd been salivating over the vision for the past hour.

The barman hands me my scotch, "Have you a sandwich order to place, sir? We are extremely busy in the kitchen and it would be best to place your order now as it might take a while."

"Sandwiches of my choice," muses I while massaging my chin. "I would like sliced beef with horseradish, mushrooms and fried onions. I would also like sliced and minted new potatoes in very thickly buttered bread. And could you kindly do me a dish of peas on the side."

"Um… sorry, sir no side dishes allowed if eating up at the bar."

"Very well. Then I would also like a sandwich of peas."

He looks askance at me. "A pea, sandwich?"

"Yes. With mint sauce."

"Mint sauce?"

"Thank you."

"Brown or white bread?"

"White, please."

He writes it all down on a note pad, tears it off and turning around opens a small hatch and hands the note through. I hear an amazed voice say, 'A potato and a pea sandwich?'

"Both with mint sauce," says the barman as the hatch is slammed shut.

Two hours later I am half cut and stuffed to the gills having eaten six rounds of sandwiches, which were delicious. I also started a new craze, as several people who came up to the bar where rather enthralled with my pea and potato sandwiches and promptly ordered the same. The expected storm turned out to be a few cracks of thunder, a couple of lightning flashes and a quick downpour before fading away. Head and Chloe went up to bed just after ten, having come up to the bar to say goodnight, which left

Betty sitting on her own looking miserable and lonely. I had contemplated going over but thought better of it. And I'm glad I didn't because; just before eleven, by which time the bar was near empty, she passed by me without a second glance to hopefully go to her bed and not to someone else's. At eleven the barman closed the bar and asked everyone still hanging around to leave so it might be prepared for breakfast.

"I believe you are checking out tomorrow," says the barman as he wipes the bar with a cloth.

"Right after breakfast. Do you wish me to settle my drinks bill now or in the morning?"

"In the morning please. Right, sir I must ask you to leave as the bar is now closed."

"I was hoping for a nightcap."

"That isn't a problem, sir. But it will have to be sent up to your room."

"Fine. I'd like an Irish coffee sent up to room six of the budget rooms."

"Yes of course, sir," says he obviously having been informed of my new address.

"Could you send young Andrew up with my order?"

He gives me the 'are you one of them?' look.

"I want to personally reward that studious young man with a large tip for all his service to myself, my friends and especially to my wife, in case I don't see him tomorrow."

"I see, sir. Very kind of you."

Fishing around in my jacket pocket I take out my purse and find half a crown which I give to him, thus getting him on side.

"I shall send Andrew up with your order immediately. And thank you, sir for your generosity."

"You are welcome. And thank you," smiles I as I swing my legs off the stool and head off to my room, where I stop outside at the entrance to wait beneath a half moon and a flickering oil lamp. Sure, enough five minutes later a yawning Andrew comes around the corner carrying a small tray with my drink upon it. He is oblivious to what's awaiting him and doesn't even notice me until he's barely two feet in front of me. I take the tray from his trembling hand and set it down on the step.

"Andrew," says I to his wide-open eyes, the fear in them so clearly defined as they reflect the light. "Fear not, young man. I have no intentions of harming you. I merely wish to ask you a few questions about your relationship with my wife."

"Oh…" says he now appearing to be absolutely terrified. "I'm sorry, sir I must go I need a wee."

"Well wee up the wall, because you are not going anywhere until I am satisfied you have answered my questions fully and honestly. Do you understand me?"

He nods, turns away to face the wall, extracts his winkle and starts relieving himself. Of course, I don't look for more than a second and then wish I hadn't. There is no justice in the world sometimes. The skinny sod has the equivalent of, not one, but two sausages hanging out. No wonder Betty fancied him so much. Controlling my temper, I wait until he has finished and turns to face me.

"I suppose, Mrs Potter has told you of my foolish act?" trembles he.

"She did," lies I. "Even so, I wish to hear your side of the story."

"It was all Daniels fault."

"Daniel the barman?"

He nods and drops his eyes, "He said it was obvious Mrs Potter wanted to take my virginity. He said he'd known similar women before who lust after young lads, and he'd had several when he was younger." He meets my eyes and swallows hard.

I am already horrified, upset and furious. Even so as I see the tears welling up in his eyes, I know I must hear him out and not do anything foolish. He's just a boy, while Betty is a full-grown woman who should have had more sense.

"Go on, Andrew," says I placing a friendly hand on his shoulder.

"I… I thought she asked me up to her room that third time because she'd planned to seduce me. Daniel had teased me as I went to take up her coffee and biscuits. 'This is it and this is what you must do,' he'd said. I went up, the door was open and I went in. We talked while I poured her coffee. She got up from the chair as I turned to face her, she stroked my hair and gazed into my eyes. She looked strange, kind of sad, it was an odd look that I thought meant she was going to do it to me. Daniel had said, 'They'll get a strange look in their eyes just before they start tearing off your clothes.' Pl…please, sir I don't think I can…"

"You can and you will," says I injecting menace into my tone.

"I… I then acted as Daniel had instructed me. I pulled her close to me, kissed her and pushed myself into her. She… she then shoved me away and slapped my face, which really hurt. Then she burst into tears and I ran for it. Since then she hasn't looked at me or spoken to me, and refuses to allow me within a yard of her."

I am utterly confused by his story. Too much booze and dead on my feet, I realise I am not capable right now of trying to fairly analyse all this. "Thank you, for your honesty, Andrew. Go on, get yourself off to bed."

"I am sorry, sir. Truly I am…"

"Get, before I change my mind."

The Big Day

I've had bad nights and rotten nights, but as I shave in the smallest bathroom ever built, while some prat is banging on the door to get in, I swear last night was the worst ever. When the old boy wasn't snoring like a demented wart hog, he was tossing and turning, grunting and moaning. His breath sounded like a thousand rasps scraping as he ground the few teeth he had left, and his constant farting and burping filled the room with the heady aroma of cow pats and rotten fish. Even worse he slept on top of the bed, because even with the little window open the room was as stuffy as hell, with his night gown way up his legs allowing the moon to highlight his knackers, the other bit being too shrivelled up to notice.

"Oy, mate," sounds whoever's outside, "'ow long are ya goin' ta be? I'm desperate out 'ere, an' I got a lord ta do for."

Enough is enough. Taking my revolver out of my bag, I open the door and point it at a skinny lad whose hands immediately shoot up into the air having been behind his back and were, no doubt, holding his cheeks together. "Go find somewhere else to crap," snarls I while realising it wasn't such a good idea to terrify someone who's as desperate as he is. I quickly shut the door to keep out the smell. Finishing my ablutions, I go back to the room, pick up my bag, say good bye to the old boy and head down for breakfast.

Betty, Head and Chloe are sat together in their usual place by the window, and judging by the spotlessly white table cloth they are as yet to be served. Head and Chloe greet me with enthusiasm while Betty gives me the cold shoulder. I sit down just as a waiter comes over for our orders. Its coffee and full English for me and Head, tea and poach eggs on toast for the girls. The waiter goes off and we all go and help ourselves to a bowl of prunes and a glass of fruit juice. At last, Betty looks at me.

"You look tired, Detective Inspector. Did you not sleep well?"

"Dreadful night. I had to share with the farting snorer from hell."

"Now you know how I feel," giggles Chloe.

"Be careful now, Mrs Head," grins Head.

At least they have cheered me and Betty up. Sitting back down we spoon in the fruit while I ponder over what Andrew told me last night, but still it alludes me. Whatever is wrong it isn't right. I shake the cobwebs from my brain and put it aside for now. I must concentrate on the investigations and not allow personal problems to cloud my judgement.

An hour later we are heading for the castle having been picked up by, Simmonds. The sky has clouded over but it is still bright and very warm. Everyone is quiet during the journey while content to just enjoy the scenery, the clean air and the world going lazily by.

As we near the castle the traffic picks up, and we are passed by several well healed gentry in lighter carriages, who glance at us, but don't acknowledge us, as we are obviously from a lower order. Head and I are expected to doff our bowlers, but neither of us do. 'Always remember this,' my old man used to say as I stood bare foot before him in my dirty ragged clothes while scratching my scabby face. 'You're as good as anyone in this world.' Easy said, but not so easy to attain to.

There are three carriages in front of us unloading their passengers and bags; so many bags you'd think they've come for a month instead of, for most of them, just the one night. Simmonds pulls the horses up and gets down to drop the steps. Chloe is helped down first and then the rest of us step down. A junior footman, pushing a sack barrow, comes running up to us. Simmonds loads our bags onto it, and except for Simmonds, we all tramp inside the castle to find the entrance hall more akin to a hotel than a private residence; it's packed with people and their luggage. However, the ever-efficient Smithers is overseeing everything and no doubt all is going smoothly. After standing around for a while it is at last our turn to be 'checked' in. Smithers greats us all with his usual aplomb. I introduce the girls and after informing me that Clump will meet us in Roberts office for ten thirty, Smithers assigns Jackson to assist us. Carrying our own bags, we follow Jackson, who's assisting Chloe, up the stairs, down the hallway and past all the best rooms to arrive at the far end where the up-market servants, lady's maids, valets and whoever, usually kip down while often having to share several to a room. Jackson shows Head and Chloe into their room first so Chloe can take the weight off her feet. She really struggled up the stairs while puffing and panting, and I'm thinking she might be an awful lot nearer her time then she realises.

"Sorry to keep you waiting, sir," says Jackson ten minutes later as he unlocks the door to our room and we go in. "This is the best we could do under the circumstances," says he going over to a small window and opening it to let some air in.

The room is small, sparsely furnished with a single wardrobe, a small chest of draws, a chair and a small table where sits a single oil lamp with little room for anything else.

"Do you want me to push the single beds together, sir?" says he apologetically.

"No need," smiles Betty throwing me a look that says it all. I won't be sneaking into her bed tonight.

"Bathrooms across the hall, two of, shared between the eight rooms. Each has a bath, flushing toilet and sink. I will have a maid bring you towels and toiletries. They should have been here, but as everyone's so busy you've been overlooked."

"Thank you, Jackson," says I.

"Thank you," smiles Betty.

"I'll leave you to it," says Jackson. "If you require anything, please do not hesitate to ask."

"What a polite, pleasant young man," says Betty the second Jackson had gone.

Taking off my hat I take a seat on the bed and give it a bounce, "Nowhere near as soft and bouncy as the one in the Smugglers."

"And it squeaks like mad," says Betty giving hers a try. "Never mind, as nothing much is going to be happening on either bed other than sleeping, it shouldn't be a problem."

"Indeed not," grates I. Taking out my fob watch I note the time. "Is there anything you wish to talk about before I go and meet Clump in a few minutes?"

"Yes. How long are we expected to remain in our rooms? What time will the festivities begin? And what time will you be back?"

"I would think you and Chloe can come and go as you please. Try a tour around the castle, that should entertain you for a few hours. Festivities will commence after a short remembrance service for Rose Bush and John Chambers, at about two o'clock, from whence you and Chloe will be with us for the remainder of the day, unless something untoward drags us away."

"What if we're hungry whilst your gone?"

"Just tell one of the footmen what you want and they'll bring it to you. Anything else?"

"Such as?"

"A quick row on the ridiculous situation we currently find ourselves in."

She shrugs and gives me the sulky look, "Well, you started it all."

"I did not start anything, Betty," sighs I getting to my feet. "I merely asked you something and you exploded…"

"Rubbish! You have bullied me, accused me, belittled and embarrassed me, what you haven't done is ask me."

"I bloody well did ask you. You were the one who lost their temper…"

The knock on the door and Heads shouting out, "Are you ready, Gerald?" takes the fight out of me. Slapping on my bowler I go out, slamming the door behind me.

"Not going so well then?" says Head.

"Not going at all, Richard," grates I. "At this rate we shall be at the divorce courts before too long."

We find Constable Burroughs in with Clump when we arrive at the office. After the usual greetings we sit down. I for one am pleased to see there's no scotch out.

"Right men, let me update you. Last night I questioned Elizabeth, Algernon, Robert and Matilda to find out just how much truth there was in Percy's confessions yesterday. Apart from, Matilda they all agreed, more or less, that Percy had told us the truth." He raises his eyebrows while searching mine and Heads faces as if we might challenge him. "Matilda is adamant that Percy had been blackmailing her just as she'd stated and I believed her. However, that still leaves Percy very much in the clear. I haven't questioned the vicar as yet," a broad grin fleetingly crosses his mouth, "but will do so as soon as possible. I also intend to give Smithers a grilling, but not today as it would be impossible to do so. For today only, I have suspended investigations for the obvious reasons. But once Sunday worship is over, we shall be going at it like bulls in china shops. I want the fear of Christ put up everyone's arse, and I mean everyone's. We need someone to crack, someone to let something slip that's significant enough to set us off onto the right track. No one, not even the countess, shall be exempt from a grilling. Is that understood?"

We nod.

"Good. I shall be inside the castle once the service is over, where I will remain with Percy alongside me. Detectives, you will be outside enjoying the festivities with your good ladies, while all the time keeping your eyes and ears wide open for any snippets of information and suspicious signs of shifty goings on. Constable Burroughs will police the outside events to ensure everyone's behaving themselves. Do you all understand your duties?"

We nod.

"Good. Although finding our killer, or killers, is naturally top of our list, today is protect Percy day. We cannot bring those young people back, but we can, and will prevent any further killings. Enjoy the day as much as you can, but do not get drunk or into any fights. Detectives, I want you armed for the day. Any questions?"

"Where is Percy right now, sir?" asks I.

"Locked in his room from the inside and hopefully taking a well needed bath and a shave. He will remain there until I go and fetch him. He has been told not to open that door to anyone except me. That includes Smithers."

"So, have you come around to thinking that Smithers is a viable suspect?"

"No, sir, I do not and remain convinced of the man's innocence. Anything else?"

"Will the family and the gentry be walking around outside the castle?" asks Burroughs.

"They may be, Constable. If so then you are not to approach any of them unless requested to do so. You will not approach Lady Matilda for any reason whatsoever. Is that clear?"

He drops his head, "Yes, sir."

"What if my Chloe goes into early labour?" asks Head.

"What if the Queens drawers slip down her legs while she's addressing parliament?" grates Clump. "As your wife has at least two months to go, Sergeant it is unlikely she will kick off early. Just as it is unlikely the Queens drawers will slip down her legs. In short, should such unlikely events take place we will deal with them as only professional's can."

"If the Queens drawers did slip down, sir," says Head deadpan. "would it be alright for me, a mere sergeant, to rush forwards and hoist them up for her, or should it be left to someone more important; like the royal drawers puller upper?"

"Sergeant, shut up. The castle will be out of bounds to any of you from two o'clock onwards, unless I call you in, Mrs Head is uncomfortable or you want to go to bed. There will be plenty to eat and drink outside and should it rain there is plenty of shelter. You are not to bother Mrs kemp or any of the indoor servants unless it is of extreme importance…"

"In other words, Chief" says Head. "Know your place."

"Exactly. Right, I suggest you all relax until the service starts. Do what you like but keep out of trouble and out of the way as much as is possible. That's it, bugger off."

We spend the next two hours showing the girls around the outside of the castle, in between sitting down for long periods to allow Chloe to rest. At one o'clock we go back to our rooms with tea and sandwiches supplied from the kitchen. By two o'clock we are outside the castles chapel along with the villagers, most of the castle's servants and the estate workers. The Bullingtons and their honoured guests stand facing us a good twenty feet away. The Reverend Hardpuzzle conducts a short but emotional service, everyone sings The Lords my Shephard followed by saying the Lord's Prayer. Constance then thanks the world and his dog for all they've done to enable this: 'Most glorious of events to take place.' She then formally declares commencement of the festivities. Everyone cheers, most of the men along with half the women, abandon their kids and rush off to the beer tents, while the Bullingtons and their guests cram into the chapel for the reverend to, no doubt, conduct a short sermon to Matilda and Trout on the seriousness of the promises they are about to make to each other. Matilda looked absolutely ravishing in a snow-white dress and floppy white hat with feathers, while holding a white parasol to keep the sun off her radiant face.

"If you had stared any harder at that girl your eyes would have popped out of their sockets," hisses Betty as we amble towards the beer tents with Head and Chloe following behind.

Not to mention the buttons on my trousers, thinks I. "Can we not just enjoy the day, Betty. I have no wish to quarrel with you. It is going to be a long day, especially for me and Richard. You and Chloe can go off to bed whenever you wish, but us men will have to remain on duty until Clump tells us to stand down, which won't happen before Lord Percy is safely locked up in his room. Clump is convinced that someone will try and murder Percy this very day. We could be up until well past midnight, and in truth I am so tired I could go to bed right this minute."

She links her arm around mine, "Just so we at least appear to be happily married, Detective Inspector. A truce until we are back in the Smugglers. Which is when?"

"Tomorrow night." I stop and face her. "If this case drags on, you Chloe and Richard may well have to travel back home without me."

"How convenient would that be for you, Detective Inspector? Me in London and you all alone down here with nothing to do except lust after a girl who's nearly half your age."

"Hurry up, Gerald," says Head catching us up. "Get the beers in before the barrels run dry."

"Just lemonade for me," says Chloe, whose face I note looks hot and clammy.

"And your poison is?" says I meeting the venom in Betty's eyes.

"Whoa there," says Head. "Why not call a truce for the day?"

"We have," grates I. "But Betty is determined not to honour it."

"For good reason," says she. "Never the less I do not wish to ruin Richard and Chloe's day. Our second truce begins right now. Let's get drunk."

"We've got orders to remain sober," moans Head. "Haven't we, Gerald?"

"We also have orders to keep our eyes and ears open for shifty goings on and snippets of information, which are most likely to happen where there's copious amounts of free alcohol on offer. Tongues loosen and folks begin to misbehave. I fear therefore, Sergeant it is our duty to mingle amongst them and gain their trust."

"And all in the line of duty," grins Head. "What are we waiting for?"

Come midnight, I finally make my way upstairs while assisting a very drunken Percy who's wobbling and swaying all over the place, he is incapable of normal speech and may well have wet himself. But at least he'd enjoyed himself. How did I end up chaperoning Percy? Simple, Clump, having decided he'd had enough of Percy, called me into the castle at ten thirty and handed Percy over to my care, so he could go and play billiards, which pissed me right off as I'd just been about ready to retire. By then the outside festivities were over, near everyone had gone home, and peace had been restored to the castle's grounds except for a few snoring drunks, who'd decided to stay the night having dropped off where they sat or lay. Betty, Chloe and Head all went off to bed leaving yours truly to manage Percy on his own. For over an hour we sat in the music room, with Percy still drinking champagne from the bottle while gabbling on about God knows what. All I could do was try and stay awake while trying to encourage him to get to his bed, but, having been imprisoned for weeks he was savouring his freedom and refused to go anywhere, until at last he was so drunk he had no idea what was going on.

At last we reach his bedroom and I bundle him inside. Now I am not about to spend the night with him, so after a few slaps to his face, I manage to bring him around enough for him to understand he must lock his door before I can leave. Remaining outside I put an ear to the door, and after what seems like an age, I hear the door bolt being rammed into place. Getting the key into the lock proves even harder for Percy. I hear his slurred curses and his head constantly banging on the door, as he obviously keeps falling forwards while struggling with the task. At last the key is turned and I check the door. Safe and secure. Now, at last I can go to my bed. Every other lamp along the hallway has been turned off, the rest have been turned low, giving out enough light to just see your way, which gives an eerie feeling to the silence that now prevails now that everyone else has gone to bed. So, the last thing I expect, which makes me jump, is Matilda's door opening a foot, just as I am about to walk past it, and her face to appear.

"Gerald, come in for a moment I have something very important to tell you," whispers she.

I shake my head, "Keep it until the morning, Matilda," whispers I putting my face close to hers. "It is very late. I am exhausted, and besides which there is no way I'll enter your room when you are obviously alone. You are alone, I take it?"

"Of course, I am, silly boy. Quickly now, do you want to save someone's life or not?"

"Whose life are we talking about?"

"Come in and I shall tell you."

Against my better judgement I throw caution to the wind, and slip inside to a room as near dark as the hallway. Matilda locks the door behind me and lays back against it as I turn to face her. Her eyes are full of sparkling intent, her breathing is hard, and her breasts oh so clearly visible through a sheer white cotton nightgown that is buttoned all the way up from her feet to her neck. With her hair tumbling over her shoulders, her curvaceous lips wet and slightly parted I can't help but run my eyes all over her. She steps right up to me, takes off my hat, throws it onto her double bed and slips her hands inside my jacket, around my waste and pulls me tight to her, the heady scent of her sending erotic waves cursing through my body.

"Whatever is so hard?" says she.

"It's my revolver," says I as I place my hands onto her upper arms and push her gently back to arm's length. "Tell me what you must and then I must leave."

"But you don't want to leave, do you? Besides it is I whose life needs saving. Will you not help a damsel in distress?"

"You're not in distress, Matilda. You're just playing a very dangerous game for the sheer excitement of it all. Please stand aside and allow me to leave before whoever is next door hears you have someone in your room."

"I have grandmama one side who's as death as a post, and Percy the other side, who no doubt is so unconsciously drunk even an earthquake couldn't wake him. Seize the opportunity, Gerald, it may never come again."

"This is madness, Matilda. What exactly do you want from me?"

Her hands cover my wrists to move them off her arms, down over her breasts before she pushes them together to rest on the heat between her thighs as she gasps oh so softly, "I want you inside me. I want you to be the first. But I do not want to beg you. Either you want me or you don't."

Not many men would turn down such an offer from such a beautiful little vamp as she, and I am no exemption. Breaking away from her I take off my jacket, remove my holster and lay them on a chair that's up against the oak panelling that goes halfway up the walls, the same as it does in Percy and Claude's rooms, it is this stupid thought that brings me partly to my senses. "Does this panelling go right around the entire castle?"

"No," says she. "If you must know it's only in the family rooms. Stop stalling and let me help you undress."

"This ends right now," says I with determination as I reach for my holster.

"It doesn't end until you have taken me," says she wrapping her arms around my neck and clinging on so tight it would take not a little force to break away from her. "But first I want you to play with me."

"Play with you?"

"Yes. Play with my button."

"Which one, there's lots on your gown?"

"You know which one." Her voice is so sultry, her eyes so mesmerising and her lips so delicious as they meet mine, I know there is no going back. Her hands move down to open part of her gown before taking one of my hands and guiding it into the warmth of her soft down, her legs part as she thrusts her hips forwards and gasps in ecstasy. Her hands explore my back, down over my buttocks and then around to my front and search for my fly buttons. This is so wrong but so right, let the world judge us tomorrow, tonight is lost to passion.

Taking my hand away she pushes it between our lips and cries, "Taste it. I give you the nectar from my Venus. Devour it and then you will want more. Then you will enter me."

Still that voice inside my head tells me to stop, think, imagine the consequences of what you are doing. Be strong and regain your self-control. I push her away just a little.

"This is so dangerous, Matilda. What if it comes out?"

"It won't if you push it right up."

"I mean, what if we are exposed? Can you image the damage it would do to your family?"

"Who cares. The Bullingtons will soon be finished socially anyway. The papers are already sniffing around for more scandal, and before long someone will let enough slip out and then everything else will follow. Can you image how the entire world will just adore reading about all the scandal that's been going on at that 'little castle' in the back and beyond. We'd collapse like a pack of cards. Live for the moment, Gerald. Be the first to take me while saying to hell with the consequences."

"I don't have any protection."

"Neither do I. We don't need any as everyone knows you can't get pregnant the first time."

I push her further away, "That young lady is a cruel myth spread by rakes, just to get their own way with innocent virgins."

"Really! Another reason not to marry Jeremy." She tilts her head oh so prettily, "Do you want me or not?"

I nod.

"Starting from the top, unbutton my gown and kiss every inch of my body right down to my toes."

"And then?"

"Then I will do the same to you."

Closing her eyes, she slips her hands under her hair onto her swan neck and tilts back her head, as I slowly begin undoing the tiny white porcelain buttons that feel cool to the touch. Her skin is so soft, creamy white with a scent of wild flowers. I kiss her neck; she sighs and moves her hands to run her fingers through my hair. The buttons that cover her breasts open at a single touch to reveal nipples so dark… We are interrupted by a boom of thunder so loud I near bit one of her cherries off. Still I continue, until at last I open the buttons to reveal her most secret place. She forces my mouth right into her silky down. There follows the flash of lightning from hell itself. "Bloody hell! That was one hell of a crack," gasps I jumping to my feet.

She clamps her body to mine, "Rip off my gown, I can't wait, I want you now, let the sky open, let the lightning power your loins to love me like no man ever loved a woman before, while the tempest drowns out the world and thunder thrusts your love inside me."

It is all so poetic, the trouble is the storm will wake up the entire household, leaving me stuck here, while no doubt at least someone will question where the hell I am? "I have to go right now," says I as I hold her again at arm's length.

"You can't leave me half fulfilled."

"I must." Grabbing my holster, jacket and hat I make for the door.

Matilda blocks my way, "We may never get this chance again. Stay, love me while you can."

With my free hand I cup her chin, bend my head and kiss her on the lips, "We'll find a way to consummate our love, but for now you must accept tonight is impossible."

She kisses me again, opens the door and peers outside, "Go now, my true love."

I slip out just as there's another bang of thunder, followed by a crack of lightning that lights up the entire hallway, as an eerie face appears further down the hallway before vanishing. A ghost, a man or just a figment of my imagination? A shudder of fear careers through my body as I hurry to my room, where I pause before going in, to put on my holster, jacket and bowler, before doing up my fly buttons. Going into the room I find the window is open with a powerful wind flapping the curtains around. Going over I shut the window and turn to find Betty is sat up in her bed.

"Your back then?" says she with indifference.

"A brilliant observation worthy of Holmes," says I.

"I left the window open because it's so stuffy in here," grates she.

"It's going to tip it down, stuffy or not the window stays shut."

Another flash of lightning followed by an ear shattering bang of thunder so loud, it threatens to demolish the roof. Betty holds the covers up to her chest as I take off my hat, jacket and holster, setting my revolver down on the small table. Kicking off my shoes I lay back on the bed and rest my arms behind my head. Suddenly, I am not the least bit tired. Matilda fills my mind's eye as I try to shut out the guilt, I feel for the woman I have loved for so long laying just inches away from me, who I know is glaring at me through hate filled eyes.

"I can smell her on you," says Betty. "Smell her scent and her sex. You rotten bastard!"

Saying nothing I turn away from her just as another bang of thunder, even louder than the last one, shakes the room and threatens to smash in the window, followed by a scream that's even louder, making me jump and sit up

"Heavens, someone's terrified," cries Betty just as reflected lightning invades the room to snake all around the walls.

Then there are more screams, screams of sheer terror. "We may have been hit," says I getting to my feet as a roar of thunder punches my ears.

"Fuck this," says she chucking the covers over her head.

"I'll go and see what's happened. Get up and put something on in case we have to evacuate."

In my socks, I'm out the room and heading towards the family rooms, passing doors that are wide open or part open, with quests in nightwear standing just outside or peering through gaps. An elderly couple, lord and lady something or other, are holding each other tight as I near the major's room. His door is wide open. "What's happened?"

Lady something or other points towards the stair end of the hallway, "He went that way."

"Who went that way?"

"The earl. And... and he had a sabre in his hand!"

"With blood running down the blade," adds her husband. "We were only going for a pee..."

Clump appears in a dark dressing gown, "What is all the commotion about, Inspector?"

"This couple have just seen the major heading down the hallway with his bloody sabre in his hand."

"Christ!" says Clump. "Everyone, go back inside," he orders waving his arms around. "Lock your doors. Leave this to us"

"What's happening?" says Constance stepping up to Clump while holding her dressing gown tight to her chest.

"Claude's running amok with his sabre."

"He wasn't running," cuts in lady something or other. "He was walking while holding up his sabre. Like… like he…"

"Was walking into battle," adds her husband. "His eyes were strange."

"Thank you, Lord Dent," says Clump. "Please go to your room. Inspector, go and get your shoes on, get your revolver and get the sergeant here. Constance, go back to your room, shut the door and lock it."

"But I can help…" is all I catch as I hurry back to my room to the sound of doors slamming shut and being locked.

"What's happening?" asks Betty as I slip on my shoes.

"We don't know yet. Just lock the door behind me and stay inside."

"I'd rather go in with Chloe."

"Do that then," says I not meaning to sound so flippant. Holster on with revolver, I go out again to find Head standing outside his room while holding up a very pale, breathing hard, Chloe.

"I think it's coming," gasps she.

"What is?"

"The baby!" says Head. "Her waters are about to break!"

What a stupid time to have a baby thinks I. "Can't you hold it back for a while?"

"Don't be stupid, Detective Inspector" snaps Betty pushing her way past me and taking hold of Chloe's other side. "Go and do your job while we look after Chloe."

"Fine, but you best get back in the bedroom and lock the door."

"She needs help," pleads Head. "Help only the right person can give."

Chloe's perspiring face says it all. So white, so scared, utterly lost. "Grab your revolver, Richard then bring Chloe along. Constance will know what to do."

We're halfway to the major's room when Clump comes panting towards us, "What's taking you so long, Inspector?"

"Mrs Head is going into labour."

"What now!" grates he. "Christ! She should be on a bed not going for a bloody walk!"

"I'll handle this, Arthur," snaps Constance coming up behind Clump. "You and the Inspector get going while we take Mrs Head down to the infirmary. It's downstairs, Mrs Head, do you think you can make it?"

Chloe nods.

"Good, Arthur, knock on Roberts door and tell him to send someone for Dr Brent. Quick now, go."

"What about me?" asks Head to Clump.

"Stay with your wife, Sergeant. If the earl appears and waves a sabre at you shoot the bugger."

"What the sabre?"

"No, you fool, the earl. Shoot the earl."

"Where?"

"Any bloody where. Incapacitate him, shoot him in the leg, kill him if you have too. Come on Inspector."

Smithers, still in his butler's uniform, is standing outside the major's room as we draw near, while holding up the major's sabre by the hilt between a finger and thumb.

"I found this at the bottom of the stairs, Chief Inspector," say he his eyes looking suitably horrified.

"Did you see the earl?"

He shakes his head, "I was just making my way to my room when I found..."

"We think the earls gone mad, Mr Smithers. In here."

Stepping into the major's room which is near in darkness, Clump shuts the door and gingerly taking the sabre from Smithers he sets it down on the chest of draws. "Can you send someone to fetch Dr Brent, Mrs Head is going into labour. Knock, Robert up to go with you, the earl may be dangerous, best not to be on one's own."

"Very good, sir," says he glancing around the room before making for the door.

"And get someone to turn up the lamps," orders Clump as lightning flashes, thunder roars and rain starts pelting on the window.

I turn up a lamp on the wall, flooding light onto a gold coloured bedspread that has blood stains on it as I notice a small door, barely three feet high in the wall panel, is open.

Clump is staring at the floor, where there are even more blood stains, and says, "What the hell has been going on here?"

"The answer could lay in there," says I pointing to the wall.

Picking up a candle in its holder, Clump sets it alight and hands it to me, "Take a look, Inspector."

Going over I bob down and shine the candlelight into a recess that heralds a passageway that goes along both ways. The candle flickers from air that is circulating, fanning the light around, there are pipes running along the walls, "It's a passageway, Chief. There's footprints in the dust, odd, they're only going one way but have been stepped over by the same footprints."

"You are not making sense, Inspector," grates Clump as he bends to peer over my shoulder.

"Whoever went along this passage went in forwards and then came out backwards."

"How odd, well let's get up there, lead the way McDuff."

Still bobbed down I shuffle in, with my back bent I stand up as best I can. The air smells somewhat feisty and my sides brush dust and cobwebs from the walls as I shuffle along.

"I am right up your arse," says Clump. "So, do not let rip or I shall have you demoted to a beat constable."

Ignoring him I carry on, there's a sick feeling of dread now in my throat as I see a light ahead of me, and I can sense that Clump is also feeling the same way. I come to a stop at another small open door where I bob down and shuffle into what can only be Percy's room. Stretching up I turn to grab Clump's hand and help him in. He straightens up as his back gives out a crack, we stare at the scene before us.

Percy is only wearing pants while laid back on his bed, his arms are stretched out by his side, his throat has been cut so deep he is near decapitated, blood is still bubbling out and trickling down onto a sheet that is swamped with the stuff.

"Heaven help us," gasps Clump. "My poor, poor, boy."

"We must apprehend the major right away, Chief," says I turning away from the scene.

"Yes. Yes, come on, Inspector."

After unbolting and unlocking the door we go out into a now well-lit hallway, shutting and locking the door behind us, I slip the key into my pocket and lead the way back into the major's room, where, for a moment, we stare at the blood on the major's bed. Clump goes over to the door and takes out the key. I follow him out, he shuts the door, locks it and pockets the key.

Fear shows on Clump's face as he stares into my eyes, "We have a mad man to capture, Inspector,"

"A mad man who could be anywhere, Chief. And worse, we've ordered everyone to lock themselves in their rooms having had no idea that our mad man might just pop out of the panelling, anywhere at any second, kill someone else and then disappear again."

Clump spins around and throws up his arms, "Christ, what if that passageway goes all around the castle?"

Smithers and, Robert in a black dressing gown, come up to us, both appear anxious.

"We have sent someone for the doctor, Chief Inspector," says Smithers. "Meanwhile, Mrs Kemp and Mrs Bellows are assisting Mrs Head, Mrs Bellows has midwife experience."

"Good," says Clump. He is chewing his lip unable to decide what to do next for the best. "Any sign of the earl?"

"None," says Robert.

"There are passageways around the walls, sir," says I to Robert. "Where do they lead and why are they there?"

"They were put in when the castle was rebuilt in expectation that one day gas pipes would be fed around the castle along with the hot and cold-water pipes, perhaps eventually, even electricity. They go right around the castle and can be accessed from every room, but only the family rooms have a passageway high enough for a man to nearly stand up in."

"So, you wouldn't get far if you went down them?"

Robert shakes his head. "What exactly is going on, Uncle? Has father finally completely lost his mind? And what is this about blood on his sabre?"

"Where's your mother?"

"With Mrs Head in the infirmary."

"Right, Inspector check on the rest of the family, take Mr Smithers with you. As they are the most vulnerable bring them downstairs to the drawing room. Safety in numbers and all that. I'm going down to talk to the countess. Everyone, keep your eyes peeled for the earl, do not tackle him if he is armed in anyway, best to talk him into coming with you if you can. If not drop him."

Clump goes off with Robert, Smithers heads to Prune's and Algernon's rooms to give them a knock while I head in the opposite direction towards Elizabeth's, apparently two bedroomed room, at the end of the family rooms. Then we shall all meet in the middle, more or less at the major's room.

One knock on Elizabeth's door and it is opened almost immediately by her maid, the indominable Priscilla Thornberry, who glares at me and barks, "Yes, what is it? Have we been struck by lightning?" Dressed in a tweed twin set she'd scare the balls off a highland bull and may be some months pregnant, but no one would know, she's that big a woman.

"Who is it, Prissy?" sounds Elizabeth's voice.

"It's that scruffy copper from London. I think he has come to evacuate us." She gives me even more of the evil eye. "Well, have you come to evacuate us, little man?"

"You are all to come down stairs right now; by order of Chief Inspector Clump."

Elizabeth steps up and manages to squeeze herself past Priscilla, she is also fully dressed, "Have we been hit by lightning, Inspector?"

"No, Miss. Please gather up your children and come with me."

"They're asleep in bed. I'll have to get them dressed. What is this about?"

"All will be explained by the chief. Please hurry, just throw something on the children while I go and give Miss Matilda a knock."

"Just one moment," orders Priscilla as she steps aside to let Elizabeth hurry past her.

"What is it, madam? I haven't got time for silliness."

"Who do you think you are coming here and ordering my lady around?"

"Shut up, you rude, dopey woman and go and help your mistress, or else!"

"Or else what? I am not afraid of any man, especially a little gelding like you. There isn't a man on earth who can order me about and think they shall get away with it."

Drawing out my revolver I point it straight between her eyes, "Lady, if it weren't for the fact you are pregnant, I'd wrap this barrel around your earhole. Now, do as you are fucking told, or I'll arrest you for causing an affray."

"Oh," says she giving me the self-same odd look that Matilda gave me before she made it clear she desired me. "At last, a real man." She gives out a girly giggle and then disappears.

Bollocks to the very thought of Priscilla bouncing up and down on me and probably breaking my back. I step up to Matilda's door as it hits me. Why the hell didn't it hit me a few minutes ago? What if the major went further along the passageway and entered Matilda's room just after I left her? Feeling sick to my stomach I rap hard on the door.

"Who is it?" sounds Matilda's voice through the door.

"Inspector Potter, Miss. Please open the door," says I sighing with relief.

The sound of a key turning in the lock precedes the door being opened barely three inches.

"You've come back," smiles she. "I knew you would. That's why I'm still up."

"I'm not here for that, Matilda," says I sounding suitably sorry. "You're to come downstairs right now with the rest of the family. Orders from the Chief Inspector."

She opens the door a little wider, wide enough so that I can nearly see all of her as she states the obvious, "But I'm stark naked."

"Then throw something on, anything so long as it is decent. Hurry now."

"You're very serious, Gerald. What on earth's the matter?"

"All will be explained. Please, Matilda just do as I ask."

Leaving the door on the jar she spins around and hurries to her wardrobe and I get to see her long hair right down her back, her firm buttocks and her perfect legs. Not that I'm looking that hard. Hearing footsteps I turn away to see Elizabeth and her brood heading towards me. The half-awake children are being practically dragged along, one each side of their mother while Priscilla brings up the rear. Matilda steps out doing up buttons on a waxed riding coat that stretches down to her ankles. Thank God she didn't put that flimsy nightdress back on or I'd have passed out.

Up ahead I see that Smithers, Prune and Algernon are waiting for us outside Constance's door. As we pass Percy's door Matilda grabs my arm, "You didn't give Percy a knock."

"No need," says I walking on.

"No need because…?"

"The chief will explain," says I unable to look her in the eyes. Smithers and Algernon are supporting a wobbling Prune between them, she looks a right mess with her starchy white hair spiked up and her face covered in some sort of muddy brown night mask, while her watery eyes beam out like coach lamps. Algernon is sporting a short, purple smoking jacket that exposes very hairy knees and a pair of red velvet slippers, over his mop of hair he has a hair net.

"What going on?" demands Prune. "Have we been hit by lightning?"

As she hasn't got her ear trumpet in, I don't bother answering her and merely nod just to hopefully shut her up.

"I knew it. What wonderous fun. Let us hope this dump burns to the ground."

"Oh, do shut up sprouting your vile crap, Grandmama," snaps Elizabeth.

"Yes, I did crap at last," smiles Prune. "Thank you my dear for your concern."

"Right downstairs everyone," says I. "And stay together."

As our entourage reaches the top of the stairs, Robert comes bounding up to us, "Father's been found," gasps he. "He's in the music room with the 'bubbly boos'."

We follow Robert downstairs with Prune moaning that she's being handled too roughly by Smithers and Algernon, who are practically dragging the old bird along. When we reach the drawing room, I order all of them to go in and wait. I head for the music room. Clump is stood outside with Constance.

"You're here, Inspector" says Clump. "Good. Draw your revolver then we shall go in."

Constance faces Clump and says, "Whatever is going on, Arthur?"

"All in good time," says he, taking hold of her hand he turns the doorknob with his other hand and pushes the door open. Claude, dressed in black trousers with his braces off the shoulders of his white shirt, is sat cross legged on the oak floor holding up a 'bubbly boo' by its tail and peering at its backside. The rest of the dogs are watching, but are unusually silent as if they know something dreadful has happened. They don't even acknowledge Constance.

Constance steps closer towards Claude. "Claude. What on earth are you doing?"

He gazes up at her, his eyes vacant. "Just checking their waste parts, old dear. Can't stand the buggers rubbing their bums all over the floor and leaving behind stinky stains. Dirty little beggars. Anyway, what's all the noise about? I heard some woman scheming out…"

"Dear God!", cries Constance. "Is that blood on his shirt and hands?" She stares into Clumps eyes. "What has he done, Arthur?"

Clump looks at me, "Watch him, Inspector while I go and talk to the family. Come with me Constance."

I close the door behind them and slip my revolver back into its holster. I doubt I'll need it.

Claude brushes his hands over his shoes and gets to his feet, "So, what's up, Who old chap?"

"Let's wait until the chief returns, Major. Just relax for a few minutes."

Wandering over to a harp he plucks a couple of strings and says, "Can you play, Who?"

I smile and shake my head.

"Nor I. Never learnt to play anything. Tone death, don't you know? But I can't half swing a golf club. And when I hear that thwacking sound, as it hits the ball, then it is my kind of music. What say you, Inspector Who, don't you just love the sound of golf balls being whacked?"

"I do indeed, Major," lies I having never swung a golf club in my life let alone having watched someone play. "Footballs my favourite, Major. I love the sound of footballs being well and truly booted."

"Footballs alright I suppose," says he picking up a violin and strumming it. "But it'll never catch on like rugby. Now that, sir is a game for real tough men. Played it a lot when I was a lad and had the cauliflower ears to prove it."

A sudden scream pierces my ears, making me and the dogs jump and prick up their ears.

"What the hell was that?" demands Claude throwing away the violin and marching towards me. "Sounded like the old duck. Somethings up."

"It is indeed," says I holding up a stop hand. "Just go and sit down, Major until the chief comes back."

"But I don't want to sit down."

"Let's play a game then."

"A game? I'm up for that, Who old chap. What game is it?"

"It's called, I spy."

He rubs his chin, "Sounds intriguing, Who. How do we play it?"

Grilling Claude

Twenty minutes later it is just me, Claude and Clump in Claude's room. I take off the bloody bedspread, wrap the sabre in it as best I can and set it down on the floor.

"Take your clothes off, Claude," demands Clump.

"Whatever for, Arthur?"

"We need to bag them up for forensics."

"Foreign what's?"

"Just undress down to your underwear," growls Clump.

"I say, bad show ordering a chap to undress," says Claude plonking himself down on the bed and bending down to undo his shoelaces. I step forwards to help him as he seems to be struggling. I take charge of the shoes as they come off.

"See if they match, Inspector," says Clump.

Taking the shoes over to the passageway I find they match perfectly. Standing and facing Clump I nod. Clump pulls off a pillowcase and holds it out, I drop the shoes into it. Then I help Claude take off his shirt and trousers. Clump places the pillowcase by the door and then fetches a dressing gown and a pair of carpet slippers for Claude. I help him into them.

"What is going on, Arthur?" snaps Claude." Here I sit before you while you stand there looking all menacing and grumpy, alongside Who, who is also here invading my privacy. What exactly do you want with me?"

"You have murdered your son," says Clump.

"Which son was that?"

"Percy! You have murdered Percy!"

"Are you sure?"

"We are certain of the fact."

"How odd. Why would I murder my son and heir?"

"We were hoping you could tell us that."

"Can't say I know. Are you sure I murdered him?"

"Yes! Now, shut up asking questions and start answering some."

Claude holds up his hands, "Is this Percy's blood on my hands?"

"It is," sighs Clump. "Sorry, you may go and wash your hands."

I follow Claude into the bathroom. He washes his hands and then wipes them on his dressing gown. Marching back into the room he goes for Clump, "Look here, brother in law. I know nothing of this murder. I've been set up by that bloody Percy, the turd. It's his way of getting rid of me so he can become the next earl, the rat." He stabs a finger at Clump. "The bastard has faked his own murder just to get me hung…"

Clump grabs Claude's finger with one hand and his dressing gown with the other, twisting it tight around his neck. He glares into Claude's eyes, "It won't wash any more, Claude. Your pretending to be mad is over. Now, if you don't answer my questions properly, I will forget you are an earl and my brother in law to treat you like any other cold-blooded killer." He shoves Claude back onto the bed.

"How do you treat other cold-blooded killers?"

Clump shakes his fists at Claude, "With these buggers. Right, tell me what happened, Claude or by God I'll beat it out of you."

"I don't remember, Arthur."

"Well, let us see if we can jog your memory by taking a look at your handy work. Come on, up on your feet." Clump opens the door, we step out into an eerily quiet, deserted hallway. Clump locks the door and steps up to Percy's room, I hand him the key, he unlocks the door and we go in. "Now do you remember?" snarls Clump.

Claude's mouth is wide open, his eyes are bulging, he has turned deathly white and looks about to pass out. He looks away and I don't blame him, it is a gruesome sight even for a seasoned gruesome sightseer like myself.

"Well!" demands Clump. "explain yourself, Claude. Why in God's name did you do this? You, mad, evil bastard!"

Head in hands Claude begins to sob, his legs wobble like jellyfish on a stick as urine dribbles down onto the carpet.

"Bastard!" screams Clump as that big fist of his slams into the side of Claude's head. Claude drops like a stone, but Clump isn't finished, he goes to put the boot in.

"Enough," demands I. "Remember who you are, sir. And just who you are laying into."

Fists clenched in fury Clump glares into my eyes, "Keep out of this, Inspector. I'll have the truth from him if I have to beat him to a fucking pulp!"

"Through me first," says I stepping between him and Claude.

"Do not tempt me."

"I'm not trying to. I'm just trying to get you to calm down before you go too far."

Breathing hard he turns away and punches the wall, which shudders from the impact. I help a groaning Claude to his feet. He is semi-comatose and utterly out of it.

"Alright," snaps Clump. "Let's take him back to his room."

Smithers comes up to us just as Clump slips the key into Claude's bedroom door. Smithers looks to have aged ten years; his ever perfectly groomed hair is all over the place from no doubt repeatedly running nervous fingers through it. He glares with hatred at Claude before turning to Clump. "I came to tell you that Dr Brent has arrived and is in with Mrs Head right now."

"No signs of the head yet?" says Clump matter of fact.

"He is also in with Mrs Head."

"Not that Head, the babies bloody head."

"Not yet, sir. Apparently, Mrs Head is having a very rough time of it."

"Aren't we all, Mr Smithers. How are the family coping?"

"In shock, sir. As we all are. They remain in the drawing room and I believe will be there for some time."

"Good. Encourage them to get drunk, Mr Smithers. It kills the pain. Right, off you go we are busy."

"Anything I can fetch…"

"No thank you," snaps Clump. "We'll ring if we need anything."

Back inside the bedroom Clump raids the drinks cabinet and comes out with a bottle of single malt and smacks his lips together. "Where there is darkness so shall I show you light," grins he as I pray that he doesn't intend doing the down the throat torture on Claude. "Right, Inspector, get three glasses and fill them up." He hands me the scotch, pushes Claude onto the bed and pulls up a chair as near to him as he can get. Claude is fidgeting with his dressing gown cord in between rubbing the side of his skull.

"Bit brutal even for you, Arthur," says he. "I may have to press…"

"Shut up, Claude. Let's begin. Rose Bush and John Chambers, you killed them as well, didn't you?"

"No, I didn't. Why would I?"

"Because you had to get rid of them. You lied in your original statement. Rose did see you going up or coming down from the roof. You told her to keep quiet about it and she did until she knew we were coming. Constable Burroughs wouldn't have fazed her, she had known him all her life, but detectives from London were a different matter. She started panicking and you realised she'd spill the beans, so you urged her and Chambers to flee rather than get arrested for perverting the course of justice. Then to muddy the waters you put on walking boots slightly too small for you, but if you had worn thin socks, I don't suspect they would have been that uncomfortable, unlike the second time when you wore them, when, according to my Inspector, you wore thick socks full of holes to no doubt ensure you got blisters. Wearing thin socks with the boots you tracked poor Rose and Chambers, like a cold and calculating demented Red Indian, and executed them both with arrows."

"Why arrows?" amazes Claude. "Why didn't I just shoot them with my hunting rifle?"

"Because Sam' Jenson, who's often out and about at night, would have heard the shots and been on to you in no time while believing there were poachers abroad."

"Oh, I see. That explains that then."

I pass the scotch around. Clump swallows his in one gulp and passes his glass back for a refill.

"Claude," says he softly. "Why not save us the trouble of trying to work this all out by simply confessing?"

"About what, old chap?"

Jerking forwards in his chair Clump looks about to thump Claude again as he shakes his fists at him, "Don't you, old chap me, you bastard! Talk or its these for you."

"Have you nothing to say, Major?" puts in I while passing Clump his glass.

Claude nods, "Do you think they'll be able to stitch Percy's throat back together? It looks so awful as it is."

"Give me bleeding strength," groans Clump slumping back in his chair. "Claude you will either hang for this or spend the remainder of your days in a nut house. But, if you cooperate with us you might only have to go into a nut house for a short while until you are cured of your, 'temporary madness'. Why you could be home for Christmas, in a few years' time."

Claude takes a sip of his scotch, "If I killed that girl and that fellow, what's his name, why would I have confessed to trying to kill Percy with that big brick?"

Exactly, thinks I.

"To take suspicion off yourself. What if Rose or Chambers had have told someone else that you were seen that day? By keeping quiet and then later being found out you would have sealed your own fate. Clever, very clever." He pauses to down his scotch and then passes me his glass. Lighting up a cigar he stares into Claude's eyes as if trying to read his mind. "Your planting of those shoes and the bow and arrows on yourself was an act of genius, Claude and not the act of a nut case."

"Can I ask the major something, sir?"

Clump looks askance at me, "If you must."

"Major, where were you intending to go when you left this room while wielding your sabre?"

Exhaling he says, "I'm not sure, Inspector Who. All I remember is waking up holding the sabre and feeling very odd. I thought someone must have shaken me awake and so I set off to find the old duck to ask her what was going on."

"Bloody liar," snarls Clump jumping to his feet. "I am sick of your ramblings, Claude. Start telling the truth. Or I'll, I'll…"

"Before you start thumping him again, one more question if you please, sir."

Clump falls back on his chair, "One more and no more."

"Major, can you remember coming up to bed?"

Claude sips more of his scotch, scratches his head and then says, "I think so. I do so. That girl of mine, the youngest one, what's her name?"

"Matilda."

"That's the one," smiles he. "She helped me up the stairs." He winks. "I'd had a few too many, Who. Bit wobbly on my feet. Yes, I recall, Matilda helped me to get ready for bed. She took off my jacket and tie, shoved me back on the bed and said: 'Go to sleep Father.' Then she went off having not taken my shoes off, the rotter."

"The self-same shoes we took from you a few minutes ago?"

"Yes, those were the ones, I think." He points a finger at Clump. "Can't abide sleeping in my footwear. Had to in the army, when camped out in bandit land, in case you came under attack in the middle of the night. No good struggling to put on your boots when there's bandits attacking. By George you'd be dead before you got your damn socks on. Hated sleeping in my boots, can't stand it too this day and everyone knows the fact. Can't understand why that girl didn't take them off."

"Perhaps she did," sneers Clump. "Only for you to put them back on just before you went and slaughtered Percy. This is just more smoke and mirrors, Inspector. Let us just take him down to the dungeon and lock him up until the morning. Don't forget, we have a body next door to sort out."

"Bear with me a while longer, sir, if you please. Major, can you remember who helped you to get ready for dinner?"

"I can. No one. I had to dress my bally self. That snotty valet chap was too busy to help, so he said, but I think he was just being lazy."

"So, no one helped you?"

"That girl tied my shoelaces up properly when I went down to the dining room. What was her name again?"

"Matilda."

"That's the one."

"Where on earth are you going with this, Inspector?" grates Clump.

"Will you bear with me, Chief. I need to speak to Miss Matilda. It won't take long."

"It better not, Inspector. If you're not back before I've finished that bottle of scotch and with something worth hearing, you'll find me down in the dungeon giving Claude a taste of my fists. Hurry up before I change my mind."

Heading down the stairs I make for the drawing room, tap gently on the door before entering to find the family so engrossed in what they are doing no one notices me. The general aura is one cf quiet contemplation, but judging by the amount of glasses and spirit bottles laying around, a lot of booze has been drunk. Constance is sat on the sofa holding hands with Elizabeth on one side and Matilda on the other. Their eyes say it all, red ringed and full of pain, with their makeup smeared they are lost in their own thoughts. Algernon is vacantly sat nursing a brandy glass while Prune is sound asleep with her head back and her mouth wide open, but at least she isn't snoring. Only Robert and Smithers are standing while facing each other and quietly conversing. Side on I note their profiles as a strange thought crosses my mind. Smithers suddenly turns his head and spots me; he comes right over.

"Can I assist you, Inspector?"

"Sorry to interrupt, Mr Smithers, can you inform Miss Matilda that I'd like a quick word with her, please."

He gives me an odd fleeting look, a flash in his eyes that says he knows about me and Matilda, "Of course, Inspector."

He goes over to Matilda and whispers to her, she wipes her eyes with a handkerchief, gets to her feet and comes over to me. I lead her out into the hall where we face each other.

"How are things?" asks I taking in the heady scent of gin and tonic.

"Alright I suppose. Mamma has been in a terrible state, but she's calm, now. To be honest, I'd say certain of my siblings aren't too upset about Percy's death."

"And you, how are you coping?"

She shrugs, "What can I do for you?"

"I have a few questions to ask you. They may seem strange and trivial, but could be of immense importance, so please bear with me. Did you retie your father's shoes when he came down for dinner?"

Her eyebrows go up as a smile crosses her lips, "That is indeed an odd question. Yes, I did retie his shoes. Father never could tie his laces neatly. But then, until recently, he has never had to. May I ask why you wish to know this?"

I shake my head, "Can't say right now. Did you remove your father's shoes when you helped him to bed?"

She nods, "Father cannot bear sleeping in any kind of footwear. Goodness, if I hadn't have removed them and he woke up and found them on, he would have my head for it."

"Thank you, one more thing, will you accompany me upstairs I wish to show you something?"

She moves dangerously close to me, "I thought you'd never ask. Do you want to go to my room…?"

"It's nothing like that, Matilda. Please, just come with me. It won't take long."

"You don't intend taking me then?" asks she gripping my arm and pouting oh so prettily.

I gently remove her hand, "Not tonight. We have a killer to catch who may well strike again before the night is through."

Frowning she says, "We were told father is the killer. Are you saying…?"

"I'm not saying anything. Come on."

Side by side we make for the stairs, passing Jackson asleep in a chair, obviously he's the poor sod stuck with night duties. As we climb the stairs, Matilda's thigh pushes its way out from her coat, and it's all I can do to stop myself from taking her in my arms and crushing her to my body.

"You know how much I want you," says she pausing at the top of the stairs and facing me.

"I do," says I as I stroke her cheek. "But not tonight." Have a bit of decorum thinks I.

We walk on, it's so quiet you'd think no one else was in the place. Even the storm has passed, and the rain has stopped. At Claude's room I tell Matilda to stay outside while I go in and reach for the pillowcase.

"What's happening?" demands Clump over Claude's snoring, as he's dropped off.

"One minute, Chief and all will be revealed." Taking the pillowcase, I slip back into the hallway, closing the door behind me. Taking out the shoes I show them to Matilda. "Are these the shoes your father was wearing when he came down to dinner?"

She takes one and holds it up closer to the wall lamp, "They certainly look like the same. Same style, size and colour." Turning it over she inspects the heal and shakes her head. "They're not the ones father wore at dinner, or the ones I took off when I helped him to bed." She points to the back of the heal. "The ones father wore to dinner were worn a little on the heals where he digs them in as he walks, well marches really. There's no wear on these heals."

"Thank you, Matilda." I take the shoes from her and put them back in the pillowcase. "One more thing, did you lock your father in his room after putting him to bed?"

She shakes her head, "I asked Jackson to look in on him periodically throughout the night to check that he was alright.

Father can be prone to sleepwalking, plus I was worried he might be sick as he'd drunk so much."

"Thank you. Please do not say anything to anyone about what I have questioned you about. And I mean no one…"

"You're scaring me now."

"You'll be fine if you do as I've asked. If questioned, just say I asked you about how Mrs Head is getting on with the birth. How is she getting on?"

"She's been more relaxed between pushes now the doctors with her. But apparently it's going to be a long hard labour."

"Right, let me escort you back to the drawing room."

"No need. I shall be fine. Besides wouldn't it look odd if we pass someone. Alone I could say I just nipped to my room to fetch something, should I meet anyone."

"Just be careful and go straight there."

"I will. Kiss me."

I am close to kissing her when the door opens and Clump sticks his head out, "Matilda, what on earth are you doing up here?"

"Helping you with your enquiries, Uncle Arthur. Must go, mamma needs me."

"This better be good, Inspector," says Clump as we watch Matilda walk away.

"It is, trust me."

"Well," demands Clump once we're back in the bedroom with Claude snoring even louder.

"I don't believe Claude is our killer."

"Because?"

I pour myself a scotch and pull up a chair close to Clump. "Matilda is adamant that the shoes in that pillowcase are not the shoes that Claude wore to dinner, or the ones she took off when she helped him into bed. Not only that the laces had been tied far too neatly, something that Claude struggles to do." I pause to see his reaction.

"Go on," says he somewhat impatiently.

"I believe our killer snuck into this very room while Claude was out for the count. They took his sabre, opened the little passageway door and went into Percy's room, murdered him, and then, making their first mistake, they walked backwards into this room while holding the sabre out, to ensure no blood would run down the blade onto their hands or clothes. They dripped blood onto Claude's hands and then laid the sabre down beside him. They then took off their shoes and put them on Claude's feet, mistake number two, they tied the laces too neatly. Then they slipped into Claude's shoes and snuck away, but not before they gave him a good shake to wake him up. They took one hell of a risk of being seen, despite the fact nearly everyone was in their bed, and were lucky that the Dents didn't see them. I believe that Claude has been set up since the outset by someone so clever and ruthless, he will stop at nothing to get what he wants. The same man who murdered Rose and Chambers."

"And his name is?"

I tell him, he doesn't appear over excited by my theories. "You are becoming a veritable Sherlock Holmes, Inspector. You may have something, but of real proof and possible motive you have none."

"I have a notion as to the motive, but admit it is only a notion. I need proof and intend searching for that proof."

"But not tonight," says Clump with finality. "The family have suffered enough, and we can't have you rampaging through the place at this time of night," he pauses to check his fob watch. "Bloody hell, it's two thirty, the bloody cockerels will be crowing before too long. I think you are almost certainly pissing up the wrong tree, but even so your suspicions cannot be ignored. Right, I will stay here with Claude. You better go and see how Mrs Head is and then get your head down for a while. You must be dead on your trotters."

"Mrs Head is still trying, apparently."

"Right, well get off to bed, and lock the door behind you, as I shall lock this one once you've gone."

"Do you want Claude handcuffed to the bed, sir?"

"No… He won't cause me any trouble. You know, Inspector I've always thought the world of my brother in law and I do hope he is innocent of these heinous crimes, but you have to face the facts, he may well be innocent of killing Percy, but could easily be guilty of killing the other two, just as we said. The trouble is, everyone will be blaming you for not charging Claude in the first place with the attempted murder of Percy, and then not locking him up, thus, saving Percy's life."

On that sobering note, I bid him goodnight and head back to my room.

Laying back on the bed, minus just shoes, hat and jacket, I had hoped to instantly drop off, but too much was going on in my head. Betty and Matilda along with the murders were all jumbled up together in a quagmire of thoughts. By now dawn is breaking, seagulls screeching, cockerels crowing and the beautiful sounds of the dawn chorus, but none of them do a thing to ease my discomfort for what I have done to Betty, and for what I'm about to do to the Bullingtons if my theory is proved right. At last the door opens and Betty creeps in, now, hopefully I can settle one problem to allow me to concentrate on the dirty job I have to do.

"You're awake," says she flopping down on her bed and running her hands over her face and through her hair. "How long have you been back?"

Sitting up I can see she is dead beat; her eyes are wet, she's been crying, and a sense of deep sadness fills the room. God forbid that Chloe and or the little one didn't survive. I go over to her bed and risk putting an arm over her shoulders and hug her to me, but am unable to speak. She puts her arm around my waste and then buries her head in my chest and begins to quietly sob. There is nothing more I can do until she is ready to speak. After what felt like forever, she lifts her eyes and gazes into mine with that look I know so well, she still adores me. Cupping her chin, I softly kiss her on the lips, and she responds instantly. Breaking away I wipe the teardrops from her eyes and then wait.

"Richard and Chloe have a son, Gerald. He is beautiful. Both are doing well. Chloe is exhausted but serene in her joy. The doctor is pleased with them and said they'll be fine. Mrs Kemp and Mrs Bellows were wonderful, such lovely, lovely ladies. I… I," she faulters and kisses me again before saying, "am so happy for them."

Sometimes I believe I must be the most stupid man on earth! I should have known exactly what was wrong with Betty, and it's nothing to do with anything other than what she is going through right now.

She takes my hand and squeezes it tight. "When I first met Andrew, I marvelled at just how much he reminded me of you when you were his age, handsome, shy, polite and friendly. I thought, that had we been blessed with a son he would now be about Andrews age. I allowed my imagination, my hopes and dreams to cloud my judgement, I was acting like a loving mother while he, naturally took it the wrong way," she half grins, "and thought, as randy young men do, that I wanted him for a lover. I should have told you how I was feeling instead of allowing you to suspect I was making eyes at the boy. It was my fault that I pushed you into Matilda's arms…"

I put a finger across her lips, "You are not to blame, my darling, I am. I was everything you said I was, and to my utter shame I took advantage of your anger to try and convince myself that it was acceptable to flirt with a woman nearly half my age."

"Have you been intimate with her?" she asks me in a way that says she knows the answer anyway.

I nod.

"Jeremy Trout. I had a long conversation with him, a heart to heart. He said I was: 'A woman of the world.' I said: 'I've never been abroad,' and he said: 'You don't have to go anywhere to become a sage.' In the strictest privacy he told me that Matilda had seemed almost desperate for him to take her virginity and take it now, even before the engagement. That was the real reason she turned up at the Smugglers. Not to size me up as I had believed, but to try again to get Jeremy in bed. Jeremy is a staunch believer in remaining chaste until wed and has refused several times to bed Matilda. She then came to me and made it clear, as you know, that she had set her sights on you…"

The bells finally ring inside my idiot brain and at last it is the kick in the balls that I thoroughly deserve. "So, Matilda is pregnant and was desperate to cover it up by hopefully bedding Trout and passing it off as his, followed of course by a hasty marriage. But as he wouldn't play ball, she decided to latch on to me. Which doesn't make sense because I'm married and nowhere near in her class."

"It does when you realise; she is genuinely infatuated with you. It does when you know that you are a real man, Gerald, strong, dependable and very loving. You're also very stupid at times, but then no one's perfect. Matilda no doubt thought it was better to be with a man like you, who would stand by her come hell or high water while believing she was carrying his child, then go with whoever the child's real father is."

"Constable Burroughs is the most likely candidate. Nice lad, shows promise, but not ready for a child and marriage, and would be even less able to cope with the repercussions of what he's been up to. You don't mess with the aristocracy and walk easily away. As a couple they'd end up destitute, she has no idea about real life, and he isn't seasoned enough to get anywhere."

"Exactly. So, there is a conundrum for you, Detective Inspector. Do you divorce me and marry Matilda, thus at last becoming a father, after all if she can have one, she can have more? Or do you stay with a woman who can never give you a child, boy or girl?"

Having called me Detective Inspector, I am thinking I am near home and dry. Even so I better not fuck the next bit up. "I stay with the only woman I have ever truly loved. I will not lie and say I don't dream of being a father, but what will be will be and you and I are forever, children or no children."

Betty starts yawning, I start yawning, there's a lot more to go over but I need at least some sleep, or I'll not be up to the task ahead. Getting up I lay Betty back on her bed and take of her shoes, she's asleep before I have laid back on my bed. The sun is now penetrating through the curtains, the birds are going chirp mad outside, but for me, at last, it is deep-deep-sleep.

Nailing a killer

I am rudely woken by someone banging on the door so loud it threatens to wake half of Cornwall. It can only be Clump.

"Not ready yet?" grates he when bleary eyed I open the door.

"Sorry, sir. What time is it?"

"Eight o' bloody clock. Christ, how much sleep does a man want? Get cleaned up and meet me in Claude's room in half an hour. I'll knock up the sergeant."

With that he strides up to Heads door and bangs on that. The man isn't human, not only is he raring to go despite having had hardly any sleep and God knows how much booze, he has obviously forgotten that Chloe has just had a baby. I go inside, pick up my toilet bag and head for the bathroom. After a dodgy shave, a quick plop and a thorough strip wash, I go back to the room and put on a clean white shirt, and black trousers. Betty wakes up rubbing her eyes.

"What was all that banging, Detective Inspector?"

Turning away from the mirror on the wall I continue tying my tie and say, "Clump. You do know that Percy was murdered during the night?"

"Yes. It's dreadful. Sorry, I um haven't even asked…"

"I haven't time to talk," says I. Holster on, revolver in holster, jacket and hat on. "I must go, Betty. If I am right, today is the day the Bullingtons face social destruction. But then nothing comes up to having your throat cut or being shot dead by an arrow." I make for the door.

"Haven't you forgotten something, Detective Inspector?"

I nip back and give her a hurried peck on the lips, "I love you."

"I love you too. But you still need to put your shoes on."

Shoes on I go out the door. I spy Head stumbling towards the bathroom and call out to him.

"Gerald," says he turning to face me.

"Congratulations, Richard," says I noting he's got more bags beneath his eyes than I have.

"Thanks' Gerald. I best hurry, Clumps in one of his: let's get the bastard mood."

I nod and stride down the hallway to Claude's room, knock on the door and get 'bellowed' in.

"Good man," says Clump. "Only two minutes late."

"Sergeant Head will be a bit on the drag, sir."

He shrugs, "New father, new priorities. He'll get used to it. Right, as you can see Claude isn't here being currently ensconced in the dungeon for his own safety. The Countess lost it around three o'clock this morning, having slipped out of the drawing room unseen, as everyone else had either gone to bed or dropped off where they sat, she grabbed a medieval axe from the wall and went looking for Claude intent on burying it in his skull. She's been sedated by the doctor and is locked in her room with her maid. The doctor has been to see the victim and will issue a death certificate. Burroughs arrived at seven and I've sent him to the village to telegram Truro Station. I have demanded they get their forensics up here right away, no excuses, and help with our investigations. Now, between us we will move Percy to the icehouse for now to keep him fresh. Then we shall clean up the mess and bag all evidence. If your theory doesn't work out, then we are left with no option but to formally arrest Claude for the murder of his son, along with the suspicion that he murdered Rose and Chambers. Then it's question everyone time, daunting though it is. But first let's go and grab the sergeant and get some breakfast."

We go and knock on Head's door; he opens it immediately but is still in a state of undress.

"Congratulations, Sergeant," says Clump. "How is the wife and child?"

"Well, thank you sir. They're still in the infirmary being watched over by Mrs Bellows."

"Good, hurry up and get dressed and armed. We'll wait for you in the servant's hall."

As we plod on Clump says, "Those little doors to the passageway require a key to open them, something we didn't spot earlier. The key will open them from the inside and the outside. The trouble is it is believed the only person who holds such keys is the head of maintenance."

"Jeffery Cornish."

"Mm… What do you think?"

I shake my head as we descend the stairs, "I don't believe he has anything to do with it, Chief. But if my theory doesn't bear fruit, we shall have to question him."

There are surprisingly few people about as we head up the corridor to the servant's hall, going past the infirmary I would have liked to have popped in to pay my respects to Chloe, but Clump is in too much of a hurry. On entering the hall, we come face to face with Smithers who is not looking his usual smart self, he looks as if he's been attacked by a hedge.

"Good morning, gentlemen," says he without conviction. "I have sent Mrs Kemp off for a couple of hours to get some rest. Someone else will have to look after you."

With that he slopes off. Clump marches into the kitchen with me on his heals where we find it isn't so much buzzing as deflated. There's barely a servant about and the few that are appear too tired to help themselves, let alone anyone else.

"Grab three of those plates," orders Clump pointing towards the drainer where cleaned crockery is piled up high. "I'll grab some knives and forks and a tray."

Duly done, I'm holding a large tray with the plates and cutlery on while following Clump into the pantry. Half a sliced leg of ham is unceremoniously shared out on the three plates, followed by giant wedges of cheese, half a crusty loaf, a lump of butter, a jar of chutney and a jar of marmalade.

"That'll do us," grins he. "Let's get scoffing."

Settling down at the table in the hall, we set too enjoying our food just as Head comes in to join us.

"Get someone to make us a pot of tea, Sergeant," says Clump. "And hurry up about it."

Head is back in a minute and sits down to join us. "Five minutes, sir," he yawns. "If the girl can stay awake long enough to boil a kettle."

Twenty minutes later we have mopped our plates and emptied the pot. Clump is now ready to brief us while sat back and enjoying a huge cigar.

"I have come up with a plan, gentlemen. While the quests and family are in the dining room having their breakfast, that's those who can face it or even get up for it, we shall be tidying up the mess upstairs once we've transferred Percy to the icehouse. At eleven, by which time we should have completed our task, I shall gather the family in the drawing room to enable you two to go about your business."

"What business is that, sir?" says Head, as obviously he doesn't know sod all about sod all.

"All in good time, Sergeant. How long do you think you will need, Inspector?"

"Judging by previous searches, I'd say a couple of hours."

"Do it in one hour. I don't believe I'll be able to hold their attention any longer. Assuming the door will be locked, how do you intend getting in? If we ask for a key, we'll lose the element of surprise, and I won't, at this point, sanction your breaking down the bloody door."

I ask Head, "Did you bring your set of lock picks with you?"

"Up in my room. Why…?"

"Shut up for a minute," snaps Clump. "You keep asking stupid questions and I shall lose my thread. Where was I?"

"Keeping the family in the drawing room," says I.

"Correct. Once you have, or have not, found what you hope to find you come and tell me and we shall take it from there. I have told Smithers to ensure that all quests and servants, who were inside the castle around the time of Percy's murder, must not leave the building without my express permission, on pain of arrest. Jackson, who is currently guarding the dungeon to hopefully prevent anyone from trying to kill the earl; will remain there until we can relieve him. Believe me when I say that Constance may stop at nothing to get at Claude, she's that out of her mind with grief. Hopefully when she wakes, she may have calmed down to just wanting to see Claude hang in place of splitting his skull with an axe, castrating him, slicing off his face and having all his golfing gear made into a bonfire in front of him. Once forensics are here, they can view the crime scene, go through the evidence, and most importantly, see if they can find any finger prints on the panelling in the bedrooms, and any other finger prints other than Claude's, Matilda's and yours, Inspector, on the shoes that we have bagged up. And before you smirk, Inspector, I have not changed my mind over the value of fingerprints, but will give them a chance in this instance. Burroughs will stand guard outside the drawing room once he returns. Questions?"

"How do you intend keeping the family in the drawing room while we're about our business?" asks I.

"I intend asking them if they have any idea why Claude carried out this dreadful act, and do they have any idea if he was involved in the murders of Rose and Chambers? I shall string it out as best I can, but be warned it is going to be difficult holding their attention for too long. They are traumatised, devastated and likely to just want to go off and do anything to take their minds off what's happened. I'll do my best while hoping that you won't be too long."

Quite suddenly his eyes go all misty as they become transfixed on something behind me, turning my head, I see he is gazing at one of the photos on the wall where Percy can be seen standing amongst the family, oddly there is a shadow across his face.

"Percy was a sod," says Clump with a sniff. "He lived life to the full and was sometimes bad, sometimes good or somewhere in between. He should have been punished for all the times he'd taken advantage of those considered lesser beings than himself, like the servant girls he'd seduced. However, even he did not deserve what he got. Let's get on."

The stage is set; I have the evidence in a bag at my feet, only it's not enough to convict my suspect. Head is sat handcuffed beside

Claude on high back chairs. Clump, having kept the family occupied for over an hour while Head and I conducted a room search of our suspect, is sat out on his own on another high back chair. I am standing between them, we are facing the family, with Robert and Algernon on armchairs either side of the sofa where sits Prune, Elizabeth, Constance and Matilda. Smithers has set down coffee on the coffee table and is pouring it into fancy blue flower-patterned cups on saucers. After serving the family he hands, Head and Clump their coffee's, I having declined. Job done, Smithers bows to Constance before about to take his leave.

"Please remain, Mr Smithers," says I. "Pull up a chair and sit down beside Mr Robert."

Robert holds up a hand. "I must protest, Inspector. Without disparage to Smithers we do not wish to have a member of staff present in what is, after all, a family matter."

"Smithers stays," says Clump with finality.

"As you wish, Uncle," grates Robert.

Smithers carries a chair over to Robert and sits down beside him, looking I must say, rather pleased to be allowed to remain.

I begin, "Lord Percy's life was an enigma. In many ways he was nowhere near are dark as he was painted, in other ways he deserved the vitriol he received. However, we are here to unmask a killer and not to slander the deceased. What I am about to present to you may cause distress and anger amongst you, but it is unavoidable. The earl did not kill his son. That said, then who did and did that same person also kill Rose Bush and John Chambers? In this room there is a killer; who may well have had others present, who aided and abetted in the murders. Certainly, this family have a good many secrets it wishes to keep from the outside world, secrets that gave motives to everyone here to want to see Lord Percy dead. But first I will explain to you how Lord Percy met his demise. The killer waited until he was certain no one was around and most likely asleep in their beds. Like a thief in the night he slipped into the earls room where the earl was sound asleep, taking the earls sabre he went over to the service hatch in the panelling, unlocking it he went into the passage way and made his way along it until he came to Lord Percy's service hatch, he unlocked it and went into the bedroom, where he found Lord Percy laid on his back on his bed, and sleeping the sleep of one who has had far too much to drink. The actual murder was over in one swift action, Lord Percy would not have felt a thing. Deed done the killer made his way back down the passageway, but he went backwards while holding the sabre at arm's length to ensure no blood dripped onto his clothes, or ran down the blade and onto his hand. Once back in the earl's room he allowed the blade to drip blood onto the earl's hands and shirt before smearing blood onto the earl's bed cover, then he laid the sabre down beside the earl. He then removed the shoes he was wearing and put on an almost identical pair that the earl had worn to the banquet. After putting the shoes he'd taken off, onto the earl's feet, he gave the earl a few shakes to wake him before slipping unseen out of the room and hurrying away. Lord and Lady Dent were on their way to the shared lavatory, when they came face to face with the earl covered in blood and holding the sabre. Lady Dent screamed and thus raised the alarm. Detective Chief Inspector Clump and I were quickly on the scene and initially were convinced of the earl's guilt. After all, he had already earlier confessed to trying to murder his son. However, once we had the earl in our custody and began to question him, we started to have serious doubts about his quilt."

"Not us, you," cuts in Clump. "It is you and you only who must take the credit for doubting the earl was guilty of this heinous crime."

"Thank you, sir. I went downstairs to the drawing room to speak to Lady Matilda to find out if she could corroborate what the earl had told us, and she did. But it was what I saw when I first entered the drawing room that set my mind into a fever. Mr Robert was stood talking to Mr Smithers. I only briefly saw their side profiles, but it struck me that they appeared so alike they could well be father and son…"

Constance is up onto her feet, horror etches her face, yet she is unable to speak and sits back down while Smithers just glares at me. The rest of the family gape at me, no more so of course then Robert, yet Claude remains calm, calm as if he had always suspected.

"You are saying the butler and my daughter-in-law have been at it for years?" smirks Prune. "Well, didn't I tell you as much years ago Claude that she wasn't the one for you? Too flighty, too common and far too randy. But would you listen…?"

"Balderdash!" shouts out Robert. "Ronald Smithers did not even join the household until I was about six years old. What you are implying, Inspector is utter rubbish."

"Just over thirty years ago, Mr Robert, your mother went over to India to be with your father."

"I can confirm that," cuts in Claude, "Because I was there."

"Yes, thank you Major," sighs I, if they keep interrupting, I shall lose my thread. I continue, "The countess wasn't enamoured with India and so she headed back to England, with just her personal maid, having secured a birth on a passenger liner. Which is where she first met Ronald Smithers, a well-respected chief steward who also doubled up as head of on-board entertainment. He and the countess quickly became friends and then lovers, and she became pregnant with her second child. During the voyage the countess no doubt maintained an outward appearance that befitted her station in life, as she made friends with other well-heeled ladies in a similar position as herself. As a group, for proprieties sake, they joined in the onboard entertainment. The croquette on the false lawn on the deck. The exercise routines and the clay pigeon shooting at the stern of the ship. Most importantly, for our investigations, she joined in the archery lessons that were overseen by Mr Smithers, for who it seems is an excellent bowman. Are you not, Mr Smithers?"

He says nothing and just glares at me. In fact, everyone is either glaring or still gaping at me, but at least I have a captive audience.

"The voyage over, the love affair between a lowly steward and his aristocrat lover would also seem to be over. The countess went home, and Mr Smithers set sail for more adventures and possibly more seductions of lonely, high society women who were away from their husbands. Only it wasn't over, because Ronald Smithers had fallen in love with the Countess of Bullington. He held out for close on a year, but still unable to let it go he finally wrote to the countess and begged her to meet him. She wrote back and refused. However, she was also still in love with him and could not resist informing him that they had a son named Robert. After that initial letter they corresponded on a regular basis, until, unable to keep away any longer, and over five years since they'd seen each other, Ronald Smithers, who'd by now left the merchant navy and taken up employment in an upmarket restaurant in London, replied to an advert in a London paper for a trainee butler; at one Bullington Castle. He secured an interview and travelled down to Bullington were he was interviewed by the earl himself, who was impressed with this smart, polite young man's demeanour, and offered him the job there and then. Smithers quickly rose up the ladder and within three years had been promoted to head butler, by which time he and the countess had literally taken up where they had left off on the passenger liner, while obviously being extremely careful to keep their affair secret."

"Good Lord," cries out Prune while waving her arms about. "So, none of these buggers, except possibly for Percy, could be the spawn of a Bullington. There you are Claude, I told you she was a bad one."

"If you do not keep quiet, madam," snaps I. "I will take away your trumpet."

"Take it away, Who, old chap," says Claude. "Then shove it up her rotten…"

"Quiet!" bellows Clump." Or, I shall have you all gagged." Instant obedience. "Please continue, Inspector Potter."

Meeting Smithers still glaring eyes I continue, "The trouble is, Mr Ronald Smithers, after years of taking a back seat you became ever more disillusioned with your lot. You believed that you, yes you, should decide where this household was going. The earl was becoming ever more erratic, while Lord Percy was becoming ever more degenerate, so you set about a course of action that would push the earl and Lord Percy into the background, while promoting your own son to the fore, and the countess went along with it for the good of the Bullington estate and the families future. The earl was to be treated as a fool, while Lord Percy was to be treated as if he were the devil incarnate, in order to promote your own son and thus ensure that the reins of the estate were safely in Mr Roberts hands, thus making him the Master of Bullington even if he couldn't be crowned earl. This action would ensure you remained forever in the place you love so much; alongside the woman you love even more. That love could never be made public, but you would be content to stay in the back ground while manipulating everyone you could to maintain the modus operandi that you had engineered. However, even that wasn't enough, and as fate took an unexpected turn you seized upon it. In a moment of utter madness, confusion and temper, the earl attempted to kill his eldest son, which set in motion a wicked train of thoughts in your obsessed mind of a way to get rid of Lord Percy, along with the earl forever, thus leaving the way clear for your son, Robert to become the earl. You murdered Lord Percy and framed the earl for it. Do you wish to say anything before I arrest you?"

A smirk flicks across his mouth, "Yes, I do, Inspector. I suspect that having gone through my personal possessions you have all the evidence you need, to back up what you have said, in that bag at your feet. I am indeed my lady's lover and Robert, is my son." He gazes with love into Roberts horrified eyes before looking back into mine. "The dates match, and yes, side on we are a perfect match, but from the front you can see so much more of Robert's mother in him. And yes, I have indeed, as you put it, engineered my son's promotion to ensure the family seat continues to thrive, and I and my love can be together for life."

"You, dirty rotten butler, who else have you fathered?" bursts out Claude as he attempts to go for Smithers, only to be restrained by the handcuffs and pulled back into his seat by Head.

"No one else, except perhaps, for Lady Matilda," says Smithers with indifference. "Lady Elizabeth and Mr Algernon where conceived while I was at sea, so no doubt they are yours."

"I say," says Algernon getting up on his feet. "May I say something, Inspector?"

"Please do, Mr Algernon."

"With Percy dead and Robert not a Bullington, surely that leaves me the heir apparent?"

"I doubt it, sir."

"You do?" amazes he. "Why so?"

"You must ask your mother that question, sir."

"Why me?" snaps Constance. "You appear to have all the answers, Inspector why don't you tell him?"

"Very well, ma'am. I suspect, Mr Algernon that you were fathered by none other than Samuel Jenson the head gamekeeper."

His eyes seem to revolve in his head as he says, "Fucking Jenson? Mamma, you, dirty rotten cow how could you do it with that scruffy wastrel? Now I shall never be earl."

"I knew it," puts in Claude. "I always said he was far too hairy to be a Bullington. I say, Inspector Who, well done. What's next on the menu?"

"What about me?" pleads Elizabeth.

"What about you?" says Claude. "Probably the daughter of a pig farmer I shouldn't wonder."

"Fear not, Elizabeth" says Constance while glaring at Claude. "You are your father's daughter, and thus, at present, your son will be next in line for the earldom."

"Oh goody," smiles she.

"And me?" croaks Matilda standing up and glaring down at her mother. "Who is my father? The butler, the earl or some miscreant who just happened by?"

Obviously resigned to it all Constance's answer is negative, "I don't know. You could be a Bullington or you could be a Smithers. But you definitely are one or the other."

"Oh… Whoopy-do, you, dirty rotten bitch! You rotten hypocrite. I hate you." With that she whirls away and storms towards the door.

I block her path. "You will remain, Miss until I say you may leave."

"Get out of my way!"

"No. Go and sit down and control yourself. Change places with Algernon if you want."

"I'll tell all," she whispers.

"Then do so, Miss," whispers back I. "Tell them that you are pregnant by the local plod. Tell them that you became engaged to Trout while knowing you were pregnant. Tell them that you had hoped to seduce Trout into bed, thus blaming him for your condition, but when he refused to give you one before marriage, you tried it on with me, as you were desperate to convince some mug they were the father before you began to show."

Spinning around she holds up her arms and calls out, "I have a confession to make."

Ears prick up and eyes widen, they have no idea what's coming next, but judging by their faces they are terrified they might not like what they are about to hear. Nor I, as she may be about to discredit me, which could be detrimental to the case and would see me thrown off the force with two black eyes, curtesy of Clump.

"I am pregnant," says Matilda with defiance.

"What!" shouts Constance jumping to her feet. "Why, that's wonderful news. At last there is light in our current darkness. Of course, Jeremy will have to marry you right away. Oh, joy of joys."

"It isn't his."

"It isn't? Who the hell is the father then?"

"It's that man who's currently standing guard outside the door to prevent anyone from coming in or leaving."

Now Constance appears absolutely horrified, "The Village Constable? You've given your chastity to the Village 'fucking' Constable? Why you stupid, stupid girl."

"Slag heap," spits Prune. "Always knew the girl would be a tart like her mother."

"Shut up you, old fool," spits Constance. "You are finished, Matilda. You will be cast out or committed to an asylum…"

"You hypocrite, Mamma. If I am to be cast out then surely you also must be cast out along with Algernon and Robert. Why you don't even know who my father is, but at least I know who my babies' father is. I love Albert Burroughs and he loves me. It would be best for all concerned that you swallow your missed placed pride and welcome him into the family once we are wed. Perhaps you could give him a title, say head of security or something." Going over to a crest fallen Algernon she thumbs him out of his seat and sits down with a smile on her face, then does the unthinkable by somehow managing to cross her legs despite all her petticoats and stuff.

"Shall I continue, sir?" says I to Clump.

"Let's have a real drink first," says he getting to his feet. "Matilda, come and give me a hand."

"I'll have a scotch in a glass," calls out Claude. "I say, Sergeant What, now that I'm proven innocent can't you take off these chains, they're hurting my wrists somewhat?"

"Sorry, Major. I have strict instructions to keep them on until you are absolutely proven innocent, and the culprit is absolutely proven guilty."

Claude points at Smithers, "Well it's obvious that valet chap is the culprit and should be clapped in irons in place of me."

"Why so?" demands Smithers. "I have confessed to being my lady's lover and to being Mr Roberts father, but of murder I deny everything." His sneering eyes fix themselves back into mine. "Afterall, Inspector, where is your proof? Do you have any proof at all?"

"Rest assured, Mr Smithers that we soon will have." Going over to a corner of the room I take an aspidistra plant from its waist high wooden pedestal and carry the pedestal back, ready to set out my evidence. Clump and Matilda start handing out drinks. It looks like neat brandies all around. Matilda comes right up to me and hands me a brandy.

"Thank you, Matilda," smiles I.

"Thank you, Gerald." She smiles the sweetest of smiles. "You do know that I did truly want you, don't you?"

"I do. But I'm so glad we did not take things any further."

"And I."

I watch her go back to her seat before glancing to the side to see Clump hand Claude and Head a drink, after that he fetches the bottle and a glass and walks right up to me, his eyes are stormy with accusations, he knows or he has guessed, either way he will say nothing until we are alone and I'm thinking he will then rip me to shreds.

"Continue if you please, Inspector," says he re-taking his seat.

I take a long swallow of the brandy; it is silky smooth with a nice kick. Setting it down on the pedestal I pick up the bag and hold it up for a second. "In this bag are albums full of photos and short anecdotes of Ronald Smithers sea faring days; along with photos of him overseeing the on-board entertainment while interacting with the passengers." Removing one album from the bag I set it down. "There are also letters, letters between you and the countess from the very first letters you sent each other, up until you, Mr Smithers took up employment here at the castle. They prove beyond a doubt that you and the countess have been conducting an affair for over thirty years."

"Dirty buggers," spits Prune.

Clump is up, marching over to Prune he wrenches the trumpet from her hand and then marches back to his seat.

"Give it back, Arthur Clump or else!"

Or else what? thinks I while noting the flash of panic in Constance's eyes. I flick a glance at Clump, the old sod, who appears quite calm and collected as he meets my eyes.

"Please continue, Inspector," says he with a wink.

Taking out a small bundle of letters in their envelopes I set them down. "You are correct in your assumption, Mr Smithers, that I do not as yet have any real evidence to arrest you for Lord Percy's murder."

A sinister smile crosses his mouth while his eyes mock me, the man is so cock sure he will get away with what he's done, he is not in the least worried about anything. Throwing back his brandy he says, "If that is all, Inspector, perhaps I may leave to go about my business?"

"Stay and have another drink first," says Clump going over with the bottle.

With a careless shrug, Smithers holds out his glass. Between finger and thumb, Clump takes the glass by its rim, turns away and heads for the door where he gives it his customary kick. The door is quickly opened and Burroughs sticks his head in, Clump hands him the glass and Burroughs also takes it between finger and thumb. The door closes and Clump retakes his seat. It looks like no more brandies for Smithers. Smithers is now glaring at Clump, whether he suspects what's going on I don't know. I continue.

"In truth everyone sat before me is still a suspect for Lord Percy's murder. Lady Matilda and Constable Burroughs had a motive to want to see Lord Percy dead. Mr Algernon, Mr Robert and even you, Lady Elizabeth all had motives to want to see your brother dead. Regardless of whether or not Lord Percy was blackmailing any of you, you all knew he may well have done in the future, depending on how short of money he became. Get rid of him now and save yourself from the constant worry that he may open his mouth or bleed you dry. The problem we detectives have is in uncovering the absolute truth. If Mr Smithers is our killer, was he in collusion with others? After all, you all had something to gain by getting rid of Lord Percy with Mr Robert having the most to gain. Did you, ma'am, not only know what was going on, but was actively involved in a conspiracy to get rid of your husband and your seriously flawed, eldest son, so that your beloved Robert could become the next earl? Thus, saving the estates future while ensuring that you and your lover would be together for life. We must have answers to these questions and rest assured that we will have them no matter how long it takes." I pause to look each one in the eye, Smithers and Constance are defiant, the remainder just stare at me through blank eyes. "Mr Algernon, you did not appear too horrified to find out who your real father is, nor I suspect were you Mr Robert. Lady Elizabeth you were content with the knowledge that you are a true Bullington. Lady Matilda, you of course were shocked to find out that your mother doesn't know who your father is, and for that I sympathise with you."

"I know who her father is," pipes up Claude. "She's mine. Isn't she old duck?"

"I have said that I don't know!" spits Constance before chucking down her brandy like a seasoned brandy chucker downer.

"Oh yes you do?"

"Speak up," yells Prune. "I'm missing all the juicy bits."

"Shut up you, demented old crow," says Claude giving her a two fingered salute. "Look here old duck."

"Do not call me old duck, ever again, for I cannot stand it."

"As you wish, from now on I shall address you as old fuck, because that is all you seem to be good at. Now, where was I? Oh yes, after that hairy boy was born, I didn't get back in your bed for some years because I wasn't invited. But I didn't know back then that that treacherous valet chap," he points at Smithers, "was the one getting all the invites. When you did invite me in to take my rightful place on top of you, I'm know thinking it was because he," he points at Smithers again, "had buggered off for three months to sort out his parent's estate, having received a letter informing him that they had been killed in a train crash. Or was it a coach crash? Or did they jump off a cliff? I recall at the time questioning why a servant should be given so much time off to go and conduct personal affairs at our expense."

"His parents lived on the Isle of Man and he was their only child, that's why. Ronald was gone some time, but that still doesn't prove that Matilda is yours, does it?"

"It does because I have other evidence. I know she's mine because she removed my shoes, while knowing full well, I hate sleeping in my bally footwear, and you can't say fairer than that."

He shoots me a smug smile, "How's that for detective work, Inspector Who?"

"Excellent, Major," grins I.

"So, I am officially a Bullington," smiles Matilda.

"Of course, you are," sighs Constance. "Now, can you all shut up and allow the inspector to continue with this ridiculous charade?"

"It is no charade, ma'am. And you would be well served to take this much more seriously. Should I receive the evidence I am hoping for it won't be long before someone is swinging from a rope."

She folds her arms while still holding on to her glass, only now is it sinking into her mind just how serious this all is. What sticks in my throat the most is the lack of empathy from any of them for a son and brother who was so brutally murdered. There was much more empathy for Rose and Chambers.

"When we searched your room, Mr Smithers, we had hoped to find Rose Bush's diary. No such diary was found. However, my sergeant and I did not have the time to conduct a thorough search, that is being conducted at this very moment by forensic officers from Truro, who hopefully, will uncover enough evidence to convict you for Lord Percy's murder, if not for Rose and John's murders. Even though I am convinced that you committed all three murders."

"Still to prove a single thing, Inspector," smirks he. "And if you don't, what next?"

Then I'm fucked, thinks I, up the creak without a boat let alone a paddle and covered in rotten eggs, still I state the obvious, "Then we shall have to interview all suspects again and dig even deeper until we uncover the evidence we need."

He laughs while running his mocking eyes from Clump across to Claude, "By God, Inspector that's half of everyone who works in and around the estate and no doubt several of the villagers. And surely Seb' Bush and Samuel Jenson would be high on your list?"

"For Lord Percy's murder, they would indeed."

"It is obvious to me, Inspector, that Percy killed Rose and Chambers because he believed that Rose had tried to kill him, and that she and Chambers were plotting to have another go and so he did them in before they did him in. Percy was then killed by Jenson who knows this castle inside and out, and is in truth a master at sneaking around in the dark." He looks around the family to find that Robert, Elizabeth and Constance are nodding in agreement. "That, Inspector is how it was and required only the simplest of logic to work it out. Perhaps I should be conducting the investigation while you go off and investigate who's been stealing ducks from the village pond."

"Perhaps," says I as there comes a knock on the door. Clump goes over and opens it, Burroughs hands him a note, he glances at it before bringing to me and handing it over with another wink. I read the note and take in a long deep breath as I hold it up for all to see. "Forensics have matched your finger prints Mr Smithers with prints found on both the panel doors in Lord Percy's room and the earl's room. They have also matched prints on the shoes you wore when carrying out the murder of Lord Percy, before putting them on the earl's feet. They found a small key, in a secret draw in your bureau, that fits the locks for the panel door's. They have also found spots of blood, on the trousers you sent to the laundry this morning, that no doubt will turn out to be human blood. They also found a book in your room that records member of staff's indiscretions, misdemeanours, disobediences and so on. On John Chambers: you wrote that you suspected him of stealing small items of jewellery and money from the bedrooms of family members, and that you would deal with him accordingly once you have proven your theory. This of course is insufficient evidence to arrest you for Chambers murder. However, Ronald Smithers, I am formally arresting you for the murder of Lord Percival Bullington. Do you have anything to say?"

Constance jumps to her feet, "Tell him that it isn't true, Ronald. No, tell me it isn't true."

Standing up he looks broken as he smiles miserably at her, "I did it for us my darling. For our son and for this place that I love so much. It is over for us, for all of us. I am sorry."

"Release the earl, Sergeant," demands Clump. "And clap the cuffs on Smithers. We shall interview him in Mr Roberts office before we convey the bastard to the cells in Truro. Inspector, well done. Constance, dear sister in law, I shall send your sister to you, perhaps together you may gather the family around you for comfort while deciding where you will go from here. There is no need for this to go beyond these walls for now, but be prepared; this amount of scandal can never be fully covered up."

"What do you intend doing now, Major?" asks Head as he takes the cuffs off Claude.

"I think a game of golf is in order. What say you, Arthur?"

Clump smiles a very sad smile, "Perhaps later, Claude. Officers grab the prisoner, another bottle, and follow me."

Our jubilation at catching our killer swiftly abated once we'd shoved him into Robert's office. Snake like and smug, Smithers changed tack and refused to admit he had murdered Percy.

"What do you have, Chief Inspector?" he'd drawled. "Inadmissible finger prints. A key that I would testify that I never knew was there, having inherited the bureau when I first moved into the head butler's room over twenty years ago. Blood spots on my trousers? Why, I'd swear under oaf, that I'd had a nose bleed due to all the stress I'd been under while overseeing the arrangements for Miss Matilda's party."

Clump had wanted to give Smithers the drowning treatment with the brandy, showing just how frustrated he was if he was prepared to empty such treasured nectar down Smithers' throat. However, for some reason known only to him, he decided against any form of torture. Left with no option, he released Smithers who sauntered away as if he had not a care in the world, and deluded beyond belief, stated that he intended to carry on as normal.

"We're buggered," Clump had said once Smithers had gone. "If we put him on trial and it collapses, we'll not be able to retry him.

We need a plan and further evidence to add to what we already have."

"Why not just accidently kill the bastard?" Head had suggested.

"Nice thought, Sergeant but too risky. What else?"

"We could carry out a full-scale search for Rose's diary," I'd suggested.

"Brilliant, Inspector. But first we better inform the earl that we had to let Smithers go, and for now, he must allow the bastard to continue in his current role while we gather evidence."

Only Claude would have none of it, he wanted to sack Smithers on the spot and throw him out of the castle. However, he relented when Clump pleaded with him to use his head, if Smithers was made jobless and homeless, what was stopping him from re-joining the merchant navy and sailing off into the sunshine, and thus escaping justice forever? Claude settled for demoting Smithers to under-head of service, a position that would see him overseeing those who served meals and such to the family and their guests. Effectively, it kept him mostly confined to the kitchen and servant areas, and away from the family. He even had to give up his luxury room in exchange for a small, lower status, servant's room.

Gathering together as many willing hands as we could, we had led a search over the route that Rose and Chambers took on that fateful night they were murdered. Over hill and down dale, across meadows and through woods, along the grassy banks of the brook and even amongst the reeds. Nothing. Plan two was to interview everyone again along with a serious grilling of the entire family, including Prune. Nothing new materialised. Smithers new post didn't faze him and his arrogance was such; he constantly bragged to anyone who'd listen that he would be back in his exalted position before Christmas.

Claude was becoming more coherent by the day now that Smithers was off his back, and no longer manipulating him into believing he was going insane. He'd decided to maintain the status quo by allowing Robert to continue in his role as estate manager, even though Robert now knew he would never be earl or inherit the estate. Life carried on in much the same way as it had always done. Matilda and Albert set a date for their wedding for three weeks' time, once the funerals and inquests for Rose, John Chambers and Percy were over.

Constance and Claude spoke only when it was absolutely unavoidable. Claude had stated that he was considering divorcing his wife because of her dirty habits, but would leave it for now because he had a major golfing tournament coming up and needed lots of practice. Despite an oft aura of gloom, things settled down quite quickly.

All those required had attended Rose and Chambers inquest to hear a verdict of unlawfully killed. Percy's inquest was set for the following Monday and was also to give a verdict of unlawfully killed. John Chambers funeral was a solemn occasion, while the wake was a jolly do that lifted spirits while celebrating the lad's life. Roses funeral was heart-breaking, tears fell like rain while sobbing and wailing loved one's cries echoed around the valley. Practically everyone from the village and the estate attended; along with all of the family. Even Smithers attended, but then why not? He had become a hero to the villages who by now fully believed that Percy had murdered Rose and Chambers, and would have gotten away with it had Smithers not slit his aristocratic throat. Of course, Smithers rigorously denied having had anything to do with Percy's death, but no one believed him, certainly we didn't and by now he had become almost a celebrity amongst the working classes, especially the villagers. He was so popular, if he ventured into the Rams Head, he would not have to buy a drink all night, with his new best friends, Seb' Bush and Sam' Jenkins always first to dig into their meagre funds. Walking on air and supreme in his victory, Smithers was laughing in our faces. Once Percy was buried the day after his inquest, Clump had sent Mrs Clump, Head, Chloe and their new baby, who'd already been christened Thomas in the village church, home together. Betty stayed with me in a pleasant room in the castle, whiling her time away knitting and helping out in the kitchen where she and Gloria became firm friends.

Clump received a telegram from Scotland Yard ordering him to wind up his investigations and hand the cases over to Truro police, and then return home with D. I. Potter. This was a bitter blow to Clump and he telegrammed back and begged for an extension. The Yard relented and gave him one more week and no more, despite the fact we had gotten nowhere with the cases.

Two days later Betty and I were sitting in the servant's hall having enjoyed a hearty lunch of ploughman's, scones and pots of tea, and were just about to leave when Claude himself walked in.

"Ah… There you are, Inspector Who. I have an old army comrade waiting in the drawing room. I think you need to speak to him. Come on old chap, no time to lose. How are you, Mrs Who?

Betty had giggled, "Fine thank you, sir."

"Good show. My, aren't you a beauty. You're a lucky chap, Who old boy."

"I am indeed," I'd replied as I followed him to the drawing room where he introduced me to a Captain Soames, retired. A round faced, balding man with thick bushy grey sideburns who was dressed in a quality tweed suite and exuded an air of worldly confidence. He was also an expert in hand writing and was intrigued enough, by what Claude had told him, to want to examine the scrap of paper evidence that we had found in Rose's bag at the scene of her murder. Clump at the time was in his room restudying the case files, in the hope of turning up something we may have missed, and didn't want to be disturbed. In truth, I believed he was so mentally frustrated by it all he just wanted to lay his head down and forget about everything for a while.

All the evidence for the investigations were still locked in a sturdy cabinet in Roberts office, for which I held the only key. Claude, the captain and I went there immediately. I dug out the scrap of paper and a letter written by Rose for a member of staff who could not read or write, something apparently, she did a lot of.

Soames compared the scribbled handwriting on the scrap of paper with Rose's in the letter, and declared that although very similar, the scribbled writing on the scrap of paper definitely wasn't Roses. He'd then gone on to explain why he had reached this conclusion. I'd then produced Roberts ledger which had a good many paragraphs written by Smithers, who had often updated it whenever he wished with the latest staff misdemeanour, or whatever. Soames compared the writing to the scribbled writing on the scrap of paper and declared, without a doubt, that they were from the same hand.

"I'm so glad to be going home at last, Detective Inspector," says Betty dreamily as the train pulls away from the station.

"And I my love. I had begun to believe I'd be here forever."

"It's been lovely, but there's no place like home and one's own bed. Right, you were too tired when you came to bed last night to tell me all. Tell me now."

"In brief; as I haven't the mental strength to go over it in detail. Once I'd told Clump what Soames had come up with, he was ecstatic in the belief that this single piece of evidence could well turn out to be Smithers nemesis. Even so, we knew it wouldn't be enough on its own to make Smithers crack. We had to somehow out fox Smithers while piling on pressure to break his resolve and force him to confess. Claude came up with a plan of action, he would use everything that Smithers held dear to attack him and crumple his defences, so he had no option but to surrender. "After all, gentlemen," he'd said. "What is Smithers? Why he's a peacock who believes he is so captivating, so admired and respected he is untouchable. Pull out his tail feathers so he has nothing to display and he will crawl off and die. Do you understand where I am coming from?"

We'd both said yes, but in truth, at the time, I hadn't a clue what the devil he was on about. Even so, following Claude's advice, Clump and I set off for the kitchen where we arrested Smithers in front of everyone who was there, so that word would quickly spread, and judging by the shocked faces that quickly turned very nasty, Smithers knew he had instantly gone from being a worshiped hero to the most hated man who ever drew breath. Even if he beat the courts and got away with Rose and Chambers murders, mud sticks and he'd never be able to show his face within a hundred miles of Bullington Castle. Frog marching him out to boos, jeers and even Gloria hitting him on the head with her soup ladle, we took him into Roberts office to grill him. He denied the handwriting on the scrap of paper was his, and demanded, as would a defence barrister, a second and even a third opinion. Just one shred of doubt and with nothing else to back us up Smithers would walk. For two hours we relentlessly grilled him, while constantly tormenting him with the cold hard fact that his life at Bullington was over for ever. Still he wouldn't budge.

"I have put away a good amount of money," he'd casually said. "Enough to start out again. Perhaps I might open a restaurant in somewhere like Scarborough."

That's when the door flew open and slammed against the wall, shaking the entire room. Enter Claude; red faced, eyes popping and practically foaming at the mouth, "Now you swine!" he'd spat. "Now that the detectives have you in their clutches, I want you to know you are sacked."

Smithers had laughed, before sneering, "So what, you, old fool?"

"So what? I'll tell you so what. Now that I no longer have to pander to you just to ensure you don't run off, I shall tell you what else I intend doing. I shall announce, after tonight's evening meal and in front of the entire family, that your son, Robert the Bastard, will also be losing his position. Once he's had his dinner of course, you know, allow the condemned man his last supper and all that. Then Robert the Bastard, will be physically thrown from the premises before he has time to wipe the strawberries and cream from his quivering lips. Taking nothing with him except for what he is wearing. I shall also ensure that doors will forever slam in his face, so he cannot ever take up gainful employment beyond that of a shit shoveller. I shall be divorcing my wife for adultery while naming you as her main co-respondent, along with Jenson, who by the way will keep his position as he lovingly looks after my dogs. I may even accuse my wife of having it off with a devilish goat. Her name shall be tarnished for ever. She'll never again be accepted in high society anywhere in the civilised world. Not only that, she shall be cast out penniless, and no doubt end up having to sell herself down the docks' as she has a penchant for seedy sailors. Even better; I may have the Dirty Gertie committed to an asylum for life. That done I shall have yours and their memories wiped from the castle's archives, all photos destroyed and any semblance of you swine's ever having been here go up in smoke. So, there you are valet chap, buggered and virtually butchered. That is all I have to say for now, but rest assured I may well return and have another go, should I think of anything else. Oh… I shall also ensure that you will not get to say au revoir to your tart or to your bastard. Good afternoon to you, sir, whatever your name is."

Smithers, self-serving as he is, utterly ruthless and remorseless is also a man of passion, who would walk on hot coals for everything he holds dear, his son, the countess and of course for Bullington Castle. We were certain we'd cut his Achilles Heel, but still he held out for a further four hours, but as the clock ticked ever closer to dinner time he began to sweat, to appear incredibly tired and morose, until at last, barely forty minutes before the family would be making their way towards the dining room, he fell right into the trap.

"If you'll kindly fetch the earl," he'd said, "and providing he'll make a deal and swear to abide by it, I will give you what you want."

"Go fetch the earl, Inspector Potter," Clump had ordered.

I did so. Claude was waiting in the library in expectation of my coming while reading one of Algernon's dirty little books.

"Good show, Who," he'd said snapping the book shut and stuffing it in his jacket pocket. "Whatever happens, I think I shall allow Algernon to remain in the family, providing he keeps me amused. Right, off we jolly well go to deliver the coup de grace."

Smithers put his demands to Claude, who made a lot of fuss, a fine bit of acting I must say, before reluctantly capitulating almost entirely. Robert would remain in his position for as long as he wished, he would have the run of the estate, a substantial wage and a large house on the estate in his own name. However, Claude refused Smithers demands that Robert be crowned the Thirteenth Earl and inherit the estate once Claude had passed on. Claude agreed not to have sex with Constance while Smithers was alive, as Smithers couldn't bear the very thought, having never gotten over Constance being 'unfaithful' with Claude; when he was away sorting out his parent's estate. Despite their marriage being over, Claude also agreed not to divorce Constance while keeping up the pretence that all was well between the 'devoted couple'. Oaths were sworn and the deed was done.

"I am now ready to confess all," Smithers had said the second Claude had left.

And he did so. Rose and Chambers were murdered to keep a secret and to help frame Claude. Chambers was indeed stealing from the family, and was inside Constance's bedroom nosing around when someone began to open the door, he darted behind a curtain. Constance and Smithers entered the room, shutting and locking the door behind them. They then began talking sweet nothings, kissing and caressing each other. Smithers then realised someone was hiding behind the curtain and Chambers was exposed. What then was to be done? Report Chambers to the police and have him tried for theft? But then Chambers would let the cat out of the bag thus destroying Smithers and Constance. Smithers gave it some thought and came up with a plan. He would forget all about Chambers little indiscretions provided he kept quiet about what he'd witnessed, only Smithers wasn't about to trust Chambers with such an important secret. He needed to silence him for good, while knowing he would also have to silence Rose, as no doubt she would be the first-person Chambers would tell his secret too. He then went on to convince Chambers and Rose that they must run off before we arrived. If not, Rose would find herself being charged with attempting to kill Percy, after all she had the opportunity and the motive to want Percy dead, with Chambers charged with aiding and abetting her. It was well known the couple hated Percy with a vengeance. Chambers was on night duty the very night he and Rose ran off so no one was about to see them go, except Smithers, who was hiding and waiting outside the castle for their departure having armed himself with a bow and arrows. The rest you know."

"I still don't understand about the scrap of paper."

"Smithers told us that having shot Rose with an arrow, he'd then crossed the brook, via a make shift plank bridge, with the intention of searching her bag in case she had a diary with her that might contain damning evidence against him. On finding the diary he then decided to further incriminate Claude by adding to Roses last entry. Rose wrote: He told us we got to go before them coppers from London come. He said he'd help us get away. But I don't trust him. I think he's evil. Smithers then added in a hasty scrawl: If someone finds this note please tell the police that the earl is chasing us and has already killed John. It was then that a cloud covered the moon and hampered Smithers vision, so that when he ripped the page out of the diary, put it in the bag and covered it over, he'd failed to see that he'd left the most incriminating part of the note that named the earl still in Rose's diary. Later on, he read the diary and then disposed of it in the boiler rooms furnace."

"Poor Rose, so innocent, guilty of nothing and murdered just in case she knew about Smithers affair with Constance. At least Smithers will hang for his wicked deeds."

"Not just Smithers. Certain members of the family will also hang, metaphorically speaking. You can't cover up that many secrets. Roberts intended will be forced to end their relationship the second her father hears, from a duty-bound Claude, that Robert isn't a Bullington. Eyebrows will raise and the gossip-mongers will go bonkers when Matilda marries her Albert. Especially as she is determined that the union appears in all the best society magazines. The rest will follow; estate workers, villagers and even the odd greedy copper from Truro will be only too willing to talk to the press, once money is on the table."

"But not you, I hope."

"Not this time. The money would be too bloody, even for me. Besides, I've got two crates of free brandy in the guard's van. Things will settle down eventually. The old boy network will close ranks to at least protect Claude, and as such life at Bullington Castle will carry on more or less as it always has."

"Going back to that little vamp, Detective Inspector. You have still to confess how far you went with her."

I feel my face going red and sweat creeping around my shirt collar. I play for time. "I thought we'd agreed to put that behind us."

"You may have agreed, but I didn't. As honesty is the best policy, start talking."

"Will you still love me no matter what I say and promise to at least try to forgive me?"

"I thought I proved how much I love you last night."

"You did. I'm just worried you might change your mind once I've told you all."

"I love you and I promise I'll try to forgive you and put this all behind us, especially as it wasn't entirely your fault. But I still want the truth, and don't lie because I'll know if you do."

"I know you'll know. Very well, I shall begin."

"I've changed my mind. I don't want to know after all. Just swear again that you did not go too far with her."

"I swear that I did not go too far with her."

"And you'll never do anything like that again."

"I swear that I'll never do…"

"I accept your swearing. Now, as you've secured us this private compartment with its little beds, all be it bunk beds, let's pull down the blinds, put a do not disturb sign outside the door and start catching up. We've got several hours before we reach London."

9 781916 405042